THE ADVENTURES OF TOM FINCH, GENTLEMAN

by Lucy May Lennox

The Adventures of Tom Finch, Gentleman
ISBN 9781688904507

Copyright © 2019 Lucy May Lennox
Cover art by Avery Kingston

CONTENTS

BOOK ONE: THE MUSIC MASTER

CHAPTER ONE: DIDO AND AENEAS

London, 1735

> London is a dainty place,
> A great and gallant city.
> All the streets are pav'd with gold,
> And all the folk are witty.

Singing this tune quietly to himself, a tall, lean figure rapped with the chased silver head of his walking stick at the stage door of the Rose, a small worn-out theater well past its prime, if indeed it could ever have been said to have had one. The company within was rehearsing for the latest production, a revival of *Dido and Aeneas*, an opera as superannuated as the theater itself. Still, a job is a job, and the rent must be paid.

"What cheer, Mr. Finch?" said the young stagehand who opened the door.

By way of greeting, Tom Finch doffed his tricorne hat and held it out for the boy to take.

"Thank you, Frankie," Tom said as he stepped inside. The boy plucked the hat from his hand. Tom did not, however, surrender his walking stick, as it was no mere fashionable ornament, but his primary means of finding his way as a blind man, and he was almost never without it.

"I say, Frankie, what is Mr. Betterton cracking on about?" Tom cocked an ear toward the interior of the theater, listen-

1

ing to the racket issuing from the stage.

The stagehand looked up at him in surprise. "Ain't you heard, Mr. Finch?"

"Heard what?"

"Miss Fenton quit the company. Mr. Highmore engaged her to sing Rosamund at Drury Lane and off she goes. She only left a note for Mr. Betterton this morning."

It was not so unusual for a theater of higher standing to poach the talent of a lower company, and Miss Margaret Fenton was widely admired for her wit and charm, if less so for her skill at singing.

"Oh ho, and why should our esteemed Mr. Betterton inform me? I am only the lowly conductor," Tom muttered as he set off down the hall toward the stage, with Frankie trailing behind.

In point of fact, his position in the company was significantly less exalted than conductor. He had been hired only recently to conduct during the rehearsals and train the singers and musicians in place of the gouty maestro Mr. Holden, who would resume his lofty position in the pit once the performances began. If there was now to be any performance at all.

"Pardon me, sir, but the painters left the boat in the hall to dry," Frankie called out, pulling at Tom's sleeve, and preventing him at the last moment from running at full speed into the large but flimsily constructed replica of a boat that would carry Aeneas away at the start of the third act. With Frankie's guidance, Tom skirted around the boat, wrinkling his nose at the sharp odor of wet paint.

Shaking loose of the boy's anxious grip, Tom swung open the door to the auditorium. Within was a scene of even greater confusion than usual. Rather than arranging themselves in neat rows on the stage for the rehearsal, the singers and dancers were pacing about, gossiping in small groups, and the musicians had ventured out of the pit to lounge among the stalls, while three finely-dressed men argued loudly to the right of the stage. Mr. Betterton, the manager, was conferring at top volume with Mr. Holden, the conductor, and Mr. Brookings, the first violin. Holden had squeezed his bulk uncomfortably into a chair with one leg painfully extended to the side, while Betterton paced about in agitation, scratching at his head and setting his wig askew as Brookings hovered anxiously.

"Ah, Mr. Finch, late as usual I see," Betterton rounded on Tom as he entered. "How kind of you to join us for the rehearsal."

"Your servant." Tom ignored the sarcasm in the manager's voice and executed an abbreviated bow. "Is the production to go forward, then?"

"And how are we to mount a production of Dido and bloody Aeneas without a Dido?" Betterton thundered.

"Sir, your language," wheezed Holden from his seat. "There are ladies present." He glared meaningfully in the direction of the stage.

One of the said ladies took this as her opportunity to step forward, a sweet-faced light soprano named Jane Carlyle, who sang the part of Belinda. "Sirs, if it please you, I have a suggestion," she called from the edge of the stage.

Betterton stopped his pacing. Jane was not very high in the company, this role being her first promotion from chorus girl to comprimario, but her father was sergeant-trumpeter to the king, and a man of some importance in the musical world.

"Well, what is it?" Betterton demanded.

Jane curtsied. "If I may make so bold, sir, my father has through family connections been introduced to an excellent soprano who has just arrived in London from the continent."

Betterton made a dismissive sound and waved his hand at her, but Brookings, a small man with a kind face, whispered urgently, "Begging your pardon, sir, we should at least give her an audition, as we have no other options at the moment."

Betterton sighed dramatically. "Very well, send for her."

"But sir," said Jane, "she is already here." She gestured behind her on the stage, where a young woman with brown curls dressed in a modest blue striped casaquin stood hesitantly. She appeared to be in her mid-twenties, rather on the short side, but with large, expressive brown eyes and a comely round face. The entire company—owner, musicians, singers, stagehands, all turned to gape at her. Jane gestured again with more of a flourish.

"May I present Mistress Tessa Turnbridge, just returned from a tour of the continent."

Tess stepped forward to the edge of the stage with a show of more confidence than she felt and regarded the company. The shabby old Rose was not what she imagined the theaters of London to be, and the company seemed far less professional than what she was accustomed to, but she found she could not pass up the unexpected opportunity for a leading role with even a second rate theater.

Tess curtsied very low with a formal, studied air. "Mr. Betterton, Mr. Holden, I am at your disposal." Her voice was strong and steady but the color stood out on her cheeks, betraying her nervousness.

"Yes, yes the continent, so you say, but your accent suggests that you are a Londoner. What exactly is your training, pray tell?" Betterton demanded impatiently.

Tess straightened her back. "I spent my childhood in London, but I have trained these past eight years in Naples. Perhaps you knew my mother, Giovanna Battista."

Astonished whispers circulated about the company. Naples was the very seat of opera seria, home to the most exalted composers and the most accomplished singers. Among these, Giovanna Battista had been much fêted in London as the Italian coloratura, until her retirement to marry a British composer.

"Oh indeed!" Betterton exclaimed. Tess noticed his attitude towards her warmed significantly upon hearing this. "I did not have the pleasure of hearing her sing in person, but I know her by reputation. And your father must be William Turnbridge. I know his works very well. My dear Miss Turnbridge, that is a remarkable pedigree."

Tess colored even more, although this reaction was not unexpected. "You honor me, sir, but you must also know that they are both dead these many years, and have left me only their good names to recommend me."

"That's no small portion. Come now, let us hear your audition directly. You know the part of Dido, I trust?"

"I have studied it, yes," Tess replied.

"Then why are we still wasting time?" Betterton demanded. He clapped his hands, waving impatiently at the musicians to resume their places. "Mr. Finch, if you please!"

Tess watched as the musicians shuffled back to their instruments and the latecomer who had been scolded by the manager leapt to attention from the seat on which he had been lolling during this exchange. She had taken no notice of this Mr. Finch when he came in, but now she observed curiously as he stood, one hand gripping his walking stick and the other reaching out into the air. He followed Brookings to the pit as the other musicians scrambled back to their neglected instruments. There was something unusual about him but she could not say exactly what, and in any case she had no time to reflect before starting her audition.

As Betterton cursed the orchestra for their lazy and slovenly ways, the music master took his place on the conductor's box and rapped on the stand. The cacophony of dissonant notes quickly resolved as the orchestra tuned up.

The music master raised his head toward the stage, and for the first time Tess looked straight into his face. It was a remarkably well-formed face, but what struck her above all else were his eyes—they were completely scarred over, and where the irises and pupils should be were flat blue-white orbs that twitched and rolled slightly. His expression was unreadable. He was unlike anyone she had ever seen before.

"Very well, Miss Turnbridge, if you are quite ready, let's have 'I Am Press'd with Torment.'"

Tess nodded distractedly, but of course he did not see it. Before she could collect herself, Mr. Finch started the orchestra playing, and she missed her cue to come in by half a beat. Flustered, she stumbled through the first bars awkwardly, for while ordinarily she was as at home on stage, now with this strange blank gaze aimed in her direction, she felt her throat constrict and her breath come but shallowly.

After a few more bars, Mr. Finch frowned and rapped again on the stand, stopping the orchestra. Tess quivered with shame and frustration. To her surprise, he did not comment on her poor performance, but instead pointed his baton unerringly at the hautboy.

"Mr. Hart, tune up for God's sake!"

The youth on the hautboy mumbled an apology as he adjusted his reed then blasted out a few strangled notes.

"Very well, that will have to do," said Mr. Finch breezily. "My apologies, Miss Turnbridge. Shall we begin again? On three—"

With a clearer cue, Tess came in on the beat correctly. This time, she looked away from the odd music master and sang out with more confidence, feeling the breath move through her easily.

Holden leaned toward Betterton, who was seated beside him in the stalls scrutinizing Tess's performance. "Finch did that on purpose to give her a second run at the aria, the sly bastard," he hissed.

Betterton smirked. "No doubt. How does he always know which tarts are the prettiest?" he replied in an acid tone.

"He'll be seducing her before the rehearsal is ended, mark my words," Holden added, shaking his head.

As Tess came to the end of the aria, she hazarded a glance at the music master's face and found he was smiling.

"A very solid technique, d'ye think, sirs?" he observed, turning to where the manager and conductor were seated. "Our Jane would do well to emulate it, hey?" he added, causing Jane to turn away in a pique.

"She'll do," Holden intoned.

"Not that we have a choice," Betterton muttered, then

called out in a louder voice directed at the stage, "Very well then, Miss Turnbridge, welcome to the company!"

The theater was instantly abuzz as the other singers, the dancers, the musicians, even the stagehands and the costumers weighed in with their thoughts on Tess's talents, her countenance, and any idle gossip, real or imagined, attached to her person. The second violin heard from a cousin in Naples that Tess had come to England under somewhat scandalous circumstances. An aged costumer was eager to share the tale of a dress she had once sewn for Signora Battista. It took Betterton shouting and cursing at top volume, threatening to sack the lot of them, and dire reminders that there were dozens more singers and musicians waiting to replace them, before order was restored, with the singers seated in rows on stage and the dancers behind them awaiting their cues.

The music master rapped his baton on the empty music stand before him and started the orchestra in on the overture. Tess sat stiffly in her seat beside Jane, watching him, her head whirling. Just yesterday she had stepped off the carriage that had carried her to London, the last leg of her difficult journey from Naples, with nothing more to her name than a letter of introduction to Mr. Robert Carlyle. She had never dreamed that the very next day his daughter Jane would send for her with news of a possible role, much less that she would be cast already, and in such a curious company. This music master, for example. What a singular individual.

As the orchestra droned on through the overture, Tess leaned towards Jane seated at her right. "That man," she whispered, indicating with her chin. "The music master. Is he blind?"

Jane glanced at her with an expression of incredulity at the overly obvious question, then gave a quick nod. "It don't seem to bother him none," she added with a shrug.

Tess stared at the music master. About thirty years of age, he was very tall, smartly dressed in a dark blue surcoat with just a bit of heavy gold trim, his sandy brown hair tied back with a wide black ribbon. He had a thin but handsome, well-proportioned face, with a long nose that looked like it been formed by nature to be straight as a razor but was now slightly crooked, as if it had been broken more than once. But those opaque eyes above all caught her attention. Beholding that one deformity in an otherwise pleasing countenance gave her the queerest sensation in the pit of her stomach, like pleasure mixed with pain. It was not pity, but more like a kind of attraction she could not name.

The music master led orchestra as surely as if he were sighted, pausing here and there to point to the various players.

"You there, the second violoncello. Forgive me for not knowing the measure number, but at the part that goes tum tum tiddle, I think you'll find it's an F sharp, not an A." He sang the phrase perfectly on pitch, naming each note.

"Yes, sir," said the second violoncello, staring down at the score in consternation. "You has the right of it, sir."

"Right then," Mr. Finch said, pointing his baton toward the first violin. "The measure number, Mr. Brookings?"

"Thirty-two, sir," the first violin replied.

"At thirty-two," he ordered, and they were off again, with the music master smiling and nodding as he waved his baton.

Tess leaned over to Jane again. "You know the gentleman? His name is Mr. Finch?"

Jane gave a quick laugh. "Aye, Tom Finch, but I wouldn't call him gentleman."

"Why ever not?" Tess raised her eyebrows in surprise, watching as Mr. Finch again with good humor chided the hautboy for falling out of tune. Instead of answering, Jane gave a rather unladylike snort, just as the overture came to an end.

"Silence, if you please!" Mr. Finch snapped, never losing the rhythm as he conducted. Tess turned dark red and clapped her mouth shut. "Now then, Belinda, Dido!"

Tess stood up along with Jane, and again her first notes came out in a tight, thin voice, to her shame. This was not how she had envisioned her brilliant career in London at all. She had imagined taking the opera world by storm, quickly rising to the most prestigious stages just as her late mother had. But here she was at the Rose, a lucky break to be sure, but in this strange company, and even worse, giving a poor performance. She would never fulfill her lofty ambitions like this. If only that odd music master were not distracting her.

Again she shifted her gaze away from the music master's frowning face and fixed instead at the empty space at the back of the theater, forcing herself to put him out of her mind. At last she was able to relax and let the notes flow out of her with a rich, open tone, giving voice to the lament of the unhappy Queen Dido.

By the end of the rehearsal, Tess was faint with exhaustion, but at least she had managed to sing through her part passably well. As she was preparing to leave, Mr. Betterton the manager stalked over to her, never dropping the scowl affixed to his face throughout the entire rehearsal. Jane repeated the formal introductions and Tess curtsied low, thanking him for giving her the part.

Betterton looked her up and down. "You're comely enough to sell tickets, but Holden has made it a condition of your casting that you take lessons with the music master."

"I beg your pardon?" Tess said faintly.

Rather than replying, Betterton gestured impatiently for her to follow him down from the stage and into the pit.

The music master was deep in conversation with Mr. Brookings, the first violin. Mr. Betterton clapped Mr. Finch roughly on the shoulder without warning, causing him to jump slightly in surprise.

"You're to give the new Dido lessons," he commanded. "See to it." He strode off to bark orders at the dancers, leaving Tess gaping after him.

"Ah, Mistress Turnbridge? Are you here?" Mr. Finch asked, his blank eyes searching sightlessly. The color was so very blue. Tess again felt a sharp, twisting sensation.

"Yes, it is I. Very pleased to make your acquaintance, Mr.

Finch," she murmured.

He gave an elaborate courtly bow, showing a leg very neatly, and Tess curtsied unthinking, carried on by force of habit. Was it proper to curtsy even though he couldn't see her? What ought she to do?

At these close quarters, she could see his clothes were of a fine cut, but perhaps a bit threadbare. Real silver buckles on his shoes, white silk hose, with silver buttons at his knees. His close-fitting dark blue surcoat flared stylishly at the waist and wrists, but the gold trim was frayed and the elbows were shiny and worn. A few stains stood out here and there.

"My dear Miss Turnbridge, I am delighted to make your acquaintance," Mr. Finch said and put out a hand.

Tess extended her hand as well, then paused for an awkward moment as she realized he would not grasp it unless she put her hand into his own. He waited patiently, and when at last she placed her hand on top of his, he pulled her unexpectedly close. He brought the back of her hand to his lips, caressing her palm at the same time. Even when he lowered it again, he did not let her go, but stroked the back of her hand and wrist with his long, slender fingers. Tess felt the blood rise to her cheeks, but made no move to escape.

"Sir, I must beg your pardon most sincerely for disrupting the rehearsal," she said, but he only laughed.

"My dear, think nothing of it!" He flashed long white teeth in a grin so artless and honest Tess could not but feel more at ease. "The company is lucky to have you. Just returned from the continent, have you? I thought I detected something Italianate in your voice." As he talked, his eyes gazed upward of their own accord, as if he was looking up over her head. It was so odd, yet Tess could not help staring at him. He seemed prepared to continue with their conversation, but Brookings pulled him away with a pressing question, and Jane swooped into tug Tess in the opposite direction.

Jane gave her a sharp look as she led Tess back to the stage to collect their cloaks and scores.

"I'll give you a bit of advice—I would watch yourself with that one," she warned. "I tell you, he's a terrible rake."

"Is he now?" Tess replied a bit defensively.

The music master was joined by a man much closer to the profile that Jane had painted of Mr. Finch: a shorter, heavier man in flashy brocade, with colorless hair tied into a queue, and a curved mouth that moved easily into a sneer. Now there is a rake, Tess thought. Mr. Finch greeted the man as if they were the best of friends.

"And who is that?" Tess prompted, for by her disapproving look, Jane clearly knew him as well.

"Jem Castleton, an unrepentant rogue. You see what sort of company your Tom Finch keeps."

Tess watched as Betterton handed Tom a small purse of money, which he weighed in his hand then pocketed, under Jem's considering gaze.

"My Mr. Finch?" she mused, her eye still on Tom.

"Don't say I didn't warn you," Jane replied darkly.

CHAPTER TWO: THE LABOR IN VAIN

The two friends departed arm in arm to a chophouse in Covent Garden not far from the Rose to take their supper, where Tom generously offered to pay, in celebration of his recent employment.

"And how is old Purcell?" Jem asked around a huge mouthful of roast beef.

"Wretched and dull as ever. But we are to have a new Dido, the most remarkable change! She seems a bit unsure of herself but I think she is a promising talent."

Jem shrugged, uninterested, but Tom mistook his silence for encouragement. "A fine clear voice, full of character, and a firm, lively hand. I'll wager she is a rare beauty..." Tom trailed off in a reverie, and Jem snorted in derision. "Mark my words," Tom said, coming back to himself. "In a few seasons, she'll be the toast of the beaux."

"Never mind all that," Jem said as they were finishing their meal. "Now we really must make a proper night of it. Say, where is Sal?"

"I haven't heard from her in weeks. I thought perhaps she had gone to Bath."

"Never! Ain't you heard? She's been seen all around town with Ned Ward. Think they're going into business together, then?"

Tom sat up straight in alarm. "That infamous thief! Whatever is she thinking? She's already been burned in the hand for lifting a packet of lace from that mercer's shop in Southwark."

"Hmm, yes, if she's taken up for housebreaking, she'll be hanged as an old offender for sure," Jem agreed with considerably less concern.

"Then we must find her!" Tom declared, thumping the table with the flat of his hand.

Jem sighed, regretting opening this topic of conversation. He found Tom's sentimental attachment to Sally Salisbury, a common, thieving trull, rather foolish, if not downright dangerous. Jem certainly held no moral qualms about intimacies with whores but as one who considered himself an expert on the professional ladies who plied their trade around the Piazza of Covent Garden, he found it best to keep the more adventurous type at arm's length. He had been endeavoring for some time to convince Tom to give over his hopeless infatuation. He had no desire to see his friend throw himself away on Sal.

Smacking Tom on the back, Jem cried, "The devil take her! Let's go see Betsy Careless instead, hey?"

Tom agreed, if only because the two were sisters in the trade, as it were, and Betsy was likely to know where Sal was to be found.

Mistress Careless was passing the evening at the Labor in Vain, a public house in Crown Court. The main room was not very large, decorated only haphazardly with a few paintings of famous demireps on the walls near the low ceiling. The floor was unfinished and smoke from the fireplace hung in the air. Jem guided Tom through the crowd, around the dirty plates and goblets dropped on the floor, to a large round table. A number of women sat around the table, all in lace caps with ribbons, with a great many black patches affixed to their faces. They toasted Tom and Jem familiarly as they sat down. Betsy served them each a pint, which they downed gratefully, then seated herself impudently on Jem's lap.

"Say, Betsy, have you seen Sal?" Tom inquired as Jem

13

wrapped an arm around her waist.

Betsy put a finger to her dimpled cheek. "Now that you mention it, no, I ain't seen her this age."

"D'ye suppose she's given up the trade?"

Betsy gave a bark of laughter, revealing a mouthful of crooked teeth. "Not her! If she's given up whoring, it'll only be for some worse crime, ha ha!"

Jem was ready to put aside this talk of Sal and pass the time with Betsy, but as he had no money of his own this evening, she had no use for him. As she departed, two ready bawds approached them and attempted with great persistence to offer their company in place of the absent Mistress Careless and Mistress Salisbury, but Jem looked them over and saw clear evidence of the pox, while Tom declared they seemed to be of the thieving sort, for he had already caught one trying to reach into his pockets. They left the place feeling even more dejected.

Tom was in favor of going over to the Duke's Bagnio in Salisbury Court to look for Sal, but Jem countered that it was too far, and instead suggested the Essex Serpent on King Street, which was much closer. They argued it back and forth heatedly for some time, but in the end Jem won out when he reminded Tom that they might find a posture moll at the Serpent, that is, a girl who would take off her clothes for a shilling, which was enough to distract him for the moment from Sal.

It was already quite late by this time, and the Serpent was filled with a noisy, riotous crew. Jem found them a seat in a corner, where they downed one pint after another in quick succession. They soon found a wench who was willing to join them, but after stripping off her outer gown, she stopped and declared that to remove any more would cost them extra. Unwilling to pay more, Tom attempted to reach into her petticoats by means of jesting and tickling, while Jem looked on, slightly bored. It was so dark in their corner that he could hardly see any better than Tom, and there were no upper rooms to which they could retire. The girl proved adamant, so they sent her away, downed one last pint, and quit the place.

Once out in the street, Tom admitted defeat in his search for Sal, and with arms flung about each other's shoulders, they staggered the short distance back to number eight Maiden Lane, just off the Piazza of Covent Garden. Tom fumbled for a long time with the key. When he at last flung open the door and they stumbled up the stairs, Jem found that Tom's only servant, Stinson, had long ago closed the shutters and gone to bed, leaving the whole house shrouded in darkness.

Jem was accustomed to this, however, and as Tom felt his way easily to an armchair in the front parlor, he followed after with slightly more difficulty, for there was as usual a great deal of clutter on the floor. Jem cursed loudly as he collided with a chair and knocked it over. At last he discovered the box of candles and flint he kept on the mantelpiece for just this purpose. After lighting two candles and stoking up the fire, he then found another bottle of rather decent claret on the sideboard in the dining room, which served well enough between them to blunt the sting of a disappointing evening.

They awoke the next morning to find themselves still in their armchairs by the fireplace. Stinson was creeping about the house like an aged, slow-moving shade, opening the shutters to let in the sun. The rays of light pierced through Jem's swollen eyelids like a knife and he groaned loudly. In the chair next to him, Tom stretched stiffly.

"What, is it daylight already?" Tom asked, yawning hugely.

In response, Jem only groaned again and let his aching head hang back limply. At last he sat up sharply and gave his companion a close stare.

"By God, Finchy, you look a dreadful sight."

"I do?" Tom asked with some alarm. He struggled to straighten his shirt and stockings, and ran his fingers over the sleeves and front of his surcoat. He had to admit it was unpleasantly sticky in several places. "But Stinson assured me he brushed it just yesterday," he said woefully.

Jem shook his head. "That jacket is far beyond brushing, my lad. Now that you is flush in the pocket, it's time you had new togs."

It was Jem who kept Tom rigged out in the first stare of the mode, and Tom trusted his sartorial judgment above all others. Call it vanity, but Tom had no wish to be pitied on account of his appearance, and went to some lengths to be certain that he was at all times dressed as other men.

"Very well then, let's be off," Tom said, standing up with a great show of vigor, then sinking immediately back down in his chair, looking greenish, with his mouth turned down. A moment later, he jumped up again. Kicking aside empty bottles, he dashed downstairs to the jakes, to flay the fox, as they say, leaving Jem laughing uproariously in the front room. He was gone a considerable while; in the meantime, Jem found one of the bottles of claret was not quite empty, which answered well enough for the purpose. Just as he was considering looking for more, Tom at last returned, declaring himself quite empty and ready for breakfast.

After a heavy meal at the White Wig, a tavern hard by, they headed down the Strand and over to Temple Bar, from whence they boarded a wherry to take them over to Southwark. There may have been tailors closer to Covent Garden, but Tom was in the habit of visiting this one in particular, which found he served his needs to a nicety.

They spent the better part of the morning debating cuts and colors, fabrics and finishing, but just as Tom was beginning to find their errand intolerably wearisome, Jem and the tailor came to an agreement and the order was placed. And since they were there together, it seemed only right to add two new shirts, silk stockings, and a pair of breeches for Jem to the order as well, as thanks for his assistance and companionship. As he counted out the reckoning, feeling each coin carefully to be certain of its value, Tom discovered that between this and the night before, he had spent the money he had got from the Rose entirely.

"I say!" he exclaimed. "How the devil did it all go so quickly?"

Jem did not answer, but offered to pay for the wherry back across the river, which was not exactly generous of him, considering it was the first of his own coin he had laid out since they had met the night before. Still, they parted on very good terms, for Tom was far too good-humored to allow the small matter of cash to come in the way of friendship. And as it was Jem who had convinced Betterton to hire him, Tom was pleased to be able to share this new windfall. Tom knew very well that Jem might have kept the position for himself, and that his friend had argued rather strenuously on his behalf to convince Betterton to employ a blind man as music master. Tom found the necessity of such an argument tiresome, but he was grateful to have a friend willing to make his case on his behalf. A night of drinking and a few new articles of clothing seemed trifling in return.

When they reached Aldwych, Jem bade him farewell and returned to his lodgings in Broad Court by Drury Lane, a considerably less respectable residence than Tom's, which is to say, a rather low place indeed, and left Tom to find his own way back to Maiden Lane. An outside observer might have found this strange, but Jem knew very well that Tom was perfectly capable of walking about town on his own. Jem never hovered nor fussed over him but treated him as an equal, the same as any sighted person, and it was this easy attitude which Tom valued in his friend above all others.

As Tom strolled along the cobbled street, he held his walking stick not out to the side like the fashionable beaux, but close against his body at an angle. Every few steps, he struck it hard against the ground, listening with a cocked ear for the echoes from the buildings all around him. At times he was brought up short by a carriage whizzing by, or stumbled over a loose cobble, but he knew the streets around Covent Garden as well as the inside of his own home, and his progress was slow but unerring.

He tried to put aside his concern for Sal. She would re-appear when she wanted to be found, and not a moment be-fore. He knew she would only scorn him for his worry.

The purchase of his new clothes gave Tom an idea for an-other verse to the song he had been composing the previous day. As he tapped along Bow Street, he sang to himself:

There's your beaux with powdered clothes
Bedaubed from head to shin,
Their pocket-holes adorn'd with gold,
But not one sou within.

Back home, Stinson prepared him for rehearsal. After Jem's comment, Tom was feeling quite anxious about his appear-ance, and his new clothes would not be delivered for some time. Discarding the dirty surcoat, which he had thought of as his best, he ordered Stinson to fetch the second-best, a coat of bottle-green broadcloth (so Jem had assured him) without gold trim, but, he hoped, at least cleaner.

"And give it a thorough brushing, for God's sake," he added to Stinson as he changed his stockings and breeches. Tom loved the old valet but he was getting on in years and per-haps not keeping house as well as he might. But Tom could not bring himself to reprove the old man, and in any case the disorder of his house rarely troubled him, unless someone else drew his attention to it. After Stinson shaved him and retied his queue, and he had exchanged his cravat and waistcoat, Tom at last felt more himself. He never wanted it said that he neglected his appearance.

Just as Tom was thinking of leaving, there came a knock at the door. His valet was fetching water from the cellar to clean his shaving things. Not being one to stand on ceremony, he an-swered the door himself, thinking it might be Jem come back for a pint before rehearsal.

He was very glad he had answered, for the moment the caller spoke he realized it was his landlady, Mrs. Bracegirdle, a middle-aged widow, on the whole a decent sort, but given to haranguing him on the disordered state of his household. "Bachelor's Hall," she called it, and Tom had rather not let her in if he could help it. He held the door tightly against his side, only his shoulders and head protruding.

"Ah, Mrs. Bracegirdle, what an unparalleled pleasure." He gave her a disarming smile. "I regret I cannot receive you at the moment, as I am about to depart on business. Perhaps you might call another time?"

Mrs. Bracegirdle took a step back. She was never quite sure what to make of this odd tenant, and vacillated between solicitous charity for his affliction and stern disapproval of his dissolute and slovenly ways, more so when he was in arrears on the rent, which was not infrequently, as indeed was the case today. Something about the blank look in his opaque eyes was disquieting, particularly when she stood so close to him. She rather felt like she was talking to a shut door.

"Th-the rent," she stammered, not sure where to look as his eyes would not meet hers. "Mr. Finch, may I remind you the rent was due last week."

Tom's smile never wavered, "Ah yes, indeed. My deepest apologies for the delay, but I must ask you to wait another week." She started to protest, but he cut her off. "I assure you the delay is only temporary. Have I ever failed to deliver the money to you in full?"

She conceded that while that was true, the lack of punctuality was a trial to her spirits. He countered that was he not the most steady, reliable and upright of her tenants, which in truth he was not, but neither was he the most disreputable. She was loath to turn him out and risk a worse tenant, and they both knew it. Tom plied her with more assurances, and she at last departed.

After he was certain she had gone, Tom took up his walking stick and departed for the Rose, although perhaps with not quite as light a step as the day before, for would not receive his salary again for another two weeks. There might be, he reflected, a few shillings lying about the house that had gone un-detected by him. It might do for dinner, but would not come close to paying the rent. As for that, however, he put it out of his mind. Something would turn up; something always did.

CHAPTER THREE: ST. JAMES'S SQUARE

In Tom's estimation, the next rehearsal of *Dido and Aeneas* proceeded tolerably well. He only had to remind the hautboy that he was out of tune five or six times, and the violins missed their notes only in the trickiest passages. Even better, during the break, he was able to put off Brookings pestering him with notes and avoid the prickly Miss Carlyle long enough to have a moment of private conversation with the new Dido.

Tess greeted him hesitantly, a reserve that Tom guessed was due to her wounded pride at being forced to take lessons. In an effort to put her at her ease, he invited her to meet for a walk in Pall Mall the next day, before beginning formal lessons later. To his surprise, she agreed.

With some anticipation, Tom picked his way down Maiden Lane, away from Covent Garden, across Charing Cross Road and Haymarket, and thence to the Mall. He judged by the tenor of the crowd–the more refined accents, the wafting per-fumes–that he was in the right neighborhood. He pulled out his pocket watch, lifted the glass, and carefully brushed his fingers across the face. Right on time. He paused for a moment, letting the crowd flow around him, then strolled indolently along the walkway. The new Dido would have to find him her-self.

He did not have long to wait.

"Mr. Finch! Mr. Finch!" A warm, pleasing voice rose above

the din of the crowd. He stopped and turned towards it, then felt a firm plump hand take his. He bowed formally and brought her hand to his lips, breathing deeply as he did so to catch the lush, fresh scent of her. He straightened with a smile.

"Mistress Turnbridge, I can't tell you how delighted I am that you agreed to join me for a stroll."

Tess found herself utterly disarmed at the sight of him. He still clasped her hand in both of his, keeping her close to him. His expression was the most unguarded and unstudied she had ever seen, and now his friendly grin only communicated to her unalloyed pleasure in her company. His face pointed in slightly the wrong direction, as if he were looking over the top of her head, his brows lifted in anticipation, his opaque blue eyes darting right and left, as if searching for her.

She felt confounded, not merely because Jane had warned her to stay away from Tom, while her position in the company demanded she seek him out. Having spent her life on the stage, Tess was hardly one to be scandalized easily, or to shrink from the company of men. But she was only too aware that the division between the actress and the whore was a slender one. If she was to fulfill her ambitions as a singer, she would have to walk the knife's edge of pleasing men, perhaps even taking a patron, while not allowing her reputation to become too sullied. She would never be a fine lady, but she had to pass for one on stage. This odd music master did not figure in her plans for her career. However, resisting temptation had never been her strong suit.

She withdrew her hand from his. "Shall we take a turn about St. James's Square?"

Tom replied that would suit him very well, but Tess made no move forward. Guessing at the cause of her hesitation, Tom held out his hand invitingly.

"Come now, my dear, if you will allow me to hold your elbow, I trust you will steer us clear of any collisions and we shall proceed quite easily. I promise you, none shall think it improper."

Somewhat stiffly, she held her elbow far from her side, allowing Tom to settle his left hand in the crook of her arm, and led him into St. James's Square. As they walked, Tom ran his thumb along her sleeve. She was wearing a glossy silk gown that crinkled and rustled as she moved.

Tess carefully steered them through the well-dressed crowd on the promenade, now and then stealing a glance at Tom. He had his head cocked to one side, with one ear pointed forward, and he held his heavy walking stick at a slant in front of him. Yet his posture was relaxed and confident, not hesitant. A few people stared, but most either nodded politely or ignored them. Walking with Tom on her arm rather than with her on his, that is, with the natural order reversed, Tess found a curious sensation, one she rather enjoyed. Even through her dress she could feel the warm pressure of his hand on her arm.

"Tell me, Mr. Finch, how long have you been with the Rose?" Tess asked as they began their second turn about the square.

"Only since the start of this production a few weeks ago. I assisted here and there in previous productions but this is my first formal appointment. So you see Miss Turnbridge, it is the maiden voyage for both of us."

"Oh indeed," she said faintly.

"I understand that you are not best pleased with the requirement to take lessons from me."

"No, I—"

Tom cut her off with a wave of his hand. "Miss Turnbridge, I sympathize with your position. It were inconsiderate of Holden to make such a demand on you, an insult to your talent to be sent to study with a lowly music master, and one of so little experience to boot."

"Mr. Finch, please, you put words in my mouth. I mean no offense to you."

"Not at all, in fact I agree with you. What could I possibly have to teach the daughter of the exalted diva Signora Battista? And d'ye know, my true profession is not music master at all, but composer of broadsheets."

"I'm sure it is a lively profession," Tess said politely, for this was indeed a very low position. Still he did not seem at all ashamed of it, but never wavered in his laughing good humor.

"It's the trade given me by my uncle, although he was in life a bit of a rover. I believe you have seen my friend, Mr. Castleton? He is a composer as well, of no little talent, but he is kind enough to assist me by writing down my compositions, and we give them to a publisher to sell. Should you like to hear my latest endeavor?" he asked eagerly.

Tess nodded, but as he continued to wait expectantly, she prompted herself, "Yes, I should like that very much."

He sang another verse of the tune he had been working out all week:

There our English actors go
With many a hungry belly
While heaps of gold are laid
God wot! On Signor Farinelli.

The tune was quite charming, and Tess found herself relaxing enough to laugh a bit.

"So I take it you are not among those entranced by the heavenly Farinelli?" she teased. She was not quite ready to admit it to Tom, but it vexed her that lately the best parts all went to the men with high voices. Men already ruled in every other area; why did they have to take the soprano roles as well? It would not do to speak too loudly against the most popular opera singer in all of London, but Tess was secretly delighted that Tom was not afraid to tease the great Farinelli.

"Ha! There are those who would call me afflicted, and believe I rise every morning lamenting my fate, but I tell you, I had rather be blind and a bastard than a castrato."

Tess burst out laughing, then caught herself. "Oh! I did not mean—"

"Did not mean what? Perhaps you hadn't noticed, but it's

true, I cannot see at all."

"Mr. Finch, you tease me!" Tess protested, blushing slightly.

"Oh, did you mean the other?" Tom continued in a playful tone. "It is also true that I am a bastard. I make no secret of it. I believe all of London knows the story of my infamous birth. In fact, I assumed Miss Carlyle had told you already."

"No, never," Tess lied. Jane had whispered in her ear before rehearsal that Mr. Finch was the natural son of a person of some importance, although she didn't say who.

"Hmm, did she not?" Tom drawled in a tone that clearly conveyed he did not believe her, but he did not press her further.

They continued on their revolution around the square in silence for a time, their shoes crunching on the gravel. Tess was a bit taken aback at this frank confession, but his easy, guileless manner encouraged her to ask the question that had been on her mind since she first saw him.

"If I may ask, I have seen you arrive at the theater unaccompanied, and leave again on your own..." She paused, uncertain how to phrase it.

Tom smiled. "You are going to tell me it is unsafe for one such as I to walk the streets unescorted?"

"Why, no, nothing of the sort. I was merely going to inquire how you do so."

"My dear, you may take it as boasting, but it really is the most singular thing," Tom said, his smile broadening. "I tell you, I can hear everything about me, by which I mean not only the footfalls of other people, but even the buildings and other obstacles all around me. Even here, I know that St. James's is a large open space, but we are surrounded on all four sides by tall houses joined together, several stories, and in the center is a large fountain, for I can hear the water."

"That is indeed remarkable," Tess replied.

"And as for the direction," Tom continued, "nothing could be simpler. I have a map of most of this part of London in my head. I have walked these streets so often, I know exactly how far it is from place to place."

Tess marveled at his skill and confidence. "And have you always been thus?" she asked, "since your childhood?"

Tom nodded. "When I was a young child, I could see, but only dimly, the shapes of objects and colors, but by the time I was a lad, even that had faded. Now the brightest sunlight or blackest night, it is all the same to me. As my uncle always said, what can't be cured must be endured." He admitted this with such apparent unconcern that Tess was strangely moved to compassion.

"Then it is really no affliction to you?"

"Not at all, my dearest Dido," Tom replied. "On the contrary, I consider myself the luckiest of men. For observe, were I not a bastard, but my father's legal heir, I should almost certainly have been disinherited for my *affliction*, as you call it, so there is no great fortune I have lost. I have three older brothers who, like me, are also bastards. Two of them are in the navy and one is in the army. Were I not blind, that would certainly have been my fate as well, and a worse one I could not imagine. However, as it is, I was raised gently and with the greatest kindness, and now have the freedom to pursue a musical career, which I should never have been afforded otherwise."

They both laughed heartily at this, and Tom was greatly encouraged to hear a lack of restraint in Tess's laugh, which suggested she was not an innocent in the world.

"A girl on her own on the continent, without any to protect her—surely you enjoyed a great many adventures."

"I did no such thing," she rejoined with some heat. "I was at all times under the guardianship of my mother's relatives. I assure you it was all perfectly proper and dull." This last point was not quite true, but she had no intention of expanding on it at present.

Their discourse was interrupted by a change in the weather, the sun gradually giving way as they walked slowly around the fountain, to skies that turned darker, and now it began to rain.

"Oh dear, shall we hire a carriage?" Tess suggested.

"Yes let's, only you must hail it, for I am fairly useless at such a task," he told her, not mentioning that he hoped she would also pay for the carriage as he was equally unable to do so.

Unwilling to cut short their conversation, Tom directed the carriage to take two more turns around the square before taking them back to Covent Garden. As they settled back into the swaying gloom at the back of the carriage, he grasped both her hands in his, then slid his hand up the side of her arm to the shoulder and toyed with the glossy ringlets he found there. A sudden jolt of the carriage brought him closer to her, his face directly beside hers. His eyes shone white in the darkness.

"Tell me," he said, his voice much lower than before. "What color is your hair?"

Tess's voice was equally husky. "It is dark brown, like my mother's," she replied. "I'm told I am her very image."

"I'm sure you are," he said, moving his hand to her neck and then to her cheek. It was wonderfully soft and smooth. With both hands, he carefully traced the outlines of her face, from the gentle curve of her eyebrows and thick lashes to her shapely nose, her full round cheeks and soft lips. As he had expected, she was an enchanting combination of bold and delicate, her prominent features softened by a lush, fleshy femininity. Under his long, sensitive fingers, she shuddered slightly, then exhaled, blowing a sweet heady breath at him. With a slight moan, he buried his face in her neck, wrapping one arm about her waist.

Tess froze. The sensation of his face against her neck was unbearably sweet, and she was seized with a strong desire to pull him closer, for she was no innocent, but something of a libertine due to being brought up in a rather unconventional musical family. Why did God grant us pleasure, if not to enjoy it? But bitter experience had taught her that if she were to fulfill her lofty ambitions as a singer, she needed to take greater care of her reputation. Already she had ruined her chances in

Naples. She could not make the same mistake in London.

The carriage gave another sudden jolt and brought her back to herself. She pushed him firmly off and rather breathlessly said, "Mister Finch, you mustn't compromise me like this."

He leaned back immediately, although he continued to clasp her hands tightly in his own.

"Never, Miss Turnbridge, I assure you, I hold you in the highest esteem, and would never seek to compromise you in any way." Although uttered in a tone of utmost concern, his sincerity seemed questionable as he kissed her hand lingeringly on the palm, breathing in her scent as he did so. "No, nor would I for all the world compromise the friendship which has grown up between us. If it will set your mind at ease, I shall alight at once."

Tess glanced out the window. "Are you certain? How will you find your way home? Even I am unsure what street we are on."

Tom laughed. "I don't mean to impugn your superior powers of perception, but you must allow that I know the city better than one who has just arrived here."

Tess was about to argue further but just then the carriage rounded a corner and the Great Piazza of Covent Garden came into view, which she reported to Tom. He rapped on the floor with his walking stick, which caused the driver to pull up.

"I thank you for a lovely afternoon," Tom said, pausing halfway out the open carriage door. "I understand your reluctance to take lessons with me, but let us think of it as merely for show to satisfy Mr. Betterton, just between us, hey?"

Before she could reply, he touched his fingers to his hat and stepped down to the street. She called a hasty farewell as the driver slammed the door and jumped back up onto the box. As the carriage turned towards her lodgings in Aldwych, she leaned back on the seat, running her fingers along her neck, still hot from his touch.

This odd music master did not figure into her plans in any way. She would speak to Mr. Betterton again. If she must have lessons, surely he could find someone more suitable. She did not reflect until she had returned home that Tom had left her to pay for the carriage on her own.

CHAPTER FOUR: SOVAY

Tess, despite her resolution to put the music master out of her mind, found herself thinking on him, unable to take her eyes off him during the rehearsal. Tom, however, had no thought to spare for her. He had consumed the remaining bread and cheese and wine in the house, and Stinson assured him there was not a penny nor groat to be found anywhere. Throughout the rehearsal, Tom was increasingly aware of his empty belly, although this distraction made it easier for him to keep his distance from Miss Turnbridge, which seemed to be what she desired.

Jem was lately engaged as a violinist at Vauxhall Gardens, so Tom found himself walking home from rehearsal alone. At last, having forgone both dinner and supper, Tom realized this could not go on for another week. He swallowed his pride and sent to his aunt, the Lady Gray, his father's elder sister.

Tom tapped along from Maiden Lane to Soho Square with a heavy step. Listening to the passing crowd on the street made him think of Sal. With each day that passed, he was more certain that she was getting up to some dangerous mischief. As his feet found the familiar path to the residence in Soho Square, his spirits sank even lower. Lady Gray often provided for him; indeed she had once rescued him from the direst of circumstances, but while he was grateful for her generosity, it always seemed to come at great personal cost to himself. A dowager of upright moral fiber, she never missed a chance to comment on his character. It oppressed his spirits to be forced to ask for her assistance yet again.

A footman opened the door and led him through a maze of echoing hallways to a small room where the august lady greeted him with formality, layered with an undercurrent of genuine affection. Tom executed a careful bow, doing his best to display his genteel manners.

Although the hour was quite late, Lady Gray invited Tom to join her for supper, already laid on the table, for she was under no illusions as to the reason for his visit. Tom accepted gratefully.

At Lady Gray's direction, one of the footmen made a detailed description for Tom of the contents and position of each of the dishes set before him, although he hardly seemed to notice. She watched with dismay as Tom wolfed down his meal as if he had not eaten all week, and sighed inwardly. While she excoriated her younger brother's excesses, she thought it against Christian charity to visit the same disapproval on his natural children. She took a particular interest in Tom, whom she felt had suffered inordinately for the sins of his father. Yet her nephew's behavior was a trial to her spirits.

But rather than browbeat him for his spendthrift ways, she merely said, "Pray, Tom, how goes the rehearsal for *Dido and Aeneas*?"

Around bites of cold roast beef, Tom regaled her with the details of the production, for Lady Gray was also a great lover of music. Sharing this with her, Tom's natural good humor reasserted itself. She watched his normally rather blank countenance become more animated as he spoke. He was the very image of his father, she reflected, not for the first time. There could be no mistaking his parentage: he had the same spare, tall frame and the same lean, narrow face, as well as, unfortunately, his father's libertine ways.

"When the show opens, you must come see our new Dido, Auntie," Tom said, as ever taking a rather childish attitude when speaking to her. "She is quite the go. A lovely, rich voice and very handsome, too."

Lady Gray sniffed in disapproval. "I'm sure you are already well acquainted with the girl's physical charms." Tom merely smiled devilishly but did not reply. "Really, Tom," she continued. "It's far past time you started thinking of honest Christian marriage. Will you not allow me to find some suitable girl for you?"

"I will not," he said, returning his attention to the pudding before him.

"And why not?" she persisted. "Don't tell me you still have an attachment to that trollop who has styled herself after Lady Salisbury?"

"I shan't tell you, if you don't wish to hear. Pray don't ask me any more about her," Tom replied.

Lady Gray turned her eyes heavenward as if appealing to the Almighty for intervention. There had been a brief time, about ten years previous, when she had taken Tom in, after the last of his mother's relatives had died, leaving him alone in the world. The sight of him appearing suddenly on her doorstep, thin and bedraggled, had moved her to tears, and she had resolved to look after him in her brother's place. However, after some time, it became clear that Tom's bachelor ways were not in keeping with Lady Gray's conception of an orderly household, so she set him up in the house on Maiden Lane. Still, she sometimes wondered if that had been the best course of action.

"If only you will come to church with me this Sunday..." she tried.

"I will not."

She regarded him through narrowed eyes. The footman cleared away the last of the meal. It was time to come to the reason for his visit.

"Very well then, but what of your income? Have you enough? Or are you in difficulties?"

Tom's demeanor changed instantly, for he was incapable of the slightest guile.

"I have a fair salary from the Rose," he started somewhat defensively, "but only one more installment, and that not until next week. Jem informed me that my carriage was not commensurate with my current position, that is, I was, he informed me, in dire need of a new suit of clothes. And the rent, that is, I find—"

Lady Gray threw up her hands, "Jem Castleton, forsooth! Upon my honor, there was never a worse rogue. How much are you short, pray tell?"

"A month's rent."

She sighed mightily and launched into an extended lecture on the moral value of thrift, the importance of living within his means, the limits of Christian charity, on and on. Tom sat up straight in his chair, wearing what he imagined was an expression of polite attention. As she warmed to the subject, she admonished him to become more self-sufficient, and not rely on the natural instinct of his betters to take pity on him. He felt his ears grow hot, but tried not to otherwise react to her words. The old busybody. What did she know of self-sufficiency? She had never had to choose between a new suit of clothes or dinner. By the time she worked her way around to suggesting that if he was unable to support himself, it were better if he live with her, Tom could stand no more.

"You must excuse me," he cut in, rising from his seat with an abbreviated bow. "The hour is late and I have already imposed too long on your hospitality. It's been a pleasure as always dining with you but I must be off."

He picked up his cane from where he had leaned it against the table and made for the direction of the door, then jumped slightly as he felt the unaccustomed touch of her papery old hand on his. "My dear boy," she said in a thick voice. "You know I would never leave you in want. It only pains me to see you as the author of your own ruination. Pray think on your reputation, or if not that, on the state of your immortal soul."

"Hmm," Tom replied noncommittally, rather than admit that he cared not a whit for either. He stood awkwardly toying with his walking stick while his aunt bustled off, then returned to press a small purse into his hand.

"Please take care," she entreated, kissing him on either cheek. He did not know it, but it was a greater gesture of affection than she showed her own grown children.

Tom strolled along the darkened streets, wielding his walking stick and whistling carelessly. He was very glad to quit Soho Square for Maiden Lane, and gladder still for the cash in his pocket. The interaction with his aunt was unpleasant, but never mind. Now that the rent was sorted, he began to think again on his latest composition.

London is a dainty place...

As he crossed St. Martin's Lane, he ducked into a dark and narrow street, by way of a short cut. The moment he turned into the alley, he felt a cold, blunt prodding at his back, the unmistakable jab of a pistol against his ribs.

"Stand and deliver!" the owner of the pistol shouted, in an oddly hoarse and strangled voice.

Rather than reply, Tom twisted about slightly and drove his elbow sharply down against the hand holding the pistol, forcing his opponent to drop it with a clatter on the cobbles. Just as quickly, he grabbed at the wrist, prepared to put up a greater struggle if need be, but the moment he grasped the wrist, he stopped his attack, his mouth dropping open and his brows shooting up in surprise. This was not the rough hand of a thorough-paced villain, but the narrow one of a woman. As his opponent gave no further struggle, he pulled her towards him, running his hands over her form somewhat frantically. She laughed, and then he was certain of her identity.

"Sal!"

She leaned forward and kissed him mightily on the mouth. He returned the kiss gladly, but when she pulled back again, he said, "Dammee, Sally, what d'ye mean by all this? Was you truly about to rob me?"

Sal laughed again. "Oh ho, of course not, Tommy dearest, I

knew it were you. It were only a joke. I never intended to fire on you. But you should take a little more care at night. These streets ain't safe."

Tom drew himself up haughtily. "I think I know how to look after myself," he replied, "and may I remind you, it was I who disarmed you."

"Aye," said Sal, retrieving her pistol from the ground, "but where's your boung?"

Tom reached for his pockets, finding the purse he had just received from his aunt missing. He lunged wildly at her, shouting, "Hussy! Give it back!"

Sal tossed the heavy purse back to him with a look of amusement. As the purse struck his chest, he caught it and held it tightly.

"Come now, Tommy, don't be cross with me. It's only a bit of fun," she said. "I've been having a rum bite. Look!" She grasped his free hand and placed it impudently on her rump. Over her lean, familiar form, he found she was wearing not the usual layers of petticoats and skirts, but a man's breeches and jacket. Tom again demanded explanations of her, but Sal refused to say more until they had retired to his home.

Number eight Maiden Lane was dark and shut up for the night, but Sal, like Jem, was a frequent visitor, and she quickly found the candles and stoked up the fire. Tom bade her find some bottles of wine and glasses in the sideboard, and while she was in the dining room, he paced anxiously on the carpet of the front parlor.

Sal was a hoyden, to be sure, a forward and wanton girl. She had never shared many of the details of her past with him, but he gathered that she had been born to a whore in Covent Garden, bred to follow her mother's profession. She was intermittently allied with Mother Needham, an infamous procuress, but she never seemed to stop for long at any address. Although Sal was popular enough to command a rather high price, still the money was not enough for her, so she frequently supplemented her wages with thievery.

Tom knew of none, man or woman, who was bolder or more fearless than Sal. He envied and admired her utter freedom, the way she did and said whatever she wished, with no thought of propriety or what others might think. But even more than that, he loved her because she never treated him differently from any other man. With the other whores, he could always detect a note of pity or fear in their voices, but not Sal. If that meant she was sometimes rough with him or treated him with indifference, well, that only made him wish to pursue her more eagerly.

When Sal had returned from the dining room and handed him a glass of wine, Tom said, "I've heard from Jem that you've taken up with Ned Ward. Sal! Is it true?"

Sal turned away and played with the fire tongs, rolling the burning embers over. "Now Tommy, don't be jealous. Ned's a rum cove and a right clever cracksman."

"So now you've turned to housebreaking?" Tom cried. While he esteemed her adventuresome spirit, this was taking things rather too far, even for her. "Sal, you know very well if you're taken up, you'll be sent to the gallows for sure."

Sal shrugged and discarded the fire tongs, then took Tom's hand in her own. "Oh Tommy, ain't it the cleverest bite! I dress like a boy when we go crack a crib, then after put on my own proper rigging. The cullies are looking for two men, not a man and a woman, and I pike off with none the wiser."

"Is that so? Then why have you got pistols?"

"Ned wanted to try his hand as a toby."

"A highwayman?" Tom burst out, even more agitated. "Housebreaking ain't exciting enough, you would turn to highway robbery?"

Sal laughed. "But my dear, we already have! Why d'ye think I'm here?" She pulled something from her pocket and placed it in his hand. "It's a gold necklace, worth ten pound at least. Oh Tommy, 'twas the jolliest prank, and it's certain they never seen our faces. We got a hundred pound in ready cash. The rest is easy enough to pawn, but we was thinking the necklace might be recognized."

"So you want me to fence it for you."

"I knew you'd help me," said Sal happily, leading him to a chair and seating herself on his lap. Tom ran his hands over her strange attire. She was a lanky girl, more angular than round, and the clothes made her form more readily apparent to his searching fingers. Although still concerned that she might be in danger, he had to admit there was something rather exciting about her latest scheme, or bite, as she called it, and her high spirits were infectious.

"It were a dirty trick to come at me with a pistol," Tom said, but now more teasing than reproving. "I shall call you my dear Sovay." He sang the first lines of the ballad:

Sovay, Sovay all on a day,
She dressed herself in men's array.
With a brace of pistols all at her side,
To meet her true love she did ride.

Sal laughed, for she knew the song well. She sang the last verse:

I did it all for to know,
If you would be a man or no.

Sal had but an indifferent voice. No matter how high her fortunes, still she retained the coarseness of the street–she talked flash and did not pretend to gentle manners. Nor was she any great beauty, having a squarish face and lank blonde hair that would not hold a curl. Such a creature was not of the usual sort sought out by the beaux among all the other bawds in the Piazza. Her blue eyes were hard and calculating, and unlike the other whores, she did not whine or plead or hang on a man, but made it clear she had no use for him. Yet her careless attitude made the beaux more eager than ever to seek her favor. Tom knew he was but one of many admirers, but he flattered himself that she somehow esteemed him above all others, and the fact that she sought his help on such occasions as this only confirmed this impression.

The thought of his own lovely Sovay overwhelmed his fears for her safety, and inflamed his passions. They kissed lustily, if a bit awkwardly, in the heavy, stiff armchair, then retired to the comfort of the bedroom upstairs. Tom removed her jacket and ran his hands over her cotton blouse. Without any stays to conceal them, her small breasts poked enticingly through her man's shirt. Pulling the shirt open, he pressed his face against her and inhaled deeply. As always, she had a slightly smoky odor that was far from the flowery perfumes of love poetry, but he found it intoxicating. With a groan, he pulled off her trousers, exposing her narrow hips and slender waist to his touch. How strange that she should be more alluring in men's attire than in her richest dresses.

He felt her rough hand reach around to grasp his queue and pull his head back, then her mouth was on his, kissing him urgently. He gripped her tighter, groaning slightly as he pressed his hips against hers. Her utter abandon and aggression drove him to even greater pleasure.

They sported thus undisturbed for some time, until they were both satisfied and weary, but despite his entreaties, Sal demurred at sleeping by his side until morning. It would not do, she said, to be seen walking about in what she called her high toby rigging in broad daylight. They were both of them too well known around the Piazza; if she were discovered and recognized, it would spoil the ruse. But the truth was, for all her nighttime visits, Sal never stayed until morning. By way of apology, she promised to take him shooting the next day. After one more forceful kiss, she was gone.

Tom rolled over with a sigh, inhaling her scent from the pillow and running his hand over the bedsheet still warm from her body.

The next morning he rose earlier than usual which, it must

be admitted, was still not particularly early at all. After Stinson dressed and shaved him, he left the purse he had gained from his aunt in the hands of his valet, with instructions to pay the rent in full to Mrs. Bracegirdle when she came calling.

As promised, Sal appeared at his door, once more clad in her own clothes, she assured him. She was riding a fine white mare and leading a bay for Tom, post horses she had hired for the day with some of her ill-gotten gains. Taking his two pistols with him, Tom swung easily into the saddle, and they set off to the north, away from the city to the quiet meadows of Hampstead Heath.

Tom's Uncle Jack, his mother's brother, had seen to it that he learnt to be a gentleman. He knew Tom was unlikely ever to inherit his father's name or be introduced in polite society; still, he did not want the lad to be at more of a disadvantage than he already was. He taught Tom to ride a horse, to shoot a gun, and occasionally hired tutors to teach him fencing and other manly pastimes. Fencing proved to be something of a disaster, as Tom could not fix his opponent's position with any accuracy, and at last, his uncle abandoned the idea. On the other hand, Tom had taken to riding with great enthusiasm, exulting in the sensation of unfettered speed and motion, although to his regret at the moment he could not afford to keep a horse himself. He also did tolerably well in target shooting, and owned a fine brace of pistols he kept in a cherry wood box. The time it took to load and ready them, however, made them impractical for any sort of self-defense, and he was not in the habit of carrying them about.

Finding a secluded spot on the heath, Sal tied their horses to a tree, and set up along a low stone wall some pewter mugs she had riffled from Tom's sideboard before they set out. They loaded their guns and took their places a few paces away. Sal fired first, hitting one of the mugs square in the center. It toppled off the wall with a loud dull ring. Having fixed the location of the target, Tom took a turn, but hit the wall instead.

"How is it that you have bested me in this already, when I

have been practicing for years? When did you learn to shoot?" Tom demanded.

Sal laughed. "Neddy taught me," she said. "Here now, listen closely." She fired and knocked down another of the mugs. Tom followed her and this time managed to hit one, although he could tell by the sound he did not hit it squarely in the middle.

They continued on until all of their powder was spent. To Tom it was the pleasantest of days–the warm sunshine, Sal's raucous laughter, her hand on his arm, correcting his aim, the powerful kick of the pistol as he fired, and the gratifying ding that told him he had hit the target. Tom did not often compare himself to other men, nor did he care for manly pursuits such as hunting, but there was something deeply satisfying about having this skill, being able to do this thing no one expected of him. Having Sal along with him, even if her aim was much better than his, only made it more enjoyable.

After they had finished shooting, Sal gathered up the mugs and they lay in the grass, drinking ale they had brought with them out of the now sadly battered mugs, which had a tendency to drip and slosh unexpectedly. Tom lay with his head on Sal's lap. He treated her to several songs, the one he was composing, as well as several he had picked up on the road with his uncle many years ago.

When the reckoning is paid, who cares for the landlady?
Farewell and adieu to the worries of life.

Sal toyed with a lock of Tom's sandy hair, not really listening. She was not musically inclined, and would rather kiss and tease with him.

Tom traced his fingers along the sharp line of her jaw. "Will you really not give up this, ah, business venture?" he asked hesitantly.

She pulled away from him and sat up. "No, and why should I?"

"But Sal—" he paused, knowing that if he pushed too hard she would only pull away again. But his concern for her was too great. "If it's money you're worried about, you can always stay with me. My house is large, and I have a regular salary now —"

Rather than answering, she stood abruptly and declared it was time she was off. She rode with him back to Maiden Lane, depositing him back at home and departing with the two horses.

"Now don't forget the necklace," Sal reminded him as she left.

CHAPTER FIVE: THE GOLD NECKLACE

Tess found herself at the door of number eight Maiden Lane, against her will. She had tried in vain to talk to Mr. Betterton and Mr. Holden, to persuade them that she was not in need of lessons, or at the very least to entreat them to find a more suitable teacher. But they made it clear that her preferences mattered not in the slightest, and if she valued her position in the company, she would make no demands of any kind. Reluctantly, she arranged to meet Tom for the first lesson, but she brought Jane with her, to ensure Tom did not again try to take liberties with her, or perhaps to remind herself not to give in. And who was he, anyway, to intimidate and discommode her? She was here only on business.

Tess rapped the door, and they both stood for a long moment, Jane shifting impatiently from foot to foot. The three storey house was built right up next to its neighbors, and all had the same brick facades with white doors and window frames in the Palladian style.

Stinson at last opened the door, looking at them incuriously as Tess stated their names and business. Without a word he crept slowly back up the stairs in the entryway to the first floor, leading them to the front parlor, where Tom was playing on a spinet, a kind of small portable harpsichord without legs, that sat directly on the table.

"Mistress Turnbridge, Mistress Carlyle here for the music

lesson, sir," Stinson wheezed.

Tom stood and greeted them with an elaborate bow. "Jane, what an unexpected pleasure."

She turned up her nose at his overly familiar address. "I ain't here for a lesson," she declared icily. "Only to accompany Tess."

As they spoke, Tess looked about the room, which was rather dark and gloomy, even with the shutters open. The fireplace smoked badly and the walls were bare. A great profusion of articles were scattered all about, on the mantle, on low tables, on the floor—half-empty bottles of ale and wine, dirty glasses and plates, bits of clothing, belts, laces, a tipped-over chair. A fiddle half out of its case lay by the hearth. In the dining room just off the parlor, she could see ink-stained papers scattered all over the table and the doors of the side-board standing open.

"My God, Mr. Finch! You've been robbed!" she burst out without thinking. Tom jerked bolt upright in alarm.

"Have I? What is missing?"

Tess found herself at a loss to answer. Behind her, Stinson cleared his throat.

"If you please, sir, the house looks no different than it ever does," he croaked in weary tones.

Jane smirked, but Tess blushed deeply. "My apologies, I did not mean to imply...that is, I did not expect..."

Tom laughed and gestured for Tess to be seated. "Never mind, my dearest Dido. As you can see, we do not stand on ceremony here."

"But... but, such disorder, and in your condition, is it not an impediment? However do you find anything?" Tom shrugged, clearly undisturbed by the state of his housekeeping. "And those mugs!" Tess persisted. "What happened to them?"

"Which ones?" Tom asked.

"Those pewter ones on the mantle, they are all dinged and dented."

"Oh, ah, target practice."

Tess looked to Jane to share in her amazement, but Jane only shook her head with an irritated air and sat down in a chair in the corner, after first brushing at the seat briskly to clear away the dust. "The lesson, Mr. Finch," Jane said testily.

Tom ushered Tess into a drawing room beside the dining room, a room smaller but no less cluttered than the front parlor. Musical instruments of various sorts lay scattered about, and the spinet that she had seen him play previously was moved by Stinson to a table in a corner of the room. Tom traced his hand along the wall until he found it and seated himself on a chair before the keyboard.

"Let us begin with arpeggios to relax the voice," he suggested, playing several with a flourish. But Tess found she could not relax. No matter what she tried, deep breathing, waving her arms, rolling her neck, her voice remained pinched and tight, with none of the ring it usually commanded.

Sensing her increasing frustration, Tom said, "The voice is but the string of the violin—it requires the entire body to act as the instrument. Are you breathing quite deeply into your belly, and maintaining it extended as you exhale?" Tess replied firmly that she was. Tom made to place his hand on her belly, but Tess took a step back in alarm, and his fingertips only brushed her dress slightly.

"Mr. Finch!" she exclaimed. "Is there no sin to which you will not stoop?"

To her annoyance, Tom merely laughed. "I swear to you I do not gamble or play at cards."

"Only because you can't see them!" Tess blurted out without thinking. She could hear Jane snickering from her seat in the front parlor. Tom laughed again and allowed that perhaps that was true.

"Begging your pardon, I spoke in haste," Tess apologized. "But your teasing vexes me. May we please continue with the lesson?"

Tom played a few indolent chords on the spinet, still facing her. His eyes moved back and forth, as if searching for her. She could not be easy standing so close to him. That handsome face and long sensitive fingers... her hand moved to her neck as she recalled the way he had touched her in the carriage. No, it would not do, he was utterly unsuitable.

Tess forced herself to think only on her breathing and relaxing her throat. As she sang the arpeggios more easily, Tom sat up at attention. Without a word, he shifted from simple scales to the opening lines of "Dido's Lament," Tess's most important aria at the end of the opera.

"When I am laid, am laid in earth," Tess began. She hit each note exactly right and with a good, rich tone, but secretly she felt something was lacking. This old-fashioned opera was so boring—low, repeated notes, with none of the dash and complex melisma she was accustomed to in opera seria. How was she to show off her art with something so dull?

Tom paused after the opening bars. "If I may make a suggestion..."

Tess nodded, only realizing her error when he failed to continue. "Yes, please," she said, again feeling flustered.

"Purcell has written the lamentation into the notes themselves. We have only to bring it forth," he explained. "Listen—"

Tom played the chromatic fourth at the opening of the aria, repeating the run of notes, lingering over each one, until it sounded like weeping.

"Do you hear it? Each time you sing this word 'laid' you need not sing it the same way, but increase this tone of weeping with each repetition." He sang the lines an octave below her, adding color to convey the emotion of the unhappy queen before her suicide. His light baritone voice easily filled the room. He reached the higher notes effortlessly, but with a silky richness in the lower register and great expressiveness that bespoke subtle breath control.

Tess's eyes widened in surprise. With a voice like that, he could sing on the stage himself, but of course a blind man would never be cast in an opera. How unfair, she thought.

Tom came to the end of the line then played the chords again, waiting expectantly for her to begin. Tess shook herself slightly, bringing herself back to the lesson. She sang the line repeatedly, with Tom helping her to modulate the tone by increments until her voice ached with sadness.

"There!" he said. "Sing it like that and there won't be a dry eye in the house."

He was right, Tess could feel it. Her teachers in Naples had never instructed her to convey emotion quite like this, and with such sensitivity to the slightest variation in tone. How remarkable to learn it from the most unlikely of teachers.

As they retired to the front parlor, Tess thanked him, then delicately brought up the matter of payment, for she well knew that a musician must never under any circumstance give his work away for nothing if he intends to put food on the table.

"Did Mr. Betterton offer to pay you for the lesson? Or must I pay you directly? My salary, that is...my store of ready cash..." she stammered, not certain what kind of fee Tom might command, or if she could afford it.

"I tell you what it is," Tom offered, smiling and reaching into his pocket, "I will waive the fee if you would grant me a favor."

He drew forth a thick gold necklace from his pocket and handed it to her. She took it in her hands and stared at it. Each thick shining link was worked with a dotted design and from the chain hung an elaborate filigree flower. It was heavy and seemed far more valuable than any jewelry she had ever owned.

Tess froze, the necklace dangling from her fingers. Was he truly offering to make her his mistress in exchange for one lesson? She had regretted allowing Tom to take liberties with her in the carriage, but since he had not come at her again, she had resolved to speak of it no more. A woman in her career could not look for an honest marriage, but she did not intend to offer her favors so cheaply. She looked up to see Tom still smiling expectantly at her.

"What do you think it's worth?" he asked.

The color rose in her cheeks and her mouth gaped open in surprise, but before she could answer, Jane stepped between them and snatched the necklace from her fingers.

"For shame, Mr. Finch!" Jane snapped. "Worth? Worth! She's worth much more than this, I tell you."

Not wanting to let Jane speak for her, Tess added angrily, "I may be a poor girl with no relations, working in a second-rate theater, but I'll have you know, sir, I am no beggarly trollop!"

Tom's smile fell away, "But my dear, you misunderstand me. I wish to sell the necklace for ready cash, and I was asking if you knew the worth of such things, or where I might sell it. Or indeed, if you might undertake to sell it for me. Please, you mustn't think I meant any impropriety. I hold your person in the highest regard."

On hearing this, Tess's anger cooled a bit, replaced by concern. "Are you really in such straits?" she asked. "If you have such a need for cash, I might lend you a little. It would be too bad to sell such a lovely necklace. Was it your mother's?"

Tom shook his head. "No, nothing of the sort. I was given it by a friend who asked me to sell it for her."

Jane narrowed her eyes. "Is this friend the infamous Miss Salisbury?"

"The very same."

She flung the necklace to the floor in a passion. "Oh, so you would have Tess act as a servant to your whore? And I suppose then that the necklace is stolen." Tom did not answer, but his implicit guilt only enraged her further. "My father was right about you."

Tess shot Jane a questioning look. She had not mentioned this to Tess before. "I'll tell you later," Jane whispered to her. "I told you, he's not to be trusted."

"Oh ah, Miss Carlyle, hm," Tom mumbled, clenching and unclenching his hands in a guiltily nervous gesture but making no move to apologize or explain himself.

"Would you really have me risk being taken up and transported for receiving stolen goods? I took your profession of friendship as sincere, but now I see how little you value me," Tess said, her voice rising in anger.

"My dearest Dido—" Tom started, but Tess cut him off.

"No, you may not call me that! Our intimacy is at an end!" Tess was sorely tempted to continue haranguing him, but shame at how easily she had allowed herself to be duped stayed her words. Instead she stormed down the stairs, followed closely by Jane.

Tom sank down to the chair behind him, passing a hand over his face as he heard the front door slam angrily. A moment later, however, he heard the door open again. He sat up expectantly, but then slouched down again when he heard a heavy foot on the stair and Jem Castleton shouting out, "Finchy!"

Tom waved a greeting but did not stand up.

"You're looking awfully low, by God. What happened?" Jem asked, righting a chair and seating himself in it.

Tom leaned back wearily. "There's a gold necklace on the floor somewhere. If you could find it and pawn it for me, I would be much obliged." He then related the entire story, ending with Tess's angry departure.

"So that's it, hey? I saw her on the stoop as I was coming in, and she gave me the blackest look I ever saw. I thought she'd strike me down. And Jane Carlyle, ain't she the one whose father threatened to horsewhip you for trying to debauch his daughter during the production of *Venus and Adonis*? Dammee, Tom, but that was poorly done." Jem laughed as he retrieved the necklace from under a chair. "Why did you not ask me to take the necklace from the first?"

Tom shrugged. "I don't know. I thought perhaps a fine girl like Tess would know its worth. What do *you* know of jewelry?"

"Enough to know not to flash it about to just anyone like that. Come, let's go have a pint, then we can find a pop-shop that won't inquire too nicely where this come from." He clapped Tom on the shoulder and pulled him from the chair.

The opening day of *Dido and Aeneas* some weeks later found Tom arriving at the Rose early to warm up the orchestra, but after he had put them through their paces, his work was done, and Mr. Holden resumed his exalted position as conductor. Frankie led Tom to a seat in the stalls on the left-hand side closest to the stage where he could listen to the performance. He was pleased to hear from the noise of the crowd that it seemed to be a full house.

Tom sat with his head down and ear turned toward the stage, listening in particular for the tricky bits, but on the whole it was a creditable performance. He noticed a few missed notes, and the orchestra had a tendency to get ahead of the singers, but that could be corrected tomorrow; at least there were no great mistakes or disasters. Tess acquitted herself remarkably well, her voice expressive and rich, the tone clear as a bell. Promising indeed.

Her rendition of the final aria, "Dido's Lament," was the most moving Tom had ever heard, with a note of deep sadness he had not heard in rehearsals. It pained him to think that it might be due to more than the lesson he had given her. He was accustomed to the stormy anger of actresses, but still he felt badly that he had so wounded her. She had not spoken to him since, but by way of apology, he had lied to Mr. Betterton on her behalf, saying that Tess had come for lessons daily.

Tess finished her aria to thunderous applause. As the chorus began the final movement, Tom slipped from his seat and felt his way along the wall out of the stalls as quietly as possible. No doubt Holden and Betterton wanted to consult with him after the show, but he had no wish to cross paths accidentally with Tess backstage, or even worse, Jane Carlyle. As the chorus sang, "With droo-ooo-ooping wings, ye cupids come, to scatter roses ..." Tom descended the stairs and out to the street.

From the Rose it was but a short distance to Crown Court, and a pint at the Labor in Vain. One pint became two, then three, and the company was most agreeable. Several hours later, he was still taking his ease there, with a wench seated to either side of him, joking and teasing. Suddenly, above the din of the crowd, he heard a rasping voice he knew very well.

"Tom Finch!"

"My lovely Sovay!" he cried with great pleasure, although he did not rise.

"I thought you was at the theater," said Sal reprovingly. "I looked for you over half the bowsing kens around the Piazza, and here you are lushing it at your ease. I might have known!" She curled her lip at the girls seated beside him. One had her hand half inside his open shirt, but withdrew it under Sal's stern gaze.

Sal tossed something at him that hit his chest with a dull chink. Tom grabbed it, and found it to be a small purse with three guineas, ten shillings. "Your regulars," Sal explained. "Your cut of the swag."

"What, you mean the necklace?" Tom asked. "But I never... I gave it to Jem..."

"Jem told me what a damned muddle you made of it," Sal replied, her amusement evident in her voice. "I reckon I owed you something for your trouble." Tom saluted her as genteelly as possible in his half-dressed condition.

"Now take my hand," Sal commanded, extending it to him. Tom waved his hand about until he found it, and she hauled him to his feet. Laughing heartily, she led him upstairs to a private room, with the crowd around them hooting and shouting lewd encouragement. Before morning, word had gone all around the Piazza of Covent Garden that Sally Salisbury had lain with Tom Finch at the Labor in Vain, and that she had paid him for the privilege.

CHAPTER SIX: THE MUSIC LESSON

Tess stood on the doorstep of number eight Maiden Lane, delaying knocking on the door as long as possible. Pride warred with practicality as she brought her hand to the door then hesitated a number of times.

After the moderately successful run of *Dido and Aeneas* had ended at the Rose, Tess had been surprised to be called upon by Mr. John Highmore, manager of the Theater Royal in Drury Lane. He invited her to appear as a soloist in the entr'acte of the current run of *Acis and Galatea*, on a sort of trial basis, with the understanding that if she did well, he would cast her in a more substantial role in the future. In spite of its location in a less than respectable neighborhood, the Theater Royal was far more prestigious than the shabby Rose. Tess had hastily accepted Mr. Highmore's offer, and was dismayed when he added that her position was again contingent upon her continuing with the same lessons as she had taken at the Rose.

Tess had conferred with Jane, and they were both outraged that Tom was continuing to manipulate her in this way. Surely it was he who had given the idea to Highmore. Jane related, not for the first time, the details of how Tom had attempted to seduce her when she was a lowly chorus girl, but her father put a stop to it. Tess was touched by Jane's fiery concern for her, as she vowed to accompany Tess to confront Tom directly.

And now here was Tess still arguing with herself silently, shifting from foot to foot on the stoop, shillyshallying when she ought to be more bold. Jane gave her a sharp look, her grey eyes flashing, and rapped the door herself.

After a very lengthy pause, during which Tess began to wonder if anyone was at home at all, Stinson opened the door and showed them up the dark stairs into the front parlor.

"Mistress Turnbridge, sir, here for her lesson, and Mistress Carlyle," Stinson croaked. Tess noted with disapproval that the house was in the same state of disarray as in her previous visit. His valet did seem rather aged and infirm—was that the reason why he did not tidy up?

"Ah, Miss Turnbridge, Miss Carlyle, how lovely to see you again," Tom said, emerging from the dining room. He kicked aside an empty bottle as he crossed the parlor to greet her with an elaborate bow and an extended hand. Slightly flustered despite herself, Tess unthinking placed her hand in his, but quickly snatched it away again before he could kiss it. Tom seemed to sense her mood immediately, for he straightened again with a business-like air, and fixed her with his opaque stare, his face unreadable. Tess felt her stomach clench with a painful intensity. Only a few weeks had passed, but she had forgotten the powerful effect he had on her. She stammered out a greeting.

Tom favored her with a disarming grin, and invited them to take tea with him in the dining room.

"No, Mr. Finch, we are not here to take tea with you," Jane rounded on him immediately. "For shame, pursuing poor Miss Turnbridge even when she has been employed at a better theater."

Tom's mouth dropped open in surprise. "I? I'm not sure I follow—"

"Come now, Mr. Finch," Tess said hotly. "I know very well it were you who told Mr. Highmore that I am to have lessons with you. You must go to him and explain that you are not available, and recommend a different music master."

"But Miss Turnbridge, I assure you I have done nothing of the sort. Please, come sit down and we can discuss this more civilly."

Warily, Tess agreed, and Jane followed even more reluctantly.

Tess watched as he crossed the cluttered floor with a peculiar shuffling gait he did not use elsewhere. He kicked aside the same bottle again, which now rolled off into a corner. Tess, who was of an orderly bent, resisted a strong urge to pick it up and throw it away. How could he live with the house continually at sixes and sevens? If only he had better servants...but no, she reminded herself firmly, she was not here as a friend.

The dining room table, as before, was littered with papers.

"Just clear whatever you please. You may sweep it all onto a chair; it don't matter," Tom said, anticipating her question. As she and Jane gathered up the papers, Tess could not help glancing over them. It was all sheet music, written in a very good hand, but with many corrections and revisions. As if he knew that they were stealing a look, Tom explained, "That's all Jem's doing. He is so kind as to write out my compositions and deliver them to the publisher."

As Stinson prepared and served their tea, Tom continued to make small talk about his broadsheets, and about the Rose, where he had just begun music rehearsals on a production of *The Grub Street Opera*. Tess watched as Tom added a liberal portion of sherry to his cup, but declined when he offered it to her.

Jane also refused more forcefully. "Mr. Finch, I remind you that this is not a social call," she added sharply. "We are come to insist you leave Miss Turnbridge alone."

"Very well, Miss Turnbridge," Tom said evenly. "I must apologize for my indiscretion on the occasion of our last meeting. You have the right of it—it were wrong of me to implicate you in any impropriety. But I had hoped your visit today was a sign that you had forgiven me."

"Nothing of the sort. I am only here on Mr. Highmore's orders," Tess replied in an icy tone.

"Yes, Highmore, indeed. But surely my actions on your behalf might have gone some ways towards repairing your opinion of me?"

Tess narrowed her eyes in suspicion. "To what actions do you refer?"

"Did Highmore not tell you, then? It were on my particular request that he attended the last performance of *Dido and Aeneas* to see you."

"You did that for me?"

"Why, of course. Miss Turnbridge, have I not told you I hold your person in the highest regard? Your turn as Dido was most impressive, and I have done everything in my power to further your career, even at the cost of losing you at the poor old Rose. So you see, I have acted entirely in your interest, with no thought to my own."

"Did you now," Tess mused, reluctant to be won over. "I find that quite out of character. Now that I have made more acquaintances in London, I have heard tales of your scandalous reputation, and indeed seen for myself that you regularly visit every low establishment in Covent Garden."

Tom laughed and struck the tabletop with his hand. "So you have been spying on me, hey? I heard you have removed from your lodgings in Aldwych, and set up house with Miss Carlyle here," Tom said. "Are you nearby?"

"Yes, we have taken rooms above a shop on Harte Street, to be closer to the theater," Jane said defensively.

"Harte Street! But that's very close by. We are nearly neighbors!"

"Yes, I have often seen you walking about the Piazza," Tess said.

"Have you!" Tom exclaimed. "And yet you have never addressed me. My dear Miss Turnbridge, that was most uncivil of you. I had not thought you would be one to take advantage of my blindness to sneak about undetected." He said all this in a gentle, teasing tone, but Tess felt herself blushing with shame. He was right, she realized. There had been times that she had passed directly in front of him and chosen not to greet him. Instead of apologizing, however, she covered her embarrassment with anger.

"Uncivil indeed, it was uncivil of you to tell Mr. Highmore I must have lessons with you, in order to lure me here."

Tom's eyebrows shot up in an unstudied show of surprise. "But I tell you, I did not. He must have heard it from Mr. Betterton. If the thought of lessons with me troubles you so, I will do as I did before and tell him that you have been, but you need not actually come if you don't wish to."

Tess was stunned. "You lied to Mr. Betterton about the lessons?"

"Well, yes, why do you think he kept you on even after you disobeyed his orders?"

Tess exchanged a look with Jane, who only shrugged.

"Although," Tom continued, "Mr. Betterton expected you to pay for the lessons yourself, whereas Mr. Highmore has paid for you in advance, so I admit I feel a prick of conscience bilking the poor gentleman like that. But never mind! I would not have you here against your will. Only you must promise me that the next time you see me in the street, you must greet me as a friend and not remain concealed by silence, for you will always have the advantage of me in that regard."

"I will greet you, Mr. Finch, as a music master, but not as a friend. Ours is a business relationship, not an intimate one," Tess replied stiffly.

Tom laughed again. "Very well then, I can see that is the best I can hope to expect from Miss Turnbridge. Shall we shake hands on it, then?" He extended a hand in her direction and waited for her to take it. When she had done so, he gave it a firm, brisk shake, releasing her immediately, with no attempt to draw her closer. "But since you are here, and under the protection of Miss Carlyle, I offer my services if you care to run through your solo."

Tess hesitated. Pride made her want to say no. But she had to admit that his instruction had made all the difference in her performance as Dido. Her pride and concern for her reputation were nothing compared to her ambition. If she could impress Mr. Highmore with her singing in the intermission, he might give her a proper role in the next production. And if not, well, poverty and ruination awaited her if she could not find a role. But the solo he had given her, "Nymphs and Shepherds," was a ridiculous dull art song, and in English. How was she to show off her art with such a trifle, and with such ugly harsh consonants—none of the clear open vowels of Italian. Here was a teacher who could help her polish it up, never mind his questionable character.

As Tess hesitated, beside her Jane was gesturing silently that they should leave. Tess frowned, her mouth turned down at the corners. Tom's rebuke about remaining silent before him still stung. She disliked this ill-mannered miming, and it pained her that Jane, whom she esteemed so highly, would be so disrespectful.

She stood decisively, giving Jane a stern glare. "It's very kind of you, Mr. Finch. I should be happy to accept your offer."

Again Tess left Jane in the front parlor to wait while she practiced with Tom in the music room. Jane flipped idly through the broadside drafts. She had to reluctantly admit they seemed quite lively, if rather low.

As the hour was drawing to a close, they heard Stinson let in a visitor. Jem Castleton immediately made himself at home, returning all the papers to cover the dining room table. Tess and Jane greeted him curtly as they together swept through the house, down the stairs, and out the front door.

"Ain't she forgiven you yet?" Jem asked, as Tom seated himself at the table and called for Stinson to bring them claret.

"Aye, well, I did my endeavor to gain her a position at Drury Lane, but you see the gratitude with which she rewards me."

Jem nodded absently as he shuffled through the papers. "I've been seeing them both about the Piazza nearly every day, but they don't say a word in greeting."

"They've taken up lodgings together in Harte Street," Tom replied.

Jem hooted with laughter. "Better leave off then, they'll be forming a witches' cabal against you."

"Oh, it seems they already have. The word all around the Rose is that they engage in shameless tribadism."

"Do they now! Well then, perhaps your case will not go so hard. They may even invite you to join 'em, ha ha!"

"Not likely," said Tom with a careless shrug. "Now are you not here on business?"

"Yes, we must finish off that broadside, the one you call 'London.' It wants two more verses." Jem paused for several moments, thinking on Tess's figure as she flounced out the door. "What d'ye say to this?"

There's your dames with dainty frames
Skin as white as milk
Dressed each day in garments gay
Of satin and of silk

"I'd say it's damnably dull," Tom said.

"Kiss my arse," Jem shot back. "It don't matter. We just have to finish it. I told Brown we'd bring it him in an hour."

"You what?" Tom leapt up in surprise. "Are you mad?"

Jem continued shuffling through the pile of papers until he at last found his earlier draft of the song. "You promised him delivery a week ago, didn't you? I ran into him in the street this morning, and he was mighty hot, I tell you. Nothing would do but that I swore upon my honor we would bring it today. Now would you have me disgrace my honor?"

Tom felt that he would, and heartily, and moreover that Jem's honor was no great thing. But it was true that he was late with the draft. As Jem said, there was nothing for it but to dash it off as quickly as ever they could.

CHAPTER SEVEN: THE CHOPHOUSE

The publishing house of Shaloe Brown in Henrietta Street was filled with the acrid scent of printer's ink, the dull thud of the presses, and above that, the noisy chatter of the apprentices. As Tom arrived, holding Jem's elbow, a small wiry man dressed all in black, from his round hat to his tight-fitting jacket and breeches, appeared from an inner room and emerged to greet them.

"Ah, Finch, Castleton, here you are at last," Shaloe Brown said with ill humor. He had a croaking voice and a thin, pinched face. "And only a week late this time! Fortune is surely smiling upon me!"

"Aye, and it's certain you intend to keep the fortune for yourself," Jem muttered, as Tom elbowed him sharply.

"My apologies for keeping you in suspense, my good man," Tom said in a louder, more jovial tone. "The delay was regrettable, but it seems my services are very much in demand lately. Why, just this morning I was giving a private lesson to one of the divas of the Theater Royal."

Tom heard one of the apprentices further back in the shop say, "I'll wager he's taught her a rum jig," and another reply with an even more vulgar comment.

Ignoring them, Brown stretched out his hand. "Well, let's see it then."

"Oh, I think you'll find it's quite the go," Tom said enthusiastically as Jem produced the score, holding it where it could be seen but not handing it over. "A fair tune and themes of topical interest, all on the subject of our great city!"

Brown glanced over it, his manner changing at once from irritation to fawning obsequiousness.

"Quite, quite! And that fling at Farinelli, very daring! You've outdone yourself, Finch." Still Jem hung on to the manuscript. Brown ushered them behind the counter to a room where they could negotiate the price in private.

"I'll give you five pounds today," he offered, when they were seated at a small table.

"Four pounds today, and fifty per cent of all profits for as long as you sell the broadside," Tom countered.

The printer made a sour face. "Come now, Mr. Finch, have I not always dealt fairly with you?" This was not at all certain, but Tom did not say so. Shaloe Brown continued to expostulate on the poor state of his business, the pitiable condition of his wife and children, and various indulgences he imagined he had granted Tom in the past. Still Tom remained adamant—he would have a percentage of the eventual profits. At last Brown exclaimed in exasperation, "What's all this about, then? You never made such demands before."

Tom smiled confidently. "My services are much more in demand, as I said. I am no longer a beggar to be content with payment up front and nothing afterwards. Besides, it has come to my attention that some of my other work has generated a handsome profit, which it seems only right I should partake in."

"This here is the best work we've given you, and well you know it," Jem added, but Tom silenced him with a wave. At last they agreed to three pounds today, forty per cent to be paid monthly, and one pound advance for the next broadside to be delivered in two weeks' time. As Tom said, his work was selling briskly, and as much as it pained Shaloe Brown to pay him so well, this was outweighed by his fear that Tom might seek another publisher. He was determined to get as much work out of Tom as possible before his cleverness was dissipated in drink and debt, as he had seen happen so often before. It would do no good to say such things aloud, however, so in the end, all three shook hands, Jem handed over the manuscript, and Brown placed a heavy purse in Tom's waiting hand.

Now that they were once again flush in the pocket, Tom and Jem retired directly to a chophouse nearby to celebrate their success with a fine English beefsteak. It being the middle of the day, the chophouse was full with the usual noisy crowd, but as they sat eating, Tom discerned a familiar rasping voice rising above the din.

"Say, Jem, d'ye see Sally about?" Tom asked.

Jem never paused in his attack on his beefsteak, but obligingly scanned the room, spotting her almost at once.

"Blimey! She's sitting just one table over, with her back to you. I can't believe I didn't chop on her when we come in."

Tom nodded, his head turned away from Jem and his ear cocked to listen to her. "Who is she with?"

Jem leaned around Tom to look. "With Ned Ward, the villain." Ned did indeed have something of the villain in his appearance, despite his fine clothes. He was a small but thick-set man with the shadow of a heavy beard and a jutting lower jaw.

"She is wearing a dress, ain't she?" Tom asked with concern.

Jem turned back to Tom and laughed. "Of course! What else would she be wearing?" Tom had not shared with Jem the details of the bite Sal had concocted with Ned. He did not reply, but only kept his head down and his eyes half closed as he listened to their conversation. By this time, however, Sal had raised her voice in anger and could be heard through most of the room. From what Tom could gather, it seemed that Ned had contracted an intimacy with a girl named Moll.

"Who is the blowen?" Sal demanded. "Is she your wife?"

"No she ain't," Ned replied, but Sal seemed dissatisfied with this answer and let loose a stream of curses.

"Listen to her pass him under the harrow," Jem said, awed.

"Your girl has a vulgar tongue in her head, hasn't she? Did you ever hear such professions of love?" Tom ignored him, still listening to the conversation behind him.

"And what of our bite?" Sal was saying. "Was you planning to chouse me out of the swag and give it to her?"

"Hold yer mag, ye daft mort, d'ye want everyone to hear?" Ned hissed back at her. "And about that anyway, we can still play the high-toby, you and me."

"Aye, and if we're taken, she'll post your bail and leave me to rot in Bridewell," Sal retorted, her voice somewhat lower but still angry. "D'ye have to take a flyer with every chit who crosses your path? Now leave off with that slut or you'll send us both to the gallows."

Ned banged on the table with his fist. "Shut yer gob, you sorry wench! Don't pretend to give me orders. I ain't leaving Moll and that's that."

"Then we're finished," Sal retorted.

"No we ain't," Ned replied in a threatening tone. "You know too much of the bite. Stay with me or I'll impeach you myself."

Tom clenched his fists, for this was exactly what he had feared, that Ned would gain a pardon for himself by testifying against Sal. What could he do to protect her? For a moment he seriously considered standing up and threatening Ned, blindness be damned. But he knew that Sal would not thank him for meddling in her affairs, and the thought of facing her contempt stayed him more than concern for his own safety.

In the moment Tom sat vacillating, he heard a scuffle behind him. Sal give a shriek of anger, followed by more curses from Ned. There was a second of silence, then suddenly the whole room erupted in bedlam—plates clattering, crockery falling, women screaming, men shouting, chairs and tables being pushed aside, and a great hurry of running feet.

"What's going on?" Tom cried, desperate with worry for Sal.

Jem had already leapt up from his chair and was making for the table behind them. "Sal stabbed Ned with her steak knife," he explained.

"What! Has she killed him?"

But Jem had already gone and did not answer. Tom stood up as well, uncertain what to do, or even which way to move. He took a hesitant step towards where Sal had been sitting, his hand groping the air.

Amidst the din and rush of bodies, he heard one set of footsteps moving towards him.

"Sal?" he cried out, reaching towards her, his fingers just brushing her sleeve for a moment before she stepped back out of reach.

"Oh, it's you," she said calmly, heedless of the chaos just behind them.

"Sal, come with me!" he begged her, reaching forward again.

"No."

"Think, Sal! What have you done? If he dies, you'll be tried for murder. Come with me. I'll hide you at my house."

"No, I'm good as cheese on my own. Never fret over me," she said, kissing him on the cheek, then disappeared, not a moment too soon, for now the crowd was crying out to find the jade, and to send for the constable to take her up.

Tom lingered awkwardly before the table, running his fingers around the remains of his meal. He hated that he could not do more for her, or at the very least follow after her. He was still attempting to get his bearings amidst the noise and chaos when a familiar hand clapped him on the shoulder, making him jump.

"Come on, we'd best pike off before the constable arrives," Jem said as he returned.

Tom grabbed at his arm. "But what of Ned? Tell me, did she kill him?"

"Not yet. She done him in the shoulder, and he fainted for a spell, but now he's awake again. Can't you hear him cursing her?"

Tom turned his head slightly but could not make out Ned's

voice above the hubbub. He would have lingered, but Jem hurried him along, half dragging him out of the chophouse.

Saying that he needed something to steady his nerves, Jem led Tom on to Moll King's for a cup of coffee with a flash of lightning, that is, a shot of gin. As they tossed back their drinks, Tom pressed Jem to recite the details of the affair repeatedly.

"Was he badly hurt?" he asked. "D'ye think he might die yet?"

"Who can tell?" Jem replied, already bored with this discourse. "Sal's a clever girl. I'm certain she can fend for herself." Tom was not best pleased with this answer, and was all for going off in search of her, on his own if need be. He discovered, however, at the moment he stood to storm off dramatically, that he had left his walking stick at the chophouse.

"It's no use going back for it now," Jem pointed out. "Someone's likely made off with it already."

Tom sat back with a frustrated sigh. He downed the rest of his drink silently, running his fingers along the rough edge of the table restlessly. "D'ye suppose Sal's gone back to Mother Needham?"

Jem glared at him in irritation. "How should I know! I tell you, Sal will be fine on her own."

"But—"

"No, enough! You may throw yourself away on that ungrateful jade if you like, but I shan't go along with you. I won't speak of her any more tonight."

Tom turned down the corners of his mouth and did not reply. Jem finished his drink and set down his mug with a clink.

"I'm off to the Labor in Vain to find Betsy Careless," Jem declared. "Will you come with me, or go home?"

Feeling reluctant to walk the streets on his own without his walking stick, Tom elected to accompany Jem to the pub. Jem disappeared with Betsy, but Tom waved off the attentions of the whores, preferring to down pints of beer on his own.

The next morning, Tom was awakened by the sound of hammering at the back door. He had only the vaguest memory of how he had managed to return home. Had Betsy assisted him? Or one of the other bawds? He rolled over with a groan, feeling ill with drink and a short night's sleep.

He had just decided to order Stinson to say he was indisposed and send whoever it was off, when he heard the squawking, childish tone of a familiar voice asking Stinson if the flash cove was within. It was Frankie, the young stagehand from the Rose. Tom hurriedly descended the stairs, the dressing gown he had thrown on over his shirt billowing over his spare frame and his hair hanging loose about his shoulders. He followed the sound of Frankie's voice into the kitchen.

"What is it, boy?" he inquired anxiously, pushing his unkempt hair out of his face. "Have I missed a rehearsal? What time is it?"

Stinson cleared his throat. "Sir, it's only eight o'clock in the morning."

"Oh, is that so?" Tom sagged against the doorframe in relief.

"I'm sorry to trouble you so early in the morning, Mr. Finch," Frankie said. "I only come to return this to you." He stepped forward and Tom felt something strike the center of his chest. Wrapping his fingers about it, he recognized his silver-headed walking stick.

"Oh!" His brows raised in surprise. "Thank you, my boy! Was you at the chophouse last night?"

"Yes," Frankie replied. "I seen it on the floor and knew it was your own, sir. I says to myself, you'd be right buggered without it, so I made off with it quick, before anyone sees me."

Stinson snorted in disapproval at such vulgar language, but Tom took no notice. "So you know about the happenings there last night, then? Tell me, what has become of Ned Ward? Is he dead?"

"No sir, they called in a doctor but he declared it were no mortal danger, and they carried him off home." Tom was relieved at this news, even more so than on the return of his walking stick. Recalling that there was no food in the house, he sent Frankie off with a few coins to buy some bread and cheese for breakfast, and gave half of it, along with a shilling, to the boy as a reward. Frankie, beside himself with delight at a reward much greater than he had imagined, departed with effusive thanks and pledges of undying loyalty.

After Stinson had seen Tom shaved and dressed, there came another knock at the door, this time at the front. It was Shaloe Brown. Tom, somewhat surprised by the unexpected visit, greeted him formally in the front parlor. The publisher had never before called on him in person, but had only sent messengers to harass him over late delivery of a manuscript.

"Mr. Brown, to what do I owe the pleasure of your visit?" Tom asked, attempting to affect the air of a man of business, and not one who had been up drinking until the wee hours.

As usual, Shaloe Brown came straight to the point. "I heard you was at the chophouse where Sally Salisbury stabbed Ned Ward with a steak knife."

"Why yes, so I was. News certainly travels apace around Covent Garden," he remarked warily.

"Yes, quite. Mr. Finch, this is an ideal opportunity! You must write us a broadside describing the altercation, the sooner the better. If you can deliver it today, I'll run the presses overnight and we can have it on the streets by tomorrow. Only think! An eyewitness account of a bloody event still fresh in the public memory."

"I think you'll find me a poor eyewitness," Tom said drily.

Shaloe Brown shuffled his feet a bit nervously. "Oh, ah, well, that don't signify. I know you can come up with a clever rhyme and a jolly tune. That's all that matters. What say you?"

"No."

"What? Come now, I'll give you ten pounds now and fifty per cent of the profits after."

"No."

"Mr. Finch, would you bankrupt me? Fifteen pounds now

and sixty per cent later." This was far in excess of anything he had been paid before, but still Tom refused. Shaloe Brown continued to remonstrate with him, hardly believing that he could turn down such a generous offer, more so as Tom would not explain his reasons. At last Brown gave up in frustration and took his leave.

He then went straight to Jem Castleton, who had no such niceties of feeling about the incident. Jem consented on the spot, and for a much lower sum. As promised, the broadside titled, "The Tragicall Ballade of Sally Salisbury and Ned Ward: The Account of an Eye Witness," was being hawked all over the Piazza the very next day.

Tom did not begrudge Jem the money, but he was not pleased when he heard the song being sung as they drank together at the Essex Serpent several days later.

"How could you do that to Sal?" Tom berated him. "To make her a public spectacle, the subject of a low ballad."

Jem snorted in derision. "She makes herself a public spectacle. I'll wager she's happy that I've increased her fame."

"But what you put in the song is not what happened," Tom protested. He recited one of the verses:

Sally cried, what have I done
Ned he cried, now I am undone
Sally tore her yellow locks and sighed
I've killed my own true love, she cried.

Indeed, Jem had altered the ending as well, with Ned dying on the spot and Sal pining away for him after. He finished off with a well-worn verse of Sal professing her intention to join him in death:

Go dig my grave both wide and deep
Put a marble stone at my head and feet
And at my breast put a snow-white dove
To tell the world that I died for love.

"Come now, Finchy, you know it's better this way. Would you have me put in all the foul curses they flung at each other? That weren't fit to be written down. Besides which, I only had an hour to write it. You can't expect all the verses to be original."

"That's as may be. But did you have to end with Ned dying? He ain't dead, you know."

"He ain't?" Jem was only mildly surprised.

"No, the doctor said it weren't mortal. Would you have her tried for murder?"

Jem took another swig of ale. "Whether he dies nor no, that girl will come to a bad end one way or the other, mark my words."

CHAPTER EIGHT: ALCINA

Tess Turnbridge continued to appear at number eight Maiden Lane every few days for her lessons. Now that they had settled into a routine, she found she was much easier in Tom's presence. She was enjoying her lessons far more than she had anticipated. She had even stopped bringing Jane with her, as Tom had not come at her again, and she found it easier to concentrate without a sullen companion sighing in the front parlor.

Her solo in the entr'acte was earning her eager applause each night, and she had once glimpsed Mr. Highmore nodding approvingly from the wings. This was due in no small part, she was certain, to Tom's instruction. He showed her how to cheat the tricky English vowels to open up her voice, and how to add color and nuance to the repetitive runs.

At her latest lesson, however, she found Tom uncharacteristically low in spirits, his face drawn and wan.

"Are you unwell, Mr. Finch?" she asked with concern, as he played a wrong note, his head drifting down and to the side in what she had come to recognize as a sign of inattention.

He sat up straight immediately, pointing his face more nearly in her direction. "Forgive me, Miss Turnbridge, I'm merely tired." He did not add, sick with drink from the night before, although she could easily guess. "But I fear we both grow weary of these art songs," he continued. "Would you prefer to sing something different?"

Tess agreed and proposed singing in Italian instead, which suited her better. At her insistence, they began with "Le Violette" by Scarlatti. Tom found it was easy enough to improvise an accompaniment on the spinet.

Tess ripped into the opening stanzas of the Scarlatti with gusto, enjoying the swelling anticipation of each phrase, and the satisfying trill as she rolled her rs: "*Ruggiadose odorose, violette graziose…*"

She broke off suddenly, noticing with chagrin Tom laughing as he played the accompaniment. "Mr. Finch, you mock me!"

"My dear Miss Turnbridge, I admire your *brio*, as your countrymen would call it, but pray do not attack the top note in each phrase quite so hard. As the song says, you have too much ambition. You will frighten off the delicate violets with your stomping about." He demonstrated the phrase she had just sung. "Let each word flow smoothly thus," and he sang the phrase again in his clear light baritone. Tess tried again, producing more of a ring on the top note with less strain.

After they had worked through "Le Violette" and several other songs, Tom suggested she rest her voice and called for Stinson to bring them tea.

Tess observed Tom as he moved easily from the spinet to sit before a small round side table, feeling the edge of the table and the back of the chair before sitting. She was no longer so completely distracted by his uncanny gaze, or the way his long sensitive fingers were constantly in motion, feeling out the objects around him, although she still found his artless smile utterly disarming.

When Stinson placed the tea tray before him, Tom reached for the teacups with the back of his fingers, so as not to knock them over, then poured each of them a cup. She did not mind that he extended a finger into the cup to ascertain the level of the tea as he poured. To the contrary, she was impressed by how well he managed without sight. She recalled his words, what can't be cured has to be endured. She could not help but wonder how he had fared as a child, what his family was like, but it was indelicate to ask.

"You may sit here if you wish," he offered, gesturing to the chair opposite his beside the round table.

"Oh, I—yes, of course…"

"If there are papers on the chair, just shift them anywhere, it don't matter," he said with a smile, guessing at the reason for her hesitation.

Tess moved the papers to join the large collection of folios, manuscripts, and loose broadsides that were stacked haphazardly on an enormous bookshelf against one wall of the drawing room.

"My uncle's library and publications, which I inherited on his death," Tom explained. Tess hesitated at first to riffle his inheritance, as it were, but Tom encouraged her, saying, "He would be pleased for you to look at them, for as you might guess, I can neither read nor write myself."

Tess pulled down a yellowed broadside and read the title aloud: "The Brown Girl."

"Ah yes, that was one of my uncle's compositions. He took a very old Irish tune 'Slane' and set new English words to it. More or less new words, that is." Tom felt for his saucer and set down his teacup, then turned to play the melody on the spinet.

"The tune's quite lovely," she remarked. She returned to leafing through the collection, setting aside several to look at in more detail. "What a treasury!" she exclaimed. "You could write your own *Beggar's Opera* ten times over."

"Aye, and be shut down by the law within a day," Tom said, laughing. "I had rather try my fortune with the broadsides for now. But the real music you'll only hear over there in the countryside, not written down in any score."

"What? You mean in Ireland? Have you been there?"

"Yes, as a boy. After my mother died, my uncle took us both on the road, collecting songs and learning to play in the old style. Would you like to hear?"

"If you're not too tired," she replied, for he still looked a bit pale.

"Never," he said with a smile. He turned to a shelf behind him and felt about for a battered old fiddle. After testing the bow and tuning up the strings, he began to play a lively tune in a style she had never heard before, his bow flying over the strings, briskly scraping out the notes.

Tess was delighted, not only by the music, but also by the look of pure happiness on Tom's face. The color rose in his cheeks and the care lines faded away.

"Why, it is the cleverest music for dancing!" she exclaimed. "Did you learn the dances as well?"

"I cannot dance," he said lightly, jostling against the spinet as he set the fiddle down with a discordant crash. It was the first ungainly gesture she saw from him since the lesson had begun.

"Oh! I didn't mean—I am sorry—" Tess felt herself blush to the roots of her hair.

Tom only shrugged. "It's my lot to provide the music, not to dance."

"And mine as well," Tess said softly.

Tom laid the fiddle back in its case, then turned back to the spinet and played some chords. "Hm. Perhaps, perhaps not, if you find a wealthy patron."

Tess sighed. This was a question that had weighed on her mind since her arrival in London. Should she use her singing to catch the eye of a wealthy old man and become his kept mistress? It seemed her only route to financial security, and everyone seemed to expect it of her.

"I'm not ready to give up the stage yet," she admitted, "before my career has hardly begun."

"Oh, ho! So you are ambitious!" Tom laughed, his face breaking into a pleased grin. "I like that! Come, let us return to the lesson, and we shall have you a prima donna before you know it!"

Tess returned his smile, feeling a warm glow in her heart to know that he understood her ambition and supported it.

At the end of the lesson, Tom proffered her an unexpected invitation: his aunt, the Lady Gray, had a box at the Haymarket Theater, for the première of Mr. Handel's latest production, *Alcina*, on the next evening, if she was pleased to accompany them and not otherwise engaged. As it happened, that was a night on which Tess was not scheduled to appear at Drury Lane. She wondered a bit at the felicitous timing, but replied that she would be pleased to accept. Surely there could be nothing improper about attending the theater with Tom if they were accompanied by an elderly lady, and a highborn one at that.

"Of course, my lady aunt will be traveling incognito, as they say. I'm afraid we shan't make a grand entrance with her, but must instead arrive at the theater separately and make our own way to the gallery," Tom explained. Tess thought this was a rather odd way of doing things, but Tom seemed accustomed to it, as she supposed on reflection he must be, forever obliged to call on the nobility via the back door.

For the occasion, Tess wore her finest gown, a sacque of peach-colored lustring silk, tight in the bodice and half-sleeves, set off with as much lace as she and Jane owned between them, including a very fine lace head-dress, which she hoped made up for her lack of jewels. Following Tom's direction, she proceeded to the first storey gallery, and inquired of the footmen standing at attention along the hallway until she discovered the box reserved for Lady Gray. Upon entering the box, however, she found to her mortification that although Lady Gray was already seated, Tom had not yet arrived.

As the footman bade her, she slid into her seat, feeling very much awed by the august lady, sister to James Douglas, Earl of Bolingbroke, and widow of Andrew Gray, Earl of Moray. Like Tom, Lady Gray was tall and slender, her height exaggerated by her lofty powdered hair, padded out with cushions. Tess noted the family resemblance immediately, although Lady

Gray had much more of a patrician air in her long thin face and prominent nose. Tess paused. Ought she to offer a greeting? The footman had announced her, but would the lady ignore her until her nephew arrived to tender a formal introduction?

Lady Gray turned to Tess with a piercing glance that took her in entirely from head to toe and inquired, "So you are Mistress Tessa Turnbridge lately of the Rose, and more recently of the Theater Royal in Drury Lane?"

"Yes, my lady," Tess replied, jumping up hastily to offer a curtsy.

"Oh, do sit down, child," Lady Gray said, then favored Tess with an even more searching stare that did nothing to allay Tess's nerves. At last she said, "Your face is familiar to me. Have I made your acquaintance on some previous occasion?"

"Begging your pardon, my lady, you have not," Tess replied. "But Mr. Finch tells me your ladyship is a great lover of music. Perhaps you saw my mother on the stage? Her name was Giovanna Battista."

Lady Gray's expression changed from haughty distance to excitement all at once. "Why, yes!" she cried. "She was a particular favorite of mine, and I never missed her performances in London. But that was many years ago. I was very much grieved to hear she had died. And you, her daughter! Imagine! You do look very like her," she said. They continued on in this vein, until Tom arrived at last, led in by a footman.

"Ah, Tom! Late as usual!" Lady Gray commented sternly, then rose to embrace him and kiss him as if he were her own son. She guided him deftly to the seat beside her closest to the stage, placing his hand on the back of the chair. Tom's new clothes had come in at last, and Tess had to admit to herself that he cut quite a figure. He was wearing a coat of pale blue brocade, with a bit of gold trim at the buttons all down the front, and cuffs doubled back to the elbow, and underneath that, a darker brocade waistcoat, a shirt with much lace, tight breeches and white silk stockings, also new. The cocked hat he held under his arm was trimmed with feathers, and his light brown hair was neatly tied back with a black ribbon and curled at the sides.

"Your Miss Turnbridge is a delightful young lady. Why did you not tell me her mother was the famous Signora Battista?" Lady Gray demanded, when they had all been seated again.

"What?" said Tom in surprise, rising again. "Is Miss Turnbridge here already?" Tess murmured a greeting and he bowed slightly in the direction of her voice, as much as possible in the tiny space. "Miss Turnbridge, have I not specifically requested that you announce yourself to me?" he chided her good-naturedly as he sat down again. Leaning in towards Lady Gray with a conspiratorial air, he said, "Miss Turnbridge is fond of hiding herself from me."

Tess squirmed in embarrassment, but Lady Gray merely rapped Tom on the knee with her fan. "Let the poor girl be," she ordered. "I'm sure you have been teasing her shamelessly. It's your own fault if she mistrusts you."

Tess was confounded on how to reply to this banter, but fortunately for her at that moment Mr. Handel, resplendent in a heavy brocade surcoat and full bottomed wig, took his place in the orchestra pit, and a wave of polite applause swept through the theater.

"Please refresh my memory. What is the story of this *Alcina*?" Lady Gray inquired as the orchestra was tuning up.

"I believe it's taken from *Orlando Furioso*, your ladyship," Tess replied.

Tom settled back in his chair with a smirk. "More Italianate nonsense from Mr. Handel," he muttered as the overture began. The plodding notes of the overture did nothing to improve his opinion of the opera. "The progression of each note announces itself before the measure has scarcely begun. This will not be one of his celebrated works," Tom declared in a gossipy tone, but Lady Gray rapped him again with her fan and bade him be still. By the end of the prologue, however, she was complaining as vociferously as he.

"Women in men's clothing, flying horses, and a talking

shrubbery, forsooth!" She had been attempting to narrate the action on stage for Tom's benefit, but her indignation soon got the better of her. This was compounded during the extended gavotte in the middle of act one.

"Whatever is that woman wearing!" Lady Gray exclaimed.

"I believe that's Marie Sallé, the French dancer," Tess offered.

"Yes, but in no more than a shift! It isn't decent!"

Tom suddenly took a much keener interest in the activity on stage. "Oh indeed?" he said, sitting forward eagerly. "What is it she is wearing, exactly?"

"She appears to have discarded her stays," Tess attempted to explain. "She's wearing only a simple white dress and the material is quite thin. One can see her... oh my..." It was Tess's turn to receive a blow from Lady Gray's fan.

"Don't encourage him!" she hissed.

Their agitation soon faded again to boredom, however, as the second act followed the first, and the plot became increasingly convoluted. During the entr'acte, as she was attending in private, Lady Gray did not mingle with the other patrons or entertain visitors to the box, but stayed closed within while a footman brought them sweetmeats and sherry.

"I own my Italian is not the best, but I can't make heads nor tails of the story," Tom admitted, after downing two glasses of sherry in quick succession.

Lady Gray frowned and stayed the hand of the footman who was about to pour him a third glass. "I believe Ruggiero and Ricciardo are about to duel for the affections of the sorceress Alcina," she said.

"Begging your ladyship's pardon," Tess ventured, "I believe the story is a bit more complicated than that."

"Oh indeed?" Tom inquired. "Do tell."

Tess glanced nervously at Lady Gray. "Ricciardo is the knight Ruggiero's lover, Bradamante, a woman in disguise, only the two sorceresses Alcina and Morgana have fallen in love with her, thinking she is a man, and Ruggiero is under a spell and in love with Alcina. Or so I believe," she finished a bit lamely, not wanting to show away in front of the lady.

"Ha! A woman in breeches is a rum go. You can't blame 'em for falling in love with her," Tom laughed, unaware of the odd look Tess shot at him. He turned to where he imagined the footman to be. "More sherry, if you please!"

Choosing not to comment on his drinking, Lady Gray instead remarked that La Strada was doing tolerably well in the title role.

"Hmm, yes, she has improved greatly since coming to London," Tom said.

"I think she has a lovely tone," Tess added politely.

"It's a pity, though, about her face," said Lady Gray.

Tom laughed. "You know they call her the Pig."

Lady Gray sniffed. "Well, I'm sure I don't know about that, but she does make the most frightful grimaces as she sings. Now your mother, the great Signora Battista, she never did so. She always maintained a gracious countenance, as I'm certain you do as well," she added, turning to Tess.

"That's very kind of you," Tess replied, thinking of the hours her mother had made her spend practicing in front of a looking-glass.

"I hope the next time I see you, it will be upon that stage," Lady Gray said.

"In a better production than this one," Tom added.

Tess only nodded politely. Indeed, she had been thinking of little else as she stared at the singers on the stage, imagining herself treading those very boards, and how she might have performed the soprano role at least as well as La Strada. This talk made the flame of ambition in her breast flare up. At least as well, or even better, she promised herself.

The third act dragged on, no better than the first two. When the singers took their bows, Lady Gray sat up in surprise. "What, is it finished, then?" she asked.

"And what of poor Alcina?" Tom added. "The two lovers go off and leave her to sink into the ground?" Tess had been describing the action to him in a whisper.

"Well, she is a sorceress. She couldn't very well marry the human knight, now could she?" his aunt replied.

"I suppose, but still, that's a hard fate," said Tom, and privately, Tess felt she rather agreed. Why couldn't Alcina be a sorceress and marry the handsome knight? Why did she have to choose one or the other?

As they applauded the players and orchestra, Lady Gray declared the production relied too much on spectacle, scandalous spectacle at that, and Tom added that the music was but indifferent, repeating his prediction that *Alcina* would soon be forgotten.

As they said their farewells, Lady Gray surprised Tess by grasping her arm and whispering in her ear, "My nephew says you have a promising career ahead of you. Don't let anything distract you from it, not even him."

Before Tess could reply, Lady Gray departed with her footmen, who conveyed her to her waiting carriage. As Tess descended the stairs more slowly, caught up in the crowd, she wondered at Lady Gray's feelings for her wayward nephew. Tess was strangely touched to observe the obvious affection and care Lady Gray had for Tom, yet she did not overlook his faults the way a doting mother might. He was obviously fond of her too.

Tess regarded Tom as he felt his way down the stairs, one hand on the wall beside him and the other brandishing his walking stick before him. Her first impulse had been to offer him her assistance but as he had not asked, she somehow could not find the words to suggest it herself. She was impressed with Lady Gray's attitude towards him, guiding him unobtrusively but not hovering or worrying over him. She resolved to do the same.

As they approached the main doors, Tom offered to escort Tess home, as the hour was late, but they found to their dismay that it had begun to rain rather hard. Tom suggested that Tess take a hired chair, and leave him to find his own way home. She hesitated for only a moment. The thought of walking even a short distance in the downpour was distasteful, and Tom insisted, so she bade him goodnight, trusting that he would be all right on his own.

On her return to their second-storey lodging, Tess found Jane already in bed but still awake, waiting up for her with a candle lit. Her pretty heart-shaped face broke into a smile and she jumped out of bed when Tess entered, embracing her and fussing over her wet clothes.

"How was the opera?" Jane asked. "Is Anna Maria Strada as ugly as they say?"

Tess laughed as she laid her wet clothes over a chair before the fire and pulled on her night dress. "It was rather dull, and yes, she has a great big nose and wrinkles it up when she sings, like this," Tess demonstrated. "Marie Sallé danced in nothing but a shift. It was something of a scandal."

"And what of Mr. Finch," Jane demanded as they climbed into the bed they shared and lay facing each other. "Did he take liberties with you?"

Tess shook her head. "No, he has been quite the gentleman."

"Well, you needn't sound so disappointed!" Jane retorted, her large grey eyes filled with reproach. "You're in love with him, ain't you!"

"What? No, I'm not!" Tess was taken aback. "Jane, are you jealous?"

"No, he's a thorough-paced rogue. I don't care what he do, but you," she said in a plaintive tone, stroking Tess's brown curls, smoothing them away from her face, "you shall marry him and quit the stage and go away and leave me."

"Oh, fie! Don't talk nonsense," Tess replied. "I shan't quit the stage when my career has hardly begun, and I doubt I shall ever marry, certainly not him." She entwined her arms around Jane's small waist, drawing her close. "I promise I shall never leave you. Besides, you are more likely to marry and leave me," she teased, although Jane replied passionately that she would not. Then they kissed and caressed each other with increasing ardor, until the rest of the world and its uncertainties had been forgotten.

After seeing Tess off, Tom was accosted in the lobby of the theater by a stagehand who recognized him, and conveyed him backstage where he lingered, gossiping with various singers and other members of the company with whom he was acquainted, until at last he found himself in the company of Mr. Rich, the manager. They had met on several occasions previously, but it never hurt to mention the work he had done at the Rose, his arrangement with Mr. Highmore for tutoring Miss Turnbridge, and to remind him that he was always eager for future employment.

By the time Tom left the theater, it was quite late indeed, but he walked with a light step, despite the persistent drizzle, well pleased with his conversation with Mr. Rich. A stagehand had offered to see him home, but Tom had refused, arguing that it was but a short distance, and he knew the way very well. The streets were nearly empty, and his walking stick echoed loudly off the wet cobbles, allowing him to sense his surroundings more clearly than if he had been under the noonday sun. He walked confidently and briskly. Nevertheless, he was not aware of the figures lying in wait until it was too late. One moment he was passing by a close, and the next, he felt rough hands pulling him violently sideways into the alley. His walking stick fell to the ground with a clatter.

"Sal?" he called uncertainly, trying to feel the hands that had grabbed him.

"It ain't yer Sally," said a coarse male voice, and indeed, he had already deduced that it was a man who had grabbed him, or was it two men? But before he could react, or strike back at them, he was shoved with even greater violence against the side of a building, and he felt the cold, sharp blade of a knife pressed against his throat.

CHAPTER NINE: THE RESCUE

"Give us your boung and be quick about it."

Tom felt himself pinned against a wall by one pair of hands, holding the knife, while another riffled his pockets, searching for his purse. He struggled against them, but it had all happened so quickly, and now he dared not lash out with the knife at his neck. His eyes opened wide and rolled back and forth uselessly.

"The cully's blind!" said a voice that had not yet spoken, somewhat younger and lighter than the first.

"Shut your gob," said the first, "Only draw the boung and let's go!" Tom at last freed one hand and groped for the hand holding the knife, but the man easily deflected him, and pressed the blade more threateningly against his flesh. "I wouldn't do that, my lad," he said in an icy tone. Tom felt panic grip his bowels. Did they really intend to kill him for ready cash? He struggled again, but could not break free of them.

"How he writhes!" said the younger one. "Hey, this here's a rum coat. Let's take it too." Tom felt the younger man remove his purse from a pocket and begin pulling his coat off his shoulders. All this happened in the space of a few moments, and still he could not get his bearings and resist them. Just then, he heard a third voice at the entrance to the close cry out in a rasping tone.

"Leave off, you sons of bitches, or I'll pop you!" It was Sal. Tom recognized her attempt to crush her voice to a masculine register—she must be in her high-toby rig, he realized.

"Kiss my arse," said the younger man, turning towards her.

There was a sudden explosion of noise, deafening in the echoing confines of the close. A moment later, Tom realized that Sal had fired a shot. The knife dropped away from his throat at last and fell to the ground with a clatter. Tom pulled his coat back over his shoulders and reached for the hand that had drawn his purse, but could not find it. There was the patter of running feet as the younger accomplice fled, but the man before him stiffened and thrust forward sharply. His ears still ringing, Tom guessed that Sal had a pistol shoved at the man's back.

"I said, leave off or I'll kill you right now, you filthy whoreson," Sal hissed, prodding him again with her pistol. The man gave a grunt, then at last wriggled out from between them and ran off.

"My dear Sovay, what a fortuitous meeting," Tom said, brushing down the front of his coat with a show of nonchalance, although his hands were shaking badly. "What just happened?"

"I shot at the one cove but missed, dammee, and he took to his scrapers. The other one's piked off too, when he felt my pops on his back," she said, her voice returned to its accustomed feminine register, although not much less coarse and rasping.

"Tell me, did the younger one happen to drop a purse on the ground?" Tom asked. There was a pause, then she replied that she did not see it. "Then he's made off with my money, too, the sorry wretch," Tom said. Suddenly the ground beneath him seemed to lurch for a sickening second. He leaned back against the wall with a slight groan.

Sal was upon him at once. "Was you cut at all?" she asked, with an air of concern he rarely heard from her.

"I don't know," he said rather faintly. "But I should have

looked a right flat had they nicked my clothes as well as my cash. There wasn't much in the purse neither. All that for just a few shillings..." His voice trailed off. Sal's hands were all over his face and neck, inspecting him for signs of injury, and the feel of her rough fingers touching him so gently was overwhelming. He closed his eyes as another wave of dizziness washed over him.

"You ain't bleeding, anyways," said Sal, taking his arm across her shoulders and encouraging him to lean on her. "Let's take you back to your ken, hey?" She paused to retrieve his walking stick and hat, which had both fallen to the ground, then they walked slowly back to number eight Maiden Lane, with Tom leaning heavily on her shoulders.

Once inside, Sal did not stop to light a candle, but conveyed him straight upstairs to the bedroom, stumbling in the dark over the debris on the floor. After depositing him on the bed, she went off to rouse Stinson, and bade him light a candle and find some brandy for his master. She returned to the bedroom to find that Tom had discarded his jacket, waistcoat, and stockings onto the floor and was climbing into bed in his breeches and shirt. Sal picked up his clothes, glancing them over before tossing them onto a chair.

"I reckon it's these new togs what done it," she observed. "They must have thought you was a flash swell."

Tom laughed ruefully as he settled back against the pillows. "I suppose I have disappointed them on that score," he said. Sal seated herself on the bed beside him, and placed the glass of brandy that Stinson had brought in his hand. Tom drank it down gratefully, his hands still shaking slightly, then leaned back again with a sigh.

"You rescued me," he said, sounding as if he could hardly believe it himself.

Sal took the empty glass from his hand and placed it on the floor. "Aye, lucky for you I was just stepping round to your ken when I sees them two rum coves follow you into the alley. I told you, the streets ain't safe at night," she scolded, then added in a kinder tone, "Now Tommy, don't look so hipped. You is safe now, ain't you?" She took his hand in hers. Rather than replying, he leaned forward and flung his arms about her waist. She felt so slender in her men's clothes, with hardly any layers to conceal her form.

"Dearest Sovay," he said in a low voice. "Stay with me the night, won't you?" She laid her head on his shoulder and nodded so he could feel the movement. He tightened his arms around her waist and slid a hand down to her rump.

It was the most curious thing: a moment ago he had felt utterly done in, about to slip into oblivion, but suddenly, the feel of her waist through her men's breeches, of her hair against his cheek, the musky smell of her, inflamed his passions beyond all imagining. He embraced her roughly, squeezing her against him with a low moan, then found her lips with his fingers and kissed her firmly on the mouth. She responded in kind and they grappled lustily, desperately. Within moments he had stripped off her jacket and opened her breeches. They had sported in such fashion often enough before, but never with such intensity. He gripped her hard and flung her down, but never with any fear that he might hurt her unintentionally, for she was strong and lithe, and returned his roughness in equal measure. She flipped him over handily and straddled him.

As he slid her breeches below her narrow hips, she kissed him again, grasping his cheeks in both hands and darting her tongue in and out his mouth. Never breaking the kiss, she slid her hands down to unlace his breeches.

The feel of her strong hand gripping his cock made him arch his back, his eyes rolling back in his head with a sharp intake of breath. She teased him almost beyond bearing, then suddenly her hands were gone. As she had done often before, she reached into the drawer of his bedside table and drew forth a small sheath made of the gut of a lamb. She carefully fitted it over his cock, tying the end with a small red ribbon. Both Sal and Tom had witnessed their mothers die of the pox, and moreover Sal had no notion of ever becoming a mother herself. Despite her rather careless disposition, Sal always took the precaution of using such a device, and she had passed the habit on to Tom.

He gripped her waist and entered her with a groan, and flipped her over again. At the crucial moment she sank her teeth into his shoulder, and even that did not diminish his pleasure, but rather added to it.

When at last they had exhausted themselves, Tom again entreated her to stay until morning, or even longer, but she steadfastly refused to risk being seen in men's clothes in the daylight.

"Don't take on so," she said as she pulled on her breeches and shirt. "I hate to see you look so low. You've had a nasty shock, that's all. What you need now is to flash out proper, take a frolic in the countryside. What d'ye say we go to Epsom and take the air, like we was gentry?"

Tom frowned, feeling down-spirited again now that his ardor had passed. "I don't care for horseracing. It's dreadfully dull if you can't see the horse you bet on."

"But there's other diversions besides the horses. I just come into a mint of money and I'm wanting to go on a spree. We can take Jem and Betsy with us and lush it good, the four of us." She finished dressing, tying back her hair, tucking away her pistols and putting her tricorne hat on with finality, having made her decision in spite of Tom's objections.

"Wait," Tom put in before she could leave, "What about Ned? You're not still hiding from the law?"

"What?" Sal snorted derisively. "How you fret, Tommy! I swear you is worse than an old granny. Ain't you heard? Ned's gone off with that blowen Moll and I'm well shot of him. The devil take them both. We've given up the high-toby and that's that."

Tom was about to ask her, if they were no longer in league as highwaymen, then why was she still wandering about at night in men's rigging, where had all this money she spoke of come from, and more to the point, why she had kept herself from him for so long, but then thought better of it, and merely said a jaunt in the countryside might do him good. Sal grinned and kissed him on the cheek. "I'll borrow us a bang-up prime rattler and prads. You pack up your best duds and send for Jem. I'll step round again at noon." She blew out the candle and shut the door behind her.

CHAPTER TEN: EPSOM

Sal was as good as her word, appearing the next day with a fine equipage—an elegant carriage for herself and Betsy, with a matched team, a driver, and footmen riding behind, and two fine prancers for Tom and Jem to ride beside them, for she knew Tom would rather ride on horseback than in a carriage. Tom had dutifully sent for Jem and Betsy, who now waited beside him on the stoop, along with some articles he bade Stinson to pack up for them.

"Ain't you togged in twig!" Sal exclaimed happily as she greeted Tom with a kiss. Stinson had labored all morning to clean and repair Tom's new clothes, which luckily were not much damaged from the encounter the night before.

"I might have said the same of you, milady," Jem said, kissing her hand with an ironic smirk. Sal was indeed dressed very fine in a sacque of blue striped muslin and powdered wig topped with a wide-brimmed straw hat trimmed with silk flowers. "If only your filthy tongue didn't give you away," he teased.

"Shut your gob, you poxy bugger," she replied cheerfully. After greeting Betsy fondly, she affected a haughty air and allowed the footmen to hand her up into the carriage, while Tom and Jem mounted their horses. The driver cracked his whip, and they were off with a great clattering of hooves.

Epsom lay south and west of the city, but with the equipage they could not cross the Thames by boat, which would have been the most direct route. Instead they were forced to take the Strand, through Cheapside, and thence to London Bridge far to the east before they could continue south. As the Strand was crowded with a noisy, busy press of horses, carriages, and pedestrians, Jem held the lead of Tom's horse to prevent them from becoming separated in the throng. London Bridge was if anything even more crowded. The buildings housing all the businesses that lined the bridge, packed in as tightly as possible, took up nearly all the span, forcing the traffic into two lanes with barely enough room for a carriage on each side, going in and out of the city like a trail of ants, only proceeding much more slowly. They were often obliged to stop as the path had become congested far ahead of them for reasons unknown, and all this stopping and starting was exceedingly trying. Riding abreast, Tom could feel the side of Jem's horse pressing against his leg, its ribcage swelling as the beast sighed impatiently. Tom wondered if he might not have been better off in the odious carriage.

As they passed through Southwark and then Lambeth, the traffic thinned until at last the houses gave way to rolling green hills, and the din of the crowd was replaced with birdsong. It was a brilliant spring day, and Tom turned his face up towards the sun, enjoying the sensation of warmth. There was a time when the bright rays of sunlight would have penetrated the darkness, and he could have seen vague shapes, or at least a cloudy brightness. He strained to open his eyes as wide as possible, wondering if he could sense the light at all, but at last concluded that he could not. No matter, he thought. The song of the lark singing to his mate, the smell of the warm, newly turned earth, the rhythmic tramp of the horses on the dirt lane, the huff of their breath and jingle of the bridles, all of this was indescribably beautiful to him. Was it because the alarms of the night before had sharpened his spirits, he wondered, made him glad to be alive? Or perhaps being in the countryside put him in mind of the long rambles he had taken as a youth with his uncle. With Sal in command, they took the road very easy, stopping often for a pint and a bite to eat, or merely to dismount and rest along the way.

They planned to stay at Epsom for an entire week, for Tom's rehearsals at the Rose were finished, and he had left word with Tess that he would not be giving lessons. The other three, of course, had no regular employment, or at least none from which they might be missed.

They lodged at the largest inn on the high street, which styled itself the New Tavern, although having been built in the previous age it was no longer so new; nevertheless, it was a dignified brick edifice, with large airy windows, and they rented two adjoining rooms. The innkeeper was a heavy, florid man named Johnson, who received them with a great deal of winking and jesting, making it clear he would not inquire too nicely into their private affairs, to wit, whether they be married or no, for it was yet early in the season, and business was slack. He was glad for any lodgers at all, provided they could pay the reckoning.

Epsom provided a wealth of diversions, as Sal had promised. They were obliged as their first order of business to take the waters, paying a shilling each at the Old Well for tiny glasses of cloudy water. The elderly man taking the money, who styled himself Dr. Baines, assured them it could cure every ill.

"Even your infirmity, sir," he said, addressing Tom.

"Indeed?" Tom replied in a tone of polite indifference as he downed the glass, then nearly spit the contents back out again. "Ugh! It tastes like seawater!" he cried.

Dr. Baines nodded sagely. "The salts is where the physic is, you understand. They boil it down and sell it in packets too, if you should care to try it?"

Sal discreetly poured her glass on the ground behind her then peered into Tom's face. "Well?" she inquired. "Is you cured?" She waved a hand in front of his face.

Tom shrugged unconcernedly. "Apparently not."

"It sometimes takes a few days to work at full efficacy," Dr.

Baines offered, undeterred. "If you like, sir, I can arrange to have a glass sent round to your rooms at the inn every morning." Tom declined this generous offer, much to the doctor's dismay.

Next they took a ramble around the Box Wood, a pleasant copse in Boxhill, a short ride just south of the racetrack. Jem remarked with a leer that the quiet path was so dark and overgrown, it was the very spot for trysting, and was about to suggest to Betsy that they take in the scenery themselves, so to speak, when they rounded a bend in the path and alarmed a couple engaged in that very activity. The unfortunate woman shrieked and covered her face, while Tom politely tipped his hat to her, and suggested he and his companions return the way they came. As they proceeded out of the wood again, they passed more evidence that this was no singular accident, but the common use in this spot.

Despite these false starts, however, they passed the week with the greatest delight. The food at the tavern was of the first order, and they ate heroic quantities of pheasant, venison, and duck, as well as mutton, beefsteak, and ham, puddings and meat pies, and they all agreed they had never eaten so fine in London. In the mornings, a maid brought them frothing cups of chocolate as they lounged in bed, and in the afternoons, there was tea with cream and maids of honor.

In the daytime, Jem and Betsy frequented the dicing tables in the tavern, or went to see the horseracing, while Tom and Sal went riding. In the evenings, there were plays and music on the bowling green beside the tavern, performed, Tom noted, with more enthusiasm than skill, but enjoyable nonetheless. The majority of their time, however, was spent in the tavern, or just outside it when the weather was particularly fine, sampling the local brew, and getting bloody lushy, as Sal put it.

Tom had brought along a small wooden flute and a tabor, which he and Jem took turns playing, and although the girls' voices were far from the best, they ran through every drinking song they could think of, which was no small number.

Tom obliged them with a tune from *The Beggar's Opera* which they all knew very well:

Let us drink and sport today, ours is not tomorrow
Love with youth flies swift away, age is naught but sorrow.
Dance and sing, time's on the wing
Life never knows the return of spring.

On their long daytime rides around the countryside, Tom and Sal also engaged in some target practice. After one such session, they sat down in the grass to take their ease, enjoying the sunshine and the sweet breeze. Tom lay with his head on Sal's lap, his jacket and waistcoat discarded, dressed only in his shirt and breeches. She had undone the ribbon that secured his queue, and ran her fingers through his light brown hair. He closed his eyes and sighed happily.

"You were right, dearest Sovay," he said, his eyes still closed. "This was a capital idea." He sighed again. "Would you not want to stay like this, in each other's company?"

"What, here in Epsom?" she asked.

"No, no, in London, of course. Sal, should you like to come live with me?" She did not reply, and Tom continued in haste, "We needn't be married, if you don't wish it. You shall have every freedom."

Sal only snorted with laughter and ruffled his hair playfully.

Tom opened his eyes and sat up, his long hair falling about his shoulders in disarray. "Only think, Sal, I can keep you in high style, and you need never live in fear of the law. Would it be so very terrible to lodge with me?"

"Oh Tommy," she said, taking his hand, "You know you're my dearest love, but I'm happy keeping to my own ken."

He considered asking her where exactly this house she spoke of was located, but instead assayed her on a different quarter. "Never mind, then, but will you at least leave off your criminal enterprises?" He stroked the back of her hand with his thumb, feeling the raised, twisted brand that had been burned into her skin as a token of her status as an old offender. "You don't know how I fear for you, that you might be taken up by the law. You'll be hanged for certain!" His voice conveyed rather more emotion than he had intended.

But Sal was not to be swayed. "What rot! By God, I never met such a one for fretting and worrying as you. Come, ain't we having a prime bit of fun? Why spoil it?" She rose to fetch their horses, singing as she did so in her hoarse, flat voice:

Let us drink and sport today, ours is not tomorrow

They rode back to the inn in silence, Tom's horse placidly following Sal's without the need for a lead line. As they rode, Tom berated himself for a fool. He should never have made the offer. He admired her romping, dashing ways; how could he think to bind her down with domesticity? Still, if she truly was finished with Ned Ward and had not an understanding with some other man, he had thought she might not object. How many other men would make so liberal an offer? But no, he realized, she would be no man's wife nor mistress, and he could hardly blame her for that. He tried to put their conversation out of his mind.

"How were the races?" he asked Jem as the four of them sat down to supper together. "Did you win much?"

"Lost every farthing," Jem replied cheerfully, his disappointment allayed by his knowledge that Sal would foot the bill at the inn, as well as for the equipage. As a result of this loss, and a lingering awkwardness with Sal, however, the next day Tom and Jem passed the time together, leaving the women to amuse themselves. After several pints in the afternoon, Tom announced that he wished to compose, if Jem would oblige him.

"What, just like that?" said Jem, surprised.

"No, I promised another broadside to Shaloe Brown. Don't you recall, he paid me in advance? I've been working it out in my head all week. Now I think I've got it, if I may impose on your leisure." Jem replied that he might and went off in search of pen, ink, and paper. These were not the kinds of things readily at hand in the New Tavern, but he eventually found a playbill from the previous night's entertainment on the green, the reverse of which would do for the moment. Once he had ruled the lines, Tom slowly and precisely spelled out the melody, then the words:

How can I live with no money in my pocket?
But I would let the money go,
All for to please her fancy,
And I would marry no one but my bonny blue-eyed Nancy.

"Nancy?" Jem asked, when he had written it down. "Don't you mean Sal?"

"What? No!" said Tom, making a great show of surprise. "It's another old Irish air, only I've translated the words, and changed them around to make better poetry. And the name is Nancy, not Sally."

"Hmm," said Jem, clearly not convinced.

"Blue-eyed Nancy," Tom insisted. "Why, does Sal have blue eyes as well?"

"As it so happens, she does." Jem regarded him with narrowed eyes.

"Oh, really? Well, never mind that," Tom said impatiently. "Here's the next verse."

Some people say that she's very low in station,
And other people say she'll be the cause of my ruination,
But let them all say what they will,
To her I will prove constant still.
And I would marry no one but my bonny blue-eyed Nancy.

"What?" Tom demanded as he finished his dictation, for he could hear Jem snorting and shuffling about.

"Finchy! Tell me you didn't ask Sal to marry you!" Jem burst out. Tom did not reply, but his burning red ears spoke for him.

"What are you thinking!" Jem continued in exasperation. "Girls like Betsy and Sal are good for a bit of fun but trulls ain't for falling in love with. It's her occupation to make you fall in love with her for money. What did she say to you?" He affected Sal's rasping voice in a high-pitched, mocking tone: "'Oh Tommy, you're my own true love!' Was that it?"

"I have never paid her a penny for her time nor her affections," Tom replied defensively, turning his face away.

"Then the more fool you. Just as you say in the song, she will be the cause of your ruination, mark my words."

CHAPTER ELEVEN: LORD MORDINGTON

Soon after their return to the city, Tom and Jem conveyed the song "Blue-Eyed Nancy" to Shaloe Brown, who was delighted, in his brittle, costive way, and paid an advance for three more tunes. This largess led Tom to suspect that his broadsides were selling even better than Brown admitted, but he took the money without argument. Also upon his return, Tom heard that *Acis and Galatea* had been held over at Drury Lane, and Tess Turnbridge had been promoted from entr'acte to the comprimario role of Eurilla. This was a considerable advance to her career, and Tom sent her the joy of it, in a letter dictated to Jem. Tom was pleased to hear Tess was rising quickly, as he had predicted, although this also meant she would no longer be taking lessons with him, and he found he missed her regular visits more than he would have expected.

Sal also kept herself away, and for several weeks he had no word of her. Then one evening, as Tom was drinking at the Labor in Vain with Jem and Betsy, she appeared as if out of nowhere, her familiar rasping voice crying out over the din of the crowd, "Tommy! Bloody good to chop on you like this! How're you keeping?"

Tom rose and bowed to her, saying he was keeping very well, and squeezing her hand with great affection as she kissed him on the cheek.

Betsy gazed at Sal with a knowing eye and remarked, "Ain't you looking fine! And how goes it with you, sweetheart?"

"You'll never guess," said Sal excitedly. "I'm married!"

"What!" There was general consternation round the table. Jem was the first to recover his tongue, and lifted his glass to her, wishing her every happiness. Tom, meanwhile, had gone very pale—he felt as if he had been struck with a physical blow. But he lifted his glass in her direction and joined the toast to her health.

"Married!" Tom cried after they had set their glasses down again. "Who the devil with?"

"Oh, but he's right here. I'll make proper introductions," Sal said, her voice bubbling over with happiness. She turned away from them and shrieked, "Georgie!" in a grating, carrying tone.

A tall, broad-shouldered man with black hair and a black, beetling brow rose from a table where he was speaking to several other men and pushed his way through the crowd.

"This is my husband, Mr. George Harkington, an engraver in Grub Street. With his own shop! Ain't it grand? We live above it. Georgie dear, these are my dearest friends, Betsy Careless, Jemmy Castleton, and Tommy Finch." They rose as she said their names; Betsy curtsied and the men shook hands. Tom noted that Harkington's hand was large but supple, not rough or calloused.

"Sally Salisbury, married to an honest tradesman!" Betsy teased her, once they had all exchanged greetings. "I never thought I'd live to see the day!"

"Kiss my arse," Sal replied, smiling. Harkington appeared unfazed by his wife's crude remark, but only gave them all his regards and ferried her back to their own table at the other end of the public house.

There was a stunned silence again, until at last Jem cleared his throat and said, "Ain't you going to call him out, Finchy?"

Tom scowled down into his tankard. "What, a duel? Whatever for?"

"But didn't you and her have an understanding?" Betsy asked gently, concern evident in her voice. "I thought, after Epsom..."

Tom cut her off. "No, nothing of the sort. She does as she pleases, the hard-mouthed jade."

"She did run a tick in Epsom," Jem offered. "I suppose she needed the money."

"She don't look like a girl who just married for money," Betsy observed, craning her head to get a better look at them. "See how she kisses him!" Jem shot her a murderous look across the table and gestured for her to keep quiet, but she only shrugged.

"I'm tired," Tom declared suddenly. "I believe I shall return home." He groped about for his walking stick, but could not find it, as it had fallen to the floor. Betsy retrieved it from under the table and put it in his hand.

"Oughtn't you go with him?" Betsy asked Jem, as they watched Tom tap his way through the crowd and towards the door.

Jem shook his head. "Nay, he knows his own way home well enough. Let him go."

Betsy leaned over the table and finished her pint in one long swig. "Sal married!" she burst out again when she had drunk it down. "Whatever can she be thinking?"

"The devil take her, the infamous slut," Jem concurred.

Tom found himself most wretchedly, shamefully affected by the news of Sal's hasty marriage. It did no good to tell himself he was a fool, a flat, a cull for having expected any less from a whore, and not only a whore, but a thief, and a ruthless adventuress. It was not that he had deceived himself about her moral character, or her constancy, for he knew all too well that he was but one of her many admirers. But he had believed that she was opposed to a domestic arrangement with any man, and would refuse all offers as she had refused his. Had she not said plainly she preferred to keep her own household? And why Harkington, of all people? He was not particularly rich, and seemed unlikely to countenance the sort of pranks she so enjoyed.

Damn it all, what does she see in him? He tried to put her out of his mind but the more he endeavored to forget her, the more he was reminded of all the little details about her that he held so dear: her throaty laugh, her smoky scent, her bony rough hand grasping his, the feel of her form in men's attire.

While his mind was so occupied with these thoughts, he avoided the houses of resort that she was used to frequent, which unfortunately were also his usual haunts. Rather than passing a pleasant evening at the Labor in Vain or the Essex Serpent with Jem and Betsy, most nights found him at a much lower establishment, the Nag's Head in James Street, drinking a nasty, aged brew called stingo, in the company of an ever-revolving set of bawds. It was in this posture that Mr. Holden, the gouty conductor at the Rose, found him one evening.

"Really, Mr. Finch, is this any way for a man of your standing and talents to carry on? And you beginning to rise in the world, for shame!" Holden expostulated, seating himself before Tom with a groan. He extended his right leg to the side stiffly.

"Ah, Mr. Holden, how good of you to join us," Tom replied flatly, as the scrape of the chair told him that Holden had sat down. Tom pushed the jug across the table with an unsteady hand, sloshing a good deal in the process. He detached himself from the arms of the bawd seated next to him and pulled the laces of his shirt together.

"Now then," Tom said, "How may I be of service to you? I doubt you have come all this way merely to heap recriminations on my head." His voice was steady, but his overly-careful diction betrayed the fact that he was already quite drunk. His white-blue eyes were extremely bloodshot, giving him a strangely demonic appearance. Holden regarded him with distaste.

"I have come here with a message from Mr. Betterton," Holden said. "Lord Mordington is looking to engage musicians for an assembly, a ball if you like. Mr. Betterton has put forward your name with the highest recommendation, and now

Lord Mordington desires to meet with you tomorrow."

"Indeed?" said Tom, and drained his cup.

Holden became exercised by this perceived lack of response. "I hope you are sensible what a great boon Mr. Betterton has granted you. He might have merely given this position to Brookings and passed you by entirely. This could be the making of your career, you know. You might even discover a patron. A patron, sir!"

Tom replied that he was sensible, very sensible indeed, for in fact his mind was already racing with possibilities, although his face did not reflect his thoughts. He would need two violins, and two or three players for the basso continuo. He would ask Jem, of course, but while he had a high opinion of Jem's handwriting, having never seen it himself, he had direct evidence of Jem's skills on the violin, which he held in much lower regard. Jem had an unfortunate tendency to run away with the tune; he could not be trusted to keep the tempo, or to play the notes precisely as they were written. Better to keep him to the basso continuo, where he could do less harm...No, Brookings was clearly the man for the job, if he was not too proud to play second violin...

Holden's remonstrance broke in on his running thoughts. "....tomorrow at two o'clock," he was saying. "And shave, for God's sake! You look like a scrub!"

The next day Tom, grasping Jem's elbow, and followed by Brookings, called upon Lord Mordington's new address in the northeast corner of the Piazza of Covent Garden. Tom was shaved and brushed as ordered, dressed in his best brocade surcoat and his one remaining pair of white silk stockings. They were led by a servant through a cavernous entryway into a large empty hall. Tom clicked his tongue, determining that the room was long and narrow, full of echoes. Presumably this would be where the dancing would take place, with the adjoining rooms further back devoted to the gambling tables. For many years, Lord Mordington had run a gaming house in

Charles Street, and now he was opening an even larger house in the Piazza, by law a private residence, but in fact open to the public. It was not hard to guess the reason for this assembly to inaugurate the new location: invite people of quality, and the rest would follow.

From an inner room they heard the voice of a servant calling, "The waits is here, my lord!"

"Waits!" Jem muttered. "I'll give you your bloody waits!"

Tom nudged him sharply. "Only keep silent and let me do the talking."

The same servant flung open the large double doors at the far end of the hall and announced Sir George Seton, the fourth Lord Mordington, and his wife, Catherine, Lady Mordington, without the least shade of hesitation, although everyone knew that in the eyes of the law, Lord Mordington was still married to a commoner named Mary Dillon, whom he had deserted after being arrested for debt much earlier in life. Now fat and successful, the curls of his white wig stood out all around his jowly, roseate face, with his queue protruding at a right angle in the back. The so-called Lady Mordington was a small, round woman of late middle years, although the elaborate curls of her wig and her plump cheeks gave her a strangely girlish appearance.

Prompted by the sound of their approaching footsteps, Tom showed a leg as neatly as he knew how, sweeping his tricorne hat behind him as he bowed low.

"So you are the music master Betterton has sent?" Lord Mordington asked, addressing himself to Brookings.

"Begging your pardon, my lord, but Mr. Finch is the music master," Brookings corrected him, gesturing toward Tom.

Tom bowed again, murmuring, "Your servant, my lord."

Lady Mordington said to herself in a clearly audible whisper, "A blind man! Heavens! I'm sure I don't know!"

"With all due respect, my lord, you won't find a better music master in all of London," Brookings said, and thankfully Jem kept his mouth shut. Lord Mordington harrumphed. He was less interested in hiring the best music master in all of London than the cheapest one who could still be passed off as respectable.

Tom gave them what he hoped was his winningest smile as he drew Lord Mordington into a long discussion of the particulars of the assembly, the number of guests, the sort of music and dances he desired. As he spoke, he strode about the room commenting on the acoustics and the placement of instruments, walking and gesturing with confidence, as though he could see. He might not have managed it had the room not been entirely devoid of furnishings, but in the echoing, empty hall there was nothing to trip over, and he could sense the location of the doors and windows, the general size and shape, and where the musicians should be placed so the sound would carry the most strongly. It was a bit of theatrics, in truth, but it stopped Lady Mordington's mutterings.

They came at last to the delicate matter of the fee. Lord Mordington named a shockingly low price, shamelessly adding that divided three ways it would still be a handsome figure.

"My lord, I am afraid you misunderstand. We must hire at least two or three more players," Tom said.

This did not sit well. "But you are to play a trio sonata," Lady Mordington protested. "Unless I am mistaken, trio is the Latin for three, and you are three already, are you not?"

"A perfectly understandable misapprehension, my lady," Tom replied smoothly. "But you see, a trio sonata is played with two violins, (that will be myself and Mr. Brookings), and a basso continuo, which although it is counted as one, must always consist of two or three instruments, to provide the lower voices, if you will. We must have one string, one wind, and one harpsichord. May I inquire whether you have a harpsichord?" Lord Mordington was ill pleased with this unforeseen demand, as he did not own a harpsichord or anything of the sort. But Tom insisted that the voices of the violins were thin and weak; if his lordship wanted the music to be heard at all over the din of the guests, he must procure a harpsichord.

"And may I inquire further," Tom continued, "whether your lordship would be pleased to engage a singer as well?"

"All these players and now a singer as well, forsooth!" Lord Mordington cried.

"A singer could add an air of grace and elegance at the beginning of the evening, before the dances begin," Tom suggested.

"Oh, I like the sound of that!" Lady Mordington exclaimed.

"A singer, then, but none of your damned eunuchs!" said Lord Mordington irritably, feeling himself overruled by his wife. "It's against nature, I tell you."

"Oh no," Tom reassured them. "I was thinking of a lovely young woman, a soprano. If it pleases your lordship, I can arrange to engage the prima donna of the Theater Royal in Drury Lane."

This pleased Lady Mordington very well, and she kept repeating "prima donna!" and "Theater Royal!" in rapturous tones, so that Lord Mordington was obliged to throw up his hands and declare she would bankrupt him, but in the end agreed to all that was put before him.

The preparations for the assembly lightened Tom's mood considerably, although in the midst of seeking out additional musicians and planning the arrangements, Jem reported an unexpected piece of news: Ned Ward had turned up dead in a Covent Garden alley, shot through the head.

"D'ye reckon it were Sal who done him?" Jem asked, finishing off the last of Tom's claret. They were sprawled in chairs by the fire in the front parlor of number eight Maiden Lane.

Tom gave a resigned sigh. "I have no idea," he admitted. "I haven't spoken to her since her marriage to that Harkington cove." But at least Ned could no longer save himself from being hanged at Tyburn by impeaching Sal. Tom could only hope that Sal was indeed playing the proper married woman and had given over criminal pursuits. He forced himself to put her out of his mind and turn his attention to the job at hand.

Tess Turnbridge was delighted to be asked to sing at the assembly, and even agreed to call at number eight Maiden Lane to run some pieces several days in advance. It had been quite some time since she had last visited for a lesson, and she felt a pleasant rush of familiarity as Stinson showed her into the drawing room. She greeted Tom with sincere affection, grasping his hand in a warm gesture that lingered perhaps a shade longer than was proper. Now that she had risen a bit in the theatrical world, she had come to consider Tom as more of a colleague and equal. Moreover, she fancied that her deepening attachment to Jane would serve as proof against temptation. It pleased her to think of Tom as a friend, and it was perfectly natural to feel such a rush of happiness at greeting a friend.

"I must warn you, Miss Turnbridge," Tom said, as he took his place at the spinet, "this assembly will be nothing like singing on stage. Your voice will not carry, and you must take care not to blow out. I will ensure that you sing early in the evening, before the guests become too drunk, but pray do not be discomfited if they pay you no mind and do not leave off conversing. They will not be silent as at the theater." This was a bit of polite fiction, for even at the theater, the crowd was unruly and noisy as a matter of course; the stage that Tess trod nightly was lined with iron spikes along the front to prevent any overly amorous (or critical) audience members from leaping up. Nevertheless, Tess promised to remember his advice.

"And sleep as much as ever you can the day before, for the assembly will most likely continue until the small hours of the night, or even the next morning," he added.

Tom did not mention that he had advertised her as the prima donna of Drury Lane, not wanting to alarm her with his petty deception. He knew Lord Mordington would not know the difference.

They ran through several of the arias and art songs in her repertoire, including "Le Violette," and one aria from *Acis and*

Galatea, "Hush ye pretty warbling choir."

"My dear Miss Turnbridge," Tom declared, "your talents have only increased since last I heard you."

Tess smiled happily. "You are too kind," she said. "I own I have been sorry not to sing with you more often."

Impulsively, she leaned forward and played a few chords, thinking they might perhaps try a duet. He turned his face to her in surprise, his eyes wide and searching, twitching back and forth. Tess felt again that clench deep in the pit of her belly, that odd sensation halfway between pleasure and pain. She had forgotten how profoundly his uncanny gaze affected her. Making music with him had become one of her great delights—striving together for perfection, the way he listened so carefully to her, she felt as if they were partners in art, not master and student. And to be honest, she was not insensible to his handsome features and supple hands.

He did not speak, but as the surprise faded from his face, replaced with a more intense emotion, he leaned towards her, as if he meant to kiss her.

At that moment, the door opened with an indelicate crash and Stinson entered bearing the tea service. Tess leapt up hastily, blushing and smoothing the front of her dress nervously, although Stinson took no notice of her at all as he placed the tray on a side table. For his part, Tom did not attempt to pursue her further, but even so, Tess was mortified at her own forwardness. After barely taking two sips of tea, she took her leave in great haste.

CHAPTER TWELVE:
THE ASSEMBLY

The musicians arrived in the afternoon on the day of Lord Mordington's assembly, and amid a great bustle of activity in the main hall, were shown to their assigned place. The hall was no longer bare, but lined around the edges with tables and chairs, while servants set up enormous candelabras and hung swags of rich fabrics from the walls. The hall was long but very narrow, so narrow the musicians would be in danger of collisions if the dancers grew too enthusiastic, but they set up their chairs and instruments as far out of the way as they could. Tom and Brookings were on the first and second violin, while for the basso continuo, Jem took the viola da gamba, with Stevens from the Rose on the dulcina, and a fellow named Bellamy, whom Tom had lured away from Drury Lane, on the harpsichord, which Lord Mordington had so unwillingly had brought in. Tess was there as well, to sing in the early part of the evening.

"Well then, Mr. Bellamy, let us have an A," Tom said, once they were all arranged and ready to tune the strings. Bellamy played the note, while Brookings and Jem joined in obligingly, producing the most hair-raising dissonance. Tom leapt from his seat in distress, laying his violin aside.

"Oh, oh!" he cried, "That was never an A!" He felt about for the chair before the harpsichord, and Bellamy ceded the spot to him. Tom played the note again, shaking his head in disbelief, then played a running scale, again with painful results.

"They never tuned it, the dogs!" he said with mounting frustration, reaching inside the instrument and feeling the tuning pins. "I warrant it was that miserly lord himself, not wanting to pay extra for the tuning after it was moved here, damn him. Did they at least leave behind a tuning hammer?" he asked, addressing the company in general. No one knew.

There was a great confusion as the tuning hammer was sought, but thankfully it was discovered at last, in the pocket of a maid who had been about to throw it away, not knowing what it was.

Tom played the offending note again, turning the pin with the tuning hammer and tapping the key repeatedly until at last lifted his head and announced triumphantly, "There, a proper A!"

"Why, Mr. Finch, do you have perfect pitch?" Tess asked. She had been watching the proceedings with great interest.

"Well of course," he replied, his irritation returning as he moved on to the next key.

"But however did you learn it?" she persisted. "It's a trick I have long wished I had myself."

"I suppose someone once told me the names of each note and I remembered them," Tom replied distractedly, his concentration given to the instrument.

"Remarkable," Tess said, watching him with rapt attention. Tuning the entire harpsichord was an excruciatingly long and tedious process, however, and at last even her interest flagged. By the time he had finished, their rehearsal time was sadly curtailed. Tom resumed his seat, and they tuned the violins and the viola da gamba.

"Right," said Tom, squeezing the violin between his chin and shoulder, "I must request that you gentlemen follow my lead as I keep time thus," he tapped his foot, raising and lowering the violin as well for emphasis, "and pray do not go maundering off on your own, or we shall all be in a sad muddle." When he heard no replies, he added, "I'm talking to you, Mr.

Castleton."

"Yes sir, Mr. Finch, sir!" Jem replied, rolling his eyes comically in Tess's direction.

They ran through one dance without too many missed notes, the others watching Tom alertly as he had instructed. Then Tess just had time for a few vocal exercises, before a footman informed them that the guests were about to arrive, and it was time to play in earnest.

The guests trickled in slowly, the women in their wide, almost rectangular panniers and towering curls padded out with hair cushions and festooned with silk flowers, feathers, and jewels, the men in tight breeches and white silk hose, full-skirted surcoats and gaudy brocade waistcoats. Both men and women powdered their hair and painted their faces with a thick coat of white lead, embellished with patches to hide the effects of smallpox or other more shameful conditions.

Although she was now in the company of the Theater Royal, Tess's salary had not increased by much. She and Jane had scraped together as much as they could to purchase for her a new gown, a *robe à la française* in a brilliant blue that set off her brown curls, with a closed bodice and pleats cascading crisply in a straight line from the shoulder down to the hem. Tom and the others also wore their own clothes, as Lord Mordington was not about to provide them with livery, but at least, Tess noted, they looked respectable, not like they had just been plucked from the tavern next door.

Tess was glad for Tom's warning to preserve her voice, for the conversation in the great hall did not stop as she performed. All the bodies in the room, as well as the elaborate swags of cloth lining the walls had a deadening effect. It was the most frustrating sensation, as if she were singing under a blanket. The temptation to strain was very great, but behind her, Tom murmured, "Softly, gently now." At last, discouraged and spent, she retired to her chair, while the others struck up a lively courante. She felt not a single guest had attended to her efforts.

The dancing went on interminably: the courante was followed by a stately gavotte, then a bourrée, an almain, a sarabande, a minuet, and on again, tunes by Corelli, Purcell, Handel, and the rest. The ladies just returned from the continent competed to display their mastery of the latest French dances, and Tess stifled a strong urge to show them how it was done properly. Still the musicians sawed away, unmoved by the posturing before them. If they hesitated for even a moment, to tune up or tighten a bow, Lord Mordington was upon them directly, reminding them that they were not being paid to sit on their arses, and did they think this was a bloody public house?

At last, as the clock was nearing midnight, Lord Mordington disappeared into one of the gambling rooms. After ensuring that he was thoroughly engrossed in a game of faro, Tess prevailed upon Lady Mordington to allow the musicians a brief respite and supper in the kitchen, for they were all famished.

As they were hurriedly stuffing themselves with leftovers from the dainty spread, Stevens said around a mouthful of cold ham, "Christ, what an ungainly lot!"

Bellamy nodded, snagging the last Eccles cake. "Was that really the best Mordington could do? What a parcel of flats. Who was that gawkey miss with the orange sash?"

"She looked like a stork wading through a marsh," Jem commented.

"That would be his lordship's daughter," Brookings said, looking guiltily about as one of the scullery maids gave them a reproving frown.

"I believe her name is Campbellina," Tom added, prompting guffaws around the table at the unlikely name.

"God help that unfortunate child," Stevens said, as Brookings nervously tried to quiet them.

Their hasty meal over, they headed back to the main hall, and Tom somehow contrived to ensure that it was Tess's arm he grasped on to. "It must be dreadfully dull for you to sit idle behind us," he said apologetically.

"Oh no," Tess replied. "Never fret over me, I am perfectly content. But I fear you must be quite done in."

Tom laughed. "Oh, but the assembly is only just beginning! You'll see." As they took their seats once more and tuned up, Tom remarked, "Observe how the temperament of the crowd has changed already—they are becoming drunker, less mindful of their manners. Now we shall see some capers."

"You can tell just by the sound?" Tess asked.

Tom smiled. "Of course. Can't you? And Miss Turnbridge, if you wish to dance, I believe now it would not be considered improper. Only sit out front, where you may arrange yourself to better advantage." Tess thanked him sincerely, for she had few enough opportunities to mix with people of quality, unless they were beating down her dressing-room door with indecent proposals.

They began to play again, but Tom was only half paying attention to the music. He had heard a familiar voice over the crowd, cutting through the buzzing conversation. When they paused at the end of the gavotte, the voice spoke directly before him.

"Thomas. I trust you are well."

"My Lord Bolingbroke." Tom rose and bowed to his father.

There was an awkward pause. "You are looking well," Lord Bolingbroke said at last.

Tom considered replying that he was looking well also, but the old earl always took it amiss whenever Tom joked about his blindness. Not wanting to antagonize him, Tom instead inquired blandly after his health, and added that he had dined with Lady Gray a few days previously.

"Quite, quite," said Lord Bolingbroke. "You must come down to Culverleigh and pay us a visit." Then he stalked off, obviously eager to be away. Tom sat down again and resumed playing rather dazedly. Was that a serious invitation? He had not been to Culverleigh, the manor at the family seat in Bedfordshire, since he was a boy.

Tess watched this exchange with fascination, then glanced over at Jem, who winked at her meaningfully as he played. She looked back at Tom, scraping away on the violin, with his brow wrinkled up and a blank stare of concentration directed at the ceiling. There was no mistaking that the gentleman was Tom's father. Like Tom, the old earl was very tall and thin, now somewhat stooped, with the same long face, although with somewhat heavier, darker features. She could not help but notice the look he gave Tom of guarded affection, mingled with something else, more than just patrician aloofness. What was it? She longed to ask Tom about his father, but this was clearly an inopportune moment.

As Tom had predicted, the dancers became increasingly intemperate, and he soon laid aside the more sedate tunes for country dances from Playford's, which everyone knew, and exchanged the noble violin for the more plebian hornpipe, an instrument made of two horns with a pipe for fingering in the middle. This not only granted relief to his back, aching from holding the violin, but also was much louder, and carried more easily above the increasing noise of the crowd. The pleasure of playing, of hearing the notes unreeling from his fingers faster and faster, and the answering stamp of the dancers in rhythm, carried him along, and kept exhaustion at bay. Between the bleating of the hornpipe and his concentration on keeping the other players in tempo, he hardly noticed Tess speaking to an unfamiliar man, then leaving her seat, until Jem, urging him to take a short break with a welcome glass of brandy, commented upon it. They were playing in turns now, with Brookings taking the lead while Jem and Tom rested briefly.

"Your Miss Turnbridge has done quite well for herself," said Jem in a conspiratorial tone. "If it ain't the Duke of Grafton himself who's asked her to dance!"

"Oh, indeed?" said Tom, feeling strangely nonplussed.

"Now the dance has finished, he's bringing her a glass of punch," Jem narrated. "He do look taken with her. And he a musical gentleman too, a subscriber to the Royal Academy. Didn't you hear him pay her all those compliments just now? 'How lovely you sang, Miss Turnbridge,' and 'Such a fine clear tone, Miss Turnbridge.' I say, Finchy, is you feeling poorly? It ain't like you to miss that sort of thing."

Tom stood up and rolled his shoulders, shaking his head to clear it. "I am quite well, I assure you," he said. "Come, let's give poor Brookings a rest. We still have many hours ahead of us."

They played on and on. At two and even three in the morning, the numbers of guests dwindled, as some left for home or a more discreet assignation, while others, less inhibited, pursued their amours in corners and under tables, and a few passed out drunk on the floor, but still the assembly showed no sign of ending. Lord Mordington made it clear they were to play on.

It was about this time that Tess took her leave of them. She returned to her seat to fetch her calash, ordered a servant to bring the weary musicians more wine, and bade them all a hasty goodnight.

"But you ain't been paid yet," Jem protested.

"Never mind, Mr. Finch can send it to me later," she said, as she departed on the arm of Charles FitzRoy, the Duke of Grafton.

"Leaving without her pay! Did you ever hear of such a thing?" Jem exclaimed, watching her go.

"I reckon the duke will pay her more than old muckworm Mordington ever will," Stevens said with a rude laugh.

Jem laughed as well. "Looks like Miss Turnbridge found herself a patron, even if the rest of us are left on the shelf," he said.

Tom only frowned and did not reply. Finally, with the grey light of dawn beginning to show, the last stragglers departed. Lord Mordington fell fast asleep with his head on one of the gaming tables, his wife and daughter having long since departed for their residence in Charles Street. As Tom and Brookings packed up their instruments, Jem sought out the steward and after a few heated words, extracted the whole of their pay. Stevens had disappeared into the kitchen with a scullery maid, and Bellamy they left snoring under the harpsichord. By the time they stumbled home, the sun was nearly up. Covent Garden was beginning to stir to life, with the flower and vegetable vendors setting up their stalls.

Home at last, Tom fell into bed, too weary to remove his clothes, but found himself strangely wakeful. He took up the purse from the nightstand and carefully felt each coin: fifteen guineas, ten shillings, his portion for the evening. A handsome fee, to be sure, but since Holden had put the idea in his head, he had half hoped he might have been able to put himself in the way of a patron. And what of Tess and her duke? Grafton was married, and not a young man, but if he set her up handsomely as a kept mistress, she might choose a life of ease rather than continuing her opera career. Was she now lost to him too?

With an impatient sigh, he rolled over and fell into a fitful sleep.

CHAPTER THIRTEEN: THE ROAD TO DOVER

Some few nights later, not long after Lord Mordington's assembly, Tom was awakened in the small hours by a scratching and rattling at his bedroom window. Slow to awaken, he lay for some minutes in confusion, but it soon became clear that there was a person outside endeavoring to get in. His heart pounding, he felt about beside the bed for something that might serve as a weapon. His fingers closed around a heavy metal cylindrical object—a candlestick, he soon realized, although what it was doing there, he had no idea, as he was not in the habit of lighting candles. As he heard the casement swing open, he rose to his knees in the bed, brandishing the candlestick above his head. He heard a light thump as someone jumped from the window ledge to the floor, but just as he was about to swing the candlestick in the direction of the sound, a familiar, rasping voice called out, "Tommy!"

"Sal!" he cried, struggling off the bed to embrace her. She flung her arms about him wildly, gripping him with an intensity he had not known from her before.

"Dammee, how glad I am to see you again," she said, peering at him in the scant moonlight coming in through the open window. She turned to shut it, then looked back at him more closely. "But Tommy, what's this?" She plucked the candlestick from his hand, and laughed weakly. "D'ye take me for a ken cracker? Was you about to do for me with this here glimstick?"

"Well?" Tom countered. "And what are you doing, coming in through the window in the middle of the night like a damned criminal? I thought you was a respectable married woman now." He ran a hand over her waist, confirming that she was wearing women's clothes, then allowed his hand to drift lower over her rump, giving it a squeeze. "Or are you bored of your husband already?"

Quite unlike her usual romping self, Sal only stepped away from him and said, "A thumping great glimstick but never a candle in this room, I'll wager. Just a moment and I'll fetch one." She ran downstairs to the box of candles on the mantle in the front parlor, then returned to set the candlestick on the nightstand with a shaking hand.

Although he could not see her pale, drawn face, or her troubled brow, still Tom could tell from her unsteady movements and ragged breath that something was amiss. He took her by the shoulders. "Sal, what is wrong?"

She wrenched away and began pacing frantically. "Oh!" she cried, "Oh, oh, I am scragged, dished up, undone! Oh God, undone!"

Tom's stomach lurched with fear for her. "Sal, was it you killed Ned Ward?"

"What?" Sal stopped her pacing long enough to stare at him in surprise. "No, Tommy, listen, it's nothing to do with that damned scrub, his soul to the devil. It's Georgie. Our bite's gone sour."

"You mean George Harkington, your husband?" Tom could not help adding that last word with spiteful emphasis.

"Oh, aye, as to that, well, as it happens he was married already, the filthy son of a whore, so there ain't no legal marriage," she said in a venomous tone, nearly spitting at the thought of him.

"Ah, a bigamist, how unfortunate," said Tom with false

sympathy. "But what is this bite you speak of? I take it your, ah, relationship had a profitable angle?"

"Don't come it so high with me, cully," she flashed out suddenly. "You'll have plenty of time to laugh at me when they're stretching my neck on Tyburn, oh ha bloody ha!"

Tom reached out for her apologetically. "Come now Sal, only tell me what it is, and you know I'll do all I can for you."

She did not take his hand, but resumed pacing. "So like I says, we had a rum bite at first. Georgie is an engraver, you see, a devilish good one. He set out plates for false notes, and I took 'em all over town to be redeemed, never the same place twice, and this is the cleverest part, they was drawn on the Bank of Scotland. Not many cullies know what they should properly look like, so no one was too particular."

"My God, Sal!" Tom cried, aghast. "D'ye know the punishment for forgery? Never mind Tyburn—you'll be burned at the stake! You might have done better to stick to housebreaking."

"Oh fie, that's only for forging coins, not notes. But we was in no danger, I tell you, until that poxy blowen come in. 'Oh Mr. Harkington,' says she, 'How could you abandon me, and I still faithful to you?'" Sal recited in a mocking tone. "'It's all a damnable lie,' says he. He says she run off with the butcher, and he wouldn't have none of it. And then the villainous jade, she 'peached on us both! Went straight to the magistrate with the whole story, and now the constable's sent his coves after me."

"But what of Harkington?" Tom asked, his anxiety mounting.

"He's piked off to the colonies with our cash, left me high and dry. Says, 'It were never a legal marriage, Sal,' and 'You're free to marry again, Sal,' and 'Don't come looking for me. We're finished, Sal.' And off he goes, leaving me in the house with the nappers at the door." She veered again from indignant bravado to breathless panic, ceasing her pacing to throw herself upon him. "Oh Tommy, I'm ruined! You must help me!"

He stroked her hair, which was hanging loose and disheveled, but with some care, as if she were a feral cat he was attempting to tame. "Of course you may hide here as long as you wish. D'ye need money too?"

"No, I daren't stay here. We're both too well known around the Piazza. I'm going over to France, and I want you to come with me."

"What?" Tom still had his arms around her, but now he pulled back just a bit. "To France? No! You must be joking!"

Sal entwined her arms around his neck, her bony frame tugging at him desperately. "Please, Tommy! I need you!"

These were the words Tom had longed to hear from her, although to be sure he had imagined her uttering them under happier circumstances. Still, the prospect of saving her himself, rather than being the one in need of rescue, moved him deeply, and he found himself considering her proposal, despite his better judgment.

"I'm afraid you'll find me a poor traveling companion," he said, hoping to find a compromise. "Won't you make better time on your own? If it's a question of money, I can give you what I have."

She gave him a tender squeeze. "Oh Tommy, you're so kind, but I have money. I managed to make off with most of the plate and jewels, and some cash Georgie never knew about. I brought it all here in a bundle. But I need you to come with me. I had a tip that the constable's looking for me in particular, has coves everywhere with my description. But they ain't looking for a married couple, since Georgie's piked off already. Georgie and me, we was planning to flee to France anyways, before all this trouble come up, and I nicked the traveling papers—passage on a packet from Dover to Calais under false names." She pulled a rustling sheaf of papers from her bodice. "Off we go as Mr. and Mrs. Lancaster, and none the wiser. Only you must come with me. I can't use this on my own."

This was by far the most outrageous request Sal had ever put before him, and Tom knew he should refuse her. He could hear Jem's voice in his head warning him not to trust her.

When Tom did not acquiesce immediately, Sal prevailed upon him with pleas and promises of great fun and adventure on the road, traveling in fine twig, and vague suggestions that she had a great deal of money, that they might flash out in style, if only they could cross the Channel.

But as she prattled on, Tom's thoughts turned in a different direction. It was true that they were both far too well-known in London; there was nothing he could do to protect her here. Once she was arrested, she would certainly be hanged, if not for the forgery, then for any of her previous crimes. If there was anything at all he could do to save her from being sent to the gallows, he had to try. He should feel a right scrub if he hesitated to save her merely because her plan was inconvenient to him. Moreover, he was flattered to know that of all her many friends and admirers, he was the one she turned to at her most desperate moment. He knew all too well that most people thought of him as hopelessly dependent, unable to help himself, let alone others. But here was Sal, not only choosing him but relying on him to aid her. In the end, the idea of acting as Sal's heroic savior was too seductive for him to refuse.

Tom roused Stinson and bade him pack up a trunk with some clothing and a few effects, then go round the Piazza to hire a carriage. The faithful old valet did not speak his mind, but Tom knew he was disturbed by these goings-on, and concerned for his master. When the driver had secured Tom's trunk and Sal's bundle on top of the carriage, Tom handed Stinson a purse for the rent, if Mrs. Bracegirdle should call, and told him to tell any visitors that he had gone to stay with his father at Culverleigh. Tom grasped his hand and thanked him heartily, and bade him look after the house, feeling a pang of conscience for deceiving the old man, but there was nothing for it. Sal rushed from the house at the last moment, with a veil over her face, in case anyone might be watching. Stinson handed Sal and Tom up into the carriage, and they were off, with Sal laying on the floor among the straw, for fear of being recognized, until they were past Drury Lane.

Even in the middle of the night, the passage over London Bridge was slow and wearisome. It was not an auspicious start to their journey, for they fell to arguing almost immediately. Sal attempted to construct identities to match the false names on the traveling papers, but this proved more difficult than she had anticipated.

"You is to be Mr. Lancaster, a linen draper in Spitalfields, going over to France to increase your stores," Sal instructed, reciting the plan that Harkington had contrived for his own escape.

"That will never answer," Tom replied. "No one will ever believe I am a linen draper."

"What, because you're blind? We could give out that you was only just stricken with an illness."

"Then why would I be traveling on business, and not home in bed? No, but more to the point, I have no more notion of the buying and selling of linen than a cat, and neither do you."

Sal gave a little cry of frustration. "But that's what it says in the traveling papers. We'll just have to crack on as best we can."

Tom frowned. "Very well then, if I am to be Mr. Lancaster of Spitalfields, what is my Christian name, pray tell?"

"I don't know."

"Well, what does it say in the papers?"

"Dammee, Tom, you know I can't read!"

Tom passed a weary hand over his brow. "What a sad pair of flats we are. We shall just have to avoid any close conversation or inquiry until we have crossed the Channel." He was silent for a moment, then said in a hopeful tone, "You know, Sal, if we are to travel as husband and wife, perhaps we might go before the parson and be married before we depart? It might add to the deception."

"Why bother? Besides, we ain't got the time."

Tom turned the corners of his mouth down. "Well, if you're to pass for a respectable married woman, you must stop screeching and swearing like a common trull. It ain't genteel."

Sal replied with an even more vulgar suggestion on what he could do with his genteel talk, and they fell into an angry silence. Once over the bridge in Southwark, Sal paid the driver, and they alighted at the Tabard Inn in Borough High Street to find a coach to Dover. This occasioned another heated exchange, as Tom would have preferred they hire horses and ride, but Sal was afraid of being seen, and furthermore was anxious for them to make all haste so as not to miss the packet. She was inclined to go by post, but at the last moment she saw that the carriage already had two passengers in it, and unwilling to risk hours of protracted conversation with strangers, she hung back uncertainly. As the hour was still quite early, the sky only just beginning to lighten, there were few stagecoaches about, but at last she found a driver who, for an exorbitant fee, was willing to take them as his only passengers as far as Canterbury.

Although Sal had also tipped the driver even more handsomely to make all haste, their progress along the road was far slower than she would have liked, not only because of the inevitable frequent stops to change horses, but also because Tom, as he had warned her, was a less than ideal traveling companion. Within an hour of leaving Southwark, once they were on the open road and jogging along at a good pace, before they had even reached Greenwich, the swaying and lurching of the coach made him quite ill, and they had to stop repeatedly, as they passed Blackwell, Barking, Gravesend. Sal discovered her remonstrance with the driver did no good, for the man was loath to have the inside of his coach fouled, and every time Tom pounded on the floor with his walking stick, the driver would stop to allow Tom to stumble out.

"What, catting again? Have you a padlock on your arse that you shite through your teeth?" she demanded in a mocking voice, coldly regarding him once again heaving and retching on all fours by the side of the road. He did not reply, but only wiped his mouth with the back of his hand and sullenly groped his way back to the coach.

"Ain't you empty yet?" she demanded, as they got underway again.

"Shall I go back to London?" he asked wearily.

"No, you know I can't take the ship on my own. It's just the packet leaves tomorrow. We must go faster," she said.

But they did not go faster, and night had fallen again by the time they reached Canterbury. Tom suggested half-heartedly they stay the night and leave again in the morning, but as he expected, Sal would have none of it. She marched off, still with a veil over her face, to search for a coach to Dover, leaving Tom collapsed in a corner of a tavern. His head was pounding and he still felt dizzy and nauseated. Thinking it might set him up, he ordered a pint of ale and some bread and cheese, but this proved to be a mistake, for as soon as they were on the road a short time, it all came up again.

"How ever did you travel the length and breadth of Ireland when you was a lad?" Sal demanded, after another forced stop.

"That was in no wise similar," Tom replied defensively. "We traveled on horseback or walked, and took our ease, none of this heathenish pell-mell dashing about in a closed coach." The carriage lurched sharply as the wheels settled into a rut, and Tom groaned loudly.

It took the entire night and most of the next day to reach Dover, and by this time Tom was nearly prostrate with sickness and lack of food. Sal and the driver had to haul him half-fainting up the stairs at the inn, with the innkeeper, a round red-cheeked woman of late middle years named Mrs. Broadwell, following after, wringing her hands. When Sal had seen Tom laid out on the bed, Mrs. Broadwell pulled her aside and asked if she should send for the doctor. Sal demurred, but Mrs. Broadwell was a determined comforter, and she seemed to be under the misapprehension that Tom's blindness was a temporary effect of the rigors of the road.

"Never you worry, Mrs. Lancaster," she said, patting Sal's hand in a motherly fashion. "He just needs a pint of ale and a good rest, and I'm sure his sight will return again in the morning."

Sal was sorely tempted to make a rude remark about how that would be a bloody miracle, and that Mrs. Broadwell could retire a rich woman with the healing properties of her ale if that were so, but remembering Tom's warning about vulgar language, she held her tongue and merely gave a strained smile as the innkeeper looked at her pityingly.

While Tom rested, Sal made inquiries about the town. She discovered to her vast relief that the packet ship *Acanthus* had been delayed due to a dispute between the owner and the dockyard and would not sail until the following morning. Even more fortuitously, she did not find evidence of the constable's men or any other signs of pursuit, and so with a light heart, she set about securing their passage on the *Acanthus*. She returned to their room at the inn to find that in the intervening hours Tom had recovered much of his customary good humor under the careful ministrations of Mrs. Broadwell, whose sympathies he was playing upon outrageously.

"I see you've run a tick, Mr. Lancaster," Sal said icily, regarding the remains of the sumptuous meal Mrs. Broadwell had served him in their room by her own hand.

"Oh, not at all!" cried the innkeeper, "I could never think of taking money from you in your misfortune. Shall I bring you a cup of chocolate, Mr. Lancaster?" she added in a louder voice.

Tom smiled and bowed slightly to her from where he still lay stretched on the bed. "My dear Mrs. Broadwell, I should like it above all things. You are too kind."

As she trundled off downstairs, Sal heard her muttering to herself, "Such a pity, and he so handsome!"

Sal shut the door and rounded on Tom with a sour look. "If you is done gammoning the landlady, we sail at dawn tomorrow."

Tom sat up eagerly. "But that is excellent news! I've a mind to stride about on deck like an old tar. I am certain the salt air will do me good."

CHAPTER FOURTEEN: THE STORM AT SEA

After a scant few hours' sleep, Tom and Sal rose and hurried down to the quay in the dark hours of the morning, followed by a servant from the inn, dragging their baggage in a cart. The packet ship *Acanthus* lay in port, surrounded by a bustle of activity despite the early hour as the sailors made ready to put to sea. The captain's steward was waiting for them with a lantern, and led them on board with little ceremony, ushering them to where the captain stood by the binnacle. Sal had spoken with the boatswain the day before, but this was the first time for both of them to meet the captain. He was a small, nervous man with a protruding nose and disheveled hair. If his demeanor did not inspire confidence in his seamanship, he at least did not seem particularly interested in his passengers, which would be to their advantage.

Sal produced their papers, which the captain looked over by the light of the lantern the steward held aloft.

"Mr. and Mrs. William Lancaster, is it?" he said. Tom gave a snort, and Sal elbowed him in the ribs sharply. "It says here you are conveying with you two hundred ells of linen to sell in Paris." He strained about to see the shadowy dock. "Where is all this plaguey linen, then? The hold's full already, you know. I'm buggered if I know where you can stow it."

"Oh, as to that..." Tom said, extemporizing wildly, "I, ah, was taken ill..."

"Don't trouble yourself about us, sir," Sal cut in. "We was forced to leave hasty-like, on account of an unexpected turn in our business, you see, and we ain't got but a few little things with us."

The captain looked up from the papers to peer at them more closely. They were indeed an unlikely pair: a blind man, tall and thin, dressed very handsomely but looking unshaven and rumpled, as if he had slept in his clothes, and a woman almost as tall as he, with a brazen swagger and the unmistakable accent of the London gutter in her coarse voice. Luckily for them, however, after the delay of the previous day, the owner was pressing the captain to make all haste, and he cared more about getting his ship across the Channel than the condition of his passengers. "Well, whoever you are, I won't presume to tell you your business," he said. "Joe here will take up your dunnage. Make yourselves fast, and God willing we'll have a short voyage of it, although I must warn you the glass has been falling wickedly this past hour. I'm afraid we shall see some dirty weather this morning." He hurried off, while the steward ran back to the dock to fetch their baggage, leaving them alone on the deck.

"A fine hash you made of that," Sal hissed at Tom. "D'ye call that lying?"

"I?" said Tom indignantly. "And what was that you was cracking on about? I'd have thought you of all people would be better at contriving some tale of a cock and a bull. I'm sure he is fly to us already." They spoke no more, however, as they were not really alone, the deck of the small ship being full of sailors hurrying about, although to their relief they appeared to be the only passengers.

As the first grey light of dawn appeared, the *Acanthus* slipped her mooring and slowly passed through the crowded shipping lanes. She was an aged vessel with only two masts, not particularly fast or handy, designed only to make the

122

short trip to France and back over and over. Sal settled herself on a fall of rope with a loud sigh and fixed her eyes on the horizon.

Once he felt the deck beneath his feet begin to sway and the freshening breeze on his face, Tom regained his good spirits, and declared his intention to stride up and down the deck to take the air, but in fact this proved to be somewhat more difficult than he had imagined. Nearly every inch of the deck, seemingly, was littered with obstacles: barrels, huge coils of rope as thick as a man's arm, netting, and other objects Tom could not identify, so that rather than striding manfully, he found himself picking his way slowly along. And the obstacles were not only lying on the deck, where he might find them with his walking stick, but hanging treacherously from above as well. On shore, when walking about the street or in a house, he usually knew somehow if there was a wall in front of him —even walking in a park, he could feel the loom of the trees before colliding with them. But the width of a rope is nothing compared to a tree, and he found himself smacked in the face by the rigging repeatedly, a most unpleasant and undignified posture, to be knocked backwards unexpectedly. And worse, no matter where he positioned himself, he was in the way of the sailors: first came the slap of bare feet, then the angry shoves and muttered curses.

At last the sailing master took him by the arm and offered to escort the passengers to their cabin. The master led them down the companionway, saying, "Mind your head, sir," just as Tom cracked his forehead against a low-hanging beam. He heard Sal behind him give a snort of laughter, then stifle a curse as she too banged her head. The master showed them to a tiny cabin, the size of a closet, forward on the starboard side. Triangular chunks of glass set into the ceiling let in a weak, hazy daylight from the deck above.

"It might be best if you stay below, sir, madam," the master said. "It's coming on to blow." He handed Sal a wooden bucket, giving her a significant look.

Tom ran his hands all over the tiny cabin, searching out its dimensions and features. Standing in the middle, he could touch the bulkheads on either side with each hand, and the ceiling was so low he had to stoop slightly. There was no furniture, apart from his trunk and Sal's bundle, and no easy place to sit or stand. Against the opposite wall were two bunk beds built up against the hull like two small shelves, with a board along the open side to keep the sleeper from tumbling out. Each bunk was equipped with straw ticking and threadbare quilts. Having been foiled in his attempt to pass himself off as a sailor, Tom announced that he was quite tired, and removing his coat and shoes, squeezed himself into the bottom berth, while Sal seated herself on the trunk, kicking her bundle to the floor.

They were soon very glad of the bucket the master had left them, for not long after the *Acanthus* entered the chops of the Channel, Tom became violently seasick, and Sal followed soon after. The promised storm arrived as well. The ship pitched wildly, up and down in the troughs of the waves with a hideous corkscrew motion. The sound of the wind was unbelievably loud, and the aged ship creaked and groaned with every pitch and roll. Before long, water was seeping in and dripping on them from the upper deck as it was washed by rain and seawater.

At one point at the height of the gale, Sal crept up on deck to empty the bucket into the scuppers and rinse it with seawater from the pump, attempting to stay out of the way of the running sailors. The sight that met her eyes did not inspire confidence: the ship being blown about under bare poles, with all sail furled, waves breaking high and spraying the bows, all hands at the pumps, pulling water out of the hold. As she filled a leather bottle at the water-butt, she distinctly heard someone utter the words "floating coffin," and on the way back down the companionway, she glimpsed a sailor on his knees, looking as if he were giving a last desperate prayer.

She did not mention any of this to Tom, but only offered

him the brackish water, which he drank down gratefully. With shaking hands, she pulled off her soaking cloak and climbed into the lower berth, wrapping her arms about Tom and clinging to him desperately.

"Oh Tommy," she sobbed, "are we to be cast away?"

Tom returned her embrace as another roll tumbled them against the hull, which could be felt working and buckling. "I fear we really are dished up now," he said.

Sal sobbed more loudly. "I've been a heartless jade," she cried. "I'm sorry I bade you come with me against your will. I'm sorry I said them cruel words to you when we was on the road. Oh Tommy, please forgive me!"

Tom squeezed her harder, burying his face in her shoulder. "There's nothing to forgive," he said. "I would do anything for you, Sal."

"If I'm to die, I'm glad it's with you," she said in a small voice.

"And I, you," he replied. Just then, a mighty wave threw the ship on her beam ends, and the alarming sensation of flying through the air then crashing back down silenced their talk. They lay clinging to each other for what felt like hours, tossed about in the cramped berth, wracked by seasickness, too terrified to arise or even speak, expecting at any moment to hear the hull rending apart, or the cabin filling with water.

The ship did not sink, but by the time the storm subsided Tom and Sal were in the most wretched, squalid condition. Tom was still affected by seasickness, but Sal tended him with more kindness than he had ever known from her, helping him to remove his clothes and wash off with a little sea water, and finding him clean clothes in the trunk, not too wet, before exchanging her own clothes.

The *Acanthus* had been blown far to the south by the storm; even after it passed, the wind was foul for Calais. They had to tack up the entire way, in a laborious zigzag course, the grinding and thumping of the pumps never ceasing for a moment. Expecting a journey of a less than a day, Tom and Sal had not brought any provisions with them. At nightfall, the master came by the cabin, and finding their distress, sent along some hardtack and small beer to soak it in, with the captain's compliments. They downed this gratefully, although by the second day, the gluey mass had already become distasteful. The *Acanthus* did not reach Calais until the morning of the third day, and by then Tom and Sal were both swearing they would never, ever go to sea again, even if it meant living the rest of their days in France.

On shore at last, it was another full day before the sensation of the ground pitching and rolling beneath their feet finally faded. They took a room at an inn facing the center square of the town, and for several days they were both too weary to leave it. Communication proved to be a difficulty, for although Tom spoke tolerably decent French for an Englishman, it was his first time in France, and he found pronunciation and usage varied significantly from what he had been taught. As for Sal, she had never been abroad in her life and knew not a single word of French, nor did she seem inclined to learn. The innkeeper and his family knew some English, fortunately, but this also encouraged them to keep within until they had recovered, for fear of discovery.

During this time, Sal continued to treat Tom with great kindness, arranging for their meals to be brought to their room and serving him herself, and sending his clothes out to be washed. She also had the servants bring a large copper tub up to their room and fill it with hot water so they could bathe. After the bath, she shaved him and brushed out his sandy brown hair, retying his queue with her own garter.

At night Tom embraced her with renewed passion, his ardor returned as he regained his health. She had grown even thinner and more wiry after their ordeal, but he did not mind it—the sharp angles of her hips, her small pert breasts, her bony fingers, the rasp of her laugh deep in her throat were all so familiar and dear to him. She was a tireless companion, urging him on to new heights with a flick of her tongue in his ear.

He gave himself up to her with abandon, as she pinned him to the bed with a throaty growl and straddled him, her long legs squeezing him and her rough hands holding him down. He felt even more free with her than at home, and he was very glad he had agreed to accompany her on this unlikely journey.

In the morning, nothing gave him greater pleasure than to awake with her still by his side. He felt as if they were indeed husband and wife, and again considered asking her if she would not marry him, although a popish wedding in a foreign country would never be legal in England. In the end, he said nothing.

CHAPTER FIFTEEN: PARIS

"Dammee, but I'm bored to death of this rotten old ken," Sal cried as she kicked the grate with her hard-soled boot, dislodging a log and sending a shower of sparks up the chimney. Tom only sighed deeply and did not reply. They had been in Paris for nearly a month, but already their spirits were much oppressed.

Calais had been too full of English merchants for Sal to feel at ease, so there was nothing for it but to follow Harkington's plan and continue on to Paris. They left Calais in good cheer, happy to have survived the wretched Channel crossing, with each feeling charitable towards the other. The late autumn weather was balmy, so they hired an open dog-cart and took the road to Paris very easy, enjoying the warm sunshine and the smell of new-mown hay in the rolling hills as they passed. They were certain now that Sal had escaped the law, so there was no need for haste, and in the slow-moving, open cart Tom was not troubled by travel sickness.

To guard against pursuit, they agreed to continue with their alias of Mr. and Mrs. William Lancaster, linen draper of Spitalfields, but they dared not proceed to the address named in the traveling papers, even if they could find someone to read it for them, for fear of any association with George Harkington. On their arrival in Paris they first stopped at an inn, but if they were to set up as respectable members of the bourgeoisie, they must secure their own household, and this was no easy matter in a foreign city without acquaintances or relations.

Sal had her heart set on taking apartments at the Place des Vosges, apparently because the innkeeper in Calais had mentioned it as an elegant address for people of quality. The Place des Vosges proved to be for those of a quality a bit higher than their own, however. Tom was not surprised to discover that Sal had greatly exaggerated the amount of money she had spirited away from Harkington, and with no additional source of income forthcoming, he prevailed upon her to budget a bit more carefully. They could do no better than to let a modest house with only the barest furnishings in Rue Villehardouin, a small street set at a right angle, just north of the Place des Vosges.

Theirs was not a happy household. After leaving Calais, they found far fewer people who spoke English, especially among the servant class, and those they could afford to hire spoke none at all. Neither Tom nor Sal had ever managed a house full of servants before, and they found themselves with a surly, froward bunch, who clearly had a low opinion of the master and mistress. On various occasions, Tom was sure he heard them refer to Sal as *la putain sans pudeur* and to himself as *le maudit aveugle*, but he chose to ignore these insults rather than go to the considerable trouble of hiring new servants.

As for amusements, they had none at all. Sal could see the gentry coming and going as she walked around the white colonnades of the Place des Vosges, but this only served to remind her of the vast difference between them and herself. In Covent Garden, she had been the toast of the beaux, pursued by the men of all ranks, equally admired and feared by the bawds, but in Paris there was no one to take notice of her.

Tom as well found himself sadly out of joint. His French was improving quickly—he had a natural facility with languages, as with music, but he was reluctant to make acquaintances, for fear of being discovered as an imposter. Worse, he feared becoming lost in the maze of unfamiliar streets, and so for the first few weeks he did not dare venture out without Sal. They made daily journeys to various goldsmiths, silversmiths, jewelers and pawnshops to sell the jewels and plate Sal had brought, only one small item at a time, and never the same place twice, so as not to arouse suspicion. Sal claimed these were all gifts to her from Harkington, but Tom was certain it was the swag from her previous careers as housebreaker, lifter, and pickpocket, not to mention her brief turn as a highwayman. These trips necessitated that they both be present, Tom to speak French to the shopkeeper, and Sal to lead him and to be certain they were not swindled. Once this weary task was complete, however, their day was over, and they had nothing more to do.

Tom regretted extremely having left all his musical instruments behind in London and longed for some diversion. Music, of course, listening or composing or simply practicing, was his primary occupation, but he enjoyed being read to as well. On his visits to Lady Gray, she sometimes favored him with an improving read, while he could count on Jem to share the latest scandal sheet or adventure tale. They were particularly fond of *Colonel Jack* by Mr. Defoe. Tom found he missed this simple pleasure as well, but alas, neither he nor Sal could read. It was beyond all bearing to know they were in the most fashionable, exciting city in the world, only to spend each evening sitting in the parlor listening to the clock ticking on the mantle, until Sal cried out in frustration and kicked the grate.

Sal's good-will towards Tom had likewise dissipated. "Must you make those damned noises with your mouth?" she hissed at him as they entered a shop. "It ain't natural."

Tom shut his mouth and turned it down. He had not even been aware of what he was doing, but it felt irritatingly claustrophobic to be prevented from clicking his tongue to bounce the sound off the walls and find the dimension of a room.

In the street, Sal was careless and ran him into crates or

doors or low-hanging signs, and chided him for his slowness. It was true that he was far more nimble at home in Covent Garden, where he knew every street by heart, and even every loose cobble. There, he could tell the time by the smells in the air and the cries of the crowd. Moreover, the Piazza around Covent Garden was not such a large place, and it was easy to memorize the lay of the streets he trod every day. But here everything was unfamiliar and they did not make the same trips often enough for him to fix a map in his mind. Tom was used to coming and going as he pleased. Having to hang on Sal's arm every time he stepped outdoors was shamefully confining.

When Sal had provoked him beyond bearing, he would at last reply with a curse and call her a heartless jade, at which point she would be overcome by remorse and beg his forgiveness, but within hours she would be short-tempered again.

One day, after they had been in Paris for over a month, they brought an emerald ring to a shop to sell, but the owner would not agree to their price. Tom was having even more difficulty than usual making himself understood in French, and Sal was growing impatient next to him, shuffling her feet and sighing loudly. Tom was about to give up and suggest they leave when a loud booming voice spoke next to him in very lightly accented English.

"May I be of assistance?"

Tom turned his face toward the voice. "It's very kind of you, but no, we are just leaving."

"Why yes, thank you!" Sal spoke over him, reaching a hand around to shake. The stranger laughed so loudly that Tom could feel the floorboards vibrate slightly beneath his feet.

"I'm Mrs. Lancaster of London, and this here's my husband," Sal plowed onward in her coarse way. "Pleasure to make your acquaintance."

The stranger grasped her hand and kissed it. "The pleasure is mine. I am Jan van den Staal of Rotterdam. What seems to be the trouble?"

They explained the price that they wanted for the ring, in cash, and he translated for them with the owner, who it seemed was a friend of his. Sal was overjoyed to find an ally, and one who spoke such good, clear English. He was a large man with a barrel chest and a round belly, a florid face and shaggy whiskers.

Van den Staal pulled them aside to a corner of the shop and spoke to them in a low tone. "In truth, madam, the price of this ring is not so great," he said, holding it with improbable dexterity in his meaty fingers. "The emerald is not large, and behold, it has a large flaw down the center. Monsieur Jouvenet has named for you a fair price." Sal set her chin stubbornly, clearly intending to argue, but he waved her silent. "I am less concerned with the price than with the circumstances that lead you to sell it. Was this a love-gift between you, of great sentimental value, perhaps? Come, tell me, are you in some difficulty?"

"Why, no..." said Tom.

"Yes, oh yes, sir," said Sal, speaking over him again. "It were a gift from my dear husband when he was wooing me, and oh how it pains me to part with it! We come here on business, but now it's gone sour and we ain't got friends nor acquaintances here, not a one to help us!" As Sal delivered this impassioned speech, Tom snorted impatiently, but van den Staal seemed to take this as embarrassed pride at having their straitened circumstances revealed. "Oh sir, could you perhaps give us a greater price for it? Seeing as how it's got sentimental value, as you says?" Sal asked.

Van den Staal shook his head. "Now as you know, that's no way to conduct business, neither in linen nor jewels." This was directed to Tom, although it took him a moment to realize it, and he did not react in time. Van den Staal continued more kindly, looking at Sal, "No, I cannot buy this from you; it would not be right. But I shall help you in other wise. Will you come to dine at my house tomorrow evening, if you are

132

not bespoke?" Of course they were not, and Sal gratefully accepted. "Well then, I shall see you tomorrow. I hope we shall all become the best of friends," he said, squeezing Tom's hand in a manful grip and bowing to Sal.

"Are you mad?" Tom exclaimed when they had left the shop. "A whole evening together—he will be fly to us directly, if he ain't already."

"Oh fie," said Sal. "I swear there was never such a one for worrying as you, Tom. I mean, *Mr. Lancaster*."

Jan van den Staal had let a house not far from theirs, on the Rue de Rivoli, an address far more fashionable than their own. Van den Staal treated them to a lavish meal with no less than ten removes, including hog's head, duck, beef kidneys, cassoulet, rabbit, pastries, pungent cheeses, and the most excellent burgundy.

Tom and Sal were the only guests, and their host was unmarried, so with only three at the table, the conversation was heavy going at first. Tom was extremely reluctant to volunteer any information about themselves, although Sal invented a long tale of their lives, including wholly fabricated details of her idyllic childhood in Kent, their flourishing business in Spitalfields, and Tom's supposed illness and ensuing affliction, which she situated during their voyage to France. Tom thought privately he had never heard a more unlikely and contradictory narrative, but van den Staal appeared to take no notice.

After dinner, they retired to the drawing room, richly furnished with burgundy wall coverings in figured silk. Among other curios, van den Staal revealed to Tom's great joy that he possessed a harpsichord.

"It came with the furnishings in the house," he explained. "I have no notion how to play myself."

"May I make so bold as to try it out?" Tom asked, trying not to sound too eager.

"My dear fellow, I should be delighted!" van den Staal replied, awkwardly guiding him to it in a sort of stiff-armed circular dance.

Tom ran his fingers over the keyboard, testing the tuning, then dove directly into a Bach fugue, and then another. He gave himself completely over to the music as he played, feeling his spirits lift as they had not for many weeks, not knowing or caring how much time passed, but reveling in the sweet familiarity and the satisfaction of mastering the complex interweaving themes. At one point he was dimly aware of a rustle of fabric, a sharply indrawn breath, Sal's voice saying *sshhh*, but he pretended not to notice, unwilling to allow anything to interfere with this unexpected pleasure.

When he at last finished playing, van den Staal applauded heartily. "Why Mr. Lancaster, what a talent you have! Who would ever have thought it? I shall arrange a musical evening, and you must come play again!" This plan appealed both to Tom's vanity and to his desire for diversion, which was indeed as great at Sal's, and so he put aside his lingering reservations about the danger of discovery.

The musical evening was held some days later, although again the company was rather small. Van den Staal had invited, among a few others, his next door neighbor, Charles Desmares, an *agent de change* at la Bourse and his young wife Marie, as well as a young gentleman visiting from Rouen named Henri d'Angoulême, who seemed to have no occupation in particular. Upon being introduced to Tom (who was addressed as Monsieur William Lancaster d'Angleterre), and told of his supposedly recent misfortune, Desmares drew back in horror and remarked to van den Staal in French in a rather loud whisper, "How shocking that he should reveal himself in polite society in this condition."

But Marie, a flighty, delicate little thing with a mass of ash-blond curls, was nearly overcome with pity for him. "*Qu'il a été aveuglé, quel dommage, quelle tristesse,*" she exclaimed in distressed tones, her blue eyes as large as saucers.

"Do not trouble yourself on my account," Tom replied

smoothly in French, bowing to her. "I am quite well, I assure you." She placed her hand in his and he brought it to his lips, then grasped it with both hands. "I am honored to make your acquaintance," he said, still holding her hand. It was a dainty, delicate hand, soft as velvet, with a lingering perfume of lilies of the valley.

At their host's request, Tom played the first offering of the evening, the first two movements of a sonata da camera by Corelli, which was very politely received. After he had finished, he found himself seated beside d'Angoulême, as Marie Desmares warbled her way through "Caro mio ben," while accompanying herself on the harpsichord. She had a slight, breathy voice, with the kind of untrained, hollow sweetness that would have been thrown out of the Rose in an instant had she auditioned there, but somehow in this intimate setting, he found it charming.

"*Ca-ha-ha-ro mio ben, cre-he-he-dimi almen*," she sang, laboring up and down the scale like a washerwoman huffing and puffing with a load of laundry.

"Quite lovely, don't you think?" Tom said in French as they applauded at the end, leaning towards d'Angoulême.

"Rubbish," the man replied good-naturedly. "Now you, Monsieur, are clearly a gentleman who knows about music. I should not think you would be taken in by Madame Desmares' amateurish efforts." Tom had to admit that she was not quite polished, but still, there was something pleasing about her innocent delivery. As it happened, d'Angoulême knew a thing or two about music himself, and after he favored the company with several tunes by Descoteaux on *la flûte traversière*, he and Tom fell into a lively discussion of innovations in woodwind manufacture and techniques for reducing concerti for solo performance. Feeling quite buoyed by the conversation, as well as a good deal of the fine burgundy, Tom strayed to more personal topics.

"Tell me," he asked in an undertone, "our host, M. van den Staal, is he quite handsome?"

D'Angoulême shrugged dismissively. "I don't know. I suppose in a way, although he has the figure of a bear, and those dreadful mustachios are quite out of fashion."

"Hmm, I see," Tom said. "And Madame Desmares? Would you call her a beauty?"

"My dear sir, they say she's the prettiest girl in Paris!" d'Angoulême said, laughing. "Although you must think me a puffed-up boor to crack on about my own sister."

"Your sister!" exclaimed Tom. "I beg your pardon, I had no idea." Had Tom been able to see, he might have noted that Marie and Henri shared the same blond curls, blue eyes and round cheeks.

"Oh, not at all. I tell you, she could have had any man in Paris. What a pity she accepted that villain Desmares, and she so young."

"Indeed a pity," replied Tom with feeling.

After this successful evening, Tom and Sal were frequently guests of Jan van den Staal, occasionally with the Desmares as well, but more often on their own. Tom and Sal both looked forward to these visits, and not only for the entertainment and fine wine. Their evenings at Rue de Rivoli were seemingly the only times when there was peace between them, for the greater the pleasure they took at van den Staal's household, so too did their bickering increase when they were alone. Still, Tom did not think anything in particular of it, attributing this strife to Sal's volatile nature.

Then one morning, deep in winter, Tom awoke to find the bed cold and empty beside him, and the house strangely quiet. With a sense of foreboding, he rang the bell for the bonne.

"Where is your mistress?" he demanded in French when the girl arrived.

"Madame has gone with M. van den Staal to Rotterdam, Monsieur, and she bids you not to follow after," the maid replied, not bothering to disguise the sneer in her voice.

"What?" Tom leapt from the bed and began pacing the bare

boards in his night-clothes, exclaiming to himself in English. "She never! Oh, the wicked jade! Oh, the infamous whore!"

An even darker thought occurred to him, and he rushed across the room to the escritoire that held all their ready cash. He opened the drawer and felt about inside with trembling hands. It was empty. Now he let loose with a stream of oaths and invectives that would have burned the ears of any nearby, had the servants understood English, or indeed had any been about. He discovered soon after that most of them had decamped along with their mistress, either gone with her or disappeared on their own, he could not tell. The few who were left, it seemed, had remained not out of loyalty to him, but in hopes they might be paid their salaries in full.

Tom sank down on the edge of the bed, his head in his hands. *I'm undone.* The thought rose unbidden to his mind, and he felt the icy grip of fear around his neck.

He yearned all the more for his free and easy life in London, and his dear little house in Maiden Lane. In the hazy mists of memory, he had forgotten how long it had taken him to master the crooked streets around Covent Garden, the irregular paths between the stalls around the Piazza, and even the treacherous disarray of his own house. He had not realized how much he relied on the good offices of his friends, the steady reliability of his old valet, and the familiar routines of the everyday.

Now he found there was no food in the house, as the cook had gone, and not enough firewood. It was very cold. He was confounded on how to obtain more cash, for although there was yet some plate that might be pawned, he was loath to be led about town by a servant. Ordinarily he was not so nice about such trifles, but the blow to his dignity was already so great, and the servants that remained were a mean lot. At last Tom sent a footman out with a silver saucière, although he received back far less than he had looked for. Within a week the cash was gone, and the routine had to be repeated. Word had got around the neighborhood of Rue Villehardouin that the wife of *l'aveugle Anglais* had run off with his money, and no one would extend him credit.

Living with Sal had proved more difficult than he had anticipated, but now that she was gone, he found himself longing for her, against all reason. It did no good to remind himself of how poorly she had treated him. Every corner of the house they had shared reminded him of her. As he lay alone in the cold bed at night, he yearned to feel her wiry frame next to him, to feel her rump under his hand, to hear her braying laughter.

After two cold and hungry weeks, he thought, this cannot continue. He must send to England, but how?

One frigid morning, Tom awoke with fresh determination. He had learnt his way around a few of the streets, and now he took himself to the barber for a shave and to have his hair dressed neatly, with his queue tied. Upon being assured that he looked presentable, he set out for the Rue de Rivoli. He remembered the route very well, as they had gone there often, but he had always been on Sal's arm, and had not paid close attention to the number of houses. He took a guess, feeling about the stoops one after another with his walking stick, until he was reasonably sure he had found van den Staal's former address, then went one further and knocked smartly with the silver head of his walking stick. A footman answered the door.

"Is Madame Desmares at home?" Tom inquired in French. There was a very long pause, long enough for Tom to arrive at a sinking certainty that he had the wrong house, maybe even the wrong street, but at length the footman asked for his name, then disappeared within, leaving Tom on the front step.

After an endless wait, the door opened again, and the footman said, "This way, Monsieur," to Tom's great relief. He hastened to follow the sound of the servant's receding footsteps, praying that he would not trip over the carpet or bark his shins on the furniture, or otherwise disgrace himself.

Tom managed the short traverse across the hall, although

it seemed a vast ocean, and was shown into a sitting room without incident. As the footman announced him, Marie raced across the room and grasped his hands in her own.

"Monsieur Lencastaire!" she cried. "What an unexpected pleasure!" Tom kissed her hand and bowed gracefully. She led him to a divan and seated herself beside him.

"Please, Madame," he said, "I hope we are intimate friends. Please call me Tom."

"But is your name not Guillaume?" she asked, surprised.

"Oh, ah, yes, but Tom is my second name, and more favored by my closest friends." He inched closer to her on the divan, and she drew away slightly.

"Very well then, Thomas," she said, pronouncing it in the French manner. "Although I must inform you that Henri has returned to Rouen, and Charles is at la Bourse, of course, so I am quite alone in the house. I'm not sure it's at all proper to receive you, Monsieur Len—I mean, Thomas," she said, with the wide-eyed innocence of a child.

"I'm afraid I'm not here on a social call, my dear Madame," he said, "but to throw myself on your tender mercies." With great concern, she listened as he recited his tale of woe, or at least an expurgated version thereof.

By the time he concluded, Marie was beside herself. "Oh, that was very wicked and wrong of them!" she exclaimed. "I always held M. van den Staal in such high esteem, and your lady wife as well. It is a perfect scandal, and right next door! Charles shall be enraged, I assure you."

Tom allowed her to comfort him for quite some time, but at last he came to the true purpose of his visit. "My dear Madame Desmares, I'm afraid I have been left quite deprived of cash, and with bills to pay. I do not ask for charity, however. I have money in England, if only I can send for it. You have some English, do you not?"

"Yes, a little," she replied. "When I was a little girl, my father used to take me with him when he traveled to England on business. I can say ''Ow do you do?' and 'A plaisaire to meet you' quite like *une Anglaise*," she said, laughing.

Tom did not laugh, but took her hands entreatingly and asked, "Can you write a letter in English for me?"

CHAPTER SIXTEEN: THE LETTER

20 Janvier, 1736

To M. Jaimes Casseltoun, Broad Corte, Londoun

Sir,

I write to you, my Dearest Frend jem, in the graiteste of Distrait. *As you well no*, I embarqued for paris with myne oun wyfe salle many mounths previous. We had a rottoun crossing, and *I do not hesitate to sey* that our lucque here has ben verie bad. Now I regrette to inform you that salle has departed for Rotterdamme in compagnie of a Jeuleur, a low villain *nom de M. Jan van den Staal*, and with them all myne monie.

I am not without Frends, however. The Madame Charles desmares of the *Rue de Rivoli* has ben moust kinde to me. But the Wynter is cauld, and I find I have need of cash. I shood be infinatelie oblij'd if you can sende me some Notes by Poste. Applie to ladie graie if you must, *but pray do not give her the particulaires.*

Pray make haste. I await your replie with Gratitoud.

Your affectionate frend,
Wm. Thomas Fynche Lencastaire
N°. 10 Rue Villehardouin, Paris

Jem turned the letter over and over in his hands, baffled. It was written in a round, feminine hand, on very fine paper which retained a faint aroma of lilies of the valley. He was accustomed to the common vagaries of spelling, but even so, he was hard put to make heads or tails of this letter. It must have come from Tom, despite the extra names, but what the devil was he doing in France? Several months earlier, when Jem had called at Maiden Lane, Stinson had informed him that his master was at the family estate in Bedford. Jem had assumed Tom was passing the winter there, and had been a bit wounded that he had not seen fit to inform him in person. Jem had never made a connection between Tom's whereabouts and the disappearance of Sal, but merely supposed that she had gone to ground when the whole nasty business with Harkington became public. It was not unlike her to disappear for months at stretch.

Tom, what a fool you are, Jem thought as he read the letter over again. He didn't like the sound of that Madame Desmares either. Most likely he had gone from the clutches of one thieving trollop to another. And why send to me, of all people? Jem wondered. He knows I ain't got one sou to my name that I could send.

As suggested in the letter, Jem decided to apply first to the Lady Gray. Making his appearance as neat and respectable as possible, he headed over to Soho Square, but found to his disappointment that Lady Gray had removed to her estate in Stirling for the winter. Who goes to bloody Scotland for the winter? he thought bitterly, cursing her for an inconsiderate old hag.

Next he considered petitioning Betterton at the Rose, but a judicious word over a pint with Brookings, the first violin, dissuaded him. Tom was in bad odor at the Rose for his hasty departure, which had forced a very unwilling Mr. Holden to run the rehearsals himself. Jem also considered Shaloe Brown, but quickly dismissed the thought; that old miser would see them both to the devil before laying out a farthing. Tess Turn-bridge, he thought at last, aha, now that one has a tendre for him, and has come into money too—that might answer very well indeed.

Jem was rather put out to find, upon calling at Harte Street, that Mistress Turnbridge and Mistress Carlyle had removed from that address quite some time ago. As the opera season was ended, moreover, she was no longer appearing nightly at Drury Lane.

At last after many inquiries he discovered her address in St. James's, and paid her a visit. This new address was far more fashionable and luxurious than her previous apartments. A servant answered the door and showed him in to a tastefully appointed sitting room with walls of pale blue. It had been some time since he had seen her last, but Tess was looking more lovely than ever, even in an ordinary striped day dress.

"What is the meaning of this?" Tess demanded, looking from the letter to Jem with suspicion.

"I should think it's quite plain," Jem replied. "Sal used Tom to help her escape to France when Harkington was arrested, then she abandoned him there."

"The wicked jade! How could a person be so cruel?" Tess cried, clearly distressed. "And I suppose this Madame Des-mares mentioned here is the one who wrote this for him?"

"That's what I'm thinking," said Jem. "Tom don't know one letter from another. As for the bank notes he asks for..."

"No," said Tess. "We must go to France directly."

Jem smiled at her with genuine affection. "I was hoping you'd say that, miss," he said. "I always knew you was a bang-up girl."

Despite Tess's anxiety for Tom, she found she could not leave immediately: there was His Grace the Duke of Grafton to appease. He had set her up handsomely in St. James's, and even allowed her to keep Jane Carlyle with her as a companion. He was a broadminded man, not overly given to jealousy, but she did not think he would be pleased if she sent his money to another man. She must wait, she explained to Jem, until the duke left for his estate, then tell him she was taking a short voyage to France to see a relative (for she did have a cousin in Paris), and he would give her plenty to cover the expense. All this took many weeks to accomplish, however, while in the meantime there was no further word from Tom, and letters sent to his address went unanswered.

There was one more delicate matter as well. Tess suggested to Jane that she might come along, might enjoy the sights of Paris, but she declined, as Tess had known she would. She found Jane's continued jealousy of Tom so petty and tiresome. Could she not see that Tom was only a friend and colleague? Jane seemed happy enough with their current arrangement, even with the duke's frequent visits, but at the thought of Tess going to France she pouted and hung her head.

"Come now, if you don't speak your mind honestly, I shall be forced to believe what you say," Tess told her. "Do you really intend to stay here? You're not cross with me for going to France?" she asked.

"No," Jane mumbled, staring at her shoes. Tess threw up her hands in exasperation, and continued with the preparations to leave without her.

Tess and Jem's journey was in no wise similar to Tom and Sal's. Tess arranged for their passage on a merchant snow-brig from Brighton to Dieppe, which she considered the most efficient route, as it was shorter by land, if longer by sea. They asked along the way if anyone had seen a personage of Tom's description, but no one had. Tess arranged for separate cabins for herself and Jem, which were, by nautical standards, roomy and pleasant, and their brief passage was comfortable, favored with tolerably good weather.

"You ain't worried about your reputation, traveling alone with me?" Jem asked her as they took a turn about the deck.

Tess smiled. "Mr. Castleton, I appreciate your concern for

me, but I am already a kept woman. I am undertaking this journey for Mr. Finch's sake. I trust you will not do anything to make my reputation more scandalous than it is already."

Jem promised he would not. As they traveled together, her opinion of Jem as a dissolute rake had, if not changed, at least become more nuanced. His concern for Tom was genuine, and she was touched by the sincerity and devotion she saw in him.

After the long stagecoach ride from Dieppe to Paris, they at last arrived at the home of Tess's cousin Constanza, who had married a French lace merchant and settled near the Place Vendôme. They had not seen each other for many years, but Constanza was very happy to greet Tess and make much of her. Like Tess, she was small with brown ringlets and the same flashing dark intelligent eyes. She inquired at length about Tess's career on the London stage, but Jem noted that they did not speak much of their family in Naples. It seemed to be a sore point.

On Constanza's advice, Tess and Jem proceeded first to the address on Rue Villehardouin named in the letter, but found to their dismay that the house was boarded up and the neighbors knew nothing of the erstwhile tenants, only that Madame had run off, the most shocking scandal, and as for *l'aveugle*, he too had departed, they knew not whence. Next Tess and Jem set about searching for Charles Desmares on the Rue de Rivoli, although he too was not at home, and the servant who answered the door refused to give them any more information, other than that Madame and Monsieur were not expected back for many weeks.

Days passed and further inquiries came to nothing. After these failures, Tess was becoming increasingly anxious for Tom. Where could he have gone? She imagined him lying friendless in the street, reduced to beggary, or run down by a carriage—it was too horrible. Constanza's husband, however, was quite well-connected and at last he discovered the name of Charles Desmares's clerk at la Bourse, a man by the name of Fontaine.

M. Fontaine was not pleased to meet with them, but they plied him with wine and a heavy meal at a restaurant at Tess's expense. Jem also sank several glasses of wine in quick succession, ignoring Tess's warning glances.

"Capital stuff!" Jem exclaimed, miming for a serving girl to bring another bottle. "A damned sight better than what we are accustomed to at home, hey? M. Fontaine, to your very good health!" They toasted and each swallowed another glass together.

The wine at last loosened the clerk's tongue. He conversed with them in English, for while Tess spoke excellent French, Jem had very little, and M. Fontaine did not like the idea of a lady serving as an interpreter. Yes, he admitted, a blind Englishman, a linen draper by the name of Lancaster, had come to stay with the Desmares.

"A draper? It can't possibly be him. The man we are looking for goes by the name of Finch, and he's a musician, if you please, a composer of popular music," Jem blurted out, slurring his words slightly, then jumped as Tess kicked him under the table.

"Remember the name on the letter," she hissed at him, then to Fontaine she said, "May I ask where this Mr. Lancaster is now?"

Fontaine made a sour face, and explained that as M. Desmares had gone to Brussels on business, Madame Desmares was visiting her father in Rouen, a wine merchant by the name of d'Angoulême, and had taken Mr. Lancaster with her. Having gained the information they needed, Tess was eager to depart, but Fontaine detained them, asking many questions about themselves, which to her distress Jem, now very far in his cups, seemed only too happy to answer.

After gaining this information, Tess and Jem took their leave of Constanza, who was sad to see them go, and floated on a barge down the River Seine as it meandered through the countryside towards Rouen. M. d'Angoulême, who seemed to be quite well known in the area, lived in a large, rambling half-timbered house not far from where they disembarked at Quai de Paris. In their haste to depart, they had not sent ahead, and now on their arrival, Tess worried how they might be received, appearing like vagabonds on a stranger's doorstep.

She need not have worried, however, for both Marie and Tom were at home, and received them joyfully, although with astonishment. Tess looked them over carefully. Tom appeared rosy and well, a far cry from her imaginings, and rigged out in the best Parisian mode, with snowy white hose, very tight fitting fawn colored breeches and a full-skirted green surcoat with deep cuffs over a daringly short waistcoat. Marie Desmares as well was far from the conniving old woman she and Jem had supposed, but rather was exceedingly young and pretty, with a round plump face and the wide-eyed stare of a child.

"Jem, by God it's good to see you again," Tom cried when they had been announced, embracing him and kissing him on both cheeks like a brother, then doing the same to the rather startled Tess. "I can scarcely believe you are here," he repeated several times, as they were seated in a lavishly appointed parlor, with thick carpets and dark mahogany paneling. "How the devil did you find me?"

"I assure you, it was no easy task," Tess replied acidly. Her ill humor had been increasing since the moment they set foot inside.

"You gave us quite a scare with that letter, Finchy," Jem put in.

"What letter?" asked Tom, looking blank. "Oh, yes, that! Marie was good enough to write it for me." He gave her arm a squeeze and she tittered. "But that was months and months ago. I assumed it had got lost."

"We came as quickly as circumstances allowed," Tess huffed. "We having been chasing all over Paris looking for you, and here we find you cuckolding the bourgeoisie. Had we known, we might have stayed home."

Jem gave a snort of laughter, but Marie did not react. They had been speaking in English, and Marie seemed not to be following their conversation, instead staring at Tom with a rather besotted expression.

"Ah, Miss Turnbridge, sharp-tongued as ever," Tom said with a smile. "Pray do not be angry. I am very glad you are here. I hope you will stay with us for a while."

"But this is not your house," Tess insisted.

"Oh, but Marie will not mind, will you *chère?*" he said. Marie smiled blandly. "M. d'Angoulême is most obliging, and you must meet Marie's brother Henri. He is quite the go, I tell you, an excellent musician. And you won't find better wine anywhere in France, ha ha!"

And so in the end they agreed to stay the night, having come to Rouen with no plan in particular and no other lodging. M. d'Angoulême *père* was, as Tom had promised, not at all averse to two additional guests, for the large house was always bustling with activity: clerks, customers, suppliers, and ship owners coming and going at all hours, so a few guests more or less were hardly noticed. Henri as well was very pleased to have another musical gentleman in the house, and the three men spent the afternoon happily playing and trading low ballads, of which each had a great store. Henri knew a great many sporting tunes, which he had already been teaching Tom:

Quand j'étais fille à marier j'étais belle et galante,
Beaucoup d'amants venaient me voir à minuit dans ma chambre,
Ne venaient pas ni un ni deux, venaient de vingt à trente.

In addition to the music, Henri also taught Jem and Tom some of their peculiar Norman French, and invited them to sample the new shipment of wine with him.

There was one matter that preyed upon Tom's mind, however. After a very late informal supper, he pulled Jem aside at the base of the darkened staircase, just before they were going to retire.

"Whatever became of George Harkington, the villain?" Tom asked with concern, his face pale in the gloom.

Jem blinked at him in surprise. "Ain't you heard? He was caught trying to flee the country, plucked off a ship bound for Virginia. He was sent to Newgate and hanged on Tyburn. I saw it myself. But this was all months ago, last autumn."

Tom let out a sigh. "And his criminal case? Is it over, or are they still searching for, ah, anyone else? Other accomplices?"

"His first wife was arrested too, and transported, and that was declared the end of it. Come now, never look so hipped. Ain't that good news? You're all in the clear." Jem did not add that the unfortunate woman had been punished in Sal's place. They did not speak of the matter again.

While the men spent the afternoon and evening entertaining themselves, Tess was left with nothing to pass the time. She found herself sitting with Marie, the only lady in the house, and helping her with her embroidery while making small talk. This was not the sort of amusement Tess liked best, and she found the childish Marie exceedingly dull. Marie had no conversation to offer besides exclamations of her likes and dislikes, and repeated comments on the progress of her sewing.

Tess sorely missed Jane and wished she had not been so stubborn about accompanying them. Or better yet, Tess wished she had never made the trip over to France at all. She felt foolish for assuming that Tom had been in need of rescue. Had he not told her many times that he was more than capable of handling his own affairs? She should have listened. But more than that, it irked her to see him throw himself away on women who were not worthy of him. First a common whore who abandoned him for money, and now a married woman with nothing to recommend her but a pretty face. And he can't even see it, she fumed. How could a blind man be gulled by a girl like this with no accomplishments to speak of?

Tess resolved to depart for England the next morning and

leave Tom to whatever fate he chose. The start of the opera season was not far off, and she had not been able to secure a role for herself with Mr. Highmore before she left. If she lost her position in the company at Drury Lane because of this misbegotten adventure, she felt she would never forgive Tom.

Early the next morning, however, just as they were all sitting down to cups of chocolate in the breakfast room, a frantic servant rushed up to Henri with a letter. His face grew increasingly distressed as he read it.

"It says that Desmares is on his way here," Henri told them in French. "He has heard some very shocking things about you, M. Lencastaire, that you are no respectable linen draper but a low musician, that you have insinuated yourself into his acquaintance under false pretenses and with an assumed name, and that you have, ahem, contracted an intimacy with his wife. He is enraged. You must flee at once. I'm afraid he means to call you out."

Fontaine, Tess thought, as she translated into English for Jem, who was seated beside her at the little round table. "This is your fault," she whispered to him angrily. "You should not have spoken to him so freely."

Their reactions were not as Henri had expected—Tom looked rather blank, while Jem appeared to be holding back laughter.

"Is this true?" Henri asked in English.

Jem could no longer contain himself. "Oh, he's no more a draper than I am the king of France, ha ha!"

Tom at least offered an apology in French for deceiving them, but both Henri and Marie brushed it off, unconcerned about such trifling details.

"I knew you were a far more accomplished musician than you let on," Henri said, seeming rather impressed. "But in truth, I tell you, Desmares will be here very shortly, and he is a dangerous man. You must leave with all haste."

"Oh, but Charles would never be so monstrous as to demand a duel with a blind man," Marie cried. "I'm sure I can set things right with him."

Instead of answering, Henri merely gave her a sharp look, and she fell silent. There was nothing for it but to leave at once. Tess and Jem ran upstairs to pack their bags, and Henri went off to secure them passage back to England, leaving Tom and Marie sitting alone at the table.

"I'm very sorry we must part like this," Marie said in French, grasping his hands.

Tom pulled her closer to him, his brows raised entreatingly, his milky eyes swimming. "But we need not part, dearest Marie. Come with me! Desmares is a brute. You must come to England with me."

Marie drew back, opening her blue eyes wide in surprise. "Oh no, that could never be! How could I leave my poor children?"

"Children?" Tom's mouth hung open. "You have children? Have they been utterly silent that I have never noticed them?"

Marie laughed. "No, Thomas, how you jest! They have been sent out to nurse, of course, three fine fat boys. I see them once or twice in the year."

"Once or twice...?" Tom echoed faintly. It was true most women of the better classes sent their children away if they could possibly afford to, but his own mother had not.

"Oh yes," Marie continued, "I love them dearly, so you see I could never leave. Don't worry about me. I'm sure Charles will calm himself by and by."

Within a very short time, they took their leave of Marie Desmares and Henri d'Angoulême, thanking them profusely for their generosity. The three of them were bundled down to the Quai de Paris with all their baggage and set on a barge bound for Le Havre, along with that day's shipment of wine.

Tom, wearing a round broad-brimmed hat, in hopes it might disguise his appearance, allowed himself to be led along and settled in the barge, his head still reeling. He had supposed Marie was a mere girl, recently forced into an unhappy marriage with an older man, but now he realized she had been married for quite some time and had no intention of ending it.

Their voyage down the Seine to the mouth of the river at the English Channel was uneventful. Tess and Jem breathed a sigh of relief to have escaped Charles Desmares' wrath, although Tom still appeared distracted. At Le Havre, along with the shipment of wine, they transferred from the barge to a packet bound for Portsmouth.

"I am becoming quite an old hand at these clandestine flights on shipboard," Tom remarked to Tess as they stepped on board, just before he tripped over a deadeye and went sprawling, the round hat rolling away. Tess plucked his hat from the deck, then helped him up and led him over to a quiet spot by the taffrail, out of the way of the sailors, while Jem went below to see about their cabins.

As the ship got underway, Tom sang a lively little tune he had learnt from Henri.

J'ai trouvé la caille dessus son nid
J'y marchai sur l'aile et la lui rompit
Elle me dit pucelle retire-toi d'ici
Je n' suis pas pucelle tu en as menti

"Did you know," he burst out suddenly, breaking off the tune, "Marie Desmares has three children!"

Tess gave a sharp laugh. "No, but I'm not surprised. She is a married woman, after all. What a fellow you are, Mr. Finch." Tess was heartily glad to be shot of her and on her way back to England.

Tom turned away in a pique and ran his hands along the ornate carving on the taffrail. "And what of you, Miss Turnbridge?" he asked pettishly. "I have not yet inquired about your own situation. Tell me, how is the Duke of Grafton? And Miss Carlyle, have you cast her off and quit the stage?"

Tess stiffened. "You know very well I am in His Grace's keeping," she replied. "But I shall never give up my career, and he has not asked it of me. As for Jane, she lives with me still. I would never abandon a friend."

Tom nodded without answering, his head still turned out to sea, away from her, his face twisted into a bitter smirk.

Tess felt the last strand of her patience snap. "You're coming it rather high with me, Mr. Finch!" she said angrily. "You were the one who put me in the way of finding a patron. The duke has treated me with great respect, which is more than I might say for you. And now I have risked his regard for me, and my career, all of it, to come rescue you from your own poor decisions. Some gratitude!"

"I never asked you to come!" Tom could hear the passion in her voice. He turned in her direction and answered her with equal heat.

Jem emerged from below at just that moment, to find the two of them facing off like two cats fighting. The color was high in Tess's cheeks and her dark eyes snapped with anger as she leaned forward.

"The devil take you!" she cried and turned on her heel, her skirts flying around her.

With grim amusement, Jem watched her stomp down the companionway to her cabin.

"Actresses," he muttered under his breath to Tom. "High strung, the lot of 'em."

Tom turned away unhappily, turning his face into the breeze. "I suppose you've come to also tell me what a fool I've been."

"Do you really need me to tell you?"

Tom did not reply.

CHAPTER SEVENTEEN: THE RIOT

While in France, Tom had longed to return to London, but now that he was back, he still felt somehow dissatisfied. He attempted to fall back into his old routines, but this was not so easily accomplished.

Stinson had kept the house on Maiden Lane faithfully in his absence, even going so far as to clean up the worst of the detritus, although Tom hardly noticed. Still, he was very glad to once again submit himself to his valet's steady offices. Within a few days of his return, he and Jem dashed off a few more ballads for Shaloe Brown, making good use of the French tunes they had learned from Henri, and this put them in the way of ready cash. They went directly to the Labor in Vain, where they found Betsy Careless and her companions taking their ease, although it was not yet evening. As they drank the king's health in pint after pint, Tom declared he would never again set foot outside England if he could help it.

Betsy relayed news, however, which put a damper on Tom's spirits. Word of erstwhile forger and bigamist George Harkington's execution and his unfortunate wife's transportation must have reached Rotterdam, because Sally Salisbury suddenly reappeared in Covent Garden, re-ensconced in the bawdy house of Mother Needham, and flashing out as if she had just come into a great deal of money. Betsy had not, however, seen her in the company of anyone matching the description of Jan van den Staal.

"Ain't you going to call on her?" Betsy inquired with feigned innocence. "I can send word if you like."

"I will not," Tom declared grimly, tossing back the rest of his ale and calling for more.

"That's it, Finchy," Jem said, clapping him on the shoulder. "Never mind that hard-mouthed jade."

But there was even further bad news. While his publisher did not mind his long absence, the same could not be said for the manager and the conductor of the Rose. Betterton and Holden were incensed over Tom's unannounced departure and refused to hire him back. As the pints went round, Tom and Jem abused them as grasping petty-foggers, then as blackguardly whoremongers and at last as infamous scrubs.

Tom banged his empty tankard on the table with finality and rose rather unsteadily to his feet.

"I shall go talk to them directly." There was nothing he could do about Sal's inconstancy, but he could at least give Betterton a piece of his mind and demand to be rehired as music master.

"What, now?" said Jem, who felt he was only beginning to lush it good, and had no intention of departing anytime soon. "It's nearly five o'clock. The show will just be starting."

"Even better," Tom declared. "Then he is sure to be there."

Jem shrugged to Betsy as Tom clapped his tricorne hat on his head and strode out the door, brandishing his walking stick crosswise in front of himself.

The short walk from the Labor in Vain to the Rose cleared his head well enough, so that by the time Tom arrived at the theater, he felt quite steady. The Rose was putting on a revival of *The Beggar's Opera*, and as he approached, he could hear a large, raucous crowd on the street in front of the main entrance. Excellent, he thought. If ticket sales were brisk, the theater must be doing well, and he could prevail upon Betterton to hire him to lead rehearsals for the next production.

Tom avoided the crowd at the front and tapped his way down the alley to the stage entrance, as he had no intention of paying for a ticket to enter just to speak to the manager. But the hefty stagehand loitering by the open door would not allow Tom within, and bade him depart in rather vulgar terms. Evidently the man had been hired during Tom's absence and did not know him.

"Now see here," Tom said in his most authoritative voice, drawing himself up to his full height of just over six feet. "I have business with Mr. Betterton and I shall not be put off."

"Betterton ain't here today," said the stagehand. "Now bugger off."

"Mr. Holden, then."

"Holden ain't here neither."

"Now I know you're lying," Tom said, his voice rising. "You will let me enter." He attempted to push past, but the larger man easily blocked him.

As they tussled in the doorway, Tom heard a piping voice from within calling, "Mr. Finch! Mr. Finch!"

Frankie slipped in between the two men and dragged Tom back out into the street. "Please sir, Mr. Betterton was quite particular. No one is to be allowed in without paying for a ticket."

Tom grumbled at this but allowed the anxious Frankie to lead Tom back around to the front of the theater, through the noisy crowd, to purchase a ticket. Tom was even more incensed to discover that the price of the ticket had risen from two shillings to four, but as he had come this far, he handed over the money.

"Double the price, this is outrageous," Tom complained as Frankie put the ticket in his hand. "When did this start?"

"Just today," Frankie admitted. "We ain't turned a profit since Miss Turnbridge left for the Theater Royal. Mr. Betterton insisted that if we don't increase the fee, he'll have to close. But the crowd don't like it," he said nervously, glancing behind him at the large number of people milling outside. Not all of them were purchasing tickets at the new higher price; at least half were arguing and convincing themselves that if they protested loudly enough the price might be reduced to what it was previously. Stagehands placed at the inner doors were turning away anyone who attempted to enter without paying full price.

Frankie accompanied Tom into the stalls and let him know that the seat at the end of the row closest to the stage was empty. Tom thanked him and sat down, indicating that he would come backstage when the first act was underway. Before the play started, by custom there would be three pieces of music played, called the First, Second and Third Music, introduced with speeches by Mr. Betterton. But there was no need for Tom to wait until the entire performance was over, or even for the entr'acte, to go backstage. As was the usual practice of the time, there was no curtain or anything else to separate the players from the spectators. While there were metal spikes along the front of the stage to discourage the lowest audience members in the stalls from leaping up, the wealthiest patrons enjoyed box seats along the side of the stage, and some sat directly beside the players. Those who could pay were free to go backstage as they pleased, and many of the players were happy to entertain their patrons at any time during the show. As a result, there was always a great deal of noise and activity surrounding the stage, even during a performance.

As Tom waited for the orchestra to tune up and Betterton to come out and greet the audience, he listened to the voices around him. Those that had paid the double price to enter had not let go of their resentment. There was an ugly tenor to the chatter in the stalls. Ordinarily the audience never quieted until well after the opera began, but the crowd sounded even drunker and more restless than usual.

In particular, Tom was dismayed to hear one voice he recognized, belonging to a Mr. Marcellus Loudon, a former soldier, sometime artist, sometime singer, and constant drunk.

Marcellus occasionally painted sets for the Rose and from time to time filled out the men's chorus, but after he had passed out drunk on stage during a performance of *The Grub Street Opera*, Betterton had sworn he would never be cast again. Now by the sound of it, Marcellus was sitting in the middle of the stalls with some of his cronies, shouting loudly in a slurred voice about how the new ticket price was highway robbery, and he intended to have words with that blackguard Betterton. Evidently Tom was not the only aggrieved former employee intending to speak to the manager.

"Good evening, ladies and gentlemen!" Tom lifted his head as he heard Betterton address the audience. The chatter did not abate. "My apologies, but Mrs. George Ann Bellamy will not be singing the First Music tonight as advertised, as she has taken ill. Instead we have engaged the celebrated Italian contralto, Signora Francesca Bertolli, late of the Theater Royal, Drury Lane!" He clapped his hands vigorously to welcome her, but the crowd was not having it. They had paid the inflated price to see Mrs. Bellamy, a comedic actress and singer at the height of her popularity, not some miss they had never heard of, and a foreigner no less. Moreover, Mrs. Bellamy was known to bestow her favors after the show on those in the audience who could afford it, and the same could not be said for Signora Bertolli.

The orchestra played the opening notes of the First Music, and Signora Bertolli began to sing, "*Amarilli mia bella...*"

"Get that foreign cow off the stage!" Marcellus shouted, followed by similar cries from the others seated near him.

Signora Bertolli broke off singing and fled the stage as the audience began to pelt her with objects, Tom was not sure what, until the peel of an orange hit him on the back of the neck. Tom leaned forward and gripped the edge of his seat in apprehension, as he realized that Marcellus and no doubt many others had carried rotten fruit and vegetables into the theater with them for this very purpose, and they had no intention of allowing the play to go on as scheduled.

Betterton shouted over the crowd, pleading with them to be silent. "We shall proceed to the Second Music," he declared with an edge of desperation in his normally strong voice. "May I introduce Mistress Jane Carlyle, a fine English soprano!" He placed great emphasis on the word English, but Tom knew it would do no good; the crowd was already too far gone.

Tom heard Holden in the pit cry for the musicians to attend him, and again the orchestra began to play. On stage, Jane warbled through her first line: "Let us drink and sport today, ours is not tomorrow..."

But it was too late; the riot had already begun. Before Jane reached the second line, her voice was drowned out by the cries of the audience as they shouted and rose to their feet. Having already thrown what fruit they brought with them, the crowd turned to ripping up the chairs. There was a clattering of feet, and Tom realized with sickening dread that the drunk men were rushing the stage.

Being seated closest to the stairs at the far left side of the stage, Tom pushed his way through the crowd and leapt onto the stage. "Jane!" he called, "Jane!" One hand gripped his walking stick before him while the other hand groped the air frantically. He took a few uncertain steps forward on the stage, until a small, slim hand grasped his.

"Mr. Finch!" Jane gasped.

He put his arm around her protectively. She was small, even smaller than Tess; her head did not even reach his shoulders. "Come, let's go out the back, through the stage door," Tom said urgently. "Only you must lead the way."

It seemed not many of the rioters had made it up onto the stage yet, as Jane hurriedly led him into the wings. But just as they were about to turn down the hall past the dressing rooms, Jane was suddenly yanked backwards and stumbled out from under his arm.

"Where do you think you're going?" It was Marcellus, but Tom was unsure if he was by himself or was accompanied by his cronies.

"I'm going home," Jane said, trying to twist her arm away, but she could not break his grip.

"A pretty little tit like you? I think not," Marcellus slurred, leering at her, all yellow teeth and greasy curls. "Don't be so hoity-toity with me, miss! The show ain't half begun."

Tom heard a rending of fabric and Jane gave a screech, but he could hear no other men with the drunk Marcellus. "Leave off, you wretch!" Tom shouted, taking a step closer, as Jane ducked behind him.

Out of nowhere, Tom felt Marcellus's rough hand grasp his shirt. "Oh ho, blind Cupid steps forth! Trying to keep the girl all to yourself, hey?"

Instead of answering, Tom took a swing at Marcellus with the head of his walking stick, bringing it up crosswise, but even drunk, Marcellus saw the blow coming and easily dodged it. The heavy silver head of the walking stick barely grazed his chin, and did nothing to subdue his ardor.

Marcellus pushed Tom aside, reaching for Jane's skirts. "Come miss, show us your cunny!"

"No!" Tom was accustomed to all manner of lewd behavior, but even he was shocked that a man of some learning and status would outrage the modesty of a woman in full public view, and with such vulgarity. Even the denizens of the bawdy houses showed more propriety than this. He swung the silver head of his walking stick again in the direction of Marcellus's voice, and this time caught him unawares, connecting on the side of his head with a heavy thud.

Jane screamed and jumped back. Just as Marcellus slumped to the floor, Frankie came running up, shouting, "Mr. Finch! Miss Carlyle!" His voice, only recently lowered, screeched up to a boyish soprano and cracked. "This way!" He tugged on both their sleeves, imploring them to follow him down the hall to the stage door.

"He ain't dead, is he?" Tom asked as he allowed Frankie to pull him along.

Frankie glanced behind him. Marcellus was slowly sitting

up, rubbing his head in bewilderment.

"No, only stunned. Come, the riot in the front of the house is worsening. Hurry!"

Frankie fairly danced with impatience as he tried to pull both Tom and Jane down the narrow passage, but they made very slow progress. Marcellus had ripped away Jane's lacy fichu and loosened her stays. With every other step, she paused to tug at the front of her dress, but the entire edifice was slipping, exposing her bosom.

"I can't go out into the street like this," she protested, as they reached the open door.

Tom removed his surcoat and settled it about her shoulders. She clutched it shut in the front gratefully.

They joined the small group of performers spilling out the stage door onto the street, but as they could hear the rioters at the front of the theater, they did not linger. With Frankie still holding awkwardly to both their arms, they hurried down a close, along the southeast side of the Piazza of Covent Garden and thence to Maiden Lane. The feeling of the familiar cobbles beneath his feet had never been so welcome, Tom thought.

Once they had settled Jane in a chair with a blanket wrapped around her and a restorative glass of brandy, Frankie took off for St. James's to summon Tess. Tom helped himself to the brandy as well, wondering if Tess would deign to set foot in his house again, after the way they had parted. She had not spoken to him since their return from France. He realized with a pang of guilt that he had not inquired about her affairs either.

Tom was brought out of his own running thoughts by the sound of muffled sniffling in the chair beside him. He reached his hand out rather uncertainly and Jane grasped it tightly.

"You saved me," Jane said wonderingly.

Privately Tom felt she need not sound so surprised, but he only said, "You've had a bad shock, but it's all right now." He patted her small hand reassuringly.

Tom need not have worried over Tess, for she came running directly. Before long, he heard her tripping up the stairs. She burst into the front parlor unannounced. With a little cry, Jane leapt out of her chair and the two embraced tightly. Tom twisted in his chair uncomfortably, feeling himself an auditory witness to a private scene.

Tess made Jane sit down again and knelt before her, making much of her and ensuring she was unharmed, then listening as Jane recounted their escape from the riot. When she was finished, Tess turned to Tom with wide eyes.

"Is this true?" she asked. "Mr. Finch, we owe you a debt of gratitude."

"There's no need to feel indebted," Tom replied rather stiffly. "I would never abandon a friend."

Tess's face flushed at his words, but he was unaware of it. She stared at him, but his expression was blank as ever. Perhaps she had misjudged him. Now she regretted the harsh words she had spoken to him on the journey home from France, but still she could not find the words to apologize. Instead she murmured her thanks again, then announced that she would step outside to hire a hack, for Jane was in no condition to walk home.

"Frankie can do it," Tom suggested. "Where is that boy, anyway?"

"He ran back to the Rose," Tess explained. "I'll just be a moment." She was gone to find a carriage before Tom could protest further.

"Don't be so hard on her," Jane said suddenly, as they heard the front door shut below. "She loves you, you know."

Tom jolted upright in his chair. "No, she don't!"

"Yes she do, only she's too proud to admit it," Jane said. "She gave up her position at Drury Lane to go fetch you in Paris. She asked me to go with her but I wouldn't."

"What? Why not?"

"Because I was jealous! Really, Mr. Finch, I thought you was cleverer than that. Someday she will leave me for you, and then where will I be?"

But Tom had only now grasped the full import of her words. "Wait, did you say she lost her position at Drury Lane because of me?"

"Yes, what did you think? She was gone for weeks. By the time she returned, all the roles had been cast, and Mr. Highmore said she could whistle for her supper."

"He never!"

"He did, and now she's afraid she shan't be cast at any other theater neither, and what shall she do if she can't find a part? I tell you, Mr. Finch, she cannot go back to Naples."

"What? Why not?"

"That's her private business, not for me to tell. I've already said more than she would like. She's very proud, you know. She yearns for a career on the London stage above all things, yet she gave it up for you."

Tom was deeply moved by this speech from Jane, so much so that for a time he did not reply at all, sitting slumped in his chair with his long legs thrust out before him. He held Tess in high esteem, yet he realized now he had acted selfishly. If she had not come to France and brought Jem with her, how would he have returned to London? It pained him to think he had cost her a role, perhaps even for the entire season.

"I must go," Jane said suddenly, standing up. "I hear the carriage pulling up below."

Tom roused himself and stood as well, extending his hands, which she clasped. "I am very sorry for what happened today," he said kindly. "Please take care."

She shook his hands. "I am very grateful for your kindness."

He did not let her hands go. "Please tell Tess I'm sorry about what happened to her as well."

"No. Don't tell her I discussed this with you." She removed her hands from his and took her leave. Tom listened as she trod lightly down the stairs and out the front door.

CHAPTER EIGHTEEN: ARIODANTE

Tess Turnbridge stood on the dimly lit stage of the newly constructed Theater Royal, Covent Garden, singing her heart out to the empty seats. Empty, that is, save for five finely dressed gentlemen sitting in the middle of the stalls. Of these five, the opinions of only two mattered. The first of these was Mr. John Rich, the manager, himself a top-billed comedic actor, also holder of the Letters Patent granted by the king to the theater. Mr. Rich was the man who had some years previous commissioned and produced *The Beggar's Opera*, the astonishing success of which now allowed him to open his own theater and produce whatsoever he pleased. And while for the first four years of the theater's existence it had pleased him to produce stage plays, now he issued a direct challenge to Mr. Highmore at Drury Lane by commissioning a new opera seria, titled *Ariodante*, from Mr. George Frideric Handel, the second man whom Tess would have to impress with her audition. In comparison to John Rich, with his elaborate wig and fine delicate features, Handel looked dowdy and aged. He was dressed informally in a red velvet jacket with a soft cap on his bald head, his face paunchy and tired. Tess was careful not to meet the gaze of either man as she sang, lest she lose her nerve, but kept her eyes fixed on the back of the hall.

Tess had been amazed to receive word from Tom that he

had convinced Mr. Rich to audition her for *Ariodante*, but she must appear that same day. As there was no time to prepare anything else, Tess sang "Hush ye pretty warbling choir," the same aria from *Acis and Galatea* that she had performed at Lord Mordington's assembly. Inside she was trembling to perform his own composition before the great Handel himself, but if her mother had taught her anything, it was how to appear confident on stage even when she was not. She gave her whole attention to hitting each note exactly right, with enough vocal ornamentation to show off her talents to best effect. As her voice filled the cavernous theater, she punctuated each trill with delicate movements of her hands and smiled as sweetly as she knew how.

The applause of the few spectators echoed thinly, and Tess curtsied low. She looked up just in time to see Handel give a slow nod, and her heart lifted. The five men rose, and Handel lumbered toward the exit, while Rich, followed by his retinue of conductor, assistant manager and set designer, made his way at a dignified pace through the stalls and onto the stage. Tess curtsied again before them on the stage and thanked them for their time.

"Very fine singing, Mistress Turnbridge," said Rich, standing with one hip thrust out as if he were posing for a statue. "Mr. Handel is pleased to offer you the role of Dalinda."

Tess's heart raced with excitement, but she schooled her features in neutrality, recalling the bit of advice Tom (through Jem) had appended in his note, not to offer her talents too cheaply. The Theaters Royal at Covent Garden and Drury Lane were in direct competition, and Tess intended to use that to her advantage.

"I am honored to accept," Tess replied demurely, "if there also be a place in the women's chorus for Miss Jane Carlyle, late of the Rose." The riot had destroyed much of the interior of the Rose, and part of the façade as well; there would be no more performances for the rest of the season, leaving all the players unemployed.

Rich arched an expressive eyebrow at her. "Indeed?" he drawled.

"A role for Miss Carlyle," Tess insisted, meeting his gaze boldly. "Unless you prefer I tell Mr. Highmore I am unengaged for the season...?"

Rich's jaw tightened and he smiled humorlessly at her. "Very well, I can always use another chorister as long as she's young and pretty. Any other demands, Miss Turnbridge?"

Tess took a deep breath. "Yes, I request that you hire Mr. Finch as music master." She could hardly believe the words even as she uttered them herself. She had vowed to stay away from him, but on the other hand, he was just as unemployed as Jane, and even less likely to secure a position. It seemed a fitting way to thank him for all he had done for her and Jane.

Rich gave a sharp bark of laughter. "Him? Whatever for!"

"He's the best music master in London," Tess said stubbornly. Rich's dismissive response made her more determined than ever to have her way. "I have trained with him extensively. If you were pleased with my technique, it was all due to his tutelage." She lifted her chin defiantly.

"Hmmm." Rich surveyed her with hooded eyes and a smirk. He had many years of experience managing willful divas and was not one to give in to the demands of actresses, but it might be this problem contained its own solution. "Very well, Miss Turnbridge. As it happens I have no music master yet, and Mr. Handel shall be pleased not to run the rehearsals himself. Mr. Finch may run the first music rehearsal as a trial, but if his conducting is not up to standard, he is out directly. Understood?"

Tess nodded and curtsied again, thanking him profusely.

"Well done, Miss Turnbridge! I give you the joy of the part." Tom shook Tess's hand heartily. She had stopped at his house directly after the audition to share the news with him that she had been cast and inform him of the details of her arrangement with John Rich. Tom bade her sit in the front parlor and

166

called for Stinson to bring them tea.

"*Ariodante*, is it? I hope it won't be another *Alcina*," Tom continued.

"It is another libretto from *Orlando Furioso*, yes," Tess replied carefully, sitting opposite him at a small round table. As usual there was a pile of papers on the table, as well as a small tin flute. "But I assure you it is all a love story this time, no flying horses and such nonsense. And Marie Sallé must keep her clothes on this time, or we shall be shut down by order of the Magistrate of Westminster."

"More's the pity," Tom muttered.

Stinson arrived with the tea service, and Tess shifted the articles on the table onto another chair.

"It was very kind of you to intervene on my behalf, but I must inform you, I have applied to Mr. Rich before, and he has never seen fit to grant me employment," Tom said as he carefully ran his fingertips over the tea service, then poured them each a cup.

"Why ever not?" Tess asked in surprise. Mr. Rich had certainly not mentioned this to her.

Tom shrugged dispiritedly. "To begin with, how am I to learn the music?"

"But, with *Dido and Aeneas*, you knew every note..." she stammered, suddenly unsure of herself. "And *The Grub Street Opera*..."

"Ah, but you see, Miss Turnbridge, those were revivals. I had attended many earlier performances, and so committed the whole to memory, whereas *Ariodante* is entirely new. Mr. Handel will deliver the score to the company on the day the rehearsals begin, I presume. And when will that be, pray tell?"

"In three days' time," Tess answered faintly. She thought back to her interview with John Rich, his sardonic look as she had assured him of Tom's skill. He had known all along and purposely had not mentioned it to her, she realized to her mortification. Tess had not said as much to Tom, but Mr. Rich had only promised him the position contingent on his performance at the first rehearsal, and now she understood why. How unfair, she thought with a pang. Tom was the best music master in London, to be denied a position only because he could not see the score, how monstrously unfair.

"If I may, I shall speak to Mr. Rich again and see what can be done," she said at last, with greater conviction than she felt.

Tom thanked her and bade her good day, expecting nothing more to come of it. But the next day, to his great surprise, Tess called on him again, this time bearing the immense conductor's score, with the ink still fresh, accompanied by Jem Castleton and Jane Carlyle, whom she had enlisted to aid her.

"We shall play through the parts entirely, until you have learnt them," Tess explained.

"You would do such a thing for me?" Tom exclaimed, feeling strangely moved. "I find I am in your debt once again, Miss Turnbridge."

"Oh no, pray think nothing of it," she said airily. As grateful as she was to him for helping her secure the part and for rescuing Jane, it pleased her more to be the one granting favors than receiving them.

Despite Tess's assurances, however, playing the entire score was no small task. They first ran through the entire opera, with Jem working out a reduction on the spinet, and Tess and Jane supplying the vocal parts. This was not so difficult, as the conventions of opera seria mandated that most of the arias were solos, and there were few ensemble parts. But next they played through each part for each of the main instruments, and this took much longer. The basso continuo was to be mostly improvised and so was not noted down in detail, but to play through the top lines for the strings, brass and woodwind, they each took turns on the spinet or violin, as Tom sat slouched in a chair, his brow furrowed and eyes shut tight in concentration, occasionally asking them to repeat a phrase until he had got it. They labored in this fashion for two entire days; it was tedious, exhausting work, and as there was only one score, the three of them were constantly on top of each other trying to see it at once. Jem seemed to take it all as a lark, not least because Tess had quietly paid him rather handsomely out of her own pocket. Jane, on the other hand, had been very unwilling to come out after her recent shock, but Tess had prevailed upon her, and at last she had acquiesced. Tom was exceedingly polite to Jane, refraining from his usual teasing, and she eventually lost some of her reserve, to Tess's great relief.

By the day of the first rehearsal, Tom had not heard each part more than twice, but he assured Tess that was sufficient to fix the notes in his mind. Jem came along to act as Tom's assistant, to sit beside him with the conductor's score and follow along in case of missed notes. Tess took her seat on stage beside the other singers, thinking back to her first rehearsal at the Rose as she watched Tom arrange himself at the conductor's stand. How strange, she thought; she was far more nervous this time, although not for herself, even though this was a far more celebrated company than at the shabby old Rose. Seated beside her was the prima donna, the great Anna Maria Strada del Po, known in less polite company as the Pig, who would sing the part of Ginevra, the princess of Scotland, while Tess had the role of Dalinda, her servant. Tess stole a glance at La Strada's profile, with her long Roman nose—she was not so bad looking, in truth, if only she did not grimace so when she sang.

Beside La Strada was none other than the famed castrato Farinelli, who would sing the title role of Ariodante. Did he know that Tom was the author of that fling against him? Tess wondered. The song had become quite popular; she had heard it all over town. But Farinelli maintained a lofty attitude, as if he hardly noticed the mere mortals around him, least of all the mere music master. The comprimario roles were mostly filled by German singers whom Mr. Handel had lured to England with him, including a hefty bass who had once been his cook.

Tom began the rehearsal with the same flourishes as he

had at the Rose, pointing directly at musicians who missed their notes and singing through difficult passages exactly on pitch, all the while jesting with them in a light-hearted tone. Tess watched him with wholly new admiration, realizing now how much of this was a theatrical display to encourage their confidence in him. And yet it seemed to work: by the end of the rehearsal, the singers and the orchestra were all in good humor. Tom did not miss any notes, but only called on Jem to give the measure numbers to the players. Mr. Rich complimented him, although rather stiffly, adding that if Jem stayed on as an assistant, his pay would come out of Tom's salary. Tom shook hands with all the principles, who were all exceedingly polite, even Farinelli, and that was the end of the first rehearsal.

"The Pig's hand was surprisingly small and lady-like," Tom remarked to Jem as they crossed the Piazza to the Essex Serpent afterwards. "But then again, so was Farinelli's." Jem hooted with laughter. "Tell me," Tom continued, "what does the celebrated castrato look like?"

"Not so womanish as you might expect," Jem replied. "But not like a man neither. More like a boy stretched out. All them castrati have long arms and legs, fat round bellies, and big barrel chests like a blacksmith's bellows. It's how he can hold a note as long as he does, but he's an odd-looking cove, I tell you." As they settled in to a well-deserved bottle of wine, Jem added, "A toast to your Miss Turnbridge, she has done us both yet another very good turn."

"My Miss Turnbridge?" Tom asked with a frown when he had drained his glass. "I should hardly say that."

"She has been uncommon friendly to you," Jem said.

Tom refilled his glass, holding a finger inside the rim to be sure he did not overfill it. "Miss Turnbridge has two lovers already, one of each sex, one of whom is exceedingly rich," he said with a grin. "What more could she possibly want?"

"What indeed," said Jem.

It was true that as of late Tom found himself in Tess's company more often. He realized he appreciated her charms more than ever. She had a way about her that was quick and clever, but also kind. In her company it was easy to put aside the unhappy events of his trip to France with Sal, and as for Marie Desmares, he had forgotten her entirely. Then one morning just before the opening of *Ariodante*, Jem came calling at Maiden Lane with a letter for Tom that had been delivered to Jem's address in Broad Court. It was from Charles Desmares.

"I believe it says you are a cowardly blackguard, an infamous rake, and that you engaged in criminal conversation with his wife," Jem said, summarizing the letter, which appeared to be written hastily in a mixture of English and French. "He's coming over to England straightaway, and he intends to call you out."

"Oh really now," said Tom sourly. "A duel? Is that at all necessary? I had assumed this sort of amour was even more common in Paris than here in London."

"That's not all, Finchy," Jem said, scanning down to the bottom of the letter, skipping past more imprecations and abuse. "He says that Marie is with child, and you are to blame."

CHAPTER NINETEEN: THE DUEL

It was not in Tom's nature to dwell on unpleasantness, and as the letter from Charles Desmares was unpleasant in the extreme, he put it out of his mind entirely. When Jem questioned the wisdom of ignoring this threat, Tom brushed him off, saying he thought it unlikely Desmares would come all the way to England over a matter that was already over and done with, as Tom had returned home and had no intention of going back to France.

"And what of this supposed child?" Jem asked suspiciously.

"Oh," said Tom airily, "if there even is a child, I really doubt it could be mine," but he offered no further proof of this assertion.

During the final dress rehearsal the day before the opening of *Ariodante*, La Strada had just settled into her first aria when there was a commotion at the back of the house, and a large man with a square jaw and a flashing, angry eye came striding up the center of the rows of empty seats, followed by the rather more portly clerk, with several agitated stagehands trailing behind them. Tom, his concentration devoted wholly to conducting, took no notice of them until one by one the musicians left off playing, their mouths hanging open, and their forgotten instruments dangling from their hands. La

Strada stopped singing.

As the shouting and banging drew closer, Tom recognized the voice of Charles Desmares. He set his baton down with a sigh. He could hardly believe the man had come all the way to London. Tom turned slowly and stepped up out of the orchestra pit. Desmares had reached the front of the stage and stood before him, hitting the backs of the empty chairs with his walking stick and shouting in French. Tom's blind eyes opened wide, his face fixed in what he hoped was a picture of innocent confusion.

"I beg your pardon," Tom said in English, "but this is a closed rehearsal. May I direct you to the manager, Mr. Rich...?"

Desmares charged forward and poked the head of his walking stick against Tom's chest. "You!" he shouted in heavily accented English. "I 'ave found you out! You are a liar and *un bâtard*! Oh yes, I 'ave 'eard all these things about you!"

Tom calmly pushed aside the walking stick. "I am very sorry, but to whom am I speaking? Are we acquainted?"

"You come into my 'ome on false pretenses and dishonored my wife! I demand satisfaction!" Desmares shouted, his face mottled red with anger.

Tom reached forward with an uncertain hand, groping towards his face. "You must excuse me, but due to my, ahem, affliction, you see, you have the advantage of me. Pray, what is your name?" Behind him, Tom could hear titters from some of the younger members of the chorus, all of whom had crowded to the edge of the stage to watch.

"Desmares, Charles Desmares of la Bourse, *maudit Anglais*," he said, batting Tom's hand away. "As you know very well, you villain. I will 'ave satisfaction for the shame you 'ave brought to my wife and *honneur*!" He made as if to lunge towards Tom, but by this time Jem had also climbed out of the pit, and now interposed himself between them.

"Now, now, let's settle this like gentlemen," Jem said loudly, pushing Desmares back and looking significantly at Fontaine for aid. The clerk reluctantly stepped forward.

"If it's a duel you want, you might have summoned me to Paris, rather than taking the weary trip yourself," Tom suggested. There were more titters behind him, and Desmares lunged forward again, a dangerous look in his eye. They all knew very well that dueling was illegal in France; it was clear Tom was merely toying with him.

"Let's agree on a spot, then, hey?" said Jem hurriedly. "We'll meet you in Hatchett's Bottom in Hampstead Heath at sunset. What say you? It will be easy to find a spot on the Heath where none will disturb you. Well?" He looked at Fontaine, ignoring Desmares, who had turned to pace about in agitation. Although not yet against the law in England, dueling was nonetheless frowned upon by the authorities, and if they were caught by a constable, they would likely be prevented from carrying out the deed.

Fontaine nodded slowly. "That is acceptable."

"And the weapons?" Jem asked. "Since he's called you out, Finchy, you have the honor of choosing."

"Oh, pistols, I suppose," said Tom carelessly, then clapped his hands in a brisk, businesslike way. "Well then, if that's decided, come now, we must continue the rehearsal." He bowed to where he heard the sound of Desmares' restless pacing, then found his way back into the pit and resumed his spot on the conductor's stand. Still the singers and musicians stood about, hoping for more from the agitated Desmares.

The stage manager, a small wiry man named Collins, herded the chorus into the wings, shouting, "Back to work, damn you! A fine parcel of flats you shall look tomorrow when the show opens! Come on, we ain't got all day!"

And so the rehearsal continued, although it was hardly their best effort, as everyone was rushing to finish before sunset. Ordinarily a dress rehearsal might drag on interminably, but the moment Tom laid his baton down, Collins announced the show was well enough, and there was a general scramble for the dressing rooms.

As he was leaving with Jem, Tom discovered that Frankie

was awaiting him by the stage door, with his pistols brought from Maiden Lane, and a worried message from Stinson.

"Dammee but news travels fast round the Piazza," Tom grumbled as he exchanged a coin for the box containing the pistols, with his thanks. The boy did not run off as he usually did, however, but hung about expectantly as Jem hailed a carriage. Tom did not realize until the carriage was underway that he was accompanied not only by Jem but also Tess and Jane, wringing their hands and looking anxious, and Frankie, who had slipped in at the last moment.

"You ain't afraid, sir?" Frankie piped up as the carriage lurched northward. "Your man Stinson was in a terrible taking, but I told him, I says, Master Finch is a bang-up cove. He's sure to dish up that Frenchie."

Tom turned his face up in surprise. "What the devil are you doing here, boy?"

Jem cut in, "Shall I load the pistols for you, Finchy?"

"What? No!" Tom protested. "I shall do it myself. I swear, you are the worst pack of old women." He turned towards Tess, opposite him in the carriage. "Well, Miss Turnbridge? Have you anything to add? I can hear you fretting and sighing."

"Have you got Marie Desmares with child?" Tess burst out. "I tried to warn you, but this time you have really gone too far —"

"And I tell you I have not," Tom said with annoyance. "Not that it's any of your concern. If you must know, I have always made it a practice to use Phillip's Machine, what is known in the common tongue as a cundum. I'm sure you are familiar with such devices, Miss Turnbridge."

Jane gasped, "How vulgar you are, Mr. Finch!" but Tess only blushed and looked out the carriage window.

They arrived at dusk in Hatchett's Bottom, a tiny village in a valley at the east end of the Heath, only to find awaiting them at the one tavern, called the Crown, not only Desmares and Fontaine but half the company from the theater including Collins the stage manager, Signor Farinelli, looking highly amused, as well as some other hangers-on from Covent Garden.

"How did they get here so devilish fast?" Jem wondered aloud, while Tom cursed them for a bloodthirsty rabble.

"You would think they had never heard of a fellow being called out," Tom complained. "Are there not enough hangings on Tyburn to satisfy their curiosity?"

"Please, do not talk so," Tess murmured behind him.

Desmares stalked out of the Crown and over towards them, followed by Fontaine. One of the violinists shouted, "For shame, to duel a blind man!" but was quickly silenced by a murderous glare from Desmares.

Jem sighed. "So much for keeping close. Come, let's get this over with quickly." He led them away from the village, over a rise to a more secluded spot, followed by the crowd of curious onlookers, who straggled along behind. Once he found a suitable flat grassy area, he and Fontaine measured off twenty paces and marked it with handkerchiefs, while Desmares and Tom loaded their pistols.

"You realize this is your fault, for carrying tales," Jem hissed at the ashen-faced Fontaine as they were readying the ground. "One shot each should be enough, hey? Let's not make this a damned bloodbath." Fontaine nodded, looking miserable. Unlike his master, he was not a violent man, and had never participated in such barbaric practices before.

Tess pulled Jem aside as Fontaine went to inspect the pistols and review the rules with the duelists. "What can we do?" she whispered to him.

Jem looked grave. "It's already growing dark. Tom might have an advantage if Desmares makes a noise, but he seems too clever for that, the dog." Fontaine was now setting the two combatants in their places, marked by the handkerchiefs, glowing white in the gathering gloom.

The onlookers leaned forward eagerly as Tess thought quickly. "Oh, oh, can you not settle this some other way?" she cried in her most carrying voice, pitched to reach the rafters of the Theater Royal. "Think of what Marie would say if she were here!"

"*Silence!*" Desmares shouted, glancing at her.

At the same moment, Fontaine called out, "*Commençez!*"

Two pops and two puffs of smoke: Tom's tricorne hat went flying off behind him, while Desmares fell to the ground. There were several cries from the onlookers, including Farinelli's distinctive soprano. A moment later, Desmares sprang up again, holding a hand to his face.

"*Quel salaud!*" he shouted. "Fontaine, bring me another pistol!"

Tess rushed towards Desmares, with Jane following after her. The ball had grazed his left cheek, not deeply, but the wound was bleeding prodigiously. Tess pressed a handkerchief against it. Desmares continued to rant, but they were soon surrounded by the others, including the wretched-looking Fontaine, who held him in check.

"Another pistol, damn you!" Desmares shouted in French. "I will make that bastard regret crossing me!"

"Calm yourself, Monsieur," Fontaine mumbled. "You agreed to one shot each. Now there's an end to it."

At the same time, at the other end of the field, Tom took one or two uncertain steps, the pistol dangling from his fingers, both hands outstretched. "What's going on?" he cried.

Frankie came running and placed Tom's hat in his hand. "Oh sir, you dinged him good!" he said excitedly. "And the Frenchie missed! Look, there is a great hole in the crown of your hat." Tom ran his fingers over the cocked hat; indeed, there was a hole right through the very top, its edges still charred and warm where the ball had passed through.

Jem clapped him on the back. "By God, that was neatly done, Finchy!"

"He's not hurt, is he?" Tom asked with some concern.

"Not seriously, no, but you've given him a scar on the face he won't soon forget, ha ha!"

Desmares was at last disarmed and the entire company

retired to the Crown. Several pints in quick succession aided in calming his temper, although he remained sulking in a corner with his clerk, awaiting the doctor, while the others drank Tom's health and celebrated his victory.

"I swear, it was the most remarkable feat this age," said Collins.

Richardson, the first violin added, "Was you not afraid?"

"I am impressed, Signor," said Farinelli, who seemed to be enjoying himself immensely. "Have you engaged in a duello before?"

"Ah, no, not as such," Tom answered, a bit embarrassed by all the attention.

"Can't you see anything at all?" a stagehand asked incredulously, waving a hand before Tom's face. Tom swatted the hand away with annoyance, not bothering to answer. He was feeling strangely tired, utterly sapped of vitality. His fingers recalled the feel of the hole in his hat. It had been a very near miss, but more than the attempt on his own life, he regretted that he had nearly killed a man and was filled with relief that he had not.

Tess put a hand on his arm. "Perhaps it's time we all returned home," she suggested gently. But just at that moment, the doctor arrived, and the crowd watched with interest as he prepared to dress Desmares' wound. A moment later, the doctor was followed by a disheveled and tired-looking Henri d'Angoulême.

"Charles!" he exclaimed in French, "I have been searching for you since I arrived yesterday. Thank God I arrived before you did anything rash—oh dear..." he broke off, as he saw the doctor and the blood-soaked bandages.

"I shall live, I assure you," Desmares replied sourly. "What the devil are you doing here?" Henri bowed to him. Jem and Tom had crossed the room to greet him as well, and Henri embraced them as brothers, then bowed to Tess, who was behind them.

"Oh, Messieurs, I am so relieved to see you unharmed,"

Henri said. "Marie sent me to inform you that it was all a misunderstanding," he continued, addressing Desmares in a low voice. "She is not with child." Desmares did not reply, but much of the choler seemed to drain from his face at last. Tom bowed to him, begging his pardon for the unfortunate altercation, and took his leave. As Tom and Jem prepared to depart, Tess pulled Henri aside.

"Do you mean she was never with child or is with child no longer?" she whispered to him.

"Madame, I will not impugn my only sister. Pray do not ask it of me," Henri answered, looking evasive. "It hardly signifies."

"But she is well, is she not?" Tess pressed him. "She has not done herself any harm?"

Henri's face cleared. "No, I assure you, she is quite well. But perhaps it would be for the best if your friends did not come visit again, to prevent any further, ah, misunderstanding." Tess was quite of the same mind, and they bid each other goodnight very kindly. Tom tried to convince Henri to stay in London, at least to see the opening of *Ariodante*, but Henri refused him, saying he must see to Charles, and ensure he returned to Paris without mishap.

It was a pity Henri chose not to stay for the opening, as the company acquitted itself remarkably well. Mr. Handel was fêted all over London, and everyone commented on the vigor and brio of the production. Tom of course was not on the conductor's stand during the performances, as that honor went to Mr. Handel. But the entire company, from the musicians to the singers to the stagehands, had all become extraordinarily attached to Tom, each one eager to claim a role in the famous duel, the news of which spread even faster than the reviews of *Ariodante*. Tom was a bit surprised to be greeted by shouts of "What ho, the duello!" uttered by complete strangers every time he entered a tavern or coffee house, but as this was invariably accompanied by the purchase of drinks for him and his companions, he soon accustomed himself to it.

CHAPTER TWENTY: THE SPONGING-HOUSE

Following the successful opening of *Ariodante*, Tom found life very easy. John Rich was well satisfied with his work and paid him a handsome salary, with the promise of further employment to come, although Tom soon disposed of the greater portion of the payment, with Jem's help, in the public houses around the Piazza. There were also new clothes to be purchased, as Tom had lost much of his wardrobe in his adventures in France. Together they made his tailor in Southwark a happy man.

Most evenings, Tom stepped round to the theater to listen to part of an act, just to be sure *Ariodante* was going well, then retired to the Labor in Vain or the Essex Serpent with Jem and Betsy Careless. Regrettably, he was not so much in Tess's company as when they had been rehearsing, but she would occasionally join them at the Serpent after the performance, with Jane in tow. Tom found he enjoyed Tess's companionship extremely, although he was careful not to take liberties with her, especially with Jane about.

Lady Gray attended a performance as well, declaring it the prettiest opera this age, and praising Tom's work in particular.

"I have never heard the orchestra at Covent Garden play so precisely, nor with half so much dash," she said. Tom bowed his head humbly, but he was very pleased. Praise from the exacting old dame was high praise indeed.

"Now Tom, tell me plainly, are you in need of cash?" Lady Gray asked him as they sipped their sherry during the entr'acte. Tom inclined his head again and thanked her kindly, but it was his pleasure to decline her offer for the first time in a great while.

Several weeks into the run of *Ariodante*, Tom was awakened late one morning by the sound of Frankie pounding on the back door. On being summoned by Stinson, Tom descended to the kitchen in his dressing gown to find the boy was all in a taking.

"Oh sir," he cried, "It's Miss Sally, she's been arrested for debt!"

Tom was thrown into confusion. He had not spoken to Sal since their unfortunate time together in Paris. With great difficulty, Tom extracted what he could of the story from the distraught Frankie. It seemed she had been living rather too grandly since her return—not only had she run a tick on her own accounts, but some of George Harkington's former creditors had taken the opportunity to come after her as well. Frankie averred that Sal had not sent for Tom directly, but the boy was certain no one else had yet come to her aid, and as she was still at the sponging-house beside Bridewell, there was yet time to save her from being cast into prison.

Tom threw on his clothes and bade Stinson to gather up what cash was at hand. This was not the first time Sal had been clapped on the shoulder and sent to the sponging-house, and each time he had helped pay to get her out again before she could be sent to prison, although he was nearly certain that in the past she had other benefactors as well. With Frankie leading the way, Tom headed down the Strand and along Fleet Street toward Bridewell. Tom kept a hand on Frankie's shoulder as they negotiated the busy streets, and he noted with surprise how much the boy had grown. *I must do something more* for him, Tom thought distractedly as they walked on, but at the moment he had more pressing concerns.

As Sal's case had not yet come up before the magistrate, she was being held at a private house hard by the prison, a sponging-house, where debtors might be squeezed like sponges to give up their last pennies. The house itself was a wretched place, a cross between the meanest of inns and a prison, with cramped private rooms and scant meals offered at exorbitant fees, guards at the doors and iron grates over the windows. The guards bade Frankie wait outside and escorted Tom up to Sal's room, letting him in without ceremony. Tom found himself in what he sensed was a tiny, low-ceilinged room, airless and hot.

"Oh Tommy, it's you!" he heard Sal cry in her rasping voice, a moment before she flung herself upon him. He returned her embrace, running his hands over the familiar planes of her body, nearly overcome by a mixture of longing and resentment.

"I heard of your duel with that scrub Desmares," Sal continued, as if this were a social call between the closest of friends. "That was a prime bit of business, hellish fine of you. But really, Marie Desmares? Was that hoity-toity wench worth risking your life?"

Tom thrust her away in annoyance. "I might ask the same of you, Sal," he said. "You threw me over for a damned penny-pinching jeweler." He waved his hand about, searching for a table and chair, but finding none, remained standing stiffly by the door. "How could you be so hard-hearted?" he continued, his voice cracking, to his shame. "How could you leave me without one sou to my name?"

"What?" Sal exclaimed. "But I left you everything, all the lour in the desk drawer."

Tom frowned. "I assure you, it was all gone. You left me with nothing but a few old plates."

"No, I swear to you, I never nicked the chink," Sal insisted.

"Half the servants ran off. Perhaps one of them stole it,"

Tom conceded, although privately he felt there was no way to prove who had taken the cash. Nor could he persuade Sal to give a thorough account of her affairs in Rotterdam, only that she had grown bored with the life there and come back to England under shady circumstances; it seemed to him that she had helped herself to a good deal of Jan van den Staal's money as well, but he could not bring himself to pity the jeweler. However, it was clear that although she had been living in fine twig at Mother Needham's, most of her old patrons had deserted her after her bigamous marriage and long absence.

"Oh Tommy, what am I to do?" she cried, pacing about the tiny room. "This is all the fault of that son of a bitch Harkington, running a tick and leaving it in my name, damn him."

Tom was deeply moved for her—despite all that had happened between them, despite her inconstancy and treachery, he could not bear for her to suffer imprisonment, for once she went in, it was unlikely she would ever get out again.

Sal was accustomed to squalor and even sleeping rough, but she had a horror of imprisonment, and had no intention of submitting herself meekly to the brutality of the guards, nor of beating hemp alongside the other prisoners, particularly as she was still wearing the fine clothes she had been arrested in. Furthermore, the longer she was confined with her fellow bawds, lifters, and pickpockets, the more likely she was to be recognized and made to suffer for her previous activities.

"I have the remainder of my salary here, and you are welcome to it," Tom said. "How much is the debt?"

"Five hundred quid," she whispered miserably.

"Five hundred!" Tom exclaimed. He had only twenty guineas with him. However could he get that much money before her trial? Leaving her with what little he had brought, and reassurances that he would find the rest as soon as possible, he embraced her and departed. Much to Sal's misfortune, however, the magistracy moved with unwonted speed, and three days later, as Tom was still attempting to raise the cash, Frankie brought word that she had been removed from the sponging-house and confined in Bridewell Prison.

CHAPTER TWENTY ONE: BRIDEWELL

Tom did his endeavor to raise the money to get Sal out of prison, but five hundred pounds was not so easy to come by. He and Jem put their heads together, yet they could think of no better plan than to petition Lady Gray. Tom well knew his aunt would not willingly part with such a large sum, and for a common harlot, no less, but after much consideration, neither could he lie to her about the use the money would be put to, after all she had done for him, so in the end he merely tried to put the best face possible on it.

"It's to save a young widow from imprisonment for the debts of her late husband," Tom offered a bit uncertainly over an informal supper at Lady Gray's residence in Soho Square. "A worthy young lady—only think of her rotting in Bridewell! Who knows what unsavory criminal influence she might be exposed to there," he added, warming to his story.

Lady Gray regarded him shrewdly. He may have grown, but he still looked to her like a boy, and a boy far too easily lost and led astray. "Don't be inventing tales, Tom," she scolded. "I know very well you mean that Salisbury girl, and she is no innocent, to be sure. She could teach the devil himself some tricks. If she is in prison, then it's no better than she deserves."

Tom's brow wrinkled in distress. "No, Auntie, I assure, you, she is imprisoned for debt, nothing more, and the tick was all her late husband's, not her own."

"Don't speak cant; it's vulgar," she replied, unmoved. "Say 'debt,' not 'tick.'"

"Haven't you been telling me to marry?" Tom continued, with increasing fervor. "Once her tick, I mean her debt is cleared, I shall marry her and set up as a respectable household, I promise you."

"Marry? Tom, that girl will bring you nothing but grief, mark my words," Lady Gray said coldly. Then seeing his chagrin, she added more kindly, "Pray do not look so low. I could not in good conscience condone a bad match, one that would be your undoing."

Leaving aside the question of marriage, Tom tried again on a different tack. "Have you not been campaigning for improving the usage of female prisoners?" he asked. "Think of how she must be suffering in Bridewell, that wretched place, what dreadful posture she must be reduced to."

This last assay hit its mark, for Lady Gray had indeed been concerned that poor women, particularly unwed mothers, were thrown into the most inhuman confinement, and not even supplied with food or clothing. In the end, she would only give Tom enough to buy some provisions for Sal, but not enough to pay the entire debt.

Still, this was better than nothing, and enlisting Jem's aid as a guide, Tom set out again the following day across the Strand and along Fleet Street, with Frankie trailing behind them holding a basket with bread, cheese, and meat pies. They had tried to prevent the boy from coming with them, but he was anxious for Sal and insisted on joining them. This time there was no pretension to gentility in a private house; they proceeded directly to the entrance on Bridge Street and into the prison, commonly called Bridewell Hospital, although far more died there than were made well.

This ancient edifice had once been a palace of Henry VIII, but was soon given over to the housing of indigent women, and thence, as is the way of the world, became a house of correction, where female prisoners were set to work to reform their wicked ways. From the moment they stepped through the heavy iron doors and under the barrel vaulted arch Tom could hear the cries of the prisoners echoing faintly and smell the stink of filth in the air.

With Tom holding his elbow, Jem inquired of a guard, who directed them across the quadrangle to a door on the opposite side. As they crossed the green, they passed by where a woman stripped to the waist was being whipped before a small crowd, only a few of whom were gaolers, the rest being curious onlookers. Just as hangings were public spectacles, so too was punishment of prisoners, even within the confines of the prison. Jem forbore to describe this scene, hurrying them across the quadrangle to the entrance the guard had indicated, although Tom could guess well enough what was happening by the piteous cries. Frankie pressed up close behind them. Another guard let the three of them inside down a dank, narrow hall. Once inside, the noise was much worse, and Tom nearly staggered at the fetid stench.

"If you're looking for Sally Salisbury, she's in here," the guard said, but just as he made to open the door, the din of the prisoners erupted into a hair-raising crescendo, topped by a chorus of bloodcurdling screams. The guard opened the door onto a scene of utter bedlam. As they entered, Tom was startled by several bodies pushing roughly by him to escape into the hall, while the room itself was filled with the sound of running feet, a heavy wooden thumping, the scrape of iron on stone, as well as more screams and oaths.

The guard rushed in to the room ahead of them, shouting, "You there, hold! Hold, damn you!"

"What's happening?" Tom cried, but rather than answering, Jem pushed him up against a wall with one hand and disappeared into the crowd. Tom's fingers pressed the rough-hewn stones behind him, and the cold damp seeped into his shoulders as he leaned against the wall. He wished desperately to follow after Jem but dared not venture into an unfamiliar space, not with such a confusion of women running and screaming. He strained his ears to listen for Sal, but could not make out her voice above the din.

"Sal!" Jem shouted, leaving Tom against the wall by the door and rushing into the room. "Get her down! Hurry, send for a doctor!"

The long narrow room was filled with rows of women prisoners beating hemp with wooden mallets on rough wood stands. Those who were not shackled in place were attempting to flee in the opposite direction, but a few still stood to their task, beating their mallets with stony faces, oblivious to the confusion around them. Jem elbowed his way around the remaining prisoners as fast as he could, attempting to reach the wall opposite the door.

Up against the far wall, Sal stood in the stocks, her hands forced up above her head, her face to the wall. She sagged sideways, hanging by her wrists, the front of her dress soaked with blood. Next to her, the guard who had shown them in was holding a small, wild-looking woman by the shoulder with one hand and twisting her wrist upwards with the other. A knife fell from her hand, disappearing into the straw on the floor.

"Get her down!" Jem shouted again, but as no one else moved to help Sal, he pushed open the stocks himself and caught her as she fell, groaning loudly.

"What's happening!" Tom demanded, his eyes rolling back and forth uselessly.

"Oh sir," Frankie wailed, trembling all over. "Some blowen done for Miss Sally, chived her in the belly."

"No!" Tom clutched at the boy's arm. "Is she dead?"

"It don't look that way, but there's a mortal lot of blood," Frankie replied. As Sal fell swooning in Jem's arms, Frankie gave a loud cry and buried his face in Tom's waistcoat. Tom patted his back awkwardly, feeling he lacked the fortitude to reassure himself, let alone the boy. Silently, Tom cursed in frustration at not knowing what was happening to Sal and not being able to rush to her aid.

Across the room, Jem held up Sal's head as it lolled back. "Thank ye, Jemmy," she whispered, her eyes fluttering. "I knew you and Tommy would come for me." All the color was drained from her face. Jem held his other hand against the wound in her side, so horrified by the amount of blood seeping up between his fingers that he could make no reply to her.

At last the gaoler and several more guards arrived to take away the guilty party and restore order among the other inmates. Two of the guards took the door off the hinges and placed Sal upon it. She had fallen into a faint, but as they moved her, she revived enough to curse them in a weak voice. Jem and Tom followed after them as they bore her to a solitary cell and deposited her on a bunk. Frankie disappeared, forgotten in the confusion.

Tom stayed by Sal's side for he knew not how long, holding her hand as she writhed and groaned, only ceding his place when a surgeon arrived at length to dress her wounds. She had been stabbed three times in the stomach, quite deeply. The surgeon could not vouch for her recovery, but only bandaged her up in perfunctory manner and gave her a dose of laudanum. After the surgeon departed, Tom resumed his seat by her side, stroking her brow as she gradually quieted.

"Who did this?" he asked her, once she seemed more calm.

"It were that poxy blowen, Moll Ward," she replied, her voice a reedy whisper, but still full of vitriol. "She was taken up for whoring, been locked up here in Lob's Pound near a year, like she was waiting for me. Said it were revenge for killing her Neddy."

"Ned Ward?" Tom said, somewhat dazed by this revelation. "But you only stabbed him in the shoulder, and he didn't die of it. Wait, d'ye mean it was you that shot him?" But Sal did not reply. The laudanum had taken effect, and she had fallen into a deep sleep.

Jem, who had gone to pay the surgeon and talk to the gaoler, returned to convince Tom to return home, but he would not hear of it. Jem remonstrated with him, pointing out that they could not very well spend the night in Bridewell, but as it turned out, this was not necessary. Late in the day, Frankie appeared again, and with him Mother Needham herself, along with several of her servants. She immediately set about ordering the servants to prepare for the sleeping Sal's removal.

"What is the meaning of this?" Tom demanded indignantly.

The old madam glanced at him coldly, for she had a low opinion of men who occupied her girls' time without payment. "Her debt has been cleared and she is to be sent home," she said brusquely. Tom would have preferred if Sal were transferred to his house, but Mother Needham would have none of it, and within moments, they bore her away.

Tom was left at a bit of a loss, but there was nothing else to do but return to Covent Garden along with Jem and Frankie.

"But who paid the debt?" Tom wondered aloud as they walked down the Strand. "I can't imagine it was that old Madam Ran."

"Never in life, sir!" Frankie said. "It were Miss Turnbridge. I went and told her myself, and she laid out the money as neat as you please."

"Well, well," said Jem, surprised. "Who would ever have guessed it?"

On returning to Covent Garden, Tom insisted they proceed to Mother Needham's establishment in Charles Street, but they were turned away at the door. It mattered little, as Sal was still unconscious. Tom returned home very reluctantly, and only after leaving firm instructions with Frankie to send for him when she woke.

The boy was as good as his word, coming round the next afternoon to inform Tom that Sal was awake again. This time Tom was not to be denied, although he found the application of a few coins had far more effect than mere words; he was allowed in and shown to Sal's room. The weather was warm, and the small second storey bedroom was stiflingly hot. To Tom's horror, the room was filled with the overpowering stench of bile and rot. He groped his way towards the bed where Sal lay and ran his hands all over her. She seemed far worse even than the day before, her face and neck burning with fever, but her hands cold and leaden. He felt her stir under his hands, and she let out a ragged sigh.

"Oh Tommy, it's you," she said in a thready voice. Tom knelt down beside the bed and put his hand against her cheek. "I'm glad you came for one last visit."

"No, don't say that!" Tom cried. "You will get well. Let us never part again!"

Sal sighed painfully. "No, Tommy, I'm scragged for certain this time. Only I'm sorry I used you so badly. You was the only one who was ever truly kind to me."

"My dear Sovay," Tom groaned. He felt her smile under his hand.

"It were wrong of me to leave you in Paris," she murmured. "I have a wicked heart, and now God is punishing me for it."

"Don't talk so!" Tom said, distressed. "If it's my forgiveness you want, you know I would always grant it to you freely. You are not wicked."

"Oh aye, I am," she said softly. "As you well know. We was both born in sin, you and me, but you rose in the world and I fell, only for chasing after money. I'm sorry I wouldn't marry you, Tommy, but now it's too late." Tom did not answer, but only laid his head down on her shoulder. "Stay by me, won't you," she said, and he swore he would not shift from her side.

And yet Tom was not able to keep his promise, for as soon as she fell asleep again, Mother Needham forced him from the house, so that he was not with her when she died, but only got word from Frankie the next morning. Jem heard the news somewhat later in the day and hurried over to Maiden Lane, to find Tom sunk in the depths of mourning, from which the only recourse was drunkenness; thus they passed the day and night. The following day, they went to St. Paul's on the Piazza, where the sexton laid Sal in the churchyard with scant ceremony.

Observing that Tom had not eaten in the past day, Jem led him to the Essex Serpent and forced him to take some food, even as they both resumed drinking heavily.

"I believe I am the only one in all of London who weeps for her," Tom said miserably, his head hung low over his tankard.

Jem could not deny this, but instead commented, "You know she was never a match for you, nor you for her. Was you to be married, you'd have made the wretchedest of households."

"She begged me not to leave her," Tom cried. "I can't bear to think of her lying there alone."

Jem clapped him on the shoulder. "You did all you could for her. At least she died peaceful-like in bed, and not pilloried or whipped at the cart-arse and hanged on Tyburn, which might very well have been her fate." Seeing Tom look even lower in spirits, Jem added more kindly, "There's none who could've matched her for dash and spirit. Covent Garden will be that much less lively without the infamous Sally Salisbury."

ENTR'ACTE

CHAPTER ONE: JENNY FINCH

In the year 1704, during the reign of old Queen Anne, Jenny Finch together with her elder brother Jack set out from their home village of Pitminster, Taunton Deane, Somerset, to seek their fortunes in London. They left behind their aged father, the former schoolmaster of Pitminster, in the care of their two elder sisters, their mother having died many years previous. Already eighteen, and by all accounts a girl of fine good looks, Jenny still found herself without suitors in the village, in large part no doubt due to the education she and all her siblings had received from their father. As Jenny had no notion of passing the rest of her days in spinsterhood like her sisters, she attached herself to her admittedly rather feckless brother, and declared that she must accompany him in his vague plan to embark on a musical career in London.

Upon reaching the city, they at first found life not what they had anticipated: the lodgings more cramped and dirty, the food more distasteful, the water more foul, the people more inclined to rudeness and dishonesty; in short, everything more difficult and expensive than ever they had imagined. Yet they were both of a cheerful, sanguine disposition, and being from earliest childhood strangers to despair and loneliness, they accepted these hardships with good humor, never doubting that their fortunes would soon improve.

As aspiring musicians, they naturally found themselves

drawn towards the theaters of Covent Garden, which even at that time had begun its gradual descent from a fashionable address for aristocrats to the preferred haunt of whores, pimps, rakes, thieves, and wastrels. Jack found that work as a violinist with a theatrical company, his first ambition, was subject to fierce competition and the vagaries of preferment, of which he had none at all; thus this path was closed to him. On the other hand, there was a brisk business in writing down folk tunes, which were then cheaply printed on a single sheet of paper and sold on the street. This he took to with great success, for he had a large store of ballads and dances from his native village, mostly unknown in London. It was an easy task to take his notes to one of the many printing houses near the Piazza, then hawk the broadsides on the street himself, alternating with Jenny in singing out the tunes to advertise their wares. Both Jack and Jenny were possessed of clear, strong voices, and a lively musical sense. Soon they were doing well enough to outfit themselves in the latest mode, and having wasted no time in setting aside their country accents and manners, within less than a year, they could pass for native-born Londoners. Jenny then found herself with an abundance of suitors, although none to her satisfaction: as she was obviously without means, most of the attention she garnered was of an unsavory sort. Her brother Jack, himself inclined to sporting, nonetheless protected her from the pimps and procuresses who gathered round her like bees to a cask.

One day, she was accosted by a tall, thin man who bought up all her broadsides on the spot, and pressed into her hand a ticket to a masquerade ball at Vauxhall Gardens. The man did not give his name, but gave her such a look of passion before disappearing that she was utterly undone. He was wearing a red wool surtout in the new fashion, cut wide in the skirt, and a rich full-bottomed wig of brown curls falling over his shoulders, topped with a wide tricorne hat lined with feathers. He was clearly of a higher class than any who had accosted her before, and so she resolved to go.

The masquerade was quite the finest diversion Jenny had ever attended, and also the strangest; indeed it seemed like "the world turned upside-down," as the song goes. In the garden paths, lit with flickering torches, indistinct persons in masks and the most outlandish costumes flitted by, some quite uncovered, but just who was of the better sort and who was not was impossible to tell. To the left of the gardens was a large curved building shaped like a crescent moon, and inside she found the walls all covered with looking-glass, so that the tables of fragrant, exotic foods, the whirling dancers, and lines of footmen seemed to stretch on endlessly. Having arrived alone, she wandered about in a daze, until a tall man in a domino tugged at her arm.

"Do you know me?" he asked gravely.

"Begging your pardon, sir, but I do not," she replied, not realizing that this was the ritual question to begin conversation. The tall man laughed and lifted his mask to wink at her. She recognized him as the one who had given her the ticket, but when he identified himself as James Douglas, the Earl of Bolingbroke, she thought he was joking.

Nevertheless, she danced with him the entire night, and he was most gallant, praising her beauty and talent with flowery phrases, whirling her about with light, agile steps, and selecting for her the finest delicacies to eat. She had never been the object of such attentions before—his smoldering gaze and the bewildering setting quite turned her head, such that by midnight, when the guests all removed their masks, she was quite happy to be seduced by him.

If Jack was surprised to find his sister taken into keeping by an earl, he did not say so, nor indeed would he have had much ground to object, as he himself was a frequent visitor to the bagnios and bawdy houses, and moreover was staunchly opposed to marriage, at least for himself. As for his sister, he had no desire to see her working for some grasping Madam Ran, and neither did he imagine she would marry a fat merchant.

"Better the mistress of a rich man than the wife of a fool," he declared.

The earl was a frequent visitor to their lodgings, and Jack took care not to linger when Lord Bolingbroke arrived. Although he would not admit it, Jack was intimidated by the older man, so much higher in station than himself, and preferred to avoid him. They were both alike in their libertine pursuit of earthly pleasures, but Jack was inclined to light-hearted flirting and jesting, and found the earl's brooding intensity disquieting.

"You don't understand," Jenny sighed, gazing out the skylight with a bemused expression. "Jamie is a man of feeling. It's his deep sensibility that makes him behave thus." She did not add, the earl was also an accomplished and adventurous lover. He was particularly given to flagellation, supplying her with a bunch of rushes for the purpose, and instructing her to shout invectives at him as she did so. For many months she seemed inclined to distracted reverie—she felt as if he had opened for her a world she never knew existed, and with him she felt confident and powerful.

"You're as strong as a cart-horse," he teased her, and she took it as a compliment. He had often complained of his sickly wife, and she knew he esteemed health and strength above all other virtues, in women as well as in himself. He lavished her with gifts of all sorts, which fed her vanity as well, even if she could only wear the expensive jewels and dresses in the house.

And yet she knew this arrangement could not last, as inevitably she found herself pregnant; indeed, she was only surprised it had not happened sooner. It never occurred to her for a moment that her Jamie would abandon her at this juncture, although he seldom visited after she became so large her condition could no longer be ignored. Knowing she was unmarried, official representatives from the parish began pestering her, hanging about and asking intrusive questions, so she was greatly relieved when Lord Bolingbroke arranged for her lying-in at a new address in Cheapside, and engaged the services of a discreet Mother Midnight. Jenny also took it as a matter of course that Jack would join her at the new house, where they gave out their names as Mr. and Mrs. Finch, and the landlady was paid handsomely not to question them.

The new address was quite luxurious in comparison to their former Covent Garden lodgings, a neat little house they had all to themselves, both upstairs and downstairs, furnished by the earl, and equipped with three incurious servants. Despite her precarious posture, Jenny felt she had never before been so happy.

The Mother Midnight, an old hand at her profession, had attended to countless girls in exactly the same situation, and was not easily surprised. But at her first visit to assess the expectant mother's condition, she found Jenny's dauntless good humor, now reached a pink glowing radiance, unaccountable.

"You have three choices, madam," said she. "You may miscarry, and who should say but that it were accidentally; or the child may be born sickly and not survive, again a tragic accident; or it may be healthy and sent to the parish."

Jenny stared at her in horror. "Murderess!" she whispered, barely breathing the word.

The midwife immediately changed her tone, not wanting to lose the money the earl had promised her, or worse, to be sent before a magistrate. "Now, now, sweetheart, don't take on so. I'm sure the babe will be healthy and strong, but you understand that without a father, it must go to the parish."

Jenny, usually slow to anger, flashed out at her. "No! I won't let my child be given to cruel strangers. I have heard what happens to children sent out to be fostered by the parish—it's the same as murder by another hand. I won't hear of it."

"Is that so?" the midwife replied, no longer disguising the sneer in her voice. "And how do you intend to maintain yourself and a child? Don't say your earl—I know his kind. Mark my words, see if he ever looks on you again after the baby comes."

"Get out!" Jenny shouted. "And if you wish to be paid anything at all, never speak so to me again!"

The labor was long and difficult, but at last Jenny was delivered of a boy. Her job completed, the Mother Midnight was hastily sent away, to Jenny's great relief. Jack sent to the earl with the news, but received back only some cash enclosed under the same cover. Jamie Douglas did not appear in person, not even for the christening. Knowing he had no male heir, Jenny had not expected him to recognize the child right away, and so it was Jack who went with her to the church, where they named the baby Thomas, after their father, and added their own surname.

The labor had exhausted her and she was slow to recover, but after several more weeks had passed, it was clear to her that there was something wrong with both herself and the baby. She felt pained and ill at ease in ways she did not care to define even to her own brother. As for the baby, from the first his eyes were red and swollen, pasted shut with a crust that reappeared within a day no matter how carefully she washed it away.

At last she could disguise her anxiety no longer, and Jack sent for a doctor, a fat old man in a bagwig and severe black robes topped with a white stock. The doctor looked Jenny over with contempt, asked her many questions of a shockingly squalid, intrusive nature, then glanced at the baby. He had seen similar cases far too often to be moved by them any longer.

"You have the gleet, madam," he said in a flat, unsympathetic tone, "and the child will be blind." He left her with directions for preparing a draught for her venereal disease and suggested washing the baby's eyes with a decoction of yarrow.

The foul-tasting draught eased her symptoms and the yarrow seemed to answer at least for the moment; it cleared away the dreadful crust on the baby's eyes, so that when at last Lord Bolingbroke arrived for his first visit, Jenny was able to show him some semblance of health in herself and the baby. Upon his arrival, she did not thrust the child at him immediately, but instead offered only herself to amuse him, making herself as pleasant and charming as she knew how, until she was quite sure that his affection for her had not waned. Entwining her arms about his neck, she laid her head on his shoulder.

"Dearest Jamie," she sighed, "you would never abandon me, would you?" The earl murmured that he would not, but with less reflection or conviction than Jenny might have wished.

"Promise me," she pressed him. "Swear on your honor as a man that no matter what may happen, you will always remember me and the child."

"Very well then, I swear," he said, brushing the hair from her cheek, troubled by the serious cast of her eye and the blue shadows in her face. But when she produced the baby at last, he did not hesitate to hold it with paternal affection. Jenny had hurriedly washed the baby's eyes just before, so there was no sign of infection, and she was greatly relieved to see the infant grasp his finger, then, with his brown eyes wide open and clear, he looked straight at his father, as if he recognized him.

After such an auspicious first meeting, Jenny was certain that the doctor's diagnosis would prove false, and that Lord Bolingbroke would continue to visit her as he had before, but she was to be disappointed on both scores. Bolingbroke did not return, nor did he reply to her letters, although he continued to send money. And the baby's eyes grew worse rather than better—first turning red and rheumy, then before he passed his first birthday, becoming increasingly clouded over, the clear brown irises gradually obscured by a layer of bluish-white. And yet it seemed to her that he could still see, if indistinctly, for he would reach for objects set before him, and by the time he was breeched, he could name colors and distinguish light from dark.

Jenny did not take the earl's absence so hard as she might have, in part because she was certain he would return, but in larger part because she now turned all her attentions to her son. She had never had any particular ambition in life, nor planned more than a few days in advance, but suddenly she felt the press of duty upon her: she was determined that Tom should have every advantage. Fearing how a nursemaid might choose to dispose of a sickly child, she refused to send him out to nurse, but kept him at home at close to her at all times. Theirs was a retired sort of life, but as long as the bills were paid, no one disturbed them.

Although diffident at first towards the infant, as the child grew old enough to talk coherently and enter into human discourse, Jack became deeply attached to him. Indeed, as he grew, Tom proved to be both clever and affectionate, and, apart from his eyes, quite healthy. The same could not be said for Jenny, however, whose condition continued to worsen, although she did her best to conceal it from her son and her brother. She was not one to repine or pity herself, much less lament her son's condition, and so she cultivated cheerfulness in both of them.

When three years had passed, Lord Bolingbroke once again appeared unannounced, and this time Jenny knew she could not hide the child's condition from him. As the servant let the earl into the parlor, she held Tom in her arms, so that Lord Bolingbroke looked full into the child's face as he entered.

"Your son, my lord," she said, with a slight curtsey.

"Oh God," he gasped, sinking into a chair. Tom, already bored, wriggled in her arms until she was forced to set him down, and he ran off to play.

"What have you done to him?" he asked in a stricken tone.

"I?" she cried, much wounded. "I? Oh no, sir, this is your doing and none other. Behold!" She peeled away the black patch on her neck to reveal the red chancre, then held up her hands to show the pock marks on her palms. "Shall I strip off my clothes and show you further proof? Nay, do not attempt to question my virtue, for I have ever been faithful to you, even as you led me into sin, and this is my reward. Do you seek to deny it?"

He sank back into the chair, the color drained from a face suffused with guilt. "The pox..." he whispered.

"Yes," she said, falling to her knees before him. "I can bear it for my own sake, but please, do not make the child suffer any further. You swore to me that you would never abandon him." She flung her arms around his neck, and tears started in her eyes. "My dearest Jamie, please, if you ever loved me at all, do not abandon him, I beg you."

Lord Bolingbroke detached her arms from his neck. He could not keep the look of horror and revulsion from his face, but he was a man of honor. "I promise," he said gravely.

He was as good as his word and continued to support them, but he never returned again to visit the house in Cheapside. Nevertheless, Tom's memories of his earliest childhood were all happy ones. If Jenny suffered from a broken heart, she concealed it entirely.

Although they had no callers, Jenny did not attempt to hide her son in the house, but took him with her where ever she went, or sent him out with the servants, confident that he would be treated with kindness, a confidence that tended to encourage kindness in turn. As Tom grew older, she was determined that he learn the best manners, so that he might be introduced anywhere without embarrassment. In particular, she wished him to be able to greet his father with the grace befitting the son of an earl, for she was certain they would meet again.

It was very difficult, she realized, to teach him to bow when he could not simply imitate her, but she persisted tirelessly, guiding him through the motions, until he learned to make a leg very prettily. She kept after him constantly to stand up straight, not to slouch, or grimace, or poke his eyes with his finger, or shake his head to and fro, to eat neatly with a fork and knife, and not his hands. He was an even-tempered child, eager to please, and did not seem to mind her constant corrections.

Jack also began teaching him music, and Tom was a quick study. By the time he was five, he was playing scales and tunes on the harpsichord that the earl had presented to Jenny long ago. From there, he progressed quickly to the violin and flute, and soon they were playing duettos together with great satisfaction.

At the same time, however, Jenny noted that Tom's sight was decreasing. Whereas he had once reached for her skirts or chased the cat through the kitchen, he was now more likely to trip over the cat or feel about with his hands to find things rather than grasping them directly. As he dressed himself, occasionally he would hold a jacket or a pair of breeches right up to his face to determine its color, but soon he stopped doing even that, trusting his memory and the feel of the cloth instead. At last, one evening when he was nearing his tenth year, when Jenny offered to read to him, he said, "But Mama, the candle isn't lit."

Jenny frowned. "Yes it is," she said, gently pulling his chin around until he was facing the candle directly.

"Oh, there it is," he said, unconcerned. "When I turn away, I can't see it," he explained, shaking his head back and forth to demonstrate. Jenny sighed. The doctor had been right after all, but the fear that had gripped her when he first made his pronouncement had long since faded.

It was not long after this that Jenny's health took another sharp decline. Jack wanted her to go to St. Bartholomew's Hospital for the mercury cure, but she could not bear to leave Tom behind. And so when the letter arrived from Bedfordshire summoning Tom for a visit at Culverleigh, Jack at last prevailed upon her to send the boy to his father's family while she took the salivation.

Tom wept to be parted from her, but Jenny assured him with many caresses that when they met again in a few months' time she would be cured.

CHAPTER TWO: CULVERLEIGH

"You must understand, I suggest this plan only with the greater good to the family reputation in mind, and not to vex you personally," said Lady Gray, pouring from the silver tea service for herself and Lord Bolingbroke. "Now that you have an heir, I see no reason not to bring them all here for the summer."

Lord Bolingbroke made a sour face despite the considerable amount of sugar he had added to his tea. "The last thing I want is a damned lot of children here," he said.

You should have thought of that before you went meddling with every jade who crossed your path in London, Lady Gray thought, but aloud she said, "It will only be for a short time, until we can decide how best to provide for them. In the meantime, it will do them good to be made aware of their lineage. I'll not have the sons, even the natural sons, of Bolingbroke talking like guttersnipes." This was not likely, as the three older boys, Richard, Paul, and Philip, had been sent to school at Harrow; nevertheless, Lady Gray was not one to be dissuaded once she had set her course.

Lord Bolingbroke still appeared unconvinced. "Must they *all* come here?" he asked, trying a different tack. "Even, you know, the Finch boy? Are you certain that would be wise?"

To his irritation, Lady Gray feigned ignorance. "Whatever do you mean," she said frostily.

"He isn't, ahem, he isn't simple, is he?" he elaborated in an undertone.

"Sir, you astonish me," Lady Gray replied. "I'll have you know I have already visited Mrs. Finch and the boy. He may be blind, but he is remarkably clever. He bowed to me as neatly as you please, and played the Corelli D minor on the harpsichord with surpassing skill. I see no reason not to bring him here."

"Ah, hum, yes, I see," Lord Bolingbroke muttered into his teacup, feeling uncomfortably as if he were being managed by his sister. Then staring up at the ceiling abstractedly, with a great air of studied indifference, he asked, "So he is quite well, then? Aside from, well, you know? And his mother? How does she fare?"

"The boy is healthy. Except for his eyes, he shows no signs of the foul disease, but I am afraid I can't say the same for Mrs. Finch. Her condition is very bad, I'm sorry to say. Indeed, it would be best for the child to stay here for a time while she takes the cure."

Lord Bolingbroke turned first red, then white. So even his sister knew what he had thought was his closest secret. Despite the untimely death of his first wife, as none of their three daughters showed signs of the pox, he had hoped the secret would die with her. Furthermore, as he had thereafter on the recommendation of his personal physician availed himself of the little blue pill, and as neither his second wife nor their infant son appeared infected, he believed himself to be cured.

It would have shocked him even further to know how thoroughly his elder sister was acquainted with the details of his dissipated youth, including not only the names and addresses of all his former mistresses, but also (among other things) that he had once been seen to run naked through Hyde Park in a state of extreme intoxication. However, since he had presented the crown to the king two years previous, and more to the point, since his second wife had borne him an heir at last, he intended to stand for Parliament. He reluctantly agreed it was time to impose some kind of order on his personal life, including all those damned children.

He returned his gaze at last to his sister, sitting ramrod straight before the little table, staring at him in every expectation of compliance with her wishes. She had always been a great one for giving orders, and having been widowed early and left mistress of her own estate only intensified that proclivity. Now that her own children, two sons and a daughter, were all married off, she had descended from Stirling to Bedfordshire to take charge of his affairs. He did not like that knowing look of hers, but in the end, it was easier to let her have her way than deal with the matter himself.

"Very well, send for those bloody brats then," he said.

"Sir, your language! I hope you shan't use such vulgarity in front of the children."

Several weeks later, Tom, dressed in his finest light-gray ditto suit with his sandy brown hair tied back with a black ribbon, was packed into the earl's carriage and sent from London to Bedfordshire. He found the journey painfully dull and lonely, being unable to even watch the passing countryside to relieve the tedium. Always a messy traveler, he was twice obliged to ask the driver to stop so he could be sick by the side of the road, only to be bundled afterward back into the stifling, jolting misery of the carriage.

At last, after what seemed like an eternity, the carriage pulled up a graveled drive and stopped before a large, L-shaped building rising imposingly from the rolling green hills. Culverleigh had lately been redone in the Palladian style, after Inigo Jones, with false colonnades topped with a triangular architrave over the door. Tom stumbled wearily from the carriage, to be greeted by Lady Gray, with a cadre of servants behind her in strict array.

"I am your aunt," she declared in a ringing tone, "whom you met in London. Do you recall the sound of my voice?" Tom nodded a bit uncertainly and she trumpeted, "Clever lad!" in her commanding voice. Tom, remembering himself, bowed hastily as his mother had taught him.

Lady Gray continued, "This is Josiah Stinson, whom I have assigned to wait on you in particular. He will show you about and see to all your needs." She pushed forward a stolid footman of about thirty, who put a knuckle to his forehead.

"Yes, yes, thank you Stinson," she said briskly, "Now show him inside. No, no, you must take his hand. None of your diffidence, just take his hand." She turned to directing the other servants to unload Tom's baggage.

Tom felt a large, firm hand encase his own and lead him up the stone steps into a large, echoing entryway, then up a curving marble staircase and down a wide hall to the bedroom that was designated for his use. Once inside the door, they stood about awkwardly for a few moments, each uncertain what to do.

At last the footman cleared his throat. "Do the young sir require assistance?"

"If you please, can you show me the bed?" Tom asked nervously. The chamber was cavernous compared to his neat little bedroom in Cheapside, and he felt as if he were standing at the edge of a cliff. But the footman took his hand again very kindly, and led him over to the bed and placed his hands upon it, then seeming to have grasped Tom's larger meaning, continued on all about the room, including the wash stand and chamber pot. Then as it was growing late, he brought up supper on a tray, so that Tom might eat in privacy. At last, Stinson helped him to wash his face and hands and change into his night dress, then left him alone in the great empty room.

Tom burrowed under the covers, suppressing a sob. He was ten years old, far too grown up to be crying like a baby, but he had never been separated from his mother before for more than for a few hours and he took it very hard. Indeed, even later, after she died, he would look back and find this first separation more painful, because he could not escape the conclusion that she had chosen to send him away.

Lord Bolingbroke peered through the casement of his second-floor study. Below him, the children were playing pall-mall on the ridge of a grassy slope at the back of the house, their cries echoing up faintly through the closed window. Seated on a blanket below them was Lady Bolingbroke, along with the nurse, the governess, and the baby James, who was taking uncertain steps between them. Lady Bolingbroke glanced up at the window, then looked pointedly away. She was a sturdy girl of moderately good breeding with pleasing blonde ringlets, and nearly half his age. For her part, she reveled in her title, and her political ambitions for her husband nearly outstripped his own, but her perfect happiness on providing the earl with an heir had been seriously wounded by the continued presence of his daughters from his first wife, and now she felt she had been dealt another severe blow with the arrival of the four bastard sons.

Lord Bolingbroke stared at the boys with distaste: each one, he thought, as brutish and coarse as the last. The three eldest each took after their various mothers in looks as well as demeanor. And the three girls too recalled the late Lady Bolingbroke, with their dark hair and sallow, accusing faces. His gaze fell last upon Tom, who was standing a bit apart from the rest, leaning on a mallet with his face turned up to the sun. Of the whole wretched lot, the earl thought, he is the only one with any promise, any flicker of intelligence, and more's the pity, it shall go to waste. It was true that Tom resembled him the most strongly; he had the earl's long thin features, although he had his mother's fairer coloring. As a baby, his hair had come in blond, and it was only now beginning to darken.

But those ghastly blue-white eyes, it gave the earl a stab of pain every time he looked upon him. The sins of the father are visited on the son, he thought bitterly. His deepest secret, which not even his sister knew, was that Lord Bolingbroke believed he had cured himself of the pox by passing it on to Jenny Finch. After all, was it not often said that an infected man's best recourse was to have relations with a virgin, and hadn't she been pure, against all likelihood? He had mentioned it to his personal physician, who dismissed the idea as so much superstitious nonsense, and dosed him with the blue pill, but to Bolingbroke, the evidence was plain. Of all the women he had known, Jenny had been the most fair, the cleverest and most dear to him, but he had ruined her and her son.

Below him on the green, the children continued their game unaware of their father's gaze. Charlotte, nine years old and the youngest girl, fetched Tom to take his turn. Putting her hands over his, she set his mallet before the boxwood ball and tapped it lightly. Using the mallet as a guide, Tom reached down to touch the ball before straightening to take his strike. Paul, the second oldest boy, was standing by the iron hoop. He began to yell, his round face red with indignation.

"That ain't fair! He touched the ball!"

"Oh hush," scolded Anne, the middle girl. "Only let him touch it."

"No!" Paul shouted. "It's against the rules. He loses his turn. And Charlotte moved the ball too."

"I didn't!" Charlotte protested. Ignoring them, Tom took a mighty swing at the heavy ball, which missed the hoop, instead jumping up and cracking Philip on the ankle.

Philip set up a howl of pain. "He did it on purpose!" he wailed. Only a year older than Tom, Philip was more timid than his two older brothers.

Richard, who at sixteen considered himself far too grown up for playing with children, had been lounging on the grass nearby with a look of studied boredom. As Philip began to bawl, he sprang up with a vicious glare, and he and Paul set upon Tom, who cowered down on the grass. Even Philip joined in, not wanting to be left out. Lord Bolingbroke turned away in disgust. The three older boys had been tormenting Tom since they had all arrived at Culverleigh, but it would no more occur to him to put a stop to it than to intervene in a fight among his hunting dogs.

A small form came running up the hill and pulled the boys apart, crying "for shame, for shame," and ordering all the children indoors. The one who had stopped the fight was known to all at Culverleigh, from the earl to the scullery maid, simply as Miss Betty. A second cousin of the first Lady Bolingbroke, she had been called in after the unfortunate lady's death to act as governess to the three girls. At seventeen, she was only one year older than Richard, but to Tom she seemed impossibly grown-up.

Having sent the other children away, Miss Betty led Tom by the hand to the kitchen, where she washed the cuts on his face and gave him a cup of barley water.

"There now, they didn't hurt you did they?" she asked kindly, and Tom shook his head. "You mustn't mind them," she continued. "They have had a terrible hard time at school for being illegitimate, and now they think they have the upper hand. If only you fight back, they will leave you alone."

"But I can't," Tom said, his face pointing towards his lap.

Miss Betty took his chin in her fingers and turned his face up with a little shake. "You must be brave," she said, and he nodded reluctantly.

Tom was not by nature fearful; indeed, he had a habit of tearing around the hallways and grounds of Culverleigh at top speed, only occasionally colliding with a half-open door or blundering into the shrubbery. Miss Betty was amazed at the way he seemed to know where the bend in hall or the stairways were, or a tree on the lawn, but when she asked him to explain, he only shrugged and said, "Stinson showed me and I remembered, I suppose."

But he was not accustomed to playing with other children; at home the children in the neighborhood kept away from him, and he had not sought them out. On the other hand, his half-brothers had been at school together for several years already and had studied hard at tyranny and brawling. Even if they had not formed a cabal against him, Tom would have avoided them, as he found their company exceedingly dull.

Their passionate interest was hunting: endless discussions of horses, dogs, guns, the lay of the park, and the likelihood of each boy being invited to join the hunting party they were sure Lord Bolingbroke was planning. As Tom could neither ride nor shoot, he did not imagine he would take part, and besides he felt rather sorry for the poor fox.

The girls, Sophia, Anne, and Charlotte, were more likely to tolerate his company, although the older girls were a bit shy of him. Only Charlotte, who as the baby was inclined to be tomboyish, was unafraid to take his hand. They were kind enough, but for the most part only interested in the arrangement of their hair and clothing. He impressed the girls with his playing on the harpsichord, but when any of them attempted to sing while he played, he would scold them for not hitting the note exactly right, until each grew frustrated and abandoned the activity.

Rather than the company of his brothers and sisters, Tom far preferred Miss Betty. She was of a bookish, inquisitive nature, and having been to a dame school, she seemed to him very learned. Although no one in particular had asked her, she took it upon herself to offer instruction to all the children, including the boys when they arrived. The girls she found obedient but unimaginative; they would do whatever task she set them, but only as far as duty required. The three older boys of course were far ahead of them, having been to school, but Miss Betty was impressed with how much Tom had been taught at home. In addition to music, he could recite long sections of Milton, Dryden, and Butler, along with *amas, amat* and dozens more Latin and French verbs, and he knew his times tables as far as twelve twelves. He had a prodigious capacity for memorization, and she set about imparting all she knew, much to the delight of them both.

Tom was less pleased, however, at the presence of the other boys in the schoolroom. Surely it was not necessary, as they were constantly reminding Miss Betty how much more learned they were than she. But as much as Tom wished them away, Richard seemed determined to linger, teasing and joking with Miss Betty, and wherever Richard went, the other two followed. Tom would far have preferred to have Miss Betty's attentions all for himself, for aside from his mother, she was quite the kindest, loveliest woman he had ever met, and he was not accustomed to sharing his companions.

For her part, Miss Betty was concerned that Tom was largely ignored or harassed by the other inhabitants of Culverleigh, and made it her project to watch over him. It gave her great satisfaction to adapt her lessons for him, to expand his knowledge of the world by encouraging him to touch things, and to take him on walks around Culverleigh Park. In this she found an ally in the footman Stinson, who had also grown attached to the boy, and between them they conceived of a plan to teach Tom to ride.

Lord Bolingbroke was an avid horseman and his stables were full of purebred field hunters, fine mounts for riding at breakneck speed through the countryside, but not quite the thing for a novice. Stinson had carefully instructed the groom to bring out a gentle mare, and he was dismayed to see the man leading a wicked-looking screw.

"He'll have him off in a heartbeat," he muttered, giving Miss Betty a warning glance, but she ignored him with a set look on her face. She stroked the horse's nose, murmuring reassuringly, but it only tossed its head and rolled its eye at her.

Stinson looked down at Tom, holding fast to his hand. "He's a big un," he said. "You ain't afraid, Master Finch?" Tom shook his head determinedly. "All right then, up you go," Stinson said, putting aside trepidation. With the help of a groom, he swung Tom up into the saddle. Tom had not yet begun to grow and he was small for his age. His legs stuck out to either side and even with the stirrups buckled as high as they would go, he could only just reach his toes inside.

Tom slid his hands over the horse's withers, a look of amazement lighting his face. He had heard the ring and tramp, the snorting and whinnying of horses around him all his life, but had never before touched one with his own hand, much less sat astride one. He felt the powerful muscles under the smooth coat of hair—it was so much bigger than he had imagined, the voices of Miss Betty and Stinson so much further below him. Suddenly, the horse stepped forward with a lurch, and in a panic, he lay flat along its back, his face pressed into the withers and his hands gripping the sides of the saddle.

"Come now Master Finch," Stinson said encouragingly, walking beside and placing a hand on his knee as the groom led them from the courtyard by the stables towards a paddock. "Come now, that ain't the way for a young gentleman to sit a horse." At last, after much persuasion, Tom ventured to sit upright as the groom led him around the track, but at that moment, sensing its opportunity, the horse, with the slightest twitch, no more than a careless twist of its back, dislodged its rider and sent him hurtling through the air.

Miss Betty gave a shriek and ran over to him but luckily the turf in the paddock was very soft. Tom was unhurt. Despite his protests, however, Stinson carried him back to the house, where he was forced to remain in bed and endure Miss Betty's ministrations with vinegar and damp rags to the forehead for the rest of the day.

"My lord, is it really wise to keep all these children here?" Lady Bolingbroke demanded of her husband over the breakfast table the next day. "That Finch boy is sure to do himself a mischief. Riding, forsooth! Only think if he had fallen on the cobbles rather than in the paddock. I'll not answer for his safety if he continues with these antics."

"The boy is perfectly well. No one holds you responsible for him," Lady Gray reproved her with a sharp look. Lord Bolingbroke did not look up from his copy of the *London Gazette*.

Undeterred, Lady Bolingbroke proceeded to the heart of her grievance. "Just how much longer are they all to remain here? Surely the boys must go back to school?" Lord Bolingbroke made no answer. Helping herself to her third Bath bun,

Lady Bolingbroke continued, "I know it was that Miss Betty who put the idea in his head. She's a bad influence on the children. My lord, you should dismiss her at once."

"No," replied Lord Bolingbroke, still engrossed in the *Gazette*. He had no desire to waste his time interviewing another governess, much less throwing money away by sending the girls to school.

"Well, I shall be keeping my eye on her," Lady Bolingbroke declared, and her husband averred that she may do as she pleased, while Lady Gray looked aggrieved. Lord Bolingbroke had not warmed to the boys as Lady Gray had hoped, but rather found their noise and constant wrangling profoundly irritating. As the summer was drawing to a close, the earl was planning an early fox hunt, which he intended to make into a grand affair, and he would pay no attention to anything else while the preparations were underway.

The children soon got wind of the planned hunt and were giddy with delight, the boys in anticipation of being invited along, and the girls at the prospect of the banquet that was sure to follow, with the guests coming from all over. Only Tom was certain he would not participate, especially after his disgrace at his first and only riding lesson. As it happened, however, only Richard was invited to join the hunt, leaving Paul and Philip criminally disappointed and quivering with envy.

Although Tom did his best to avoid it, every other person on the estate, including his sisters, Stinson, and even Miss Betty were swept up in the excitement of the festivities and seeing to the dozens of guests. On the day of the hunt, Tom found himself idling on the drive before the manor, eating cake off the trestle tables while listening to the distant sound of the horns and the cries of the hounds. Late in the afternoon, long after Tom was thoroughly bored and annoyed, the party returned, riding triumphantly up the drive with Lord Bolingbroke at the head, a red brush tied to his saddle.

Richard swung down from his mount and swaggered over

to where Paul, Philip, and Tom stood near the tables set out by the front door. He walked this way and that way before them, making sure Philip and Paul noticed the blood that had been painted on his forehead and cheeks. As the adults stood about drinking and talking, Richard regaled his brothers with a long detailed account of the chase, in which it seemed he had played the crucial role at every juncture, each episode increasingly unlikely, until he ended with, "It were me, you know, who found the sly bugger at the last."

"What stuff," Paul burst in, consumed with jealousy and yet still half wanting to believe him. "Not on that miserable rip. You must have gotten the queerest prancer in the stable, ha ha."

"No chance on that miserable rip," Philip echoed.

"Are you calling me a liar?" Richard demanded, giving Paul a sudden vicious shove. Paul, a chubby boy who was inclined to be ungainly, stumbled backwards, knocking into Tom, who had been standing by him but only half-listening, instead wondering if that was Miss Betty's voice he heard in the crowd.

As he felt Paul stumble against him, Tom shoved him back, saying, "Get off me you stupid fat pig."

Paul was only too glad to find a smaller target for his anger and frustration at being left out of the hunt. "How dare you, you bastard!" he shouted. As an insult, it was rather less devastating than he might have hoped.

"We are all of us bastards equally," Tom replied calmly.

Paul's round face reddened. "Maybe so, but your ma's a poxy whore," he jeered.

Tom felt as if something suddenly snapped within him, and before he even realized what he was doing, he came at Paul with an enraged roar. They grappled for a moment and Tom swung wildly with his fists. Paul dodged just as Richard came up behind him to help, and Tom's fist caught him square on the nose with enough force to send him sprawling. For a moment, they all remained frozen: Richard with his hand to his nose, looking stunned, Paul and Philip gawking beside him, Tom in confusion, hardly knowing what he had done. A second later, there was an outcry among the adults standing nearby. Stinson swooped down on Tom and carried him into the house, while Miss Betty ran to put her handkerchief to the blood trickling from Richard's nose.

No one spoke of this incident afterwards, as Lord Bolingbroke considered it beneath him to discipline the boys, although Tom found that as Miss Betty had predicted, his harassment at the hands of his brothers decreased markedly.

Lady Bolingbroke, on the other hand, was mortified by this uncouth display, which she felt reflected poorly on her household, and redoubled her efforts to rid herself of all of them. Her main strategy was to follow the movements of Miss Betty, and so it was that several weeks later she discovered Richard hurrying from Miss Betty's bedroom chamber early one morning. Miss Betty was summarily dismissed, and Richard was sent packing later the same day, Lord Bolingbroke having hastily purchased a commission for him in the army.

Tom was heartbroken and bewildered at the sudden disappearance of Miss Betty, particularly as no one would speak of her, why she had left, or where she had gone, almost as if she had never existed. His sisters and aunt claimed ignorance. Only Philip was willing to answer his questions.

"It were on account of Richard," he whispered conspiratorially to Tom in the deserted schoolroom.

"What? What did he do?"

"You know," Philip confided in an even lower voice, blushing. "Richard, he—he debauched Miss Betty." Tom had only a vague idea of what went on between men and women. Did that mean Richard had insulted Miss Betty? He was deeply concerned for her, but no one, not even loyal Stinson, would give him any word of her.

The next few weeks at Culverleigh Tom found flat and dismal. True, without Richard to stir them up, Paul and Philip left off tormenting him. Philip even made some friendly overtures, teaching him how to play bowls, and Charlotte went on long rambles with him around the park. But without Miss Betty, the days were tedious and featureless.

Lord Bolingbroke immediately regretted sending Richard to the army, which he considered coarse and corrupt, but something in the military line did seem the best way to dispose of the other boys. A month later, instead of sending Paul and Philip back to Harrow, he arranged for them to go into the navy as midshipmen. At the same time, Lady Gray, who had by now formed a low opinion of the second Lady Bolingbroke, volunteered to take the girls back to her estate near Stirling to see to their education herself.

The prospect of Tom, of all the others, being left at Culverleigh was an arrangement that pleased no one. Not long afterwards, his uncle sent for him: his mother had returned home and was desirous to see him again. The earl was only too happy to let the boy return to Cheapside. Jack Finch posted down to Bedford himself to collect him and they set off in one of Lord Bolingbroke's carriages without any ceremony. Tom took his formal leave of his stepmother the night before, but his brothers and sisters and aunt had already departed, and the earl had been in London on business the past week. Of the entire household, it was only Stinson who was on hand to help him into the carriage, and who appeared affected by his departure.

As they bounced along the road to London, Jack regarded his nephew, a slight figure in gray sitting limply in a corner of the dark carriage.

"Were they kind to you there?" he inquired with concern.

"Yes, quite kind," Tom replied unconvincingly.

"Your mother will be very pleased to have you home again." Jack was touched to see how Tom sat up eagerly at this. "She has been asking after you every day this week. But," he cautioned, "she is still not well."

This was an understatement: Jenny had undergone the most commonly prescribed cure for the pox, referred to obliquely as salivation. She had sat daily for weeks enveloped in a cloak over a pot of burning mercury, breathing in the vapors, until her skin darkened, her limbs shook, her teeth loosened, and the saliva gushed in torrents. This, she was assured, was the sign that the foul humors were leaving the body, and indeed, the painful chancres had diminished appreciably, although the cure had left her prostrate.

All this Jack did not describe to Tom, but only said, "I'm afraid you will find her greatly altered, but you must not mind it."

Tom promised he would not, slumping back in the corner of the carriage and lapsing into silence.

CHAPTER THREE: OVER TO IRELAND

Jack Finch was not by nature inclined towards a settled sort of life. As a lad in Taunton Deane he had been given to roving, often not returning home for weeks at a time. After moving to London, he was as likely to pass the night in a bagnio as in his own bed. Upon the death of his sister Jenny, he found himself at loose ends, in his middle thirties, and with his twelve year old nephew left solely in his care.

After Tom's return from Culverleigh, Jenny had lingered for more than a year, in a sadly reduced state. Jack hired a steady, matronly woman to nurse her, but the house, formerly so cheerful, took on the oppressive air of the sickroom. Tom remained by his mother's bed as often as he was allowed, but Jack, feeling the atmosphere in the house was not healthy for a growing boy, conceived of diversions to keep him away, and thus gradually took on increasing responsibility for the boy's education. While Tom had been reluctant to divulge all the details of his stay at Culverleigh, by dint of persistent questioning, Jack eventually managed to learn much of the truth, barring the disgrace of Miss Betty. In any case, Jack was less interested in the fate of an unknown governess than in the usage of his nephew, which pained him extremely. Jack was persuaded that the trouble was a lack of education in manly pursuits. To rectify this, Jack undertook to teach Tom how to fight with his fists, how to shoot a gun, how to ride a horse, and other skills appropriate to a young gentleman. These lessons had the further benefit of keeping him outdoors and active, so that while his mother declined, Tom continued to thrive.

Poor Tom was sadly affected by Jenny's death, even though the crisis had been long anticipated as inevitable. It broke Jack's heart to see the boy cry so piteously.

After this tragedy, neither Tom nor Jack could bear to remain in the house that so bore the mark of her person in every corner. Moreover, as Lord Bolingbroke had ceased to visit many years previous, he no longer sent a monthly allowance, instead settling a sum upon them. Jenny's protracted illness had proved very expensive, however, and Jack found that once she died, no one would extend them credit any longer. He was loath to petition the earl for help, and even less willing to return Tom to Culverleigh, and so instead he suggested to Tom that they might remove to Dublin, where his broadsides might sell better, and the living was far cheaper than in London.

Jack did not mention his more pressing reason for desiring a hasty departure, namely, that an intimacy he had contracted with a comely widow had taken an ominous turn—the lady had begun hinting broadly that she expected him to make good on the liberties she had allowed him. Instead, telling himself and everyone else that it was for Tom's sake, Jack sent a terse notification to the earl, sold off everything they could not carry, including, with great regret, the beloved harpsichord, and so they set out on the road to Holyhead.

Dublin proved to be a hospitable place, at least for a short time. Jack rented some rooms very cheaply, and freed from any kind of domestic regulation, they allowed their housekeeping to slide into a slovenly, careless state that Jenny would never have condoned. Jack hired a series of tutors for Tom, who kept the boy occupied while he was working, including passing hours in public houses under the rubric of research in popular song. As the tutors' expertise tended more towards riding and shooting than Latin verbs, Tom was pleased with these diversions.

After the better part of a year in Dublin, however, several truths became plain to Jack: first, that even with the cheaper cost of keeping house, the money he had saved would soon be gone, second, that the market for broadsides was even more competitive and thus less lucrative than in London, and third, that even this careless fashion of keeping house was beginning to oppress his spirits. At the same time, Jack had become enamored of the local musical traditions, so much more rich and complex than any old "Lillibulero" he might hear in London. It was represented to him that the real music was to be found in the countryside.

With the last of their cash, Jack bought two sturdy horses. They packed up their belongings and set off on the road. It was a mode of living that suited them both very well, rambling at their ease until they found a farm or public house that would let them in, where they might play and sing in return for a meal and a bed for the night, or better yet a pot of ale or a can of the local brew, for Jack was a prodigious drinker. His capacity to consume vast amounts of liquor endeared him to many of those they met, particularly at the public houses, but at the farm houses, it was Tom who excited the sympathies of the wives, who treated them far more kindly than if Jack had arrived alone. A bed was a great luxury, but a barn would do, although there were still not a few nights where they slept rough.

Jack was not above playing upon the sympathies of those who let them in; his favorite tale was that Tom's mother had been an Irish girl, cruelly seduced and abandoned by an English lord. This flimsiest of lies would not hold up to even the most casual scrutiny, as the boy's uncle was plainly English himself, but most people were too polite to question him closely, even if they did not believe it. This was not so much due to Tom's innate charm, although he was daily growing more skilled in this regard, but more so because he had learned to speak their language.

While English had been in common currency in Dublin, more or less, as soon as they ventured outside the city they found that Irish predominated. Jack had learnt his Latin and Greek, as might be expected of the son of a schoolteacher, and had a smattering of French and Italian as well, but the hard, guttural sounds and baroque grammar of Gaelic defeated him. Tom, on the other hand, with his genius of imitation, picked it up almost immediately, if imperfectly, and even as they traveled from county to county, he could make himself understood despite the not insignificant variations in dialect. He did his best to help his uncle along as well, for most of the songs they encountered were in Irish, although in the early days of their rambles in the east, they collected many in English as well. One of the first they learned was this:

Oh there was a roving journeyman who goes from town to town
And wherever he gets a job or work he's willing to set down.
With his bundle on his shoulder and his stick within his hand,
And it's round the country I'll go with the roaming journeyman.

Up from the County Carlow the girls all jump for joy,
Says one unto the other, "Now here comes a traveling boy."
She wanted me to marry her and took me by the hand,
She went home and told her mother that she loves a journeyman.

They soon discovered they were not the only musicians on the road; indeed it was common practice for blind men to be taught the harp and equipped with a horse and a guide, and to journey from place to place to earn their keep by playing and composing. Not a few assumed this was the case with Tom as well, and were surprised to discover that he could not play the harp, even more so that he had come over from England, and that Jack was his uncle, and not a paid guide. Tom was intrigued by the Irish harp, a triangular instrument with metal strings, capable of surprising sonority despite its small size, but the harpers they encountered were not eager to teach an outsider to play, and furthermore declared he was too old already to learn the necessary suppleness of fingering. So Tom contented himself with the fiddle, rare enough in the more remote areas, or the pipes, flutes, and other small instruments they had brought with them.

Everywhere they went, they saw evidence of great hardship and privation, more so when they crossed the Shannon into Connaught. Before he saw it with his own eyes, Jack had thought of Ireland as a wild, uncivilized place, but as far as he could tell, the Penal Laws had brought not order but only misery and suffering. He and Tom did their best to disavow any allegiance of politics or religion, and Jack clung to the outrageous lie that Tom's mother was Irish. They found most people they encountered were kind and welcoming, eager for a bit of diversion, and everywhere great lovers of music.

At every house they stopped they learned a new song or air, and in the most remarkable variety: tunes for every occasion, not merely the love songs that had crossed the sea to England, but songs for plowing, milking, churning butter, and spinning, charms to bring the rain or stop a hailstorm, or imitate birds. As they traveled further through Connaught, he learned the art of imitating pipes with the voice alone, making lively music for dancing when there were no instruments.

Jack was moved to pity by the hardships they saw, and before long they had traded their fine clothes for homespun. One by one their instruments went to those they encountered, even the fiddle at last, leaving them only with a wooden flute. After no more than a year, they looked like *an Lucht Siúil*, and indeed were often mistaken for tinkers or vagabonds.

When they had been on the road for over two years, and Tom was no longer a child but growing into a young man, late one night, they arrived at the house of a tenant farmer just outside the village of Turloughmore on the banks of the Clare in the County Galway, where they were allowed to sleep in the barn. The next morning, the farmer's daughter, a romping girl named Aoife with red cheeks and merry blue eyes, served them breakfast with her own hands. Setting down the tray and brushing back the locks of brown hair escaping her kerchief, she greeted them loudly in Irish, for she had no English at all. Tom and Jack rose slowly, still flecked with hay and dirt from the road. Aoife watched with interest as Jack took one of the bowls of bread and milk, still warm and frothy from the cow, and placed it in Tom's outstretched hands before helping himself. She continued to watch with undisguised curiosity as Tom wolfed down his breakfast, feeling about with the spoon inside the bowl to be certain he had got it all.

When they both had finished, she said boldly in Gaelic, "They say you're collecting tunes. I have a good one. Come here to me now," and without waiting for further invitation, she launched into a lively song with a strong, rocking tempo.

'S é'n trua ghéar nach mise bean Pháidín
'S an bhean atá aige bheith caillte

Go mbristear do chosa, a bhean Pháidín
Go mbristear do chosa 's do chnámha

Jack, who did not fully understand, nodded mildly, but Tom burst out laughing.

"That's a sporting tune," Tom commented in Gaelic.

"I have more," she answered. "Come with me while I drive the cow to the pasture by the lake, and I will teach them to you."

"I don't know," Tom said in a teasing tone. "I've heard the girls of County Galway are fierce, and from that song I know it's true. How do I know I can trust you?"

"Come with me and find out."

Jack was certainly not one to stand between a lad and a willing girl, and so Tom set out with Aoife. She held his hand in one of hers, a strong, callused hand, and in the other she drove a rachitic, slow-moving cow with a long thin switch. When they reached the shore of Lake Turlough, she left the cow to graze, and seated them both on a grassy bank beneath a willow tree. Tom could not tell how long they sat there in the warm sunshine, talking idly, but it seemed blissfully endless. The rustling of the leaves overhead, the dull ring of the cowbell in the distance, the murky smell of the lake and the calls of the birds, all these entwined with the throaty rumble of her laughter and the warm pressure of her hand, which had not once left his. Tom was entranced.

"Your eyes," Aoife said suddenly, leaning in close and peering into his face. "They're like two boiled eggs!"

Tom laughed and gave the back of her hand a pinch. "That's not very kind in you. Don't you think I'm handsome?" he teased, holding his head up in mock seriousness.

"That I do," she said, still leaning in so close he could feel her warm breath on his face. "And yourself, are you sad at all, you being blind?"

Tom shrugged. "I am not. In truth, I rarely think on it. My hands are my eyes, that's all."

"Then you must tell me how beautiful I am," she answered pertly, taking his hand and placing it against her cheek. Tom obligingly ran his fingers over her face, taking in the curve of her round cheeks, her fluttering eyelashes, her small round nose and thick soft lips. Then suddenly, impulsively, with his fingers still against her lips, he leaned in and kissed her. It was a sensation like no other, and even as he felt all rational thought receding and his body moving as if on its own, he was faintly surprised. He had felt the faces of other people before, but never had it made his heart pound so.

Aoife kissed him back heartily. One of his hands drifted down her neck and shoulder, to grasp her breast tightly, while the other twined about her waist. He had never held a girl so closely, touched so intimately, and yet it felt right, not strange. He gasped for breath and was about to kiss her again, but Aoife pushed him away.

"So?" she asked "Do you think I'm beautiful, at all?"

"*Do bhéal mar a bhfuil siúcra mar an leamhnacht 's an fion ar bord,*" Tom recited. The effect was ruined, however, by his cracking voice.

To his dismay, Aoife stood up suddenly. "Don't sing that song to me," she scolded, "You know very well it's about a dead girl. Are you meaning to bring me bad luck, then?"

Tom stood up as well, straining to hear the faint sound of her bare feet on the grass as she walked away from him. He started after her uncertainly, choosing a direction he hoped would not lead him into the lake. After a few disorienting moments, he at last heard the crack of a switch followed by the thunk of the cowbell as Aoife drove the cow back onto the road, and he walked towards her with more confidence. As he drew near, she grabbed his hand playfully again, as if nothing had happened, and they walked back to the farmhouse, their hands swinging as they went.

For the next three days, this odd sort of courtship continued, with Tom following Aoife about as she did her chores, and she flirting and teasing him. One moment she was placing a baby chick, stolen from under an indignant hen, in his hands just to see the look of wonder on his face, but the next she was laughing uproariously as he cracked his head on an unexpectedly low beam in the barn. Her attempt to show him the barn's cat went less than well, and he was left with long scratches on his arms and hands. Still her voice was like a beacon to him; he could not stay away. He longed to steal another kiss from her, but he found it devilish hard to know when he could not be seen when he himself could not see.

The second day, when they went down by the lake, he thought to have another chance, but instead of sitting quietly like before, she skipped about on the grass, singing. He joined in obligingly, singing her a lively jig with nonsense words, and the sound of her panting breath told him she was dancing.

"And now you!" she demanded, grabbing his hand.

Tom pulled away. "I don't know how," he protested.

"Why, it's the easiest thing," Aoife insisted. "Will I teach you how, then?" Tom agreed, although it soon became apparent that it was nowhere near the easiest thing he had ever attempted.

"Now lift your foot— bend your knee—not like that, like *this*—" she pushed his leg into something approximating the right position, "and now, step-two-three, and step-two-three. There you are, only never stamp your feet so, try to step lightly..." Aoife's voice grew tight with frustration, as despite her increasingly detailed instructions, his movements remained stiff and ungraceful. Perhaps he should feel her legs as she danced, she suggested. He knelt down obligingly, placing his hands over her heavy skirts, but this too proved impracticable, as even going painfully slowly, her legs moved too far and too fast for his fingers to follow, and the only result was that she accidentally kicked him in the side of the head.

"Enough!" Tom said, standing up and rubbing his temple. "I can't dance."

They walked back home feeling out of sorts and frustrated. Their good spirits soon returned, however, and later in the day they kissed again in the barn, stopping only when Aoife's mother called from the kitchen to come in to supper.

On the third day, they could restrain themselves no longer, but kissed and sported again and again. Tom felt drawn to her with a strength he could not resist, as if he were being pulled by some unknown force. That evening, their courtship came to its inevitable conclusion in a few frantic moments up against the back of the barn.

"Are you certain no one can see us?" Tom asked anxiously, as Aoife pressed herself against him.

"I am. We are hidden from the house and the fields. I promise you, no one is about," she whispered, placing his hands up under her skirts. His fingers traced the soft round curves of her flesh, trembling. She laughed and squirmed under his touch.

By this time, Tom had gained some knowledge of the intimate congress between men and women. Two years on the road with his uncle had proved a thorough education in the art of seduction, which he was a regular witness to. Jack did not scruple to take a wench even if Tom was present in the room (or more often a barn). Tom remained somewhat vague on the physical mechanics, however, until Aoife showed him. He received her instruction with mingled surprise and pleasure, as she opened his breeches and reached within.

Her hands were neither gentle nor soft, but he was far beyond caring. She leaned her face against his, blowing her hot sweet breath against him as she lifted her skirt and guided him towards her. Tom felt fire race through his veins, his body now seeming to move of its own accord. It was over far too quickly but the sense of wonderment lingered like a warm glow even after, as he laced his breeches. He felt as if a whole new world had opened before him.

Moments later, they were back in the house, taking a late supper with the rest of the household. Jack looked sharply from Tom to Aoife, sitting on opposite sides of the table, but both with the same rosy glow and the same shamefaced, guilty look. He placed his cup of usquebaugh back on the table consideringly, forgoing his usual nighttime draught. After supper, Jack bade them all goodnight and led Tom back to the barn with him, but rather than preparing for bed, he began to saddle their horses.

"We're to leave now?" Tom protested. "But it's the middle of the night! I haven't told Aoife—"

Jack cut him off. "Do you wish to marry her?" he demanded, giving Tom's shoulder a shake. "To stay here and be a farmer the rest of your life?"

"Well, no..."

Jack turned to tighten the girth on his saddle. "It's just as well. Her parents would never agree to give their only daughter to a *siúiler*, and her a papist, it's against the law in any case.

Come now, never look so low. There will be more girls, I promise you."

Jack was right, there were many more, of all descriptions, nor was it the only time they departed hastily without taking leave of their hosts. And although Tom had no particular desire to return to her, he still thought fondly of the girl with the mouth as sweet as fresh-drawn milk.

Up from the County Carlow the girls all jump for joy,
Says one unto the other, "Now here comes a sporting boy."
She wanted me to marry her and took me by the hand,
And she kindly tells her mother that she loves a journeyman.

In every town I traveled through I got a new sweetheart,
And I'm always broken-hearted when from her I have to part.
So let them all be talking, let them say the worst they can,
It's round the country I'll go with the roaming journeyman.

CHAPTER FOUR: SEVEN DIALS

After more than six years in Ireland, Jack Finch conceived of a desire to cross over to Scotland. He and Tom had spent the majority of their time rambling about from place to place, making a long, slow circuit east through Carlow, Waterford, and Cork, then west through Clare and Galway, and finally through Leitrim, Meath, and thence back to Dublin. Although they had not covered every corner of the island, as they went, it seemed to Jack more and more that there was a common exchange of songs between Ireland and Scotland, and even more musical traditions to be explored. At Jack's urging, they boarded a ship at Dún Laoghaire that took them around the Solway Firth and up the River Nith to Dumfries. Once there, however, Jack was not satisfied. He found it a small and dismal town, not at all as he had expected, and so he insisted they take to the road again.

Tom went along with his uncle's whims, although he was a boy no longer but a young man nearly eighteen. He could not recall exactly when it happened, but at some point he had shot up like a weed and now towered over his uncle, who was growing a bit stooped and paunchy with drink. Tom now found it much easier to place his hand on Jack's shoulder, rather than to take his hand, and this shift seemed to signal a change in their relationship as well. Jack expended less effort in giving Tom a well-rounded, gentlemanly education, and more in tutoring him in the practical arts of seduction and drinking, at which his nephew proved to be an apt pupil. At the same time, Tom found himself more often the leader of their tiny band, the one who charmed the householders into letting them stay for the night, composing planxties in praise of their hosts, and rolling Jack into bed at night before he lapsed into an alcoholic stupor.

They spent a year roaming around the Lowlands, as they had in Ireland, although their condition was miserably harder. They had surrendered nearly all their possessions by the time they left Dún Laoghaire, even selling their horses before embarking, and were now forced to wander on foot. The land was far rougher and colder, and the people were far less welcoming, even though Tom soon picked up their Scots Gaelic. Eventually, the many nights spent shivering in bothies took their toll upon Jack; the damp settled in his chest and left him with a persistent cough.

Tom overrode Jack's stubborn insistence that he was well enough and arranged for the two of them to attach themselves to a wool merchant delivering his stores to Edinburgh. Tom knew that despite their current poverty, Jack still had in his possession drafts on the Bank of England, useless among the crofters, but which might set them up more comfortably in the city. As it turned out, they received only a paltry sum, enough to let two tiny rooms in the neighborhood of St. Giles, and there they settled.

After their years in the countryside, the city was amazingly crowded, the air dense with smoke and the fumes from the distilleries, but the people were kind and welcoming, especially in the public houses. Jack quickly established a modest circuit between their lodgings and a nearby tavern, the Queen's Head. He also made the acquaintance of a printer who was willing to buy Jack's manuscripts as part of a larger operation selling broadsides, saving Jack the wearisome task of flogging them on the streets himself, which his health would not permit. As Jack's condition declined, the printer was even willing (for a fee) to send a boy to their lodgings to collect the manuscripts.

It was Jack who bought Tom the heavy silver-headed walking stick, suggesting it might be of use. At first, Tom was not sure what to do with it, as he had always gotten about without any sort of aid, but after much experimentation in the streets around St. Giles, he discovered that if he banged it sharply on the cobblestones, the echoes off the hard surfaces of the buildings and the street gave a useful aural picture of his surroundings.

Although the city agreed with them, their lives were sadly constrained. Jack, feeling the press of mortality upon him, was determined to transcribe as many of the songs and tunes they had collected as possible. He would spend the days writing, with Tom by his side to ascertain the notes and words, or provide translations into English. In the evenings, they retired to the Queen's Head, although after a time even that proved too demanding. As Jack took to his bed, weak with coughing fits, Tom learned to make the short trip to the tavern on his own twice a day for food and ale.

Although Tom, and Jack as well before he took to his bed, became acquainted with some of the regulars at the Queen's Head, particularly the ladies of easy virtue, they did not form any particularly close friends. For one thing, the English were even less welcome in Scotland than they had been in Ireland, and Jacobite sentiment was running high. For another, there was no disguising their identities as they had in the countryside, for Lady Gray was well known in Edinburgh, and it did not take long for the details of the family history to come out.

As the months wore on, by dint of fevered work, Jack was able to increase their material wealth slightly, but at great cost to his health. The sound of his uncle, previously so full of life, coughing and hacking day and night pained Tom extremely. Hearing that the doctors in Edinburgh were the best in the world, he prevailed upon one to come visit, whom he met through the kind offices of a whore at the Queen's Head.

The best in the world they may have been, as a body, but MacAdam, the physician, generously titled, who was willing to accept the paltry amount they could afford as a fee, was certainly not one of the more illustrious members of his profession.

Dr. MacAdam arrived long past the appointed hour, wheezing and red-faced after climbing the stairs to their rooms. Tom showed him in himself, for they kept no servants, but the doctor only collapsed in a chair and declared he could do nothing more until he had a wee drop, which Tom obligingly poured for him. After draining his glass, MacAdam sighed heavily, closed his eyes for a long interval, then at last came to himself with a shake.

"Well now, what have we here?" he rumbled, lurching forward. Tom jerked back in alarm as he felt two meaty hands grasp the sides of his face. He tried to pull away, but the doctor held him firmly, pulling down on Tom's lower eyelids with his thumbs. "Dear me," the doctor said, his whiskey-soaked breath blowing over Tom's face. "The lens is quite sclerotic, cataractous, even. The bluish tinge is, I believe, caused by the refraction of light from the outside and not by an internal pigment." He jerked Tom's head to the side to examine his hair. "Your natural eye color is brown, is it not?"

"So my mother said," Tom replied, unsure what this was all about.

MacAdam resumed his examination. "I see no obvious scarring, but the aqueous body is sclerotic as well," he observed, confirming his hypothesis with a sharp poke.

"Ow!" Tom at last jerked free of the probing fingers, holding a hand to his right eye. "What d'ye mean by that, sir?"

The doctor shook his head. "Dear me, a sadly advanced case, but I have seen worse. You must take a low diet, my lad, and a vigorous bleeding to begin. Then I prescribe a warm bath to the legs and feet with barley water, and etiolation, or as you might say, shaving of the head thrice a week, accompanied by blistering plasters, applied behind the ears, at the base of the neck, and between the shoulders, as often as may be tolerated. You shan't be bothered by marks, hey?"

"What? No!" Tom protested, then realizing the doctor was making ready to leave, he called out, "Sir, I'm afraid you misunderstand. I called you here to see my uncle."

"Is that so?" MacAdam said peevishly. "Very well, but I ain't giving a second examination for free, oh no indeed."

Tom showed the doctor into the bedroom, where he made a perfunctory examination of Jack's recumbent form.

"Consumption, no doubt caused by an excess of venery, drink, and general debauchery," MacAdam declared with a hypocritical sneer, for he himself was no stranger to excess. "There is little to be done, apart from removing to a more salubrious environment, viz., more fresh, clean air, and taking a hearty diet. Ass's milk is the very thing, four times a day, mixed with powdered claw of crab, if you please." He then proceeded to give Jack a thorough blood-letting, while Tom sat miserably in a corner, nauseated by the sound of the blood splashing into the metal basin and the thick, coppery smell that filled the room. After the bleeding was over, Jack lay back, weak and dizzy, as MacAdam dosed him with bark as a purgative.

"Very well then," MacAdam said, tossing the contents of the basin out the window, "Now it's your turn, laddie." He grasped Tom's arm forcefully but Tom wrenched away.

"No!"

"Come now, none of your palaver. Don't you want to be cured?"

Tom drew himself up to his full height, which was a head taller than the physician. "And you mean to tell me that letting my blood will restore my sight?"

"Well, not immediately," MacAdam prevaricated, "but as part of a regimen of treatment, perhaps in time. In any case, it can't hurt."

Tom disagreed strenuously on that point, thinking that it would hurt very much indeed. He indicated that the doctor's services were not required further, which occasioned a very bitter wrangle over the bill, MacAdam insisting on being paid for seeing two patients. They at last came to a compromise, but not before MacAdam had also sold them a decoction of bark mixed with spirit of vitriol for Jack and a camphorated white ointment for Tom. In the end Tom found he had paid three times more than he had expected at the outset.

Having at last shown the doctor out, Tom returned to his uncle's bedside and slumped next to him in a chair.

"I'm sorry to have annoyed you with that damned quack," Tom sighed, but Jack patted his hand reassuringly.

"Not at all, my boy. I'm grateful you brought him in. It's I who should be sorry he harassed you."

"Why must they always take on so? Why can't they let me be?" Tom cried, for this was not the first time he had encountered such usage at the hands of doctors.

"I suppose they don't like to be reminded of the limits of their art," Jack said slowly, thinking on his sister Jenny and the treatments she had endured, which he was certain had hastened her untimely end. "'What can't be cured has to be endured,' as the song goes. Still, however, that bark has set me up right well, so perhaps the old cove ain't entirely a quack. You might try that ointment he gave you."

Tom dutifully placed a tiny amount in the corner of his left eye, but it stung and smarted so unbearably that when Jack was sleeping, he smuggled the rest out in his coat pocket and flung it down the privy.

Despite Jack's immediate claim to have improved under the doctor's care, the diagnosis of consumption weighed heavily on his mind. He had suspected as much himself, but to have it confirmed oppressed his spirits, convincing him that he was dished up for certain. They had spent two years in Scotland, but with very little to show for it. It saddened him to think what a treasure of song was awaiting him just outside, and he mewed up indoors, with barely enough income to save them from ruination. He was far more worried for Tom's sake, however. He dreaded leaving the boy alone in the world, without friends, family, or means, but when he broached the subject, Tom refused to allow him to write to Lord Bolingbroke or Lady Gray.

"I will not go back to Culverleigh, to live as a dependent like an infant," Tom declared and Jack could hardly blame him.

"Very well then, but what will you do?" Jack pressed him, but Tom had no ready answer.

At Jack's insistence, they at last removed back to London, for Jack could not bear the thought of Tom alone in a foreign city. At least in London he was in his own country, and Jack had some acquaintances there, although he had not spoken to any of them in over eight years. Jack's attempts to contact his former friends were disappointed, however; they had either died or removed, current whereabouts unknown, although more than one was rumored to be languishing in the Fleet prison or lagged, that is, transported.

What with one thing and another, they ended up in Seven Dials, not far from Jack's old haunts in Covent Garden, a far less salubrious address than what MacAdam had recommended, but the best they could afford. They took a tiny room atop a public house called the Rose and Crown, a seedy, stiver-cramped establishment run by an ill-tempered couple by the name of Corder. The Rose and Crown's one asset was its location at the apex of Earlham Street and Short's Gardens, but as each of the junctions of the seven streets facing the sundial pillar also boasted a public house, this was no great advantage.

The journey from Edinburgh to London by post had been taxing for both Jack and Tom, as both had felt poorly, but the difference was that as soon as he alighted from the last carriage for good, Tom immediately recovered, whereas Jack declined sharply, more so with each setback in their attempts to reestablish themselves in the city. Not two weeks after they took up residence above the Rose and Crown, Jack slipped into unconsciousness, and within a few days, he expired.

In a state of blank disbelief, not unlike a waking dream, Tom paid the doctor and the parson who had been called in at the last moments and arranged for a burial at St. Paul's. Afterwards, Tom stood blinking at the churchyard gate, realizing that although his lodgings were only a few streets away, he was unsure of the direction, and so he was forced to expend even more from his fast dwindling supply of ready cash to pay the sexton to escort him home.

The next morning, Tom slept late, returning to the world with the greatest reluctance. As he slowly washed and dressed, he heard the strident voices of the publican Corder and his wife arguing in the taproom below.

"And I say you must turn the cully out on the street directly," Mrs. Corder was insisting.

"That ain't very Christian of you, Mariah," her husband replied. "His uncle ain't even cold in the ground, the sad wretch."

Mrs. Corder replied with a lewd comment on what he could do with his Christian charity. "You're too tender-hearted by half," she said. "Turn the boy out now, or we will be saddled with him for the rest of our days, mark my words. I won't have no beggars living here."

Tom set his mouth in a hard line. He had been about to go downstairs to find his breakfast, but now he changed his plans. Running his hands over every surface in the tiny room, he collected all their belongings as carefully as he could. He placed a few things in a pack, and the remainder in the chest they had brought down from Scotland, mainly the manuscripts his uncle had worked on so feverishly until his last days.

Taking up the pack and his walking stick, Tom marched downstairs and felt his way to the public bar, where Corder and his wife were still arguing, although they fell silent as he approached.

"There, you have the rest of my money," Tom said, slapping several coins down on the bar. "It's more than I owe you, but you can have it, and let the room out again as you please. I only ask you, take the chest I have left in the room and keep it safe."

"Well I'm sure I don't know…" Mrs. Corder said, but Tom cut her off, reaching across the bar and grabbing her husband by the arm, pulling him close and bringing his face right up to his own.

"Promise me you will keep the chest safe," he said, his voice tight with anger. "I'm leaving here now, but I will be back within the week to collect it. Keep it for me, and I will trouble you no longer."

Corder, thoroughly unnerved by the intensity of Tom's voice and his blank stare, swore he would do so. Tom released him and charged out the door, letting it slam behind him for good measure. A moment later, however, he was still hesitating on the doorstep.

Well this is damned inconvenient, he thought. As he had said to Aoife, and the many curious girls he had met since, he rarely thought on his blindness. Up until this moment, there had always been someone who would assist him if he asked. Never before had he felt so alone, and while he had stormed out with a hauteur born of righteous indignation and pride, in truth he had no plan and no place to go. To make matters worse, the geography of Seven Dials, with its round intersection of seven streets, was seemingly designed to confound him; he had not yet learned one street from another.

There was nothing for it, however; the thought of going back was far too painful. At last he stepped down into the stream of foot traffic as if slipping into a dark, rushing river and letting the water close over his head. He walked at random for what seemed like hours, although in fact he did not travel very far, for his progress was painfully slow. He paid no attention to his direction, thinking only on placing one foot before the other, and avoiding being knocked down by the crowd or run over by a carriage, and indeed he had several near misses.

As he walked, his mind grew blessedly blank, weighed down with grief and loneliness. He found it easier to just keep wandering, rather than to attempt to formulate a plan for the future. When he could go no further, he sank down in a quiet corner and slept, then awakened and continued wandering. Unseen fingers plucked at his clothes and reached into his pockets, but as those were empty already, he simply ignored them, only holding his pack close to his chest to discourage anyone from reaching inside, although this made walking even more awkward.

Being unable to tell night from day, he soon lost track of time entirely: had it been a week? or two? Hunger was a constant presence, but he hardly noticed, except as a dull background ache. Sometimes when he leaned up against the side of a building to rest, or sat down on a stoop, someone would press a bun or a pasty or a mug of small beer in his hands, but as he would not respond to questions, they soon left him to his own devices. In the back of his mind, he worried over the chest left at the pub.

Although he did not realize it, Tom was in fact walking in circles over a very small area, and inevitably, he stumbled onto the Piazza of Covent Garden. He was overwhelmed by the noise and exotic smells of the market, the jumble of fruit and vegetable stalls in the wide open square, as he stood buffeted by the throng, hundreds of people all moving in random, unknowable directions. Still, it was an exciting place, and despite himself he began slowly cataloging and mapping it in his mind.

Tom had been creeping about the market for several days when he was brought up short by a familiar voice. This was not the first time this had happened. Throughout his wandering, he was haunted by the sound of voices he knew: his uncle, his mother, people he had known in Ireland. Each time, he would stop, his heart pounding, but after a moment it would become clear that he was mistaken. This time was different, however. He sidled closer to the stall to eavesdrop on the conversation.

"...to be delivered to the residence of Lady Gray in Soho Square," the voice said. It was Josiah Stinson. Tom was thunderstruck: what was Stinson doing here in London? And his aunt? He did not know she had a London residence. If he had thought on it at all, he might have supposed she was in Stirling. He stood hesitating for a few moments more as Stinson negotiated the final details of his purchase—should he call out to him? Before he could make up his mind, it was too late. Stinson disappeared into the whirl of noise around him and Tom was no longer even sure which stall he had been at. The sudden frustration of his intent, however slight, galvanized his spirit and awakened his mind to a new sense of purpose. Despite his lingering reluctance to be brought back to Culverleigh, he realized that he had had enough of wandering, and now determined to seek out Lady Gray's residence in Soho Square.

The only question was how. By this point, he was so dirty, no coachman would have taken him, even if he had money to pay, which he did not. He had no desire to throw himself on the mercy of strangers and risk exposing himself to mischief. He would just have to walk there, as he had a vague idea that it was not very far from the Piazza, if only he knew the way. And so began a long, slow process of trial and error, asking people the way, going a short distance, then asking again. He very seldom got useful directions.

"Go down to the sign of the Goat and Compass, then turn left beyond that red brick building," a person would say before hurrying away, leaving Tom to try again with someone else. Sometimes the person would simply walk off, leaving him talking to himself.

At long last, after countless queries, when Tom asked a hurrying footman if he knew the way to Soho Square, the man replied that he was standing in the square itself, but then rushed off before Tom could ask to be directed to Lady Gray's residence. Tom sighed inwardly and began to make his way slowly around the square, counterclockwise, knocking at each door. This in no way endeared him to the servants who answered the doors, but when he had reached about half way around the square, he at last heard that familiar voice again.

"Stinson?" he said. "D'ye remember me?"

"Master Finch!" Stinson was overcome with shock, for there was no mistaking the boy, although now he was painfully thin, quite dirty, and bearing the marks of collisions with unknown objects, as well as blows from those who did not wish him to linger, including a butler from a house further down the row. Tom staggered a bit as Stinson led him inside the entry.

The next several hours were a blur; Tom found he could not return so easily from the state of waking unconsciousness to which he had retreated, to rejoin living society. He listlessly gave himself over to the gentle hands that relieved him of his dirty old clothes, washed, shaved and dressed him in a clean shirt and breeches, and put food before him. He was dimly aware of Stinson leading him upstairs and guiding him to a soft feather bed, where he sank gratefully into a long, deep sleep.

Tom awoke many hours later to discover his aunt, the Lady Sarah Gray, sitting beside him on the bed. He sat up with a start. "Uncle Jack's chest!" he cried out.

Lady Gray pushed him back to the pillows with her firm, bony hands. "Yes, yes, you mentioned it several times yesterday. I have already sent someone round to fetch it. Pray be easy. You must rest still."

Tom drifted in and out of sleep for the rest of the day, but by evening declared himself well enough to take some supper and to talk with Lady Gray again. After a brief summary of his affairs for the past eight years, he ended forcefully, "I won't go back to Culverleigh."

"Of course not. Culverleigh has been shut up these past five years and more," she answered, to his astonishment. "His lordship has been living here in London while little Jamie is away at school," she explained. "That is why Stinson is here with me, and most of the other servants as well. Although I must say, it is the most remarkable good fortune that you overheard him at Covent Garden, for he very rarely goes to the market himself."

"And my brothers and sisters?"

"Richard is garrisoned in French Flanders, and Paul and Philip are at sea, of course," she replied. "As for the girls, Sophia and Anne are married, and Charlotte is here with me."

"What, here?" Tom was even more astonished.

"Yes, until I can see her safely married off as well. She would like to see you, if you are feeling strong enough."

At the mention of her name, Charlotte burst into the room and smothered him in a sisterly embrace.

"My goodness, you are the very image of Father," she exclaimed, then turned to Lady Gray. "Oh Aunt Sarah, he may live here with us, mayn't he?"

"Of course, child, he may stay here as long as he likes. I daresay he will find life here in London more stimulating than in Bedford."

BOOK TWO: OPERA SERIA

CHAPTER ONE: THE BOTTLE OF GIN

Tess Turnbridge rapped on the door of number eight Maiden Lane, then receiving no answer, rapped again, more insistently. It had been two weeks since the death of Sally Salisbury, and in that time, Tom had disappeared from public life, not even appearing at the theater for performances of *Ariodante*, which were still continuing. At first Tess refrained from intervening in Tom's private affairs, but by the end of the second week, concern that he might cause irreparable damage to his career spurred her to pay him a visit.

After a long interval, Stinson at last appeared at the door, wheezing and squinting at her. "Master Finch is indisposed," he said and made to shut the door, but Tess interceded her person between the jamb and the door.

"Indisposed—what stuff," she declared as she forced her way in. Stinson, well aware of the debts his master owed Mistress Turnbridge, ceded his ground without a fuss, and only stood grasping his hands uncertainly as she charged up the stairs. Tess paused for a moment in the front parlor, adjusting to the dim interior. She had grown accustomed to the disarray of Tom's household, but the sight that met her eyes gave her a turn. Things were far worse than she had imagined, with empty bottles and the remains of many meals strewn about haphazardly, and smoke from the long-extinguished hearth still hanging heavily in the air.

She turned on Stinson angrily—how could he have allowed this to happen?

"Where is your master?" she demanded. Stinson barely glanced towards the second storey before she mounted the stairs.

She found Tom lying in bed, surrounded by evidence that he had been spending the majority of his time there.

"Good heavens, Mr. Finch, you have created a veritable rat's nest for yourself," she exclaimed, but instead of replying, he merely turned away from her. "Where is that Jem Castleton?" she asked, flinging open the window to let in some much-needed fresh air.

Behind her she heard Tom say crossly, "He ain't my nurse-maid, you know."

"More's the pity," she shot back. "You could do with some looking after. I understand you are bereaved, but I doubt that your current posture is doing you any good. You are ruining your health," she warned, going to sit at the edge of the bed.

Tom turned towards her, his beard unshaven, his hair lank and disheveled. "Be damned to your good health," he slurred.

Tess had seen many men in advanced states of inebriation; indeed, she had often seen Tom drink to excess, but this was something else again, and the time was not yet noon. She stood up, seeming to make a decision within herself.

"Very well then, I shall bid you good morning," she said coldly and stalked out, slamming the door behind her. Tom sat up, for a moment seeming as if he would go after her, then thought better of it and sank back down.

"Off with you then, and be damned to you too," he muttered.

But Tess did not leave. Back downstairs, she sought out Stinson.

"This will never do," she insisted to him. "The chimney must be cleaned so it will draw again, before it causes a fire. The rubbish is starting to attract vermin and the shutters must be opened." Stinson nodded vaguely, his eyes twitching nervously in a way that seemed odd, yet familiar. She gave him a quizzical look, which he did not return. Tess realized with a start that in his old age, he was becoming as blind as his master. Little wonder the household was in such shocking squalor, she thought. Just as she was contemplating how to handle this new revelation, there was a knock at the door. Stinson made as if to answer it, but Tess, striding purposefully down the stairs, beat him to it.

It was Mrs. Bracegirdle, the landlady. Holding the door behind her to prevent the landlady from entering, Tess greeted her in an imperious tone.

Mrs. Bracegirdle, a stout woman of middle years, shrank back for a moment under Tess's haughty stare, but then collecting herself, asked peevishly, "And who are you, madam?" In fact Mrs. Bracegirdle, a keen patron of the opera, knew very well who she was.

"I am seeing to Mr. Finch's affairs while he is…indisposed," Tess replied, undaunted. "I take it by your presence here that the rent is in arrears. By how many months, might I ask?"

"Only two, but I heard dreadful tales that he's letting the interior go to rack and ruin. I am a respectable woman, Mistress Turnbridge. I won't allow my property to be destroyed by any rakehell tenant…"

Tess arched an eyebrow at her. "I make it a practice never to carry great quantities of cash about, but if I send round a draft for two months' rent later today, may I have your word that you will not disturb Mr. Finch further on this matter?"

Yes, Mrs. Bracegirdle assured her she would, her whole person transforming into a rather obsequious kindness.

"I assure you I will see to the interior, so you may set your mind at ease on that score," Tess added, also softening a bit.

She was about to withdraw, but it seemed Mrs. Bracegirdle still had further business. She stood hesitating, opening and closing her mouth several times, before at last blurting out, "If I may make so bold, madam, I—my—that is, Mr. Bracegirdle is a great lover of the opera, do you see, a great admirer of Mr. Handel, and we have not yet seen *Ariodante*—"

"I'll send two tickets with the rent later today," Tess said and closed the door with finality.

With a new sense of authority, she rounded on Stinson, who was lurking stiffly behind her in the entryway. "I shall send round a sweep for the chimney and some of my own servants to assist you with cleaning. Start with the kitchen and work your way through the downstairs rooms. Don't bother with the upstairs yet. Here is some money—buy a meat pie or two and see that he eats it. I shall return late tonight after the performance."

Tess was as good as her word, appearing again close to midnight, her face greasy with residual paint and her hair still pinned as it had been under her wig, only now covered with a lace cap. Stinson let her in without comment, although she flattered herself that he was becoming at least slightly amenable to her presence. Holding a candle aloft, she quickly surveyed the downstairs: the hearths were all clean, but she had only been able to spare two maids and they had not progressed beyond throwing out the rubbish, washing the plates, and setting the kitchen in order. In the kitchen, Tess also noticed the scant remains of the meat pies; at least someone had eaten them.

Taking a basket from the kitchen, Tess crept quietly up the stairs, her candle throwing flickering shadows through the otherwise darkened house. In the bedroom, she could hear Tom snoring softly. She entered as silently as she could and set the candle on the bed stand. At least the candle will never disturb him, she thought wryly. Trying not to wake him, she set about gathering up the bottles strewn about the room, clearing away the empties, although her real purpose was to remove all those that had not yet been drained. Her basket was soon filled, but just as she thought she had found them all, she noticed a large bottle of gin, still half full, lying tangled in the sheets. Holding her breath, she leaned over him and plucked it from the bed.

As she did so, Tom rolled over with a groan. "Shush, it's only I," Tess said, adding the bottle of gin to her basket. "Go back to sleep."

Instead, Tom turned his face to her and opened his eyes. They were shockingly bloodshot. Tess felt that now familiar pang deep in her stomach. After all this time, something about him still had the power to jolt her whole being. And yet she also noticed that he was for the first time showing signs of age. It broke her heart to see his face, so formed by nature to be cheerful, now lined with unhappiness.

"I'm thirsty," he said in an almost comically childish voice. If he was surprised at her return, he did not show it.

He's still drunk, she thought with dismay. "Shall I bring you some water?" she offered. Tom nodded plaintively, then rolled over again.

Tess took her basket back down to the kitchen and set it on the table with a loud clink. Stinson, who was finishing the last of the meat pie while he waited for her, immediately guessed what she was about.

"The master won't be pleased," he muttered darkly, but Tess ignored him.

Pouring water from the pitcher into a chipped teacup, she said only, "You may retire now. I will bring this up to him then let myself out." Stinson responded with a look so pointed she wondered if she had been wrong about his declining eyesight, but shaking it off, she marched back upstairs.

She discovered Tom sitting up in bed, waiting for her. Tess placed the cup in his hands, and watched as he drained it thirstily. When he had finished, she made to take it from him, but instead he grasped her wrist and tugged. "Stay for a moment," he pleaded in a low voice.

Tess sat down beside him on the bed, feeling rather self-conscious. True, she was a woman of the world, but he was wearing nothing but his small-clothes and his hair was hanging loose. He ran a hand through it, seeming ill at ease himself.

"Miss Turnbridge, I believe I may owe you an apology," he said, his voice still rather slurred, but clearer than it had been earlier. "I can't recall exactly, but I think I may have spoken intemperate words to you earlier today."

"I hardly noticed," Tess lied.

"You did call this morning, did you not?"

"Yes, I did. I called to inform you that *Ariodante* will end its run in a fortnight, more or less, and we will soon begin rehearsals for the next opera. Mr. Rich expects you to return as music master."

Tom groaned and leaned his head back against the bedstock. "No, I cannot."

"But you must!" Tess turned to face him directly. "Mr. Finch, I implore you, please do not throw away your career. I know you have been most dreadfully wounded, but you mustn't throw it all over now, and for that woman—" Tess bit back her words, but too late. Tom's expression hardened into a frown. "I beg your pardon," she said. "I meant no disrespect. Only it pains me still to think of how abominably she used you in Paris."

Tom shook his head. "You did not know her. She had a hard life."

Tess was unconvinced. "We have all of us led hard lives," she said.

Tom sat forward, his head facing down in his lap. "No, we may have lacked some comforts, but you and I, we were raised by kind and loving hands. I won't repeat the things she told me in confidence, but the tales of her childhood would make your flesh creep, I assure you. Her mother was a bunter, a common hedge whore, the kind who cheats the bagnios and brothels by plying her trade in the open. She raised her daughter up to the trade, had her turned out before she was ten. You know what is the lot of those urchins around the Piazza. Sal had a mortal horror of being poor. If she was ever hardhearted or cruel, it was only because she never trusted that she would have enough, d'ye see. It weren't her fault."

As Tom spoke, Tess pulled the pins from her hair, which had been fastened so tightly her head ached. She ran her hands through her curls, now springing out every which way, and rewound them more loosely. "How can you defend that treacherous ja—that woman. Fear of poverty or what have you, it still gave her no right to leave you with nothing but a dog's portion, and after you helped her escape to France."

Tom's frown deepened and his face flushed. "That's coming it mighty high, from a woman who has become the kept mistress of a duke."

"What do you mean by that?" Tess demanded.

Tom's mouth twisted bitterly. "You can't say you love that fat old cully. Admit it, your liaison is only meant to profit yourself."

"You know nothing of my affairs," she hissed at him in a low voice. "And as for the money, a good deal of it has profited you as well, if I'm not mistaken. But if abuse is my reward for helping you, I shall take my leave of you." She made as if to rise from the bed, but Tom reached out toward her.

"No, I beg you, don't go," he said, his tone suddenly altered, contrite. He found her hands and grasped them tightly. "I'm sorry, my mind is in a fog. I did not mean that. I own I know nothing of your duke, but you must own you know nothing of Sal."

Tess squeezed his hands. "I'm very sorry to see you suffering so," she said. "And I think she would not like to see you in such a state either."

"I left her!" he suddenly burst out in anguish. "I left her to die alone!"

Tess put her hand on his shoulder. "It wasn't your fault. Please, you mustn't blame yourself—" Suddenly, he threw his arms around her, burying his face in her hair and clinging tightly to her, not in an amorous fashion, but with wild desperation, like a drowning man. She stroked his head, until he seemed calmer, then helped him to lay back down on the bed, but still he would not let her go.

"Miss Turnbridge, you are very good to me," he murmured into her hair, his voice muzzy with drink and sleep.

The whole situation suddenly seemed so absurd, the formal mode of address contrasted with their frank posture, that Tess gave a short laugh. "Please, call me Tess," she said.

"But you said not to," Tom said petulantly, still not moving, nearly half asleep. "You thought I would forget and take liberties, but you see I did not."

Tess stroked his head again. "I apologize for having spoken in anger. I am pleased that our friendship should resume its former intimacy," she said.

"Then you must call me Tom," he replied. He clung to her with an intensity that surprised her and moved her to pity for him, mixed with frustration that he still seemed determined to throw away his life for that unworthy woman. Many moments passed, until Tess thought he had fallen asleep, then suddenly, he mumbled, "Why did you have to go into keeping?"

Tess was startled. "Why Mr. Finch—I mean Tom, d'ye mean to say you're jealous?"

"Why did you have to go away with that fat old man?" Tom repeated, his voice even fainter, but tinged with a childish petulance. Tess paused, formulating an answer, but before she could speak again, he had fallen asleep. She intended to stay only a short while longer, but as she lay there, she too was overcome by exhaustion, and before she realized it, she had slipped into unconsciousness, with his arms still wrapped tightly around her.

Some hours later, Tess awoke with a start, but by then it was morning, the grey light just beginning to filter in through the window. As he slept, Tom had at last released his grip and drifted to the other side of the bed. Tess slid from the bed, relieved to see that he did not so much as stir, and crept downstairs with her shoes in her hand. She paused for a moment in the front parlor to put her appearance to rights, as much as possible, and to quell the uncomfortable confusion in her breast. Feeling like a thief in the night, she slipped down the stairs and out the front door, hurrying home through the early morning streets.

CHAPTER TWO: MORNING

Two days later, Tess Turnbridge again called early in the morning at number eight Maiden Lane, and this time she was not alone. Her countenance wiped clean of any traces of the storms she had just now left behind at home, and determined not to mention her unexpectedly protracted previous visit, she rapped the door. After the now expected lengthy pause, Stinson admitted her and her party, and suffered to be introduced to the cadre of new servants Tess had engaged to wait on Mr. Finch.

She had hired a strapping footman named Matthews, a sober-faced young man, tolerably clean and well-dressed, although livery was beyond the means of the new master. A squat, red-faced woman of late middle years named Susan was engaged as cook, and a toothless old crone named Dorcas as the washerwoman, who would also assist in the kitchen. The last was the boy Frankie, already very well known to the valet, and wanting a position since the Rose remained closed. A tolerably creditable lot, although Stinson, still mentally sharp despite his advanced years, noted with amusement that Miss Turnbridge had seen fit to hire only men and aged women; there was no pert chambermaid, nor saucy scullery maid. Stinson did not comment on this, however, but merely inquired as to whether Frankie possessed the dainty manners to wait upon persons of quality.

"This is a respectable house, you know," the valet wheezed.

"Of course," said Tess breezily, swatting the boy, who could not contain his laughter at this last comment, on the back of the head. "He has already been in service at my own home these past few weeks, but I know how attached he is to Mr. Finch."

Tess then set about showing them to their tasks immediately, the first of which was to scrub each room from floor to ceiling. Starting in the parlor, she began pushing the furniture into the corners, so that they might carry the carpets outside and beat them, when Stinson grabbed at her arms, begging her to stop, for the love of God. She stared at the aged valet, who was white-faced and trembling. She had never seen him in such a rare old taking.

"You mustn't—you mustn't move the furniture—the master will be furious—what if he comes to harm…"

Tess froze, overcome with remorse. Of course, she must not rearrange things; she was ashamed that she had not thought of this before. Despite the general disorder, the largest pieces of furniture remained in place, and she had often seen Tom orient himself as he moved through the house by placing a hand along the edge of a table or the back of an armchair. Chastened, and recalling that this was after all not her house, she returned the chair in her hands to its former position.

"You shall have to take care to keep things in place as you clean," she instructed them. "The furniture is not to be shifted one inch out of place. And remember your master can find his way about the house perfectly well as long as you do not alter things. Pray do not vex him by plucking at his clothing or pushing or pulling him about," she added, warming to her subject. "If he requests your assistance, let him place his hand on your arm or shoulder, but do not to take his hand like a child. He is quite capable, and if you wish to retain your position here, you must remember that." The servants nodded seriously if rather dazedly, still wary of this peculiar master they had not yet met.

Leaving more detailed instructions below, Tess proceeded upstairs with a jug of hot water from the kitchen. She had not expected Tom to be awake yet, as it was well before noon, but to her surprise, he was already half-dressed, shirt billowing loose over his breeches, and banging about the room in some irritation. He turned around in equal surprise as he heard her come in.

"Dammee, Stinson, where the devil have you been? I've been ringing for you this age."

"No, it's Tess."

She had prepared a speech apologizing for her wanton behavior, and begging him not to speak of it again, but before she could begin, he burst out, "Where in damnation is Stinson and what's all that bloody racket downstairs?"

Tess poured the hot water into the washstand. "I have hired you some proper servants, Mr. Finch, and they are bringing order to the house. Come, let me help you to dress. You must come downstairs to greet them." She glanced sharply at him. He did not ask her to call him by his Christian name again: so, they were not to speak of that previous night, just as well.

"I trust that water is hot?" he said, cocking his head to the side as he listened to her pouring the water. Tess wondered if he even remembered their late night conversation. At least now he seemed sober at last, as he found the washstand without hesitation.

"Did I hear you aright? New servants?" he asked as he scrubbed his face vigorously in the steaming water. Tess pressed a towel against his shoulder and waited for him to take it from her.

"Shall I brush your hair for you?"

"Yes, thank you," Tom said, drying his face and hands, and sitting in a chair by the washstand. "But what's to become of Stinson, then?"

"Oh, I suppose he shall retire to the countryside or some such," Tess replied carelessly, dragging the brush over his hair, which was a snarled mess. He stiffened with alarm at her words.

"You haven't dismissed him already, have you?" Tess replied that she had not, and Tom sat back with a sigh of relief. "But this will never do," he continued. "Stinson has served me since I was a boy, and has been in service to my father's family his entire life. You have no idea how much he has aided me. I cannot simply turn him out on the street."

"I'm sorry, I didn't realize," Tess said with a pang of conscience, again feeling that she had overstepped her bounds. "But Mr. Finch, are you aware how old he is? He's becoming quite infirm. I-I'm afraid his sight may be going as well." Tom fell silent, and it seemed to Tess that this news came as a surprise to him. She continued brushing; his hair was none too clean, but she brushed it until it shone, then tied it back in a queue and twirled the ends around her finger to make it curl. "Of course you will do as you see fit, but with additional servants, his work will at least be lighter. I've hired Frankie as well; I thought that might please you."

Tom stood, feeling his queue with his fingers. "Indeed? How clever, that may answer very well. I shall speak with Stinson later. But how am I to support this army of servants, pray tell?"

"I suppose you shall have to go back to work, then," she said tartly.

Instead of responding, Tom busied himself laying out some items by the washstand. Tess watched with horror as he snapped open a large razor.

"Mr. Finch! You're not thinking of shaving yourself?" she cried.

Tom shrugged. "I usually have Stinson do it, or the barber, but I am perfectly capable, I'll have you know. I have done it myself at least once or twice before."

Tess rolled her eyes heavenward, a vision of Tom opening a vein with the wicked-looking razor flashing before her mind's eye. "Please, let me do it for you, I beg you."

In the end, vanity won out over pride, as Tom was loath to sacrifice his face to the blade. Tess set his chair by the window and lathered on the soap with the badger-hair brush, then turned to sharpen the razor, which was shockingly rusted and dull.

"So, back to work, you say?" Tom said as he lounged in the chair, listening to the rhythmic scrape of the razor on the paddle. "Have you spoken to Mr. Rich, then?"

"Yes, and he agreed to increase your wages by ten per cent, and to give Mr. Castleton a separate salary as your assistant."

"Hmm," Tom mused. He knew that even with the increase, he was making far less than the previous music master at the Theater Royal; in fact, John Rich had told him plainly he thought it unfair to pay Tom as much as a sighted man. Tom did not follow the logic of this policy, yet as the pay was slightly more than he had made at the Rose, it seemed churlish to complain of this to Tess, after all she had done for him. "And how am I to learn the music for the next production?"

Tess smiled, holding up the now-gleaming razor to the light and testing it with her thumb. "Luckily, the next one is to be a revival: *Il pastor fido*, The Faithful Shepherd. You know it already, I trust?"

Tom groaned. "Not that dull old nonsense?" *Il pastor fido*, already deemed woefully out of date upon its debut over twenty years previous, had not been one of Mr. Handel's successes.

Tess tipped his head to the side and began shaving with an expert hand, making short downward strokes. "I understand it will be revised and lengthened with arias taken from some other cantata or some such. According to Mr. Rich, it is to be a wholly new production that will correct the inadequacies of the original. Regardless, it will be much easier to learn the music, I trust?" Tom conceded that perhaps this was so, and Tess promised to send Jem round with the score as soon as possible.

Tess lapsed into silence as she made a second pass with the

razor, her mind wholly concentrated on her task. The morning sun fell in through the window, making the dust motes around them shine. As she bent over him, with the sun glinting on his sandy brown hair, turning it golden, she felt a profound intimacy, far more even than when she had fallen asleep next to him the other day. Tom sat patiently, waiting for her to finish. His opaque eyes drifted lazily back and forth, and Tess found his mood unreadable, his expression blank. The second pass finished, she was debating whether to attempt a third, when he turned towards her, so the sun caught him full in the face, and she had the queerest sensation that he was looking right at her, although of course he was not.

Overcome with a sudden, unexpectedly painful sensation of longing, Tess turned to the washstand and began cleaning up.

"There, you're finished," she mumbled.

Unaware of her distress, Tom stood up and stretched, rubbing a hand over his shorn cheeks with approval, then made for the clothes press.

"Might I trouble you to find a waistcoat that matches this?" he asked, holding aloft his second-best surcoat, a showy affair with full skirts and boot cuffs stiffened with buckram, in a startling shade of red.

"Certainly," Tess replied, recovering herself, "But you're not thinking on wearing that old shirt, are you? I'm sorry, I got the collar all wet, and besides there is a vile great stain down the front."

"There is?" Tom ran anxious fingers over the offending shirt, but could distinguish no marks. Tess riffled through both the clothes press and the highboy, but the best she could find was a shirt with some holes towards the bottom; how those had been achieved she could not begin to guess, but at least they would be covered by the long embroidered beige waistcoat she had also discovered.

As she stood on her toes tying his cravat, Tom said suddenly, "Tess, you're entirely too good to me."

She was caught all unawares again—did he recall their conversation after all? With a flash of embarrassment mixed with frustration, she snapped, "You're right, I am. After today, I shall trouble you no more."

Tom caught her hands. "Nay, that was not my intention...I am grateful to you, but I fear I've become indebted to you far beyond the point of ordinary friendship, and I should be the worst kind of scrub if I could never repay you."

Tess looked down and murmured, "The money doesn't signify."

"But five hundred pounds! You did pay Sal's debt, did you not?"

"What? No, of course not!" Tess gave a mirthless laugh. "Please don't trouble yourself on that head. I merely paid a bribe to the bailiff to suspend the debt temporarily, long enough to get her out of prison, that's all."

"Oh." Tom seemed surprised by this revelation. "Well, I am glad to hear it, but it's more than the money—the new servants, and..."

Tess cut him off. "You are correct, sir. I have taken liberties with you, presumed a greater intimacy than the friendship between us can support. I merely wanted to repay you in kind for helping me in my career and for rescuing Jane, but now we may consider the debt settled. I shall interfere in your affairs no longer," she said icily.

"What? No, that's not at all what I meant, dammee. You know I value your friendship above all things." Tess tried to pull away, but he grasped her hands more tightly and would not let her go. Suddenly, he was struck by a strong intuition. "Tess, what's amiss?"

"It's nothing to do with you," she said, still trying to pull away.

"Aha, but it is something, I warrant. I could tell straight away from the moment you entered, something is weighing on your mind. Come now, out with it, for I tell you I have no wish to end the intimacy between us. Your presence has been the one happy outcome of this whole wretched affair, I find."

"Very well," said Tess with a sigh, "If you must know, Jane left this morning. She was angry that I spent the night with you, and we quarreled."

"My dearest Tess, I am very sorry to hear it," Tom said, enfolding her in a comforting embrace and planting a kiss on the top of her head, which only reached his shoulders.

She shook her head, willing herself not to burst into tears. "She'll be back in a day or two, I'm certain. It were only a little falling out. You know how she is."

Tom put a hand against her cheek, but found it dry. "You never quarreled over me, did you?"

"No," Tess lied, then repeated unconvincingly, "It doesn't signify."

She would not repeat the cruel words Jane had hurled at her: "He's only trifling with you now that his whore is dead. You may have purchased his companionship, but if you think you can buy his constancy, you're mistaken. He will take your money and spend it on the next doxy who catches his fancy."

And yet jealousy aside, Tess felt intensely guilty for staying out the whole night and not informing Jane of where she was; in her place she would have been sick with worry. And affairs would have taken a far uglier turn if the duke had called that night; it was mere luck that he had not. Tess could not fault Jane for being angry, but all at once she felt exhausted, tired of being pulled in opposite directions by her closest friends, and tired of being relied upon for everything and receiving nothing in return.

"In faith, Mr. Finch, as I say, my service to you is at an end."

Tom gave her a gentle shake, still holding her close. "My dearest Tess, did I not request you address me more familiarly?"

Tess stole a glance up at him. He was even thinner than before, and still markedly pale, but groomed and dressed at last, she found him staggeringly handsome, with his head tipped up slightly and a tiny smile tugging at the corners of his mouth. So he did recall that conversation? She was brought all up standing.

Just as she was thinking she must make her excuses and leave, his fingers, which were still cupping her cheek, found her lips; he leaned down and kissed her.

CHAPTER THREE: THE FAITHLESS SHEPHERD

The rehearsals for *Il pastor fido* did not go as smoothly as Mr. Handel and Mr. Rich might have wished. Taking pains to improve upon his failure of two decades previous, the composer was continually revising the score, but rather than writing new music, he was largely cobbling together tunes from older suites, cantatas, and even masses, which caused no end of frustration to the orchestra.

In an effort to save money, Rich let many of the more experienced members of the chorus go, replaced with younger singers who would work for cheaper wages. For the same reason, Anna Maria Strada del Po was displaced as prima donna by Tess Turnbridge, who was cast as Amarilli, while the Pig was relegated to the secondary role of Eurilla. This pleased the diva not in the slightest, as she let everyone know.

Signor Farinelli, cast as Mirtillo, found himself forced to share the stage with Valentino Urbani, cast as Silvio, whose aging, feeble voice and predilection for whimsical, bathetic acting Farinelli protested most strenuously cheapened their art. As the first castrato to sing on the London stage, Urbani commanded a respect equal to Farnelli's, which ensured that there could never be peace between them.

The costumers and carpenters had been ordered to make

use of the old costumes and sets, but to update them into a more pleasing modern style. Yet they were given precious little time or resources to accomplish this herculean task.

In short, every member of the company harbored a deeply-felt resentment or grievance. Actors being on the whole a superstitious lot, there were loud whisperings that the opera was unlucky, and not a few had taken to referring to it as *The Faithless Shepherd*, or more lewd variations thereof.

As music master, Tom was usually immune from these petty squabbles, but the constant changes in the score set his nerves on edge. He was painfully aware of Mr. Handel and Mr. Rich sitting in the seats behind him, listening to the rehearsals, alert to the slightest error, and not infrequently stopping the flow to consider amendments, or arguing about even more radical alterations between them. While the rehearsals tried his patience, Tom was secretly glad of the distraction, and grateful to Tess for extracting him from his self-imposed exile. At least when his mind was on his work, thoughts of Sal did not intrude so forcefully and the crushing oppression of spirits seemed to lift, however momentarily.

Tess. He found it impossible to say how things stood between them. She had seemed pleased, if surprised, by the unexpected kiss, yet she had not allowed things to go further, nor had she spoken of it again. Tom was not certain if Jane had returned to her yet or not. Jane was not in the cast. Her star was not rising as Tess's was, and Tom suspected that professional jealousy might be a further source of strife between them. As Tess continued to visit him frequently, to help Jem with teaching him the score, or to inspect the new servants, it seemed likely that Jane had not returned yet. Tess was polite and friendly, yet somehow distant, and careful to call only in the mornings. There would be no repeat of her accidental night with him.

It was the first day of combining the blocking with the accompaniment of the full orchestra, on the insistence of Collins, the stage manager, and Henshaw, the director. The music rehearsals had been painfully protracted, with all the changes, and new scores had been distributed just the day before. They were not running the opera in order, however. Tom began the rehearsal with the final movement, a difficult choral entrance following several dance evolutions. The chorus arrayed itself prettily across the stage as they had been instructed, but their anxiety over executing the dance movements correctly caused the music to fly right out of their heads, and the women's entrance was a sad, ragged offering of a few very timid voices.

Tom rapped the conductor's stand with his baton.

"Come now, ladies, let us have that again," he commanded. They repeated the rising scales of the entrance, with scarcely more conviction.

"Just appalling," Tom declared, in an unusual display of irritation, causing several of the younger girls to turn bright red. Here the inexperience of the singers showed baldly, as most of them were only prepared to follow the voices around them, lacking the confidence to find the notes themselves. If only Jane Carlyle were here, he thought grimly. She might not have the full rich tone of a prima donna but at least she could be counted on to sing out loudly in tune and on cue. Tom ran the chorus through their entrance several more times, with an admonishment to learn their parts before rehearsals, for God's sake. They began the scene yet again, this time with the proper blocking, but only a few bars in, the singing was interrupted by a commotion on stage.

Tom heard a screech, followed by a young soprano crying, "Jezebel!"

"Infamous hussy!" came the rejoinder. It was the powerful voice of Elizabeth Eckton, the contralto playing the role of Dorinda. "Keep you away from me, or I'll see you dismissed the company!"

There were more angry cries, along with shoves and stamping of feet, as Collins the stage manager vaulted from the seats onto the stage.

"Silence, the whole damned lot of you!" Collins shouted, his face livid with anger. "Girls, any more of these damned capers, and I'll throw out every last one of you, don't think I can't. For every one of you, ten more are lined up outside waiting to take your part, just remember that! And I don't only mean the chorus, neither," he added, glaring at Elizabeth. She sniffed haughtily, looking away. "You're lucky Mr. Rich and Mr. Handel ain't here," he added, then turned to Tom. "Carry on please, Mr. Finch."

The chorus limped its way through the finale, an even more lackluster and discreditable performance than before. Realizing he would get no more out of them at the moment, Tom banished the chorus to the wings and prepared to run the orchestra through the interminable prologue "Terpsichore" while Marie Sallé took her place for her dance solo. The chaconne went well enough, but sarabande began with the most horrible crashing discordance.

Tom rapped the conductor's stand. "Let us try the sarabande again. The movement begins with triplets modulating up from A: *tum*-te-tum *tum*-te-tum tum-tum-tum," he sang on pitch. He raised his baton to start them off, but Richardson, the first violin, jumped up from his seat.

"Begging your pardon, sir, that ain't it. It goes like this," he said, dashing off a completely different phrase.

Tom felt his heart die within him. This was what he feared above all else, that he would misremember the music and lead them astray. But before he could formulate a reply, Jem leapt to his defense, hefting the massive conductor's score.

"Finchy has the right of it: it says here plainly triplets beginning in A," he said, stabbing at the measure in question with an authoritative finger.

"And I tell you that ain't it," Richardson cried in some desperation. Snatching the sheet from his music stand, he brandished it before Jem. There followed a general outcry from the other members of the orchestra, with much heated argument, in which even the singers were appealed to, a remarkable concession, as the instrumentalists generally believed that the singers had resonance where their brains should be, and could not be relied upon to produce the same notes twice, let alone read the score with any accuracy. However, it eventually became plain that there were significant, egregious copying errors, not only in the sarabande but throughout the entire score, with no less than three distinct versions of the opera distributed at random throughout the company. Moreover, as Mr. Handel was not in attendance that day, it was impossible to determine which was correct, and so, as there was no proceeding under those circumstances, Mr. Henshaw, looking very grave, released the company for the day.

As it turned out, Mr. Handel decided that none of the three variations was exactly to his liking, but he that would rather make further revisions. Rehearsals were put on hold for an entire week as he worked through the changes, then had the scores copied out again and thrice inspected for errors.

That Sunday, to amuse themselves during this unwonted holiday, Tess called on Tom early in the morning and invited him to attend the service with her at St. Martin-in-the-fields. Tom was not by nature the church-going sort. When he lived with Lady Gray in Soho Square, she had required him to attend regularly with her every Sunday morning, a habit which (among others) had served to hasten his departure from his aunt's house. Tess herself was not particularly religious either, but she pointed out that the famous John Weldon would be playing the organ; as he was reaching advanced years, it might be the last chance to hear him, and furthermore she had heard the tenor was quite extraordinary.

Enticed by the promise of good music and the pleasure of Tess's company, Tom agreed to go. He did not mention a further reason, which was that despite his current employment at the opera, he was still producing broadsides for Shaloe

Brown and had rather hastily agreed to a composition by the week's end. As he had not yet even begun, it seemed wise to be elsewhere that day—the odious man or his agents would almost certainly come calling.

Tom, turned out smartly in his second-best red surcoat, brocade waistcoat and new white silk stockings, took Tess's arm for the very short walk along Chandos Place to St. Martin's. Once inside, Tess purposely selected for them an unoccupied pew, but just as they sat down, there followed a richly-dressed merchant with his wife and daughter. Tom and Tess were obliged to shove down along to the pew to make room, and somehow Tom ended up seated next to the daughter, a pretty girl with a lace cap, elegantly powdered curls, bright blue eyes and pink cheeks. She smiled and nodded sweetly to Tom and Tess. A moment later, her mouth went slack for a moment as she stared at Tom.

She turned to her mother and declared in a stage whisper, "The gentleman is blind!"

Tess fidgeted in annoyance and shot them an angry look that went unnoticed, but Tom seemed unaffected.

"Ladies, your servant," he said, executing a slight bow from his seat. Both mother and daughter tittered with pleasure, and the service began.

The music was indeed remarkable, the tenor with a clear, pure tone and Mr. Weldon in fine form despite his age, but Tess heard none of it. She was attuned solely to the wordless communication that seemed to be taking place between Tom and the girl, comprised mainly of little sighs and giggles. At one point, she turned to see him shamelessly holding her hand, caressing her palm with his thumb. Tess gave him a sharp blow on the shoulder with her prayer book, which caused him to jump and kick the pew in front of him.

"Oh fie, Tom, in the church? For shame!" she hissed at him.

"Let us pray," the minister intoned.

The mother at last decided that things had gone far enough; she traded places with the daughter, and that put an end to it, although by this time the service was nearly concluded.

"Really now, have you no shame?" Tess rounded on Tom angrily when they were at last out in the street again.

Tom shrugged carelessly. "She put her hand in mine, the saucy tart. What was I to do?"

"Oh aye," Tess replied in a sarcastic tone. "Well then, it was very kind of you to accompany me. I trust you can find your own way home?"

"Oh, ah, as to that, my dearest Tess, it's such a lovely day. It would be a pity to return home so quickly. What say you to a turn in the park?" Tom asked, grasping her hand, his tone quite altered.

Tess eyed him somewhat suspiciously, but it was a fine autumn day, unseasonably warm, and she had no other engagement. Taking his arm in hers, she led the way down the Strand to St. James's Park. The moment they left the street behind and entered the park, the quality of the air changed, from the rank, close breath of the city to the cool green of the grass and the trees overhead, and the slightly murky scent of the canal. Tom could hear the dull clink of the bells on the cows set to graze, the chatter of innumerable voices, rising without echo in the wide open space, and above all of them, birds singing joyfully.

It being a fine day, people of fashion thronged the mall along the center of the park, along with army officers in their scarlet and pipeclayed uniforms, and children and dogs darted about through the crowd. Tom and Tess strolled along at leisure, Tess remarking upon the fashions on display and the more singular characters she noticed. They passed by the Lactarian, pausing to buy a cup of milk, still warm from the cows grazing just beyond the gravel walk. Finding a spot by the side of the lake, that was, if not secluded, at least a bit removed from the crowds, they seated themselves on the grass.

Tom played a few country dances on a small pipe he had tucked into his pocket, then favored her with singing several popular airs.

Tess stretched and leaned back happily, enjoying the warm sunshine and Tom's rich, expressive baritone. He had instructed her in singing so often, but it was rare enough she heard him sing himself. This thought brought her mind back to the theater, and she said, "It's a pity the rehearsals are in such a sad coil, but it is pleasant to be out of the theater and in the fresh air for a change."

"Speaking of the rehearsals, what was that nonsense with the women the other day?" Tom asked. "Eckton was bellowing like a hog in a gate."

"Oh, that," said Tess, pulling at the grass. "Can't you guess? It were Peg Ashgrove. Elizabeth trod on her foot, by accident, but on purpose, if you catch my meaning. They have fallen out over a man."

"Indeed?" Tom smiled in amusement. "Who is the Don Juan in our midst?"

"Charlie Underwood," she replied, naming one of the newest, youngest members of the men's chorus.

"Underwood? You don't say! He must be ten years younger than the pair of them. What can they be thinking?"

"He said he is twenty-one, so not quite ten years younger, but close. He is very handsome, you know. Tall, square jaw, the whitest teeth I've ever seen. And he is a tenor, after all." After the exotic, other-worldly castrato, the tenor was the most highly prized and least common vocal type, afforded the best roles and the least competition for parts.

"Huh. So young Underwood dallied with Ashgrove then threw her over for Eckton. Now I can't vouch for her looks, but I do know that Eckton is older and stouter than the unhappy Ashgrove. On the other hand, he went from a mere second soprano of no great talent to an alto of much higher standing in the company, and one who regularly gets comprimario parts. Have I hit upon the reason for this defection, this reassignment of affection?"

Tess laughed. "That's about the size of it, I daresay. The

women have all been prating on about Underwood since the day he arrived. He is rather handsome, I warrant."

"So you say. Has Miss Turnbridge fallen victim to Underwood's charms as well?" Tom teased her.

"Heavens no! He is a mere pup. I only remarked that he is handsome, objectively speaking."

"And what of me?" Tom asked, striking an aristocratic pose with his head held high. "Am I handsome, objectively speaking?"

Tess scrutinized him with greater seriousness than the question demanded. His looks were more singular than classically beautiful: not only his blank gaze, which still caught her off guard from time to time, but his long face and thin features, and the boyish eagerness that so often showed through his studied air of detached amusement.

As the moments stretched on, Tom said with a smile, "Madam, you wound me with your silence."

"I—no, I—just—I'm sorry for your nose," Tess stammered.

Tom put a hand to his nose. "Is it still quite hideous?"

"No, the marks have nearly faded, but I feel somehow responsible." Matthews, the new footman, had left the door to the music room ajar, and Tom had run into it at full speed. This incident had been followed by a stern lecture to all the staff by Stinson, who was kept on in the household ex officio as it were, on the importance of keeping doors fully open or closed at all times, never halfway, and furthermore to stop leaving lit candles where the master might knock them over. The training of the new staff had not gone as seamlessly as Tess might have wished, and she felt badly about that, but Tom had made no move to cast them out.

Tom ran a finger along the length of his nose, long and thin but marred by many bumps and angles. "My dear Tess, think nothing of it. My nose has been broke so often I have lost count. I suppose it has ruined my beauty, however," he said with a laugh.

"Not at all, you are still quite handsome, I find."

"My dear, you are too kind." Tom found her hand and brought it to her lips, which also had the effect of drawing her closer. Against all reason, Tess found her heart beating faster, but just as suddenly Tom dropped her hand, his tone unusually serious. "I must not make too free with you; you are not at liberty to grant your affections."

Nor are you, Tess thought, recalling the girl in the church, not in any serious way. Still she did not move away from him, instead admitting in a soft voice, "Jane still has not returned."

"I'm very sorry to hear that," Tom said. "I know you think I dislike her, but it was never my intention to sever your intimacy with her."

Tess pulled at the grass again, heedless of the green stains on her hands. "I know. She's just being stubborn. I'm sure she has gone back to her father's house. But truthfully," she said, looking up at him, "it is a relief to be free of the bickering and sulking. Jealousy is an ugly thing. If she thinks so little of my constancy, then begone with her."

"And your duke?"

Tess sighed. "What would you have me say? That despite my pretensions to respectability, I am nothing more than a common drab, a demirep, a whore?"

Tom wrinkled his brow. "You know I would never pass judgment in that wise, and I don't give a fart for respectability. I only ask out of concern as a friend. Do you love him at all?"

"He is very good to me," she replied slowly. "He is clever and learned, openhanded and free from jealousy. He has used me with great kindness and generosity, never showing the sort of tyranny married men wield over their wives. I do not mean to avoid your question, but as I grow older I find I value kindness even over love, with its wild extremes of passion, which so quickly grows cold or turns away."

"That is the dismalest philosophy that ever I did hear," Tom declared, "and I can tell by the sound of your voice that you will not even face me as you utter it. Come now, I know there is more passion in you yet. Can I not persuade you to give him over?"

Give him over for what exactly? Tess was about to ask, but Tom put a hand to her face and drew her into a kiss. She always prided herself on her good judgment, and there were so many arguments against his suggestion. Aside from her own feelings for Jane, and for the duke, to whom she was deeply attached, whatever one might call it, Tom was in every way a poor companion: improvident, feckless, an unrepentant rake, overfond of drink. And it was not only the girl in the church that weighed on her mind. Although on this pleasant outing Tom seemed nearly returned to his usual carefree self, from time to time he fell silent, and she knew that thoughts of Sal still oppressed his spirits to a great degree. Yet all this flashed through her mind in an instant; as the increasingly insistent kiss sent heat coursing through her, she tamped those thoughts down and allowed passion to carry her for the moment.

Things might have gone very much further, but Tess was all too conscious of prying eyes. Receiving him at her house was out of the question, and now Tom's house was no longer as private has it had been previously. She might have slipped by Stinson, but Tess had no desire to be discovered in an indecent posture by the very servants she herself had hired, and for a moment she selfishly regretted having taken that step. So it was that they passed a pleasant afternoon together in the park, but the desire between them, more insistent for having been acknowledged, went unsatisfied.

CHAPTER FOUR: MRS. CARSTONE

The rehearsals for *Il pastor fido* were still on hiatus, pending the distribution of the corrected scores, when Tom received an unexpected visitor at the house on Maiden Lane. He was seated at the spinet in the music room, working through a composition that he might creditably present to Shaloe Brown, and wondering if he could reset the song "Lemady" if it were not already too much in circulation, when he was startled out of his concentration by the voice of Matthews, the new footman.

"A Mrs. Carstone to see you, sir," he said. Tom paused for a moment, trying to think where he knew that name, when the owner of the name burst into the room, abandoning all decorum.

"Tommy! By God, it's good to see you again!"

"Charlotte!" Tom leapt up and into the warm embrace of his half-sister.

"Let me take a look at you—I swear, you look even more like Father every day, just as if you was spit out of his mouth. Dammee, how long has it been?"

In fact it had been just over ten years since Tom and Charlotte had lived in Soho Square with their aunt. Lady Gray had succeeded in marrying Charlotte's two elder sisters to respectable but dull men: Sophia to a wealthy baronet and Anne to the younger son of an earl. But Charlotte had rebelled, and less than a year after Tom had come to live with them, she contracted a dubious alliance and ran off with an officer in their brother Richard's regiment, Captain Hartsly Carstone of H.M. 42nd Regiment of Foot, who had since been promoted to colonel. He married Charlotte out of hand, and off she went with his regiment, garrisoned for the most part over the years in Wallonia.

Tom noticed immediately that her stay with the regiment had had a coarsening effect on her—Charlotte had not previously been so prone to swearing, nor had her voice possessed that hard metallic edge. Still, she was his sister, and the only one among his sprawling, scandalous pack of siblings with whom he had something approaching friendship.

"You're looking very well," she continued. "But why are you wearing your own hair like a common laborer? Will you let me buy you a wig?"

"I will not," he replied firmly. "I find them dreadfully itchy, and they invariably become infested with fleas."

"Well at the very least, you must use powder. That brown color is so very *common*."

Tom disliked powder almost as much as a wig; the smell was disagreeable and it flaked everywhere: under his collar, onto his hands, into his food. But in order to deflect an argument so soon into their reunion, he instead bade her to make herself easy and called for tea.

"However did you find me here?" Tom asked when they had settled in comfortably. "I believe the last time I saw you, you was climbing out your bedroom window in Soho Square."

Charlotte laughed. "Oh but Tommy, you is quite famous! Everyone has heard about your duel. Didn't you wipe that Frenchie's eye! We was all so proud! And wasn't Mrs. Fitzpatrick jealous when I told her you was my own brother. A blind man can't fight a duel says she, but you don't know our Tommy, says I, he is the cleverest cove." She chattered on, as if Tom were intimately acquainted with the details of her life, rather than only just meeting her for the first time in ten years.

From what he could gather, it appeared the 42nd Regiment had returned from Wallonia several months ago and was currently garrisoned at Deal, from whence Charlotte had made numerous visits to London, rather on the sly, it seemed.

"Where is the Frenchie's wife, then?" she asked, looking about expectantly. "I heard you got a brat on her and stole her away from him."

"What stuff! I'm surprised at you, Charlotte, believing any old tittle-tattle. I tell you there was never any child, and as for the lady in question, I imagine she is at home still with her husband in Paris."

"Is that so?" Charlotte replied, disappointed.

From there, the conversation rambled on to family gossip. Jamie, the young heir, was supposedly in London, while his two younger sisters had not yet come out into society and were still at Culverleigh. But having long since given up all thoughts of inheritance, neither Tom nor Charlotte were much interested in the children of the second Lady Bolingbroke. Their talk soon turned to Charlotte's sisters, the daughters of the first Lady Bolingbroke. Sophia, the eldest, had five children, but Anne had none, and was eating her heart out with jealousy. All this Tom had heard already in great detail from Lady Gray, but she very rarely spoke of the other boys.

Charlotte, however, seemed far more informed when he inquired after Philip and Paul, both following careers in the Royal Navy, with varying success. Philip, the younger of the two, had already been made post captain, although he currently had no ship and was idling the years away in Deal on half-pay. Paul, on the other hand, was suffering the indignity of being a thirty-five year old lieutenant with no chance of promotion to post captain. He had fallen behind his younger brother in rank years ago, when he had been disrated and turned before the mast for insubordination. Even after being reinstated as midshipman, he had twice failed the test to pass for lieutenant. Now having achieved that rank with the greatest difficulty, he seemed destined to rise no higher. He was currently serving as third lieutenant on HMS *Antelope* in the Downs; Charlotte had seen him the previous year when the ship called at Antwerp.

"He's grown fat and stodgy," she declared. "Married some blowen in the Fleet several years back, but he'll never amount to anything, mark my words." The Fleet prison was the favored location for clandestine marriages, when the parties involved did not wish to be troubled by parental consent, banns, or the laws against bigamy. Charlotte herself had been wed to Hartsly Carstone in the Fleet, but Tom chose not to belabor the point.

"And Philip, is he married yet?" Tom inquired.

Charlotte gave a braying laugh. "Not likely! He's a regular Miss Molly, that one. A sodomite," she elaborated.

"Such fellows usually do marry," Tom observed. "Behold my lord Thistlethwayte."

"I tell you, Philip has no interest in women," she maintained. "And if he is not more discreet, he will come to grief, I warrant." Sodomy was illegal, both on land and at sea, and the penalty was death by hanging. They fell silent for a moment, contemplating this grim fate.

Having exhausted the news of their siblings, Tom ventured to ask after Colonel Carstone. Tom had never cared for the man and had tried to persuade Charlotte that he was a blackguard, but in her girlish imagination, he was her manly hero, and there had been no dissuading her from flinging herself into his arms.

"Oh Tommy!" she burst out. "He is a villain! An infamous brute! You can't imagine the cruelty I have endured. I can hardly bear to speak of it." Her voice trembled in every appearance of genuine distress. Wives of soldiers who lived in the garrison with their husbands, even the wives of officers, were expected to act as servants to the men, in return for being allowed lodging and rations, and Tom had no doubt Charlotte must have found conditions with the regiment much harder than the privileged life she had known as a girl.

And while the British Army was enjoying one of its rare intervals of relative peace, such inactivity could not but have an adverse effect on one such as Carstone, who was prone to violence.

Tom made some vague sympathetic noises, but to his dismay, this only increased her agitation. With a sob, she flung herself to the floor before his chair and grabbed his hands beseechingly. Tom was startled—the women of his father's side of the family were not usually given to such emotional outbursts.

"I can't bear it any longer!" Charlotte wailed. "The work is bad enough, slaving all day, morning 'til night for a pack of stinking drunken louts, but..." she trailed off in a series of choked sobs.

"Does he beat you?" Tom asked uneasily, disliking where this all was heading. He felt her nod against his hand, now wet with her tears.

"Please, Tommy, let me stay here with you," she begged, "When he finds I've gone, he'll try to kill me, I'm sure."

Tom's heart sank. "So this is not merely a social visit? You've run away," he said heavily. "But why come to me? I must tell you plainly, I've hardly any money. You will find things here rather uncomfortable, I fear. Why not go to Aunt Sarah? Or Culverleigh?" he suggested hopefully.

"But those are the first places he will look for me! Oh, you've no idea what a villain he is!" She sobbed some more, then added, "Please, he will never look for me here."

"Can you not talk to Richard, ask him to intervene on your behalf?" Tom asked, still not prepared to be overcome so easily.

"Oh fie, Richard will never go against his superior officer. You know, Richard is even worse than Paul, he's very near to being broke and dismissed the service. Hart is the only officer he ain't crossed, the only one who still supports him. Richard would sooner see me in my grave than say anything to Hart."

Tom agreed that Richard was if anything an even worse

blackguard than Carstone. He patted Charlotte's head awkwardly, covered as it was by vast hair cushions and a stiff lace cap. "Very well, you may stay here," he said, regretting the words even as he uttered them.

As Tom was instructing the servants to arrange for what would likely be a protracted stay for his half-sister (she had come with a large trunk, Frankie reported), Tess rapped at the front door. The lengthy break in the rehearsals was at last come to a close, and she came bearing the new score, which she intended to play through for him to review the changes. This was something of a pretext, however, as she also intended to take up the subject of their previous conversation, that is, to attempt to see if he was serious about her making a break with the duke. Since their excursion to St. James's Park, she had been able to think of nothing else. The duke had indeed been more distant of late; his wife, whom he had neglected for years, had fallen ill, and feeling pangs of conscience at last, he was spending more time with her. Perhaps the time was right after all.

With these thoughts swirling in her head, she found her heart pounding and her hand faltered even as she knocked at the familiar door. Matthews answered in a rather slovenly, careless fashion.

"Yes?" he demanded, his body blocking the open doorway.

"Let me in, you oaf," she said, "and tell your master Miss Turnbridge is here with the new score."

"Master's occupied with a Mrs. Carstone," Matthews replied undaunted, without moving from the doorway. As Tess goggled at him, he suddenly recalled his master's clear instructions not to relay Mrs. Carstone's name to callers, and he clapped his mouth shut with a guilty look, then added with careful emphasis, "I mean, the master is entertaining a *lady visitor*. I can't say no more, miss."

Tess felt her heart hammering in her chest, her thoughts running at double-time: a lady? already? what a fool I've been

—she thrust the heavy conductor's score into the footman's hands.

"Here, just give this to him. Call Mr. Castleton to read it out, and tell Mr. Finch that rehearsals start again tomorrow," she said in a rush, then fled down the street.

The next day found Tess hurrying across the Covent Garden Piazza on her way to the opera house, the chilly autumn wind catching at her wide skirts. As she dodged the urchins and hawkers, the sound of a familiar voice caught her attention: there, beyond the fruit sellers, strolling in a leisurely fashion before St. Paul's, was Tom Finch, on the arm of a lady who must be Mrs. Carstone. She was a small woman with a rather pinched, sallow face, not particularly young, and on the whole rather plain, Tess noted vindictively, and her clothes were fashionable but just a bit shabby. Tom, on the other hand, was in fine twig, done up with more care than usual, his cravat neatly tied and rakishly pulled through his buttonhole, his hair powdered. As she watched, Mrs. Carstone gave a grating peal of laughter and pressed herself up against him, while Tom smiled and nodded.

Tess felt a surge of anger. Since the embarrassing incident with the footman, her mind had been filled with self-recrimination. She knew she had been a fool to expect anything of Tom, and it was mortifying to realize how far she had been taken in. Even now she could hardly bear to admit even to herself how absurdly her fantasies had run on: shameful visions not only of base venery, but of herself running the household in Maiden Lane. Now, seeing him in person with another, her anger turned away from herself and towards him. Had he not professed his affection for her, even begged her to leave the duke for him, not only that drunken night, but just a few days previous, in the park? Her only solace was that she had not yet spoken to the duke.

Cutting across the market to avoid crossing the path of Tom and Mrs. Carstone, Tess picked her way with difficulty around the fruit and vegetable stalls and toward the theater.

The thought of endless rehearsal hours with Tom as music master made her feel even lower in spirits, but still, she was a professional, and she swore she would not give the gossips the satisfaction of making a scene.

To everyone's relief, the break seemed to have dissipated some of the tensions within the company, and the rehearsal ran smoothly for a change. With Tom busy in the orchestra pit, it was not hard for Tess to avoid him. During the breaks, she had previously been in the habit of seeking him out for a friendly chat, but now she remained backstage with the other women. Sensing a sister in frustrated amour, Peg Ashgrove flung herself down into a chair beside Tess during one of the breaks and kicked off her tight heeled shoes.

"D'ye ken that blowsy tart Master Finch come in with?" Peg asked, favoring Tess with a knowing, commiserating grin.

"I've no idea what you're talking about," Tess replied haughtily.

"Oh aye, mum for that," Peg agreed with a vulgar wink. "But between you and me, she's a plain-faced jade, no charm at all." She looked across the empty stage to the wings on the opposite side, where young Underwood was entertaining a crowd of women from the chorus. "Men, bah, no better than dogs, every last one of 'em," she declared. "They can all go to the devil for all I care!" to which Tess most heartily agreed.

Several days later, when Tess returned home late after rehearsal, there was a letter awaiting her, wafered and sealed with the stamp of the Duke of Grafton. Sending the maid away, she sank slowly into a chair in the tastefully appointed parlor and unfolded the letter with trembling hands.

5 November, 1736

My Dear Miss Turnbridge,

It is with the Greatest Reluctance and a *Heavy Heart* that I must request an End to our Acquaintance. I trust you know that I hold your PERSON in the Highest Regard, and it grieves me to think that I might cause you *pain* or in any way inflict harm upon you or your Reputation. However, I have been informed by Physicians of Good Repute that my WYFE'S condition is very much *deteriorated*, indeed that the End is not far off. This being the case, I have returned to her side & resumed my duties as HUSBAND, of which I had been so remiss over the years. She has returned these attentions with such Grace and Humilitie that I cannot but feel I have gravely wronged her, and that indeed her illness is in some way Divine Punishment for my *sinful behavior*. From this moment, I have vowed to renounce my Venal Ways, & lead a life of Virtue, as befits this NOBLE LADY, regardless of however short our remaining time may be. For I tell you plainly, I too feel the press of *mortalitie* upon me; I am not a Young Man, and may not tarry long behind her. Pray do not take this Separation as a slight against yourself, but think fondly on our time together, as I do still. I wish you a Future Life of *virtue* & happiness.

> Yours in friendship,
> Charles FitzRoy &c.

The word virtue was underlined several times. Tess let the letter fall from her hands onto the carpet. So it was done: he had jilted her at last. And yet the letter was so handsomely worded, she could hardly be angry with him. It was only right that he return to his wife to ease her suffering, and he broke with her without casting aspersions on her character. He also, she noted, did not mention providing her with any future support.

For some time, she sat alone in the flickering light of the diminishing candle, numb to all emotion, but at last the tears came in a torrent. Even as she castigated herself for wallowing in self-pity, somehow she only cried that much harder. Alone, alone, abandoned on all sides, when she had thought she was being so clever. She had a great fondness for the duke, even if it might not be called love, and he quite old and not particularly handsome, yet she enjoyed his company and his kindness. Despite the scandal, she found there were many advantages to being a kept woman, chief among them that she remained her own mistress. She had always known this arrangement would not continue indefinitely, and as a hedge against this very day, she had insisted on gifts of jewels and plate, which might be readily converted to cash. She need not fear for her income, and as an actress on the stage, her reputation was no better nor worse than expected, but the thought of seeking out a new patron depressed her extremely.

As much as she felt her tears were for the duke, however, if she was honest with herself, it was to Tom Finch that her thoughts circled back repeatedly. She knew he was not in earnest, that he was merely toying with her, as a habitual seducer of women; still the thought that she was already replaced wounded her far, far more deeply than she ever expected. My God, she thought, have I fallen in love with that man? Truly in love, so that no other could take his place in my affections? Not wanting to call her maids and have them see her in such distress, she retired to the bedroom, undressed on her own with some difficulty and fell into an uneasy sleep.

The next morning Tess awoke with a clear-eyed sense of action and firm determination not to repeat the previous night's useless display of sentiment. She resolved to dismiss all the servants, take stock of her assets, and remove from the house that was never truly her own. She must take more care of her expenditures, and in any case she disliked being an object of pity in her own home. She wrote a polite but distant letter to the duke, informing him of her intentions and leaving the sale of the house and its furnishings to him. She was just sanding the letter when one of the maids announced a caller.

"Mistress Carlyle, madam," she said with a curtsy, her eyes trained on the floor in an extreme effort to suppress any expression on her face.

Tess looked up in surprise. There in the doorway was Jane,

in a pale blue cloak trimmed with fur, her gray eyes wide with concern. Tess hesitated, uncertain how to receive her, but Jane, abandoning all animosity and even propriety, rushed across the room and embraced her tightly.

"Oh my dearest Tessa, I've heard everything—I couldn't bear to think of you all alone. I'm so sorry we quarreled! Promise we won't never part again!" Jane cried, tears starting in her eyes, and her pale, heart-shaped face flushed with emotion.

Tess returned her embrace gladly, wiping the tears from Jane's face and kissing her. "I am leaving this house today and taking rooms in Covent Garden again. Will you come with me, sweetheart?" she asked. "It will be just like the old days at the Rose." Jane agreed eagerly, and Tess put all thoughts of the duke and of Tom Finch out of her head.

CHAPTER FIVE: THE DRUNKEN MAIDENS

Tom was not formerly accustomed to taking an elaborate dinner at home, but since the installation of the new servants, most importantly, Susan the cook, and since the arrival of his half-sister Charlotte, dinner seemed to have become a regular occurrence before departing for the theater. Jem Castleton, who well knew how to press his own advantage, had taken to showing up early, nominally in his capacity as Tom's official assistant, yet somehow, without being precisely invited, he had become a regular guest at dinner.

"The end of rehearsals at last, hey Finchy?" Jem commented, helping himself to an additional mutton chop. Susan's cooking was not what one might call imaginative or stylish, but it was hearty.

"Not a moment too soon," Tom replied with a laugh. "After today that tone-deaf pack of layabouts is wholly Mr. Handel's concern, not mine." He swept his fork about on his plate, searching for any undiscovered remains of his chop. "What a damned muddle these rehearsals have been from start to finish. Serves Mr. Rich right for giving half the chorus the sack. Matthews, another chop if you please."

The footman cleared his throat, eying Jem uncomfortably. "If you please, sir, I'll just see if there's more in the kitchen."

Jem drained his wine glass without the least shade of remorse and poured himself another. "We ought to have a proper celebration tonight," he said. "Ask your Miss Turnbridge to join us. She ain't been out with us in weeks."

"You mean the prima donna?" asked Charlotte. "Are you on such intimate terms with her, then?"

Ignoring her, Tom replied, "She ain't called, or even said how d'ye do at rehearsals. She's in a fit of pique over something, no doubt, but damned if I know what it is."

Matthews reappeared at his elbow and gave a discreet cough. "Cook sends her regrets, sir, says there ain't no more mutton. But there's more souse and a lovely eel pie on the table, sir. Shall I serve you some?"

Tom nodded, and Jem said, "Well, I expect she's ashamed to go out in company after being jilted by her duke. Devilish awkward, you know."

"What? When did that happen?" Tom said in surprise.

Jem laughed. "Ain't you heard? It were weeks ago. Old Fitz-Roy suffered an attack of conscience in the end, or I should say, his wife's end, ha ha ha. Sent Miss Turnbridge a letter and that was that, the dog."

Tom, now wholly distracted, poked at the souse with his fork. "I had no idea. Poor Tess."

Charlotte looked up sharply. "Tess, is it? Dammee, but you are on intimate terms!"

Jem, realizing belatedly that the conversation was moving in an unfortunate direction, turned his attention to Charlotte.

"Tell me, Mrs. Carstone," he said, "I've heard the 42nd Foot is to be posted to Halifax come the spring. How much longer are we to enjoy your company here?"

Tom gave a warning cough, and too late Jem realized he had made a worse blunder.

Charlotte kicked her chair back from the table, making the dishes rattle. "Never!" she cried in a sudden passion. "I'll never go to Halifax! I'd sooner lead apes in hell than go back to Hart!"

"Well then, what are you going to do?" Tom asked impatiently.

"I want a divorce!" she burst out.

Tom sighed wearily. "But that's very difficult and expensive," he said. She had been hinting in this direction for some time, but this was the first time she had put it into words.

"Perhaps if you took a lover, Mr. Carstone could sue for criminal conversation," Jem suggested with a lewd wink at her.

Charlotte looked away haughtily, while Tom uttered a strange sound, halfway between a cough and a laugh. It was plain to all the residents of number eight Maiden Lane that Charlotte in fact had a lover already, a lieutenant of the light dragoons named Nathaniel Welgarth, an active young man much in the habit of climbing in through Charlotte's bedroom window at night. The first time he had attempted this, he mistook the window and arrived unannounced in the footman's room, where Matthews knocked him on the head with a fire-iron, having taken him for a housebreaker. The blow left a wicked-looking welt, but the young man, once he came round again, had borne Matthews no ill will. In any case, however, the secret was out, and it was clear to Tom that it was this liaison that had precipitated Charlotte's flight to his house, and more to the point, now that she had a secret trysting place, she seemed in no hurry to leave.

"Oh, Hart would never take me to court," Charlotte replied airily. "He says lawyers are the worst kind of scrubs. Never mind crim. con., he would demand satisfaction in the more traditional way."

"Enough of that," Tom said, passing a hand over his face. "Let us have no public scenes, hey? Matthews, where is that claret?" He drained off the glass Matthews filled for him, and another, then departed for the theater with Jem, having avoided further talk of duels or of Charlotte's domestic affairs.

The rehearsal went tolerably well, as these things go. There were the usual missed cues, misremembered lines, dropped notes, and lost properties, but opening night would serve to concentrate the minds of all the company, and most of those errors would not be repeated.

Signors Farinelli and Urbani seemed to have reached an unspoken detente which involved a code of silence offstage, and facing away from each other onstage, even when exchanging dialog, but as this had the effect of projecting their voices more clearly, it hardly signified.

Peg Underwood, having found a sympathetic ear in Tess Turnbridge, complained loudly of the inconstancy of men, particularly young coxcomb tenors who were coming it mighty high, but she seemed content to eagerly await divine punishment rather than seeking direct revenge on her rival and erstwhile lover.

In short, the company had settled into no more than the usual state of tension and frantic preparation before an opening. The seamstresses were sewing the costumes on the actors, right up to the moment before the wearer's entrance onstage, and the green room stank with the smell of the wigmakers' hot irons. At least the orchestra had at last all learnt the same notes and everyone was, in theory at least, in agreement as to the score, and from Tom's perspective that was the most that could be expected. With the audiences as raucous and inattentive as they were, talking and playing cards, parading in the aisles, calling down from the boxes and even wandering onto the stage, a few errors would hardly be noticed.

When the rehearsal had ended at last, Tom found himself lingering with Jem by the stage door that backed into Bow Street. Charlotte joined them, and Tom was eager to be off.

"Enough of this damnable delay. I am famished, my supper is calling to me," Tom said rather snappishly.

Jem did not answer directly, but made some vague noises while patting him reassuringly on the arm. Just as Tom was beginning to wonder if this was not some artful plan, Jem cried out, "Ah, Miss Turnbridge! You was in fine voice today. By tomorrow you'll be the toast of the beaux, I warrant. Won't you step round to the public house with us? We was just about to find our supper. Tom here is fairly fainting with hunger, so he says."

"Yes, won't you join us?" Tom added, directing a smile in what he hoped was her direction.

Tess frowned uncertainly. "It's very kind of you, but I'm not—I mean, I'm afraid I…" As she trailed off, Jem noticed her gaze fixed on Charlotte, who had her arm entwined companionably with Tom's.

Jem leapt forward with a capacious gesture in Charlotte's direction. "Miss Turnbridge, you must excuse poor Tom's shocking rudeness—he can't help it, the sorry flat. I don't believe you have yet been introduced to his sister. May I present Mrs. Charlotte Carstone? Mrs. Carstone, Miss Tessa Turnbridge."

"How d'ye do," Charlotte said, with a curtsy.

"Sister?" Tess echoed faintly, looking rather blank.

"Why yes, who else would she be?" Jem slapped his thigh in an elaborate show of mirth that would not have been out of place in the theater behind them. "You never thought…? Oh my, ha ha ha!"

"You will come with us, won't you?" Tom repeated, directing an earnest grin more nearly in her vicinity.

Yet still Tess hesitated. Turning to the person beside her, she asked, "Do you want to go, sweetheart?"

To Tom's astonishment, it was the voice of Jane Carlyle that replied, and even more surprising, in a mild, temperate tone she declared, "I should like nothing better."

And so they all proceeded as a party to the Labor in Vain, along with a tiny, very young girl from the chorus whom Jem had been endeavoring to seduce these past few weeks. They called for food in great quantities and cans of beer in even greater quantities, and soon everyone was rather elevated in spirits. Even Jane laid herself out to be agreeable.

"My goodness, Tom, I had no idea you had such a large and colorful family," Tess remarked, after Charlotte had regaled them all with the family gossip, with particular emphasis on her own tale of woe. "I thought you were quite on your own, apart from your lady aunt."

"Oh no, on my mother's side I am the only one left, I assure you, but the earl's various progeny are prodigious. All told, I have four brothers and five sisters," Tom replied, then added, "That we know of, at any rate. I'm sure there are others unaccounted for. I tell you, Tess, I envy your solitary condition."

Tess laughed a bit uncomfortably. "Oh no, like you it is all one-sided. True, I have no relations on my father's side here in England, but in Napoli and the surrounding area, on my mother's side I have aunts, uncles, and cousins by the score."

"Indeed?" Charlotte was excited to hear this. "I have longed to travel to Naples, but no, we must tramp around Holland and Flanders, where it is always cold and damp, a most wretched climate."

"I would be happy to make introductions for you if you choose to go," Tess offered. "You would not want for a place to stay."

Charlotte took on the martyred expression she had perfected of late. "Nay, it's no use. So long as I am shackled to that dreadful man, I am no more than a prisoner, obliged to skulk about like a common convict." She sighed dramatically. Tom cringed inwardly at this display, although at least she had cleaned up her language. It was rather amusing how awed Charlotte was by Tess. Did Tess really cut such a figure, he wondered. He still thought of her as she was in their days at the shabby old Rose.

Tess laid a sympathetic hand on Charlotte's arm. "We must find some way to help you," she said, and Charlotte brightened considerably.

"Aye, we were just talking it over earlier today," Jem put it. "Ain't your brother in the same regiment? Can't he do anything at all?"

"You mean Richard?" Charlotte asked with distaste.

"Richard is a vile blackguard," Tom said with vehemence that surprised them. Tess had never heard him speak so angrily against anyone before.

"Fie, Tom, how can you speak so ill of your own brother?"

Tess said.

Charlotte waved a hand dismissively. "Oh, it's quite true, I assure you, Richard is a blackguard. Anyway, I believe Tom still bears a grudge against him because of the incident with Miss Betty."

"Whatever do you mean," Tom muttered, shifting about uncomfortably, in what Tess realized was a fit of embarrassment. He felt about on the table for his mug, and finding it empty, called for more rather over-loudly.

"Who was Miss Betty?" Tess asked.

"Yes, you can't leave us guessing," Jane chimed in. Even Jem had never heard this story, and was alive with curiosity.

"Miss Betty was a second cousin or some such to our poor Mama, sent to look after us after she died, a sort of tutor or governess, you might call her, but very young and pretty," Charlotte said, settling into her tale with relish. "The summer that Tom and the other boys came to stay with us at Culverleigh—that's the family seat in Bedfordshire, you know—anyway, that summer Tom had such an attachment to her."

"What stuff," Tom protested.

Charlotte carried on, ignoring him. "To put it plainly, he fell in love with her. But it were Richard who seduced her. Our stepmother found them out, Miss Betty was turned out, the poor creature, and that was that. Tom never forgave Richard, even cracked him right in the nose. Dam-, I mean, my goodness but we were all surprised."

"Upon my word, what tales you tell, Charlotte," Tom said. "That time I hit Richard was before Miss Betty left, the one had nothing to do with the other."

"But you did hit him, then?" Jem asked.

"Yes, but it were only an accident. I daresay he deserved it, though. Since we are exhuming the past, dear sister, did you ever hear what became of Miss Betty?"

"No, never," she replied, and Tom fell silent, frowning a bit. Charlotte gave Tess a knowing look, as if to say, see, I told you so.

At last Tom said, "I venture you are correct, Richard would never help; in fact he is likely to take Carstone's side. But did you not say that Philip is in Deal as well? Ain't he in the military way?"

"Philip is a captain in the navy," Charlotte corrected.

"It's all one," Tom said. Charlotte knew very well it was not, far from it, but she did not attempt to explain the divide between the army and the navy to a pack of mere civilians.

Jem slapped his hand on the table. "That's a capital idea," he declared. "Let's send for this Captain Philip and see if he can't render assistance. Have you any other brothers lounging about, while we're at it?"

"None that would be of any use," Tom said.

Having made a general decision to find someone else to aid Charlotte in her marital difficulty, they all felt much relieved, and drank to her health, to the success of the opera, and to the king, draining bumper after bumper, until all were quite merry. Jem began to sing "Back and Sides," beating the table vigorously to keep the time, and one song followed another. At last, wary of straining her voice before opening night, Tess bid them good night. She and Jane departed quietly, leaving Tom and Jem roaring away, with Charlotte joining in here and there, and the little chorus girl looking quite at sea as the songs became increasingly bawdy.

There was four drunken maidens came from the Isle of Wight
They drank from Monday morning nor stopped 'til Saturday night
Saturday night it came, me boys, before they would give out
These four drunken maidens, they pushed the jug about

There came four farmers, of courage stout and strong
And giving to each maiden a prick nine inches long
A prick nine inches long, me boys, before they would give out
These four drunken maidens, they pushed the jug about

The strains of the tune followed them out the door, and Jane was still laughing when they returned home. Tess felt as if a great burden had been lifted from her breast to find Jane at last warmed to Tom as a friend. It had been a sore trial to her spirits that the two people she loved best in the world were so at odds. Tess did not know what more she could do to prove her constancy to Jane—was not Jane the one who was always leaving her? Tess was happy with her unconventional way of life, but for all that Jane complained that Tess would one day leave her for Tom, Tess suspected that it was Jane who longed for a respectable marriage.

"Well, well, so it turns out Mrs. Carstone was his sister," Jane remarked with amusement as they settled into bed together. "The field is clear, then, ain't it? Won't you tell him how you feel?"

Tess shook her head. "It doesn't matter. Maybe he hasn't taken someone new just yet, but he will soon, mark my words. You were right in what you said before, he will never be constant. It's only a matter of time. And although he may act merry on the surface, I can tell that within he is still grieved over Sal. It just wouldn't be right." Jane seemed ready to argue, but Tess cut her off with an intemperate kiss. "Besides, my dearest Jane, after all those storms, now I am wholly yours, and so happy to be so. Pray don't spoil it."

CHAPTER SIX:
CAPTAIN LINDSEY

At the same time that Tom and the others departed for at the Labor in Vain the night after the last rehearsal, the weedy young tenor Charlie Underwood was also leaving the theater. As he walked out the stage door, Charlie caught sight of Peg Ashgrove in Bow Street, still wearing the heavy greasepaint she had neglected to remove in her hurry to return home to her supper. Seeing her there, in the dirty moonlit street, her face glowing even more garishly than those of the street-walkers plying their trade all about them, he thought she had never looked so lovely.

"Oi, Peg, fancy a pint?" he called to her.

Peg turned on her heel and stared him up and down. Her rival Elizabeth Eckton was nowhere in sight. "You're footing the bill," she declared.

Charlie shrugged. "Why not?"

They together repaired to the Essex Serpent for a can of ale, and thence to parts unknown—no one saw them until the next day, when they arrived back at the theater looking rather disheveled and conspiratorial.

The story reached Elizabeth's ears even before the dressers finished helping her into her costume, thanks to a very young stagehand, urged on by several busy, gossipy choristers. Much to everyone's disappointment, Elizabeth did not fly into a full-throated passion immediately. She was a hefty contralto, and it was generally agreed that she could easily overpower the slighter soprano, but for the moment Elizabeth merely expressed her outrage by throwing a shoe at the door of her dressing room as the unfortunate bearer of the news departed in haste.

Elizabeth collected herself, however, and the show began smoothly. The crisis did not occur until that awkward bit of staging in the second act, when Elizabeth was obliged to make her entrance by crossing in front of Peg. Afterwards, the women of the chorus, who were also arranged about the stage, argued passionately for differing versions of events: some said that clearly Peg had tripped Elizabeth, or purposely trod on the hem of her gown, while others claimed with equal certainty, that no, Elizabeth had given Peg a wicked shove, or an elbow to the ribs.

Whatever the cause, within a moment they were going at it hammer and tongs, right in the middle of the stage, shrieking and clawing at each other. The other women of the chorus stood watching, slack-jawed in surprise, while the audience, for once paying full attention to the action on stage, hooted and called for more; meanwhile, the orchestra, seated in the pit, with their backs to the stage, played on for several more bars before realizing something was amiss. Collins the stage manager shot out of the wings, followed by several stagehands, and pulled them apart, as Mr. Handel, who was conducting in the pit, rapped angrily with his baton, his face livid with rage. Collins carried Peg offstage bodily, as the less essential of the two, while Elizabeth was shoved into her position, but Mr. Handel vengefully skipped right over her aria directly to the finale.

The audience was enchanted by this display of raw passion and clamored for more right through the finale. From their seats in the stalls, Jem described the scene to Tom, and both laughed heartily over it, imagining the various punishments the two women might face. At the very least it seemed certain that both women would be dismissed the company.

By the next morning, news of the fight was all over London, spread in no small part by a handbill hastily run up by Mr. Shaloe Brown of Henrietta Street, containing the eyewitness account of a Mr. James Castleton, who reported that the two women had clawed at each other so mightily that they had each torn away the front of the other's dress, revealing their breasts to all and sundry, but so transported by the rage of frustrated love that neither had shown an ounce of modesty.

That night, the theater was packed to the rafters with spectators eager for a repeat performance. Realizing this was a stroke of luck for an otherwise poorly reviewed, old-fashioned opera, and a revival at that, Mr. Rich allowed Elizabeth and Peg to remain in their roles, but with a strict proviso that if they cut any more such capers, they would both find themselves out on the street, ticket sales be damned. Over the next week, the opera played uneventfully to a full house every night, Jem received a guinea from Shaloe Brown for the handbill, and everyone was well content. Everyone, that is, apart from Peg Ashgrove, who found herself jilted once more after that single night.

As for Tom, he found this all highly amusing, but in truth he was far more concerned with finding a way to remove his wayward sister from his house.

"It's all very well to talk of familial sentiment," Tom remarked to Jem as they sat drinking wine at the Labor in Vain, "but a man longs for his privacy, if you know what I mean. She says she dares not go abroad on her own, so there she is in the house all day long, with that cove Welgarth sneaking about at night liked a damned housebreaker. It was one thing while I was taken up with rehearsals all day, but now I should like to return to composing, only there she is in the music room with the hairdresser or what have you. I tell you, it's the outside of enough."

"Still, she ain't all bad," said Jem. "D'ye know she's teaching Frankie to read?" Jem had taken to Charlotte; he admired her style and dash, so unlike actresses, given to airy histrionics.

He had succeeded in seducing the chorus girl, but though she still sent him hopeful notes, his attention had soon wandered.

"Is she now?" said Tom with surprise.

"Aye, he's a clever lad, eager to learn. I warrant he'll put me out of a job, ha ha ha."

Still, if Frankie were to take over from Jem as Tom's amanuensis, it would not be for many years, and in the meantime, it fell to Jem to draft a letter summoning Tom's brother Philip to London to assist Charlotte in escaping her husband.

As it happened, Philip was eager for an excuse to make the trip from Deal to London, and within the week Captain Moorehouse, R.N. (for he, like Tom, had taken his mother's name) was being shown into the front parlor at number eight Maiden Lane. He was a fair-faced man, no longer quite young, but still in the prime of life, with bright blue eyes. He had already lost the sunburned countenance of a sea captain after over a year on shore; instead he had a pale and rather anxious cast, the look of one prone to worry. Like Tom, he wore his own hair, tied back in a queue, although it was rather mousy and wispy. Charlotte he had seen often in Deal, but he had not met Tom since that one summer in Culverleigh over twenty years previous, when they were children. Still, he greeted Tom and Charlotte with equal affection, embracing them and kissing them both on the cheek.

"By God, you're the very spit of the old earl!" Philip said to Tom.

"So everyone says," Tom demurred as they embraced.

Tom was startled to find on embracing him that Philip was at least a head shorter than he. As children, Philip, who was a few years older, had always been taller; indeed Tom's memories of his three elder brothers were all of enormous, terrifying brutes ready to attack at any moment. True, once Richard was sent away, Philip had been more friendly, but Tom had always remained somewhat wary of him. Now Tom could hardly reconcile the small, slight man before him with his memory of his elder brother. Even his voice was utterly altered.

For his part, Philip regarded Tom with a confusion of strong emotion. Among the other marks of his profession, Philip sported a wicked scar just above his right eye, bisecting his eyebrow and giving him a permanent look of surprise. The scar was the result of an action with a band of Barbary pirates off Tripoli: amid the cannon fire, an enormous splinter of wood had struck him in the face, glancing off his brow less than an inch above his eye, stunning him and knocking him flat. The ship's surgeon had cheerfully informed him as he sewed him up that had the splinter been a hair lower, he would have been struck blind, for such injuries to one eye invariably spread to the other. It was on account of this action that Philip was made post captain, yet the surgeon's words had hung over him, putting a damper on his joy at promotion. He had always thought kindly of his brother, in a general sort of way, when he thought of him at all, which had not been often. But having narrowly escaped becoming blind himself, he found himself thinking of Tom frequently, with a mixture of horror, primarily for himself and what might have been, and respect, even awe at Tom's seemingly complacent acceptance of his affliction. Even more, however, Philip was troubled by the sad thought that he himself might not have responded to that condition with the same moral fortitude; in short, he felt low and cowardly by comparison.

These were not the kind of thoughts a man could share freely, yet they still occupied his mind, and as a result Philip remained rather diffident and reserved at this first meeting. The three took a rather formal tea in the front parlor, then Charlotte tactfully withdrew.

"A rum bit of business," Philip said quietly as Charlotte's wide skirts swept out the doorway.

"I am sorry to impose on you," Tom said, "but perhaps there might be something we could do for you in return?" He did not flatter himself that the bonds of filial obligation ran deep in his family.

Philip toyed with his teacup, which was plain and well

worn. "I appreciate the offer, but I doubt there is anything I can do for you, nor you for me," he said in the same sober tone. "You know what I desire above all else is a command, but unless you have a secret connection to the Admiralty that I was not aware of, it's no use. And as for Charlotte, well, that's a very hard case."

"There was talk of petitioning Richard…" Tom suggested.

"Oh no, Richard is a villain," Philip replied. "I know you never got on with him, especially after that ugly business with Miss Betty, but it's worse than even you know. I've heard some shocking tales, I tell you, enough to make your flesh creep. There's not a whore in Deal who will go with him, not for a mint of money." He shuddered.

"Then what are we to do? She can't stay here forever," Tom said, feeling rather vexed.

"Hm. I tell you what it is, though, the 42nd of Foot are to be posted to Halifax the minute the ice thaws and the transport ships can get through. Only let him go, and she may do as she pleases, with the Atlantic between them."

"Is that so?" said Tom. He rather doubted that would be an end to the matter, but as far as he was concerned, it might be good enough to convince her to move out.

"And you know, brother, it has just occurred to me that you might do me a great service after all," Philip added with a great show of indifference, trying to seem as if the idea had only just struck him. "I have been intending to come up to London these many weeks. My particular friend, Captain Alexander Lindsey of the Royal Marines, has been lodging here at a, ah, gentlemen's club, and I have been desirous of visiting him, as it's been a great while since we enjoyed each other's company. It would not do for me to take lodgings there myself. I was wondering if by your leave, I might impose on your hospitality for a few days or a week…?"

Oh Lord, not another one, Tom thought, but Philip's humble entreaties hit their mark, and once again he felt himself ensnared by obligation. He knew very well what Philip meant by a gentlemen's club, and it was not the sort of place where men of quality met to drink and play cards, but a much lower establishment by far: a molly-house, where he-whores and sodomites gathered, and it would indeed be best if Philip did not take lodgings in such a place. In recent years, the self-styled Society for the Reformation of Manners had raided such houses, and men of much higher rank than their own had been arrested, tried, pilloried, and even executed.

"Of course you may stay here as long as you wish," Tom offered hollowly.

"Your soul to the devil for writing that bloody letter," Tom declared to Jem the next day, as they sat drinking together at the Labor in Vain after the performance. He and Jem had already been drinking for some time, the publican having just laid in a new store of capital port, and Tom's words slurred slightly as he cursed his friend. "He says he can't help Charlotte neither, but he wants to stay with me. By your leave, he says, might I impose, and so handsomely put I would look a proper scrub was I to refuse. I looked to get rid of one parasitical relation and now I'm saddled with two." He sighed and tossed back his glass of port, then felt about the table for the bottle.

Jem pushed the bottle into Tom's searching hand. "It ain't my fault," he said defensively. "I only wrote the letter, and at your direction. Besides, he seems like a decent sort of cove." Jem had made Philip's acquaintance earlier in the day when he arrived at Maiden Lane for dinner before the show. "Although I must say, Finchy, he don't look one hair like you. Mrs. Carstone don't neither, for that matter."

Tom shrugged. All this talk of family resemblance was confounding. Did people really identify each other solely by hair and eye color, or the shape of the face? What did it mean that everyone said he resembled his father? He felt that in disposition, not to mention affection, he was much closer to his Uncle Jack. Why should that not also show?

"A right decent sort of cove," Jem rambled on, still thinking on Philip. "Handsome, too, one might say. Those white breeches with the blue jacket really set a man up prime."

"He's a sodomite," Tom said flatly.

"Is he now? Finchy, you astound me. I would never have guessed. He don't paint his face, nor prance about like a Miss Molly. Are you certain?"

"Oh, beyond a doubt," Tom replied, laughing. "He told me the name of his lover, a marine captain, forsooth, Alexander something or other. He's lodging incognito at Mother Birch's molly-house in Holborn. That's why Philip wants to stay with me, to be near him. I suppose they would be found out if they set up house together in Deal."

"I know just the place you mean!" Jem cried. "It's right at the end of Drury Lane, no more than a stone's throw from the Piazza. Well dammee, I have often wondered what capers they cut there."

"You may find out if you are willing," Tom replied. "Philip is desirous that I meet this modern-day Alexander. He wants me to accompany him there. What d'ye think?"

Jem clapped him on the back. "Oh, by all means, let us go and see what these mollies are about!"

CHAPTER SEVEN:
THE MOLLY-HOUSE

"I swear, Finchy, I'm as giddy as a country girl attending her first masquerade ball," Jem declared as they hurried down Bow Street, away from the theater, up Drury Lane towards Holborn and Mother Birch's molly-house. There Philip would introduce them to Captain Lindsey, and presumably many others as well. Tom and Jem had been obliged to put in an appearance at the opera, but they had slipped out at the entr'acte, and were now hurrying toward their assignation at the mysterious world of the molly-house, known to them only through rumor and innuendo. It was a cold night and snow was just beginning to fall as they left the theater. Tom had his hand on Jem's elbow, his face turned down into the high collar of his wool cloak to avoid the stinging wind.

"I'm only going to this place to oblige Philip," Tom replied, his voice somewhat muffled. "He seems so eager for us to meet his 'particular friend,' poor fellow. Although I must say, I don't understand how a man could forsake the embrace of a woman. Is it not generally agreed there is no greater pleasure in life?"

Jem gave a hearty laugh, waving away a very dirty-faced whore who looked up at him hopefully from a doorway as they passed. "Oh, I don't know as who could say one sex is better than the other. We had some fine sporting fun when I was a boy at school. Didn't you?"

"And I have told you before, I was never at school. Really,

301

Castleton, sometimes you are a bottle-headed booby."

"Then you mean to say you have never once tried indorsing?" Jem sounded genuinely surprised.

"Whatever do you mean?" Tom asked.

"You know, indorsing, to, ah, approach another man from the back or dorsus, as a learned cove might say."

"If you mean buggery, then no, and why should I? Men are filthy stinking brutes, whereas women are the delight of the world," Tom replied, although in truth he hardly gave the matter much thought, being far more concerned with how much longer it might take them to reach their destination. The wind was finding its way insidiously through the gaps in his cloak and the snow struck his face with the force of a thousand tiny needles.

"Now there you are wrong, Finchy, for let me tell you, there are more pleasures than a woman may provide, as I discovered at school," Jem said with great conviction.

"You astonish me," Tom said blandly, in a voice that indicated more indifference than surprise, as they came at last to the end of Drury Lane and turned onto Holborn High Street. "I wonder what sort of fellow this Captain Lindsey is? Do you suppose he is like the ephebe of the ancient Greeks?"

Jem snorted. "If he's a marine captain, he ain't no puling boy. These mollies is all alike, though. He must be a prancing, mincing madge cull, I'm sure. Here we are then, it's just up these stairs. Take care, it's icy."

Jem paused before a nondescript building, the same as all the others on the street. Unlike a public house or even a gentlemen's club, there was no signboard or placard marking the spot; not even the lights from the windows nor the sound of revelry filtered out into the street. After pausing to be sure this was the place, Jem bounded up the stone stairs, with Tom following close behind, still clutching his elbow and holding his silver-headed walking stick before him.

The door was answered by a small wiry man in a lavish *robe à la française* and a towering wig topped with false birds in a nest, although even the heavy lead paint on his face could not fully disguise the blue shadow of a beard. He regarded them with suspicion until Tom introduced them both as guests of Captain Moorehouse, whereupon the creature gave a deep curtsy and tittered with delight.

"Oooh, she'll be right chuffed to see you. She's been talking of nothing else all evening. You may call me Princess Seraphina. Follow me, if you please."

"Did he just refer to Philip as she?" Tom whispered, pulling off his tricorne hat as Jem led him down a long narrow hallway.

"Shh, it's only their way. What did I tell you? And this one here is togged in twig, a frock that would make the finest lady gnash her teeth with envy, ha ha." Jem was delighted with Princess Seraphina, the very picture of the kind of Miss Molly he had expected to see. He was deeply disappointed, then, when Princess Seraphina led them to a rather crowded, somewhat shabby drawing room at the back of the house filled with on the whole an unremarkable collection of men, the sort he might have seen in the audience at the theater that very night. To be sure most of them seemed to have put a great deal of care into arranging their clothes and powdering their hair, and many had powdered or painted their faces as well, but this was hardly out of the ordinary.

"Tom! So good of you to come!" Philip cried, rushing forward to embrace his brother and kiss him on both cheeks, then bowing to Jem with a polite "How d'ye do?" He led them to yet another inner room, this one filled with tobacco smoke and the musty, sour smell of beer. Tom heard some nervous shuffling, then Philip said, "May I present my particular friend, Captain Alexander Lindsey of the Royal Marines. Captain Lindsey, my brother Thomas Finch, and Mr. James Castleton, both of the Theater Royal, Covent Garden."

"Delighted to make your acquaintance," Tom said, holding his hat to his chest and bowing over his extended leg.

"Your servant, Mr. Finch," Captain Lindsey greeted him in

a commanding bass. Tom straightened up in surprise. Captain Lindsey was neither a smooth-cheeked boy nor a mincing fop, as they had supposed, but, as Jem later informed him, an imposing, square-jawed soldier, with glossy black hair and flashing dark eyes. Philip stood beside him looking stony-faced and ill at ease. Jem regarded the pair of them, his mouth hanging open slightly. Despite the general awkwardness all round, and their civilian clothing, both Captain Lindsey and Captain Moorehouse had an air of command; Jem could well imagine them standing on the quarterdeck of a frigate. And despite the fact that both were well favored, they seemed so far from his idea of a molly, he could not imagine them in an intimate embrace.

The silence stretched on painfully. "Very good of you to come," Philip offered at last, with a stiff smile.

"It ain't what I thought it would be," Jem burst out suddenly. "Is yon cove who calls himself a princess the only one togged like a girl? I thought you all did?" Tom elbowed Jem in the ribs, but Captain Lindsey only gave a good-natured laugh.

"It's only that you missed our festival night, which was last week. We was all rigged out as dainty as you please. You should have seen Captain Nancy here, she was quite the elegant little tart!" He laughed again and swatted Philip on the behind, causing him to blush, but smile a bit in spite of himself.

"Stop a clapper over it, you poxy old quean," Philip shot back. "You'll alarm our guests."

"Oh not at all," Tom assured him. "We're only sorry to have missed it."

"There'll be more frolics tonight if you stay late enough," Captain Lindsey promised with a conspiratorial wink, which was lost on Tom.

"Come, come, it's yet early, let us be easy," Philip said nervously. He relieved them of their hats and cloaks, and seated them at a table. As there was no tap-room, there was precious little choice in the way of drinks, only what Mother Birch, a stout older woman with a round face and a maternal air, could carry in with her own two hands. They were served a vigorous brew called huckle and buff, a mixture of gin and ale served hot, but on such a cold night it went down gratefully.

By the time they had sunk the first round, Jem and Tom were feeling quite at home, and even Philip had traded his anxiety for a sort of fevered excitement. He brought a long procession of friends and acquaintances around to their table to meet them, although as it turned out, many of these were known to Tom already as denizens of Covent Garden, and quite a few were choristers at the Rose or Drury Lane, although he was too polite to remark upon it, not wanting to put them at risk of exposure. Many more in turn seemed to know Tom.

"My dear, I had no idea your brother was so famous!" Captain Lindsey cried. "What's this I hear about a duel?"

Jem was only too happy to launch into a hugely exaggerated retelling of Tom's duel with Charles Desmares, which Tom found far too amusing to correct.

"Oh aye, he's a credit to our rotten family, no thanks to the lecherous old earl," Philip said, clapping Tom heartily on the back.

Someone placed a creaking and battered fiddle in his hands, and Tom obliged them with several stately gavottes, while the men danced with each other as elegantly as any court ladies. He gathered what was going on from a few comments uttered by Jem, who was delighted to at last see the mollies on display, but it was all very odd, he reflected as he played. A few other men in dresses had joined Princess Seraphina, but as he could not see them, but only judge them by their voices, which were decidedly masculine, it was not so very shocking to him as it clearly was for Jem. The way they all referred to their fellows as "she" and "Mrs. Girl" likewise was more confusing than anything else. Still, there was a great atmosphere of fun and abandon, far more than in the public houses he usually frequented, which sometimes resembled open warfare, with the men determined to get the women for the lowest price, and the women to rob the men of their last penny. No, this was closer to the free and easy atmosphere of a masquerade ball, and yet as far as he could tell no one was wearing a mask; quite the opposite, they all seemed open and relaxed.

After the more sophisticated strains, Tom moved on to some country dances, "Bobbing Joan" and other well-known tunes, which were greeted with great enthusiasm, as he knew they would be, the company growing more elevated in spirits as the bumpers went down.

"This is for Captain Moorehouse and Captain Lindsey, with my compliments," he said, scraping out the first notes of "Spanish Ladies," the unofficial anthem of the navy, as they roared out their approval then joined in vigorously. After they had sung it through several times, followed by more songs beloved by sailors, an older personage in a dress that would have made a Covent Garden whore blush, whom all addressed as Queen Bess, announced that it was nearly time for the ceremony to begin.

"What ceremony?" Tom asked, laying aside the fiddle.

"Didn't Philip tell you? We're to be married!" Captain Lindsey roared out, his voice still pitched for singing out hearty on the chorus.

"Married?" Jem and Tom cried at the same moment.

"Oh, it's only one of our little games," Philip put in hurriedly, coloring. "We dress up and act out the marriage ceremony. It's just a bit of fun. I must shift my clothes. Tom, will you come with me?"

"But I can't—" Tom started, but Philip was already hauling him up by the arm, and so he followed after, rather more unsteady on his feet than he expected. Surely he had drunk no more than three tankards? But then he was forced to admit he had lost track entirely.

Philip led Tom to a tiny upstairs room, where a voluminous dark blue sacque, once elegant but now rather threadbare, was laid out on the bed.

"Are you really going to wear a dress?" Tom asked, leaning against a wall to keep the floor from shifting beneath his feet.

"I don't usually, even on masquerade nights, but it's a wedding, you know, someone has to play the bride, and I'm the shorter one." He didn't add that often the wedding was followed by an escort of the entire party to witness the marriage bed, then an elaborate lying-in and pantomime birth of a jointed wooden doll, but his modesty forced him to refuse these later parts of the ceremony, despite the general disappointment.

"It don't mean anything. It's just a bit of fun," Philip repeated as he pulled off his shirt and breeches. Then in direct contradiction of his avowed indifference, he said in a much lower voice, "I really am glad you're here, Tom."

Tom smiled, rather touched by how ridiculously grateful Philip seemed. "I am sensible of the honor you do me by inviting me to your inner sanctuary, but I assure you, the pleasure is mine. Captain Lindsey seems like a capital fellow."

"Do you really think so?" Philip pulled the dress over his head, his face alight with happiness as it emerged over the collar.

"Yes, of course. However did you meet him?"

"We served together on my last command. But now what are the chances we will be on the same ship again? A captain may request his own lieutenants and midshipmen but the marines are in a separate world entirely. I know we ain't been close, brother, but you are the only one out of our whole damned family I could introduce him to."

A faint breeze from the far wall told him there was a window; Tom stumbled over to it and after some fumbling with the latch, flung it open and breathed in deep lungs full of the cold night air, which cleared his head enough that the disagreeable spinning sensation abated. He turned at last and replied, "You honor me, brother, but I'm sure Aunt Sarah would receive a marine captain. And hasn't Charlotte met him already?" There was a long pause, long enough for Tom to wonder if he had not been left addressing an empty room—he had often enough found himself in such embarrassing posture.

At last Philip replied roughly, "It ain't the same. You know what I mean. It's different to meet him here. May I ask your assistance with these laces?"

"I shall try, but I warn you I am no great fist at doing up laces. I rather feel my genius lies in unlacing women's garments," Tom replied. As a joke, it was rather weak, but Philip laughed and it went a good way towards dispelling the heavy tone and putting them both in an appropriately merry state.

By the time they stumbled back downstairs, someone else had taken up the fiddle, and Philip was greeted with raucous singing accompanied with spirited drumming on tables, empty pots, and whatever else was at hand.

Let the fops of the town upbraid
Us, for an unnatural trade,
We value not man nor maid;
But among our own selves we'll be free.

With much laughter and lewd gestures, Philip was brought beside Captain Lindsey, and Queen Bess stood before them with a sort of surplice draped over her enormous false bosom. In a wavering falsetto, she intoned the familiar marriage rite from the Book of Common Prayer, while around her the company kept up their song.

We'll kiss and we'll swive,
Behind we will drive,
And we will contrive
New ways for lechery.

When Queen Bess reached the end of her recitation, Captain Lindsey planted a hearty kiss on Captain Moorehouse, leaning him backwards with the force of his attentions, while the company burst into boisterous applause, then conveyed them upstairs, to a private room, in accordance with Philip's wishes.

At this juncture, Tom suddenly found himself alone. Jem had long ago disappeared into the crowd, which had grown quite large. As Philip was led away upstairs, Tom realized he had lost his bearings in the throng. He was just about to pluck at random at the sleeve of a neighbor to ask where he might refill his tankard, which had run sadly dry, when he felt arms linking around his from either side, and a soft, perfumed hand stroke his cheek. He stiffened in surprise, his eyes blinking rapidly and his brow twitching upward, but the hand lingered, brushing gently along his jaw line; when he had recovered from the initial surprise, Tom found the sensation pleasing.

"What have we here?" asked the owner of the hand in honeyed tones and a very high bred accent. Tom was about to introduce himself, but the fingers moved to cover his lips, cutting off his words. "Hush, no true names, if you please. You may address me as the Marquise, and to your right and left you will find my pathics, Apollo and Ganymede. Pray will you be seated with us?"

Tom allowed himself to be propelled by the young men on either side of him to a sofa, where the Marquise sat hard by on his right and the two young men on his left. Tom sat very straight and rigid, uncertain what was to befall next, yet feeling not so much apprehension as a pleasant sort of excitement. He was accustomed to taking the role of pursuer; he had never himself been the pursued. The close, heady atmosphere of the crowded room, dense with tobacco smoke, perfume, and noise, the strangers pressing close to him on either side, the strong drink still making his head spin—it was like the world turned upside down.

The Marquise placed a soft hand on his cheek again, turning his head around to the right to face him. "You are blind," he said in the same rich tones. Tom did not reply—it was more of a statement than a question, and in any case, was it not evident? Most people seemed to grasp this fact without explanation on his part. "You can see nothing at all?"

"That is so, my lord," Tom replied, wondering where this was all leading.

"They say the remaining senses of the blind are extraordinarily elevated," the Marquise continued, "and that in particular the sense of touch is unparalleled in sensitivity."

Tom grinned slowly. "I am no natural philosopher, but perhaps my lord would be pleased to discover for himself whether this be true or no."

The Marquise laughed. "I consider it a vital inquiry into the very essence of being. But you are not a habitué of this establishment; I am quite certain I have never seen you here before, or I would surely have taken note of such a singular personage."

"It is true I have never before experienced the favors of my own sex, although I assure you I am no stranger to the stews and bagnios. Some might even call me a libertine."

"Ah, but women are mere brutes who know nothing of the more elevated forms of pleasure. Only a man may understand another man, am I right?" the Marquise asked his two young men, who took this as their cue to entwine their arms around Tom's person.

"How handsome you are," one breathed in his ear, as the other tugged his jacket from his shoulders. Just then the Marquise leaned in and, holding Tom's face on either side, kissed him deeply, not a hesitant maidenly kiss, but an insistent and demanding one. Telling himself this was in the way of an experiment, Tom returned the kiss, reaching out to embrace the other man about the waist. It felt so odd—the sensation of a form roughly the same size and shape as his own, in the same heavy brocade and lace, and even, although the Marquise was carefully groomed, the hint of stubble around his face—it was like kissing himself. Yet the knowledge that this was a forbidden act, against nature and the laws of men, and could even result in death for all of them, somehow added a thrill of excitement, so that the familiar mixed with the strange and dangerous in a heady concoction.

The Marquise pulled back from the kiss, then grasped Tom's hands and placed them on his own face. "Tell me, do you find my features pleasing?" he asked.

Tom brushed his fingers lightly over the other man's face, taking in a high broad forehead, prominent nose, thin cheeks, and thin lips, but overall these never coalesced to form for him the mental picture of a face; it was simply not the means by which he identified a person—the voice was so much more expressive and distinctive. Still, the act of touching another so intimately was in itself erotic, not something he made a regular practice; in fact he could not remember the last time he had touched the face of another man.

"Very pleasing," he said at last, having made a careful study, and judging by the reactions, the Marquise had enjoyed the experience as well.

The other two men, the Marquise's two pathics or favorites, whom he had dubbed Apollo and Ganymede, then insisted on receiving the same treatment; being much younger, their features were fuller and rounder, but they were also more playful and less serious. After much kissing and toying, Tom felt himself quite transported, even giddy, with the sensation of being caressed on all sides by so many hands, pulling away his cravat, opening his shirt, loosening his queue and running through his hair.

Just as he was thinking this could not continue, the Marquise with a bold, practiced move, reached into his breeches and pulled forth his privy part. Tom gasped, carried away by the sensation of the moment, although a part of him remained uneasy at first. He had no intention of engaging in what Jem had called indorsing, although it was soon plain that his companions seemed to understand this, and did not attempt to persuade him, but maintained their attentions with their hands. Tom found his own hands likewise conveyed towards the Marquise, and again he felt that strange combination of novelty and excitement, in no way unpleasant, and judging by the sounds all around them, the others in the room were engaged in similar activities.

At last the one called Ganymede knelt before him, and performed with his mouth an act that Tom would have never asked of the even lowest slut in Covent Garden, and yet this was performed with such skill and evident enjoyment that he put aside all modesty and gave himself over wholly to it. No sooner had the paroxysm of pleasure subsided, however, than the three men kissed him with assurances that he would always be welcome in this place, and suddenly departed, leaving Tom alone on the sofa to hastily rearrange his clothing.

He had just finished lacing up his breeches when he was surprised to hear Philip's voice directly in front of him saying, "Come on then, cully, it's time to go home."

"What, already?" Tom said, casting about for his cravat and jacket.

Philip laughed. "I can see you've been enjoying yourself, brother," he said, as he helped him tie up his shirt and cravat. "But it would not do if we were seen leaving this place in the bright light of morning."

Suddenly the din in the room seemed to have abated, and Tom realized that as Philip said, people were leaving in quick succession. They bade their farewell to Captain Lindsey, and Tom invited him to call at Maiden Lane at any time, then joined the throng preparing to leave by the front door. There were many vulgar remarks among the company made about the link boys and what they intended to do with them once they were conveyed home, or even in a dark alley along the way, although Philip assured Tom somewhat anxiously that this was all talk, and he was not to take it seriously. Tom's cloak, hat, and walking stick materialized in his hands, and Jem, plucked untimely from the arms of Princess Seraphina, appeared grumbling at his side.

Philip, still concerned lest he be seen and recognized, flashed out for a hackney, which dropped Jem by his lodging in

Broad Court, before taking them the short distance to Maiden Lane, although by the time the carriage had pulled into the street, the sky was just beginning to lighten, and they were indistinguishable from the other revelers returning home from late-night debauches of the more usual kind.

CHAPTER EIGHT: THE CLOSE OF THE SEASON

The transformation of number eight Maiden Lane from disorder to respectability had occurred quite suddenly, yet Tom in his distracted way had taken it in stride so thoroughly that he himself was hardly aware of the change. Even his carriage within the house had altered: he no longer shuffled his feet about to avoid tripping over detritus strewn on the floor, but strode confidently, secure in the knowledge that the servants would maintain the passages clear and the furniture religiously in its proper place. They were a decent lot, the new servants; it had not been long before Tom could tell each of them by the sound of their footfalls. He had also grown accustomed to large meals at regular hours, and now with such a large household it seemed perfectly natural that he entertain at home, although such had never been his habit previously.

On the day of the final performance of *Il pastor fido*, Tom invited Tess and Jane to join him, Charlotte, and Philip for dinner, along with Nathaniel Welgarth and Alexander Lindsey, both of whom had taken to calling nearly every day, and Jem, of course, who would have shown up regardless, invited or no. Since receiving positive word from Philip that her husband's regiment was indeed bound for Halifax, Charlotte threw off her prior discretion, and went about with Lieutenant Welgarth in public whenever she pleased. Philip wondered aloud if this was wise, as Colonel Carstone had not yet departed, but Charlotte declared she no longer gave a fig for the vile brute.

With eight people seated about the scarred and battered old table, the long narrow dining room was decidedly cramped. Tom did not possess what one might term a proper china service or set of silver plate; the guests were forced to make do with mismatched pewter, but the plentiful food and good company, along with a steady stream of claret, was more than enough to buoy their spirits. Tom found that the sound of his guests enjoying the meal and engaging in idle banter pleased him inordinately.

"Ain't this the thing!" Tom remarked to Jem, as they tucked into fatty slices of roast goose.

"A far sight better than the rusty old chops at the White Wig," Jem agreed, referring to the food at inn hard by which had previously been their primary source of sustenance. Tom did not bother to explain he meant the entire experience of hosting his friends and relations in his own home, but only smiled contentedly. He would never have guessed he could find such satisfaction in domesticity.

From the far end of the table, Charlotte called out in her usual brassy way, "Tell us, Tom, how did you find your excursion to Mother Birch's molly-house?"

Tom tipped his face up in surprise, while Philip and Captain Lindsey exchanged a knowing look.

"What? How did you hear of that?" Tom asked, rather taken aback.

"Philip told me, of course," Charlotte replied coolly. "Fie on you, brother, for keeping it from me. I am burning with curiosity to know what goes on in such a place."

"I expect Philip could offer you a better description than I," Tom said with equal coolness.

"It is true you enjoyed the last favor of another man there?" Lieutenant Welgarth blurted out. An intemperate young man with bulging, unintelligent pale blue eyes, his tendency to wear his dragoon's uniform at all times, including cockade and spurs, as well as his habit of speaking whatever came into his mind the moment it occurred to him, had not endeared him to the others. Philip shot him an evil look, but Captain Lindsey thumped the table, laughing.

"Modesty may prevent him from replying, but the mollies was all taken with Mr. Finch. I tell you, they found him quite the go," Captain Lindsey said with a lascivious grin.

"Did they really?" Tess asked, staring hard at Tom. She found herself wishing that just this once he could look back at her, that she might communicate with him without words, or have a hint of his inner thoughts, but as usual his expression was somewhat blank.

Jane, however, knew precisely what Tess was thinking. "Does this mean you are abandoning the fairer sex? Have you become a molly yourself, Mr. Finch?" she inquired.

Tom laughed good-naturedly. "Never in life! I assure you, Miss Carlyle, my appreciation of the fairer sex, as you put it, has hardly abated."

"What do it signify, anyway?" Jem added somewhat defensively. "Can't a man enjoy himself as he pleases without having to endure an inquisition from his own friends and family?"

"I think it's against nature," Jane replied primly, holding up her pretty head and gazing down at her plate, the picture of modesty. The entire table stared at her in astonishment.

"That's coming it pretty high from one who plays at the game of flats," Jem commented. Charlotte tittered behind her hand, and Tess reddened and looked away, but Jane lifted her grey eyes to stare back at him with calm composure.

"Whatever do you mean," she said evenly.

"Oh come now, Miss Carlyle, it's no use dissembling. The whole of London knows of your connection with Miss Turnbridge. It ain't a secret," Jem teased her.

"It's not the same," Jane replied loftily.

"I think it's all pretty nearly the same," Lieutenant Welgarth laughed.

"No," Jane insisted, "a lady's companion is usual position while both are young and unmarried, but two men together is a scandal."

"Bah! Why should it be? And in any case what does it mean, 'against nature'?" Captain Lindsey added, his dark eyes flashing. "My body is my own, and I may make what use I please of it. There's a law of nature for you."

"What a noble sentiment! I thoroughly agree with you, Captain Lindsey," Tess cried with a spirited look. "My body is my own to use as I please," she repeated with great satisfaction.

"Not women," Charlotte said darkly. "Not after we marry, then our bodies belong to our husbands. I warn you, Mistress Turnbridge, if you would live by that sentiment, never marry."

They all fell silent for a moment, thinking on Charlotte's intractable predicament.

"Well, I think it's perfectly monstrous that a woman may be divorced at will by her husband but cannot initiate the proceedings herself," Tess said.

"Hear, hear!" cried Charlotte warmly, drinking to her in a glass of claret.

"I still say, was Colonel Carstone to sue your Lieutenant Welgarth there for crim. con., it would solve the problem," Jem said.

"Either that or arrange for Colonel Carstone to sell her in the Piazza, and let Lieutenant Welgarth buy her," Captain Lindsey offered, and they all laughed at the thought of Charlotte with a halter around her neck, like a farmer's scolding wife being brought to market. All, that is, apart from Charlotte, who looked ill-pleased at being made sport of.

After they had all enjoyed a fine noble pudding, the cloth had been drawn and several more rounds drunk, it was time to depart for the theater. Jane bid her farewells, saying she had promised to call on her parents that evening, and the rest of the company set out for the short walk together, as Tom had given them all tickets. As they crossed the Piazza from Maiden Lane to the opera house, Tom took Tess's arm and they pulled slightly ahead of the others. It was another wretchedly cold day, with snow from the previous night still lingering in dirty heaps. Tess guided them briskly around the mounds of snow, through the bustling crowd.

"I must confess, I am very glad you joined us, Tess," Tom said. "It seems we haven't had a quiet moment together this age. I apologize that I have been so damnably taken up with family. A plague on them all."

Tess laughed. "Is it really so bad?"

Tom sighed dramatically. While he enjoyed entertaining, allowing his siblings to reside with him was another matter entirely. "The house is a veritable bedlam—billets-doux plying to and fro, Lindsey and that coxcomb Welgarth coming and going at all hours. And I tell you, it is most peculiar how differently we three recall the events of our childhood. My time at Culverleigh was a misery, I assure you. I was set upon and bullied by the other boys constantly, even Philip. But in his mind, it was like a new Eden. Just the other day he was telling me with great delight and in all seriousness about the time we all went fox-hunting together, myself included, although I'm sure I never did. I couldn't even ride—I seem to recall falling from a horse. Yet Philip related such particulars that it made me doubt my own memory."

"How strange," said Tess. "I suppose we each amend our childhood memories to our liking. Still," she added, "he seems like a very kind-hearted gentleman." Over dinner she had caught Captain Moorehouse and Captain Lindsey exchanging a look of unalloyed affection, and it had moved her greatly.

"Oh yes, Philip ain't a bad sort at all. It's Richard and Paul are the villains."

They had reached the theater, and Tom escorted Tess around to the stage door at the back, leaving Jem to show the others in at the main entrance.

Just before Tess went to enter the stage door, Tom raised her gloved hand to his lips and kissed it. "I give you the joy of your final performance, my dear," he said, smiling. "It really has been far too long since I enjoyed the pleasure of your company. Might I ask your favor again tonight, after the performance?"

"You may," Tess replied slowly, allowing her hand to linger in his and returning his broad smile. It always pleased her how unguarded and unstudied his smile was, especially when directed at her. Yet as soon as the pleasant sensation suffused her, she tamped it down firmly.

Tom kissed her hand a second time and said, "Then I shall meet you in the green room after the opera."

"But I must warn you, I shall accompany you as a friend," she added, withdrawing her hand at last.

"But of course, I hope that you do still consider me your friend," he replied.

"No, I mean—" she hesitated, finding it surprisingly difficult to get out the words she had so carefully prepared in anticipation of this very moment. "I mean, as you may know, since we took up lodging together again, I have pledged my affections solely to Jane henceforth, and I should not wish to give you a false impression that I am at liberty to accept your...invitations."

Tom frowned, his pale eyes searching the air just above her head. Tess felt a pang—of what? Remorse? She did her best to ignore it.

"My dearest Tess, you don't mean it. I can hear it in your voice," he said.

Tess edged toward the door, all the pleasure of the afternoon now vanished. "I do," she insisted. "Behold how sweet and agreeable Jane has become. The quarreling and jealousy is behind us now, and I would not trade that tranquility for anything. As you value our friendship, please don't ask it of me," she cried, then slipped through the door.

"I shall call on you in the green room after the finale," he

shouted at her departing figure as the door clicked shut behind her, leaving him unsure if she had heard him or not.

Tom found his way at his usual slow, careful pace back
around to the front of the opera house, in through the main
entrance, and up to the first balcony, pausing frequently as
colleagues and acquaintances greeted him. They had reserved
a private box, where Matthews had already laid out on a small
table the port and biscuits brought from home. Philip, Alexander, Charlotte, and Nathaniel were playing faro to pass the
time, as the orchestra played to divert the audience before
the performance began. Jem had been relegated to watching
the game over their shoulders, but found to his dissatisfaction
that his helpful comments seemed less than welcome, and the
players had taken to shading their cards with their hands. As
Tom entered, Jem clapped him heartily on the shoulder and
guided him to a chair.

"The final performance at last, hey?" Tom said as Matthews
put a glass of port in his outstretched hand. Rather than
answering, Jem gave a noncommittal sort of grunt. "What's
this?" Tom asked. "I would have thought you'd be pleased.
Didn't you call it the dullest bit of cobbled-together nonsense
Mr. Handel had yet devised?"

"That's true," Jem conceded, sprawling in his chair. "But it's
the end of the season, and there won't be another opera for
months. What shall we do until then? If Mr. Rich sees fit to hire
us again, which ain't at all certain."

Tom shrugged. "Something will come along," he said, unconcerned, for he was in no mood for ratiocination.

The game of faro ended with Charlotte the triumphant
winner, and after sweeping up the coins on the table, she
joined Tom at the very front and center of the box. She was
dressed in the latest mode, with a flowered gown over panniers so wide and rectangular it looked as though she were
wearing the dining room table.

"Come, brother, where is all your good cheer from dinner?"
she exclaimed as she angled herself into the narrow space and

flounced into the chair. "What is it? Is it your Miss Turnbridge? Shall we see her again after the opera?" Tom did not reply, and she stared at him closely. "Aha, it *is* Miss Turnbridge, I warrant. Is it true she has an amour with that Miss Carlyle? How awkward for you. But we shall see her tonight, shan't we?"

"Do be quiet, Charlotte," Tom hissed at her. Just then Mr. Handel appeared on the conductor's stand to polite applause, and led the orchestra through the opening strains of the prolog, mercifully distracting Charlotte from her chatter. The box was rather crowded with so many guests, but they rearranged their chairs with Tom at the front corner, Jem somewhat behind him, Charlotte and Nathaniel in the center, and Philip and Alexander squeezed behind them in the back corner.

The company was in uncommonly fine form that evening, for once putting behind them all the petty rivalries and jealousies, perhaps in the knowledge that they would never again come together with this precise complement to execute these exact figures on the stage, or more likely with regret for the impending loss of steady income. But whether the cause was sentimental attachment or attachment of a baser sort, everyone, from the celebrated leads to the smallest chorus girl, from the stagehands to the musicians in the orchestra, were at last pulling together in the same direction, and the result was an extraordinary start, fully free of error, imbued with a joyful exuberance.

For Charlotte, as well as for her young dragoon, and even more for Captains Moorehouse and Lindsey, it was a dazzling evening. Their lives in the garrison or on the sea were so often constrained and uncomfortable, occasionally dangerous but more often dull and dreary, and the delights of civilian life, when afforded to them, were generally of a cruder sort in the taverns and other places of resort catering to military men. None of them had ever before beheld the splendor of the Theater Royal: the light of countless candles held aloft above the stage glittering and reflecting off the finery of the audience, the most exalted of whom sat directly on the stage or in boxes along its length. For once the players were wholly concentrated on their art rather than talking loudly in the wings with their wealthy admirers. The stage itself was arrayed in a charming rustic scene that recalled sylvan glades and meadows, and the players were a more lovely set of shepherds and shepherdesses than nature generally allowed. Together with the graceful figures of the dancers and the elegant music, all four felt as if they had been transported to another world.

Tess as Amarilli had just begun her aria, "Finche un Zeffiro soave," halfway through the first act. Tom leaned forward intently, his left ear cocked toward the stage. She was in uncommonly fine voice, tripping effortlessly through the difficult trills and the treacherous *passagio*, with a tone as clear and pure as a bell. The countertenors had more powerful voices, but for soaring clarity at the top of the register, none could touch her.

Tom was so absorbed in the sound of her voice that he only gradually became aware of a commotion behind him. At first he dismissed the shuffling and muffled voices in the hall as the usual antics of theater-goers, but when the banging and angry voices burst into their box, he jumped up in surprise. Charlotte gave a yelp.

Behind them a rough, unfamiliar voice sneered, "Well, what have we here?" while another man pushed past the first, shouting, "Infamous whore!"

It was Colonel Carstone. Tom gripped his walking stick in one hand and reached out for Charlotte with the other. She grasped his hand tightly.

Both of the intruders were dressed in their everyday regimental uniforms, and from their muddy, unshaven appearance it seemed they had been traveling hard. Carstone had the look of a once-handsome man gone to seed, his belly and jowls inflated with drink. His battered wig and stained shirt only contributed to the aura of danger that hung about him. The other man, standing behind him, had a commoner look;

greasy black hair clubbed untidily, dark stubble mixed with grey on his cheeks, and flinty eyes above a sneering mouth.

"You led me a merry chase, madam, but here's an end to it," Colonel Carstone growled. Tom heard the slithering steely hiss as Carstone drew his sword.

Where is that useless whelp Welgarth, Tom wondered, trying to discreetly pull Charlotte out of the way, although there was precious little space in the crowded box.

"Now sir, let us settle this like gentlemen," Lieutenant Welgarth offered, his voice cracking with fright. "I would be pleased to meet you at any hour you appoint, with these gentlemen here to act as my seconds."

"To hell with your gentlemen and your fucking seconds," Carstone shouted, spitting on the floor at Nathaniel's feet. "You ain't worth a duel, kiddy. I'll just be taking your prick home as a souvenir, ha ha." He advanced on Nathaniel, his sword tip aimed menacingly at his breeches. Nathaniel drew his own sword, but his face was pale and his hand shook badly.

"Now, now, Colonel, I beseech you, let us at least remove from the theater," Philip suggested from the far corner of the box. He and Alexander had also leapt to their feet, but unlike Nathaniel they had come dressed in their civilian clothes, and they both now felt keenly the want of their swords.

"Shut yer gob, Philip," said the other man. "You always was a cowardly little son of a bitch." He turned to Charlotte and grabbed her other arm. "You're coming with us."

Tom did not relinquish his grip, and for a moment, Charlotte was tugged ludicrously between the two of them. "I believe the lady would prefer to stay here," he said evenly.

"Well, well, Tom, quite the jumped up gentleman, ain't you? And here I thought you was fit for nowt but begging. The old earl is too open-handed by half."

"Richard," Tom grated between clenched teeth, identifying the other man at last.

As Tom and Richard struggled over Charlotte, Carstone advanced again on Nathaniel, laughing menacingly. Nathaniel held up his rapier defensively for a moment, but then, thinking better, he glanced behind him. He took one final look back at Carstone, saw the murderous glint in his eye, then he turned and leapt from the balcony.

With an angry roar, Carstone jumped down after him, followed by Richard a moment later, as Charlotte gave a blood-curdling shriek.

"Oh God, Hart will kill him!" she wailed.

Without hesitating for a moment, Tom tore out of the box and down the stairs. He knew the inside of the theater as well as his own home, and now he ran as fast as his long legs would carry him, with the others close behind him.

"I thought you said Hart had sailed for Halifax," Charlotte rounded on Philip angrily as they pelted down the stairs.

"In the spring, damn it!" Philip shouted back defensively. "It's still January, you stupid girl!"

Bursting into the stalls through a side door, Tom had no trouble locating them; both Richard and Carstone were roaring like bulls, and he heard the clash of swords. Luckily for them, they had landed in the aisle, narrowly missing the occupied seats. Nathaniel was attempting to hold off the two bigger men, his only advantage that there was little room to maneuver. The nearby audience members had leapt to their feet, but it was too crowded to flee easily, and in any case, many were inclined to stay and watch.

Tom had no weapon with him other than his silver-headed walking stick, but it was tolerably heavy, and while he had no particular attachment to Lieutenant Welgarth, his heart boiled over with long-held anger at Richard. He rushed into the fray, led on by the angry shouts, and hauled on the back of Richard's jacket.

On the stage, Tess had been looking up and away, so she did not at first see the fracas in Tom's box, and in any case her concentration was wholly devoted to her art. Out of the corner of her eye, she saw a strange movement—did someone just descend from the balcony into the aisle? She turned in time to see two more men leap down, accompanied by shouts and screams all around. Her voice faltered, but Mr. Handel, with his back to the audience, only conducted more vigorously, giving her a baleful look. A disturbance among the spectators was nearly a nightly occurrence, and the singers had been trained to carry on regardless. Tess resumed the aria, rather shakily, with considerably less skill than before, as she tried to discern the struggling forms in the stalls. Now there was much more shouting, and like a storm at sea the audience began to surge upwards, some craning to see the fight and others fleeing. The orchestra left off playing one by one, Tess fell silent, and even Mr. Handel turned about, his arms still raised, glaring at the unruly audience with disdain.

Then Tess saw Tom come running in through a side door, directly towards the fight, and grab one of the men by the coat, before the crowd surged up around them and she lost sight of them both. Tess uttered a piercing shriek, a note louder and purer than any she had sung thus far, but by this time the theater was in such a state of confusion that hardly anyone noticed. Without thinking, she dashed down the steps the side of the stage and down into the stalls.

Behind her, some of the more adventurous members of the company also descended into the stalls, which had become a mob of struggling, pushing bodies, as those who were trying to get closer to the fight and those attempting to flee became hopelessly entangled. At its center, Hartsley Carstone was forced up so close to Nathaniel that it was no longer possible to wield a sword effectively, and they had instead fallen to bare-fisted blows, as Jem and Alexander attempted to pull them apart, but Carstone was a thick-set, powerful man, and not easily dissuaded from violence.

Directly behind him, Tom had gotten in one lucky crack with his walking stick, and Richard was now bleeding profusely from the right side of his forehead, but as the crowd pushed them together, Richard laid hold of the walking stick, and the two grappled over it. Tom was vaguely aware of

Philip attempting to intercede; he could hear Charlotte wailing close at hand, and was that Tess's voice behind him? With all the noise and shoving around him it was hard to be certain of anything. The confusion quickly gave way to a full-fledged riot, with even those not connected to the original fight taking gleeful opportunity to rip up the seats and harass their fellows.

The din reached an even louder level, with hoarse voices shouting for order: the constable had been called. His men began laying about them indiscriminately with their truncheons, intent on apprehending the perpetrators of the fight. Suddenly Tom felt hands all about him, wrenching him away from his brother, then marching them all out through the front entrance in a body. The stage was cleared, the quality patrons along with those players that could be found were hastened out the stage door, and so the winter season at the Theater Royal, Covent Garden came to an end.

CHAPTER NINE: THE WATCH HOUSE

"My God, what a sorry-looking lot. I've half a mind to let the devil take you all," said Jamie Douglas, the third Earl of Bolingbroke, looking with distaste at the bedraggled figures behind the bars of the Bow Street watch house. Despite the early hour, he was dressed impeccably in a pale blue full-skirted silk surcoat with deep boot cuffs over a richly figured green brocade waistcoat reaching nearly to the knees and a full-bottomed wig with a deep center part. His face, however was lined and gaunt, his thin lips pursed reproachfully.

Having been plucked by the night watch from the confusion of the fight in the opera house, Tom, Jem, Charlotte, Philip, and Alexander were identified by witnesses as among the instigators, along with Tess and several other bystanders who had been caught up in the fray, and thrown in the cell at Bow Street, just behind the theater, to hold them temporarily in anticipation of the magistrate, Sir Thomas de Veil, sorting out their cases in the morning. Nathaniel, Richard, and Hartsley Carstone were also identified as among the guilty parties, but as they were in their uniforms, they were remanded to the Savoy to await a court-martial. The constable was glad to be rid of them quickly, for it was clear that no good would come of leaving them all in the same cell overnight. Philip and Alexander, however, being dressed in civilian rig, passed undetected as military men.

The cell was unheated, and the night was very cold. They slept in a heap, embracing each other with no thought of modesty. At first light, Frankie arrived bearing a small measure of dry bread and cheese, which they shared out gratefully, and also bringing with him a distraught Jane Carlyle. Tom bade Frankie to send for his aunt Lady Gray to fetch them out, but the august lady had determined that this mischief lay beyond her purview, and so it was the old earl who greeted them with displeasure before their appointed hour to plead their case before the magistrate.

They were indeed a sorry-looking lot, their clothes and hair all astray and crumpled. Tess sat on the stone floor, pressed up against the bars, holding Jane's hand, the two of them ashen-faced with worry. Tess was still wearing her shepherdess costume from the opera, which looked well enough on the stage but in the grey light of morning appeared garish and skimpy, with its plunging neckline and lifted skirts; together with the heavy paint still smeared on her face, she knew all too well that she looked no better than a common trull thrown in the lockup.

The men looked no less disreputable, with their cravats and waistcoats hanging loose and their shirts torn and dirty. Tom sported a nasty red welt along his right cheek, although this was not a result of the fight, but rather had been incurred as the heedless night watchman thrust him into the cell without sufficient guidance, causing Tom to collide with the bars as he entered. If he now had a rather melancholy cast, however, it was less due to their confinement nor the haranguing by his father, but because Tess, whom he had convinced to spend the night in his arms, for the sake of warmth, had fled from him upon Jane's appearance, and now sat clinging to her through the bars.

"...a pack of God-damned fools, bringing ignominy on the family name," the old earl continued, wholly insensible of the hypocrisy of his words, for neither Philip nor Tom bore the family name; furthermore the earl himself had been taken up more than once in his younger days for drunkenness and gambling. Lady Gray stood behind him staring at them with stern disapproval, her hauteur not cracking even at her brother's more outrageously sanctimonious statements. He elaborated upon his point at length, as they sat wretched, cold and starving, only Captain Lindsey looking somehow rakish rather than bedraggled.

At last the tirade came to an end when a surly and unshaven clerk arrived to announce that the magistrate would receive them. The clerk unlocked the cell and led them upstairs to a large sort of sitting room where the magistrate sat behind a heavy desk, attended by two more clerks.

A corpulent, florid man in a full-bottomed wig of venerable vintage, Sir Thomas de Veil received them with a barely disguised mix of boredom and irritation, as a clerk whispered the details in his ear. He was strongly inclined to bind them all over for trial at the Old Bailey to spare himself the trouble of sorting through the case, when his eye fell on Tess, who was lurking towards the back, trying to look inconspicuous. Luckily for them, de Veil was a great lover of the opera, and could scarcely contain his surprise at seeing the celebrated Miss Turnbridge in the watch house, of all places.

"Miss Turnbridge, my goodness, there must be some mistake!" he declared.

"Indeed there is, sir, if I may be so bold," Tom offered, pushing forward with a bow. "You see, my sister here," he made a sweeping gesture with his hand; Charlotte coughed discreetly and he repeated the gesture on the opposite side, "my honest sister here, Mrs. Charlotte Carstone, was attacked by her husband under the misapprehension of infidelity, as we was attending the final performance of the season. Attacked most intemperately and wrongly, I do assure you, my lord. Apprehending this from her position on the stage, Miss Turnbridge, who is of a generous nature, was fearful for Charlotte's life, the two of them being the closest of friends. Afraid for her friend's life, her *innocent* friend's life, I tell you, and in an excess of devotion to her friend, she leapt from the stage to her aid."

De Veil turned to Tess with adoring eyes. "Upon my honor, was it ever so? What gallantry!" he said. The others rushed in to corroborate Tom's story, praising Tess's courage to the heavens, elaborating on the blackguardly conduct of Colonel Carstone, and only incidentally proclaiming their own innocence. De Veil was more than willing to clear Tess of any wrongdoing, the others, less so. However, on hearing that the two principal malefactors, Carstone and Welgarth, had already been remanded to the Savoy, he was visibly relieved that the issue of Charlotte's constancy to her husband could be sorted out there. He still demanded that the rest account for themselves: Philip, Alexander, and Jem swore that they had done no more than defend the imperiled person of Mrs. Carstone, while as for Tom, it was represented to the magistrate that a blind man could hardly have endeavored to engage in a fight, and one with swords, no less. De Veil allowed that this was manifestly true, and as Mr. Rich had sent word that he did not intend to prosecute the case, the result was no more than a fine upon Philip, Alexander, and Jem for disturbing the peace. The earl, with many black looks at Philip and Charlotte, paid the fine, then with equal ill-humor hurried them all into the waiting coach which conveyed them directly to Lady Gray's house in Soho Square.

As her guests were washing up and changing into fresh clothes that had been sent for, and while they were awaiting breakfast, Lady Gray held a hurried conference with her brother in the drawing room.

"Of course, Charlotte must be removed from the city as quickly as possible. I have no doubt that villain Carstone will be free by the afternoon. You must take her to Culverleigh," she instructed in her usual imperious manner.

The earl arched an eyebrow at her over his teacup. "Must I now?"

Lady Gray nodded crisply. "Indeed you must. And you shall take all the others with you, Philip, Thomas, and their companions if they choose. Including Miss Turnbridge," she added with particular emphasis.

The earl was accustomed receiving orders from his sister, and was for the most part resigned to the fact that she nearly always had her way, but this was coming it pretty high, even for her. "What, receive that riffraff at Culverleigh? And the opera singer too? You must be joking. Lady Bolingbroke will never agree to it."

Lady Gray sniffed. "She will do as you tell her. I don't give a fig what she thinks. Only consider, brother, we must endeavor to contain the scandal, not only for Charlotte. Philip wants for a commission. It would not do to have his name in the papers over this. Tom has been employed by the Theater Royal, very profitably, I might add, and must take care not to annoy Mr. Rich. And as for Miss Turnbridge, well, I think she is a very good influence on him."

"On whom?"

"On Tom, of course, who else? Really, sometimes I think you scarcely attend to me at all, brother. Now listen, Tom can't remain a bachelor forever. He needs looking after, but his prospects, you may allow, are not the highest, so you may turn up your nose all you like at a lowly actress of mean degree, but Miss Turnbridge is of an honest musical family. She has been a steadying influence on him, I tell you, and I believe he could do a great deal worse. He came very close to throwing himself away on a common harlot, you know, and if he isn't watched carefully, he may very well do so again. Several weeks at Culverleigh, away from the distractions of the city, will do wonders. So let them bring their companions if they wish." Lady Gray did not add that in addition to her sincere interest in Tom's well-being, she had also become somewhat sentimentally attached to Tess's singing career and did not wish to see her damage her prospects with scandal, nor that she was cognizant of the nature of the relationship between Philip and Alexander, and she wished to remove them from the public eye as well until they might be sent out to sea once more.

The earl rolled his eyes heavenward. "Very well, I can see there will be no dissuading you. They shall depart for Culverleigh this afternoon."

Lady Gray's servants outdid themselves laying out a splendid meal for the unexpected crowd, but despite the luxurious repast, breakfast was but a dismal affair. As the others ate in silence, Lady Gray with many significant looks communicated that she intended to leave the explanations of her plan wholly to the earl.

"Her ladyship and I have decided that you shall all be conveyed to Culverleigh posthaste," he said stiffly, to general consternation around the table.

"All, sir?" Philip asked, glancing up at his father's stern visage, as the others directed their gazes studiously downward.

"Yes, yes, your companions may come along if you please," he replied irritably, with a dismissive wave his hand. "We think it best if you all removed from the city while we look into a commission for Captain Moorehouse."

Philip brightened considerably, and emboldened by this unlooked-for generosity, added, "Captain Lindsey wants for a commission as well, sir."

The earl favored him with a withering glance, and Philip returned his gaze to his plate. "A commission, *if* it be possible," he continued, "and Lady Gray will make a generous gift to the Theater Royal, Covent Garden, which should ensure Mr. Rich looks on the rest of you with favor." It was Tom's turn to grin with relief, causing his father to shudder inwardly. That ghastly visage, so like his own, still filled him with guilt and unease. A protracted stay at Culverleigh—he pushed the thought aside.

"And what of me, Father?" Charlotte demanded in a girlish, whining tone. "Am I to be sent back to that brute? Have you no mercy for your own daughter?"

The earl rounded on her angrily. "As for you, madam, to my mind you have gotten no better than you deserve, marrying that wretch without my permission. You ought to be sent back to the regiment and be damned to you both," he growled.

At these harsh words, Charlotte began to wail and wring her hands in the manner she had practiced on her brothers for many long weeks, although Tom could now detect a note of hysteria in her voice that had not been present before.

"Oh, how can you be so cruel!" she cried.

Tess stretched out a hand murmuring, "There now, be easy."

Lady Gray rapped out "Jamie!" making them all sit up quite straight in surprise.

"Oh, do be quiet!" the earl shouted. "Your aunt is inclined to be merciful in your case, no matter how undeserving. She has convinced me that the scandal that would attach to you was you to remain married is worse than allowing you to separate."

Charlotte turned to him with shining eyes, the color high in her cheeks. "Then I am to be divorced?" she asked hopefully.

"Of course not, a proper divorce can only be granted by an act of parliament. You practice on my good graces too far if you suppose my generosity towards you extends to using my influence in the House of Lords to provide you with a divorce from this frivolous and ill-conceived marriage. No, a divorce is not possible." The blood drained from Charlotte's face and she looked ready to begin her lamentations again, but the earl had not finished. "However, you were married in the Fleet, were you not?" She nodded miserably. "Well then, we shall have the marriage dissolved on the grounds that it was performed illegally. You never posted banns, and as for the priest, I suppose he was no priest at all, am I correct?"

"Oh no, I'm certain he was a proper priest—" she began, but Tess gave her a pinch, and Lady Gray leveled a formidable warning look at her. "Or, I, ah, I believe on reflection he may have been a charlatan, a mere pretender," she whispered uncertainly.

"Very well, then, the marriage is undone, and we shall leave

Colonel Carstone to his court-martial in a single state."

"Then may Nathaniel come to Culverleigh as well?" Charlotte ventured in a small voice.

The earl's thin face flushed with anger. "No, I should think not. He will be court-martialed as well, rot him. You will entertain no followers while you're under my roof, you trollop, or you will be turned out of doors, d'ye hear?" There was a shocked silence for a few moments.

"And Richard?" Philip asked. "Is he to be court-martialed as well?"

The earl looked grave. "I'm afraid so, he is very like to be broke."

At this, Tom could not prevent a superior grin from spreading across his face, which did not escape the earl's attention. "Oh, and d'ye suppose this is all a God-damned jest?" he roared out, striking the table with his fist and making all the dishes jump, his anger at his wayward children reaching new heights. "Brawling like a pack of bloody schoolboys, my God, what a disgrace. And if Richard is dismissed the service, what then? Have you thought on that? I shall tell you, he'll be hanging about all your houses like a parasitical dog, that's what! Is that what you'd prefer? To have him hanging about early and late?" The grin faded from Tom's face, and the earl continued somewhat more calmly, "No, the army is the only place for him, and I intend to ensure that he stays there. Now enough of this palaver. I have sent ahead to Lady Bolingbroke to look for your arrival tonight. The carriage will depart before noon. Make yourselves ready."

Before long, the seven of them found themselves bundled into the earl's carriage, bowling along the road to Bedfordshire, although not in one might call high style, rather more in the manner of parcels directed with all haste. As the carriage bounced and jolted along the frozen rutted track, a gloomy silence overhung the company, all excepting Jem and Tom, who from the outset treated this journey as merely another diversion, rather than punishment inflicted as on an erring child.

"Come, now," Tom said as the city, with its stinks and noise, fell away behind them, replaced by the fresh stillness of the countryside. "Why so hipped? Philip, did the earl not promise you a new commission?"

Philip squirmed uncomfortably, squashed between Alexander's broad shoulders and the cold window. "Huh. We shall see if it is all air or no. What preferment can we possibly gain hidden away in the country? I would far rather be posting down to Portsmouth."

"A fart for Portsmouth, pardon the expression, ladies," Jem said. "Why look for toil and hardship when we may take our ease? A month or more of high living at a manor house, carrying on in prime twig, rumtitum, what could be better, lads? Oh, and ladies too, pardon me," He gave the women an abbreviated salute from his cramped position on the opposite side of Captain Lindsey.

"Just yesterday you was singing the praises of country living to me, hunting and whatnot," Tom added, then turned toward his sister, seated by his side. "And Charlotte, you shall have your divorce at last, ain't that the thing?"

Charlotte's sallow face had been fixed in a mask of tragedy since the rebuke she had received from their father. "Yes, but without my darling Nathaniel, what good is it? You heard what Father said, we are never to be together. To think of his fine dashing figure lying in irons in the Savoy, oh, oh—" she fell into a hiccupping sort of sob, as Tess, seated on her other side, patted her hand sympathetically.

"It's very kind of you, Miss Turnbridge," Charlotte managed to gasp between sobs. "I'm so very sorry this d-, I mean, this wretched affair has been the undoing of your career, truly I am."

Tess stiffened.

"Not undoing, surely," Tom put in hurriedly. "Did not Aunt Sarah stay behind to talk to Mr. Rich? My dearest Tess, yours is the finest voice in London. He could not think to stage the next opera without you, I assure you. Perhaps this will be like the case of Peg Ashgrove and Elizabeth Eckton, and only increase the company's repute. At the very least, after several weeks his temper will have cooled, I warrant," Tom finished somewhat lamely. Tess made a noncommittal reply, as Jane placed a protective arm about her, glaring at Tom from the opposite end of the bench.

They jolted along in silence once more. Soon enough even Tom abandoned his customary good humor as the inexorable icy fingers of travel sickness clamped about his belly. The effects of this were visited upon not only himself but also on his companions, to his regret, and so it was that they arrived at Culverleigh in even more wretched and squalid a condition than when they departed London.

CHAPTER TEN:
SAMSON AGONISTES

Catherine Douglas, the second Lady Bolingbroke, was not best pleased to discover she would be required to extend her hospitality to one of the earl's daughters by his first wife, two of his bastard sons, as well as a pack of their disreputable friends and hangers-on, just at the time she was intending to prepare her own two daughters for the coming London Season. News of Charlotte's disgrace had not yet traveled to the family seat in Bedfordshire. Lady Gray had remained in London to ensure that the story, if it must circulate, did so in a form more flattering to her misfortunate niece.

Lady Bolingbroke's antipathy toward the earl's progeny had not lessened since she had schemed to have them all removed from the estate over twenty years previous. This, along with bearing the earl his only legitimate son and heir, she considered her greatest triumph. Now, as young Jamie had very nearly reached his majority with no greater deficits than a tendency towards overindulgence and a certain dullness of wit, Lady Bolingbroke had turned her attention to her two daughters, Isabel and Agnes, now thirteen and fourteen, respectively. She had no notion of them being corrupted by this importunate visit, although she did not go so far as to defy her husband openly. The best she could manage was to forbid the girls to speak to or have any other association with the guests, and as the girls were still too young to dine with the adults,

337

this was easily accomplished. Furthermore Lady Bolingbroke resolved to discourage any callers of quality; nature conspired with her in this regard, as the weather was so wretchedly cold, alternately snowy and rainy, that their neighbors all kept to their own homes.

Tom and the others were soon settled into rooms in the spacious manor house, although with Lady Bolingbroke keeping herself and her daughters out of the way, and with the weather keeping them indoors, there were few diversions to be had. Jem in particular had been anticipating meeting the two youngest of the earl's daughters, as Charlotte mentioned that the girls were as yet unmarried. On first beholding them, however, with their yellow curls standing out stiffly all about their round baby faces, he allowed that they were still very much children (and rather plain children at that), and turned his attentions instead to the upstairs maids.

Philip and Charlotte seemed pleased enough to find themselves at Culverleigh again, despite their earlier trepidation, but for his part, Tom felt strangely disoriented. He could recall voices and incidents from his time there as a child so vividly, yet now he could not even find his way from his bedroom to the breakfast room without becoming lost. On the second day, he remarked on this to Charlotte, who had come upon him wandering about the second storey gallery.

"It is the most singular thing," he remarked as she led him downstairs. "At one time, I knew every corner of the estate, but now, perhaps because I am grown, it feels to me like a wholly different house—there is not one hall or room that is familiar."

Charlotte burst out laughing. "Of course not, cully, I mean, you silly fellow." She had been attempting to recover her genteel manners, with only moderate success. "This wing is new-built. I thought you knew. The rooms we were in as children are in the old wing. It's been shut up for years."

Tom laughed with her. "I feel less of a flat then," he said, adding in a more thoughtful tone, "I shall think of this as an entirely new place."

For the first week, as a freezing rain fell outside, they played endless rounds of faro, piquet, and all-fours in one of the spacious sitting rooms, availing themselves liberally of the earl's best tobacco and brandy, and eating candied fruit from the kitchen of Lady Bolingbroke's French cook. The surroundings were far more luxurious than what they were accustomed to, and they all enjoyed the soft beds and elegant meals. Jem was packing on weight like a prize bull, while Captain Lindsey had discovered the earl's private armory and was busy cleaning and oiling his pistols and fowling-pieces.

Being unable to play cards, Tom alternately paced behind them or lounged on the settee before the fire, occasionally joining in their idle chatter. Tess watched him covertly—he never complained, but surely, she thought, it must be frightfully dull for him. He had kept himself slightly apart from her since she had rebuffed him at the stage door, notwithstanding the night in the watch house, and she was uncertain how to approach him. Still, it pained her to see him disguise his frustration at being excluded from the company. One particularly dreary afternoon, she seated herself beside him on the settee; he had perhaps been half-asleep, for he jerked up in surprise on sensing another person join him. Tess again felt that peculiar pang on seeing his blind eyes searching for her.

"It's I, Tess," she said. He nodded soberly. "Shall I read aloud?" she asked.

Tom's face broke into the unaffected grin she knew so well. "My dearest Tess, I should like it of all things."

There was little in the way of popular novels in the earl's household; the library yielded up improving, moralizing works no doubt chosen by successive generations of tutors. With some trepidation, Tess selected a yellowed volume of Milton's *Samson Agonistes*. It was the only volume of poetry in the collection.

Tess was a skilled reader: her strong musical voice and sense of dramatic rhythm brought the words of the poem to vibrant life. Within the first few lines, however, she began to regret her choice of texts. Feeling herself on dangerous shoals, she read,

O loss of sight! Of thee I most complain!
Blind among enemies, O worse than chains,
Dungeon, or beggary, or decrepit age!
Light, the prime work of God, to me is extinct,
And all her various objects of delight
Annulled, which might in part my grief have eased,
Inferior to the vilest now become
Of man or worm; the vilest here excel me.

Tess worriedly lifted her eyes from the page to glance at Tom, but he was leaning forward in rapt attention, his ear cocked towards her. She continued,

They creep, yet see; I, dark in light, exposed
To daily fraud, contempt, abuse, and wrong,
Within doors or without, still as a fool,
In power of others, never in my own;
Scarce half I seem to live, dead more than half.
O dark, dark, dark, amid the blaze of noon,
Irrevocably dark: total eclipse,
Without all hope of day!

Now painfully aware of her audience, Tess noticed that the others had left off their game of cards to listen to her read.

Since light so necessary is to life,
And almost life itself—if it be true
That light is in the soul,
She all in every part—why was the sight
To such a tender ball as the eye confined,
So obvious and so easy to be quenched...

Philip gave a strangled sort of cough. Tess snapped the book shut, blushing furiously. "Perhaps that is enough for today," she said.

By the next day, the rain at last lifted, revealing a soggy landscape lit by pale, watery winter sunlight. At last freed from the confines of the house, Captain Lindsey rode out to the village before breakfast with half the earl's armory and some vague plan of mustering the local men. Jem had vanished and none dared inquire too closely where or with whom, while Philip and Tom set out on two of the earl's hunters to see about the pheasants in the park, leaving Charlotte, Tess and Jane to stroll the green behind the house.

As the three ladies crested the small rise, Charlotte sighed so often and with such deliberate emphasis that Tess was rather reluctantly forced to ask if she was feeling quite well.

"I'm only thinking on my poor Nathaniel," Charlotte lamented, wringing her hands as she strode on ahead of them in agitation. "I've had no news of him at all."

"I'm certain he is well," Tess offered in a baseless attempt to reassure her. She had already participated in variations on this conversation several times, and was beyond weary of repeating herself. "He seems a very, ah, capable young man." As Tess said this, Jane rolled her eyes.

Charlotte sighed again. "He is capable, indeed, but I do wish he could be just a tiny bit more attentive. Behold how gallant and true Captain Lindsey is—I wish Nathaniel would be more like him."

They proceeded toward the back of the estate, skirting several large muddy puddles. As they approached the lane, a young man in a cocked hat and leather hunting frock rode up on a fine black prancer. He paused to tip his hat to the ladies as his horse stamped the ground impatiently.

"Charlotte? Is it you?" He peered at her more closely. "I heard you was here, but I wasn't certain it was true. My goodness, it's been years. Excuse me, you is Mrs. Carstone now, is you not?"

Charlotte greeted him familiarly and introduced her friends from London, omitting, Tess noted, the fact that she and Jane were both actresses upon the stage. The young man, whom Charlotte introduced as Mr. Nicolas Brimble, stared openly at Jane, who returned his gaze boldly.

"Visiting from London?" he echoed, tugging at the reins as his horse tossed its head. "But we have a house in Cavendish Square. I shall be returning there as soon as the weather clears. Please do call on me there, Mrs. Carstone." Although he addressed Charlotte, he looked only at Jane, who toyed with a lock of hair. "And please bring your friends as well," he added.

"Lovely to make your acquaintance!" Jane called to his back as he galloped off down the lane.

Charlotte set off again in the opposite direction from him. "Nicolas is the third son of Squire Brimble," she said, with a meaningful glance at Jane. "He won't inherit a farthing, in case you were thinking of setting your cap at him."

Tess fell in step behind them, eyeing the back of Charlotte's cloak swaying just ahead of her uneasily as they marched along through the damp grass. This was not an argument she wished to have before an audience.

Jane kept her eyes fixed straight on the muddy track ahead, not looking at Tess. "Why not? He seems very handsome."

"Jane!"

Tess stood rooted to the spot, feeling as if Jane had plunged a dagger in her heart. A confusion of recriminations rose to her lips—did Jane really think so little of their alliance? That it was merely in jest, a dalliance until a man came along? When Tess stopped walking, Jane also paused, and a moment later, so did Charlotte, turning to gaze at them inquisitively.

"I tire of this walk," Tess said abruptly. "Please excuse me. I shall return to the house."

Meanwhile, in the park, Tom and Philip were enjoying their

outing immensely. After some target practice and with guidance from Philip, Tom found it not so difficult to aim, especially with the birds' distinctive cry of kek-kek-kek as they rose into the air. Tom brought down one bird, and Philip two; deciding that this was more than enough for a feast, Philip fastened the carcasses to Tom's saddle-pow. Remounting, they made their way amiably back through the park. Or Tom at least was easy, whistling an air and fingering the feathers of the birds before him with great satisfaction. Philip watched him, feeling the need for conversation but not quite knowing where to begin.

"That was some fine shooting, brother," he offered, but Tom merely smiled and tipped his hat to him. There was a long pause, with no noise save the soft tramp of their horses' hooves, the gentle creaking of the saddles and the ring of the bridles.

At last Philip began again awkwardly, "It were downright rude of Miss Turnbridge to read that poem to you yesterday."

Tom was brought out of his reverie at last. "What, the *Samson*? How was that rude?"

Philip shifted in his saddle. "All those lines about being half-dead, a vile worm, just because...I mean, what it said about blindness being worse than death. Did you not mind it at all?"

Tom laughed. "My dearest Philip, it never even entered my mind that it might apply to my own circumstance. Poor old Milton, he couldn't help it, the sorry roundhead."

"Brother, you astonish me. What do you mean?"

"You know Milton was dreadfully cast down after the Restoration and the failure of the republic, that's what all those sad lines and wailing are about. And some very noble lines, too, I might add. Now that you mention it, I suppose it's true that Milton was blind too, in his old age, but I confess I never thought on it until now. And recall, the poem ends quite gloriously, with Samson victorious, and those fine heroic couplets." He recited from memory,

All is best, though we oft doubt,
What the unsearchable dispose
Of highest Wisdom brings about,
And ever best found in the close.

He paused dramatically after this recitation, then added, "That reminds me, I heard from Mr. Rich that Mr. Handel is considering setting the poem as an oratorio."

"A what?"

"An oratorio, a sort of concert, if you like. He wanted to make it into an opera, but the Bishop of London says it's blasphemous to set a Bible story on the wicked stage. As long as the musicians and singers are arrayed together, without costumes or dancing, then it may be performed in a theater and not only in a church. He already done it with *King Saul*, and it's been some of his finest work. I am alive with curiosity to hear how he might set Milton's verses."

"Indeed."

Philip had nothing at all to say about music or poetry. He was silent again for a time. Since being reunited with his brother, he had thought constantly on Tom's blindness and his own near escape from the same fate. Could it really be that Tom himself did not reflect on it at all? Did he really find it affected him so little? In comparing their two circumstances, Philip could not help but find himself wanting, yet he was at a loss for how to put it in words.

After another lengthy silence, he began again on a different tack. "It were uncommon brave of you to take on Richard in the theater."

"The back of my hand to bravery," Tom replied lightly. "I tell you, it were no such thing. I was merely angry, and over a boyhood slight, to my shame."

"Not at all," Philip said, growing more heated. "I have seen men in action, and I have learnt to tell those who are shy from those who leap forward with no thought to themselves.

344

To dash into action like that..." He paused, then in an embarrassed tone added, "I must confess to you, brother, not long ago, I had a very near miss with a wicked great splinter. The surgeon said it very nearly put out my eyes. I have been thinking on how I might have fared in that case, and I can't help but think I would have shown far less courage than you."

"What stuff," Tom replied with a short laugh. Philip stared at him, nettled that he was not taking this conversation more seriously.

"I tell you, in the service, courage is all. There is no higher measure of a man's character," he said in a strained voice.

Tom frowned in the direction of his voice. "Is that what is troubling your mind? You fear that you want for courage?" As there was no answer, he continued, "I own our recent acquaintance has been short, and my opinion may carry no weight in military matters, but I would never call you shy. To fly in the face of society and risk all, even death, only for love —why, it seems very noble to me."

"What, you mean—that—?" Philip said, disconcerted.

"Indeed, these past weeks I have worried constantly for your safety; even now I beg you to be cautious. I believe you risk far more walking the streets of London than on your own quarter-deck, and without the slightest flinch. Now that is what I should call brave."

Philip blushed. "I think it is entirely different, but you are kind. As you say, love may lend a man more courage than he naturally possesses."

"Oh, I don't know," Tom said thoughtfully. "I loved a girl once, in the face of opposition and disapprobation on all sides, yet I could not save her from herself, and so she died. I thought I loved her more than life, but here I am still living on and even happy, without her. When I think on it, it makes me feel very low."

"Well, I don't know the lady you speak of, but I can tell you Alexander was not first in my heart. When I was a squeaker in the midshipman's berth, there was a boy, another mid, and

I was closer with him than any other before or since, but he died in a storm when our mizzenmast went by the board, and that was that. I still think of him, but it does no good to go about carrying ghosts with you."

"There, you see, how can you say you want for courage? That seems a very fine sentiment. Yet I find I can't forget her."

"And what of Miss Turnbridge?" Philip asked in a slightly teasing tone. "You may say she denies you, but I'll tell you what it is, she looks at you when her Miss Carlyle does not attend, with far more than a look of disinterested friendship."

Tom shifted suddenly in his saddle, making his horse dance sideways for a moment, as Philip watched with amusement, realizing his dart had hit home more directly than he anticipated.

"Perhaps it is as you say, 'All is best in the close,'" Philip suggested.

CHAPTER ELEVEN: THE HEART'S DELIGHT

A week later at breakfast, Jane announced that she was returning to London, as she was concerned for her mother's health. Tess did not say anything. She knew Jane was hoping to call on young Mr. Brimble.

"How can you be so cruel?" Tess cried when they were alone in their room together, as Jane packed her belongings.

"I?" Her grey eyes flashing in anger, Jane paused with a fistful of lace, then flung it in the trunk. "Why should I hang about here to watch you flirt and sigh over Tom Finch every waking moment? And you call me cruel!"

"But I have pledged myself to you!" Tess insisted, tears starting in her eyes.

Jane snorted. "I didn't mind when you was with the duke. He rarely visited and he was plenty rich. And you wasn't in love with him. But why shouldn't I look out for my own interests? We can't all be prima donnas. If I haven't the skill for it, what else am I to do?"

This was an argument they had often repeated, yet it was no less painful, and Tess still had no answer. She sat heavily on the bed beside Jane's trunk, a few tears silently trickling down her face. Absently, she refolded some of the hastily tossed in chemises.

"I shall miss you, sweetheart," she said at last.

"And I you," Jane replied, squeezing her hand affectionately. "But I shall see you again when you return home. Until then, think on what it is your heart truly desires."

They had argued and reunited so many times that Tess thought it best if they passed some time apart. In any case, Tess had no reason to return to London before the next opera season resumed. Sadly, she kissed Jane on either cheek and promised she would return home soon.

Jem volunteered to walk with Jane into town where they caught the post back to London. While the company, apart from Tess, may have been rather puzzled over Jane's hasty departure, Jem's exit was easily understood: his pursuit of one of the maids had been rather more successful than he expected, and now she was making demands on him. Despite his natural inclination to take his ease at the expense of others, he was forced to retreat.

At the same time, Lady Gray and Lord Bolingbroke returned from London, and against all expectation their arrival had a strangely liberating effect. Lady Bolingbroke dared not voice her disapproval of her unexpected houseguests with her husband present. Tom took to composing again, and found Tess a quick and agreeable copyist. Meanwhile, Captains Moorehouse and Lindsey spent their days mustering the men of the village, on Alexander's suggestion, in hopes they might impress the Admiralty with their martial zeal.

In the evenings, Lady Gray encouraged Tom and Tess to provide musical entertainment, which they were pleased to do. They found it delightful to make music together again after so long, with Tom playing and Tess performing her best arias. But Tess noted with some concern that the earl did not appear to enjoy these performances as his sister did. At first Tess thought perhaps it was her imagination, or wounded professional pride. But then she offered to play the harpsichord to give Tom a chance to sing for once.

They traded places and Tom stood before the harpsichord,

facing the company. Tess began to play the opening bars of one of the countertenor arias from *Ariodante*, transposed down an octave, as Tom sang in his clear light baritone, but before he had got through the opening lines, the earl shuffled hastily from the room. As no one else remarked on it, Tess continued playing, unsure whether Tom was aware of his father's departure or not. Could it really be that the earl did not wish to see his own son perform?

After Tom performed two more arias, Lady Gray thanked them and retired, followed not long after by Charlotte and Captains Moorehouse and Lindsey. Tom and Tess lingered in the sitting room over glasses of sherry. The fire had died down to embers and the candles guttered out, save for two or three, casting the room in dim, flickering twilight.

"You were in fine voice tonight," Tess told him. "It's a pity the earl didn't stay to hear you."

Tom shrugged. "Yes, well, he is ever thus."

Tess had wondered if she was imagining the coolness between father and son and now was dismayed to hear it confirmed. "Is he ashamed of you?" she asked hesitantly.

"No, he feels guilt for being the cause of my blindness. My presence oppresses his spirits."

"What! How cruel! How can he imagine he is the cause…?" Tess was outraged.

Tom shook his head sadly. "But my dear, it is almost certainly his fault. He gave my mother the pox, and behold, she died of it. Charlotte's mother too."

Tess stared at him with horror. The dying candlelight flickered over his face, but he showed no particular emotion at such a shocking and intimate revelation.

"You're certain?" she whispered.

"So I have always been told. My eyes were clouded from the moment I was born, although as a child I could see bright lights and colors."

As Tom did not pity himself, Tess had never before thought to do so either, but learning this about him moved her deeply.

"But if this be true, he should treat you with greater kindness, not less!" she cried.

Tom gave a humorless laugh. "That is ever the way with family, is it not?"

Tess had to own that that was true. "But does his coldness not wound you?" she asked with concern.

Tom only shrugged. "It is his burden to bear, not mine."

One day late in February the weather turned suddenly cold again. They woke in the morning to find the grounds all covered in a thick blanket of snow, but the sky was already clear and the sun shone brilliantly. Dressing themselves in heavy cloaks and borrowed mittens, Tom and Tess set out for an early morning ramble. Tess knew that Tom would rather ride than walk, but to her shame she had never learnt to ride. The moment they ventured into the snow, however, him holding her arm with one hand and his walking stick in the other, they were both in high spirits.

"The snow has quite transformed the landscape," Tess remarked as they walked away from the house toward the park.

Tom nodded. "It is a singular effect—the echoes are all muffled, as if the whole world were wrapped in cotton wool."

"That's just what it looks like!" Tess exclaimed. "There are the tracks of a hare to our right, but other than that, the snow is entirely untrodden, and the sun is making each flake on the surface shine like crystal. In the trees just ahead, the snow has settled so delicately on each branch, down to the tiniest twig. It really is extraordinarily beautiful." She paused to glance at his face, which was tipped up towards the sun with a bemused expression. "I'm sorry, is it tiresome for me to prate on like this?"

Tom smiled indulgently. "Never in life! My dear Tess, I always enjoy the sound of your voice."

"You flatter me, sir," she replied teasingly. "But I meant, does my description of the beauty of the landscape mean anything to you at all, or is it only words?"

Tom paused thoughtfully before answering, "If you mean, do I see the image you describe in what might be called the mind's eye, then no, to me it is only words. But pray do not dismiss your words so lightly—your description has beauty in itself, and I am sensible of your kindness in sharing your delight with me." He slipped his arm more firmly against her, drawing her closer to him. "Very sensible indeed," he said.

Tess smacked him playfully on the arm. "What a fellow you are, Tom," she said, but her voice held only laughter. "Upon my honor, I never met a worse rake. Will these attempts at enticement never cease?"

"Never," said he, grinning broadly at her.

"It's far too fine a day to worry over such things," she declared. The shining white landscape, the piercing blue of the sky, the utter quiet, all made her feel as if they had stepped out of time, into a place uninhabited by any others. Releasing his arm, Tess ran ahead a short way, skipping through the snow and whooping with delight like a child. They had come to the edge of a stand of trees, and she ran up to the nearest, wrapping her mittened hands on the rough bark and swinging herself around.

Tom paused where she had left him, cocking his ear toward her, then leaned down to gather a handful of snow. He pitched the snowball at her with perfect accuracy; if she had not ducked behind the tree at the last moment, it would have hit her in the face.

"Oh, oh you beast!" she cried, laughing and ran back to the clearing to return fire. They stood apart for some time, launching snowballs at each other, but while hers all went wide of the mark, his aim was true, and in no time her dark cloak was spotted with snow, her attempts to avoid the onslaught by dashing about all in vain.

"My dearest Tess, you do realize that if you would only cease laughing and be still, I could not aim so easily," he remarked, but she only laughed harder. At last she endeavored to strike him in the chest, and brushing away the snow with mock anger, he strode towards her. She shrieked with laughter and tried to run, but her long skirts tangled about her ankles in a deeper snowdrift, and he soon caught her up, wrapping his arms about her waist.

"Come now, let's have a kiss," he teased.

Tess shrieked with laughter again and struggled to free herself, but in flailing about wildly, she lost her footing, and brought them both down into the snowdrift, which cushioned their fall like a feather bed.

Tess lay for a moment in the snow with Tom atop her, staring into his blue-white eyes. In the strangely muffled surroundings, there was no sound but the slight crunch of the snow beneath them. Pulling off his mitten, Tom reached for her lips with his bare fingers, then leaned in to kiss her. Tess closed her eyes, letting herself be borne away for just a moment. Just a moment; it could not last.

"My backside is frozen," she whispered, opening her eyes and returning to the world. With a smile, Tom pulled her to her feet and helped to brush the snow off her cloak and skirts.

They walked back to the house arm in arm, companionably silent. As the day wore on, however, Tess began to wrestle with herself again. She sat by the fire with Charlotte and Lady Gray, watching idly as Charlotte composed the latest installment in the serial letter she claimed was to her sister Sophia but which Tess suspected was in fact intended for Nathaniel Welgarth, while Lady Gray wrote letters of a far more mundane sort, on the management of her estate in Stirling. They were seated in one of the smaller, more out-of-the-way sitting rooms, but even here the appointments, from the delicate Queen Anne chairs to the flower-patterned wallpaper, were far more luxurious than anywhere Tess had lived, and she felt increasingly out of place. She fretted that perhaps it was all beginning to turn her head, and she began to regret her free behavior with Tom that morning. True, Jane had left her here on her own, all but pushing them together, but she still had no answer to Jane's question. What did she desire? She felt very attached to Jane, and was unwilling to give up their intimacy so easily. And having granted him this one favor, she knew Tom would come at her again. It was time to return to London.

At tea, Tess thanked Lord Bolingbroke for his hospitality, and by the next morning's coach she was gone, having avoided a private conference with Tom.

"I'm afraid I have left Jane on her own for too long," was all she said to him by way of explanation.

Feeling vaguely that the others were more than usually interested in his reaction, Tom merely wished her a pleasant journey and promised to call when he returned to London.

With Tess gone, Tom found himself rather uncomfortably at loose ends. He played on the harpsichord, testing out new melodies, but now there was no one to write down his compositions. Charlotte at least accompanied him on rambles about the park, although he found her company tedious. They were walking toward the far end of the park one day when Philip came tearing out of the back of the house and down the grassy bank, whooping and shouting, waving a letter above his head.

"A ship!" he shouted as he approached them. "I have a ship! Dammee, I never thought I should see the day!" He embraced his sister and brother, giving them each a hearty kiss in an excess of high spirits.

"I give you the joy of it," Tom said, thumping him on the back, and Charlotte did likewise. She had dropped some of her rough military habits in her father's house, but with Philip she sometimes fell unconsciously back to old ways.

"'You are hereby required and directed to proceed on board H.M.S. *Heart's Delight*, and take upon you the Charge and Command of Captain.'" Philip read the stiffly formal letter in rapturous tones. "The *Delight*, ain't that a bang-up prime name for a ship? She's bound for Gibraltar—a real commission, none of your lurking about in port, ha ha!"

"And what of Captain Lindsey?" Tom inquired with some delicacy.

Philip grinned. "He has a commission in the *Defiant*. A thumping great command for him too! He was very clever to spend weeks teaching those peasants to march in a line and point a gun. The Admiralty was impressed. But it were the old earl who came through for both of us, ha ha ha!"

"But *Defiant*, that's a different ship," Charlotte cut in with concern. "You shall be parted."

Philip paused and looked slightly more sober. "Aye, well, that is the way of it," he admitted. "Still, commissions for both of us, that's a rare bit of good fortune."

"Perhaps it's for the best," Tom suggested, "and besides which, was you to have a wife, you would be parted from her as well, such being the way of the service, is it not?"

Philip laughed and agreed that it was.

"Come, we must drink to your good fortune," Tom added, anticipating an afternoon and evening spent earnestly plumbing the depths of the earl's wine cellar, but Philip was already running back to the house.

"No, no, perhaps later, but now I must prepare to depart. There's not a moment to be lost!" he shouted behind him. In the end, Tom was denied the pleasure of a leisurely drink with Captains Moorehouse and Lindsey. The rest of the afternoon, the house was in an uproar as they turned their rooms upside down preparing their baggage, and by the evening they had set off in a tearing hurry for Plymouth in the earl's own equipage.

The next morning the house felt echoingly empty and gloomy. The snow had long since melted and the rain had returned; Tom and Charlotte sat alone at the breakfast table contemplating another day spent in idleness. The earl and Lady Gray were off somewhere tending to business on the estate, and Lady Bolingbroke had been keeping to her rooms of late, complaining of the head-ache, while ensuring that Isabelle and Agnes remained out of sight as well. Tom and Charlotte crunched their toast in silence, until at last Tom set down his teacup with an air of decision.

"I shall return to London tomorrow," he announced.

"Oh Tommy, no!" Charlotte wailed. "How can you be so hard-hearted, to leave me here forsaken and alone?"

"You ain't alone. There's Aunt Sarah, our stepmother, and an army of servants to do your bidding," Tom pointed out. "Besides which, your troubles are now at an end. Father had your marriage to Carstone dissolved, and he rots away in the Savoy, awaiting his court-martial. Even once he gets out, you are protected from him at Culverleigh; he dare not come at you here. This is what you desired, is it not?"

Charlotte sighed, scraping with a fork at the hardened remains of egg on her plate. "Aye, but my sweet Nathaniel, are we to be parted forever?"

Tom thought of the feckless dragoon; "sweet" was not a word he would apply to the young man in question. "Be patient. Perhaps if her ladyship tires of your presence here, the old earl might consent to you marrying again," Tom suggested, thinking privately, marrying again, no matter how ill-advisedly.

Charlotte knew very well that her ladyship their stepmother had tired of her presence even before she arrived, but instead she only said, "Thank you, Tom. You've been so kind to me these last few months. I shall miss you."

"And I you, but you may write and tell me how you're getting on here," Tom offered, carefully avoiding any remark that might be construed as an invitation to return to London with him. "Jem can read your letters to me, and I shall dictate my reply to him."

"Are you truly to leave?" she asked again, rather wistfully, but his mind was made up.

The following morning found Tom on the front steps of the estate, his baggage already loaded onto the earl's carriage. He bowed stiffly to his father. "It's very kind of you, sir, to allow me the use of your equipage all the way up to London."

Lord Bolingbroke nodded gravely, his face lined and old in the pale morning light. Beside him, his sister gave a haughty sniff.

"The horses can use the exercise," she said. "And that black-guardly postilion is best kept busy. See that he returns here directly, no idling about in the city. And speaking of idleness, I trust that on your return, you will apply to Mr. Rich for employment in the next season, Tom."

Tom bowed again. "I am in your debt for interceding on my behalf in this ugly business, and for Miss Turnbridge as well. Not for my own sake, but for hers..."

The earl cut him off. "Think nothing of it. I, ah," he paused, uncharacteristically hesitant, "I have heard your career—I mean your career at the Theater Royal," he clarified, purposely omitting the low broadsides Tom penned, "I have heard great things of your career. I would see you continue in it."

"You honor me, sir," Tom said, feeling strangely overcome. "I am grateful for your patronage, and for your hospitality these past weeks."

"You are welcome to visit whenever you please." Feeling the need for some accompanying physical gesture, he extended his hand, then found himself awkwardly waiting in vain for Tom to take it.

"Perhaps you should shake hands," Lady Gray prompted, being more accustomed to Tom's ways. Tom reached out his hand and the earl shook it solemnly. Lady Gray embraced Tom and kissed him on both cheeks.

"Call on Miss Turnbridge when you return," she instructed as she led him to the carriage. A footman handed him in, and he was off, feeling rather oddly like a child again for just a moment, yet it was not such an unpleasant sensation.

CHAPTER TWELVE: BLACKBIRDS AND THRUSHES

How pleasant and delightful is the midsummer's morn,
When the hills and the valleys are covered with corn,
The blackbird and the thrush sing on ev'ry green spray,
And the lark sings melodious by the dawning of the day.

As a sailor and his true love did their pleasure take,
Said the sailor to his true love, "I must you forsake,"
And while they stood embracing, tears from her eyes fell,
Saying "May I go along with you?" "Oh no my love, farewell."

Although midsummer was still some way off, the bright spring sunshine angled in through the narrow window, warming the front parlor of number eight Maiden Lane where Tom sat composing at the spinet. His long nimble fingers danced restlessly over the keys, trying out different arrangements of the tune as he sang out short bursts in his clear light baritone.

Upon his return to London after the long stay at Culverleigh, it was represented to him through some rather pointed remarks by Stinson that his household had not been left in what one might call an orderly state, viz., he was again in need of cash. Rehearsals for the summer season at the Theater

Royal, Covent Garden had not yet been announced (if indeed he could hope for employment there after the ignominious end of the last season). But Tom was not greatly distressed, as he knew his grasping publisher Shaloe Brown was always eager for a new broadside.

Tom was in mind to set down a sailor's tune he had heard his brother Philip sing, and the thought of the sad parting of Philip and his particular true love had put Tom in a creative frame of mind. He had already worked out the entire composition in his mind, and now arrived at a state of increasing agitation since Jem seemed not to be about to produce a fair copy, or any copy at all. Frankie had offered his services, but Tom had no great opinion of the boy's newfound skill with a pen, and in any case Frankie could not write musical notation. The longer Tom toyed about with the tune, the more he enamored he became of the rich harmonies possible in the repeating last line of each verse, but even this only added to his vexation. It was a long-standing argument —Tom desirous of setting down the harmonies, and disbelieving Jem's increasingly impatient explanation that it couldn't be done, not on a broadside. The last such exchange had ended with Jem flinging down his pen, shouting, "It ain't a God-damned oratorio!"

"Not a God-damned oratorio, my arse," Tom now muttered to himself as he pounded out the chords, modulating up and down the scale just to test the effect. The legs of the delicate table on which the spinet rested trembled as the strings jangled and twanged.

He was in the midst of a full-throated run: "May I go along with you? Maaaaaaaaaaay I go along with yoooooou? Oh oh, maaaay I go along with you? Oh no, my love—" when he was interrupted by a knocking at the door. Expecting Jem had at last responded to his summons, he allowed Matthews to answer the door while he finished off the verse. "Oh no, my love, farewell!"

Tom was just about to start up the next verse when Matthews burst in and announced in a dull tone, "Mistress Turnbridge, sir!" then stalked out.

"Tess!" Tom left off playing and turned away from the keyboard to smile in the direction of her footfalls. "Just the very person I was hoping to see! How delightful of you to step round. I tell you, I am in a sad way with this ballad. It is at the very moment to be set down, but where is that blackguardly Jem Castleton? Out whoremongering, I warrant, pardon the expression. And here you are at the opportune moment! Might I beg your assistance in pricking it out?"

Tess stared back at him, rather stunned, her face drawn and pale, her mouth hanging open slightly. Had he been able to see her, he might have inquired as to the cause of her distress and why she had come calling, but as it was, he merely took her silence as acquiescence. She looked into his grinning face, alight with uncomplicated pleasure, and choked back the tears that had been threatening to well up. "Yes…yes, I should be happy to assist."

If Tom noticed the slight waver in her voice, he gave no sign of it, instead clapping his hands and calling out, "Prime! Let us get started then. Matthews! Matthews, I say, some paper and ink, if you please, oh, and tea for Miss Turnbridge!"

Tess politely pretended not to notice when Matthews set out the writing materials with barely concealed ill-humor, but when he returned a moment later and slammed down the tea tray so indelicately that the milk slopped over and pooled under the dishes, she turned to Tom wonderingly.

"Whatever is the matter with Matthews?" she asked.

Tom stood up from the spinet at last and brushed the back of his hand along the edge of the small round table until he found the teapot. "Oh, take no mind of him. They are all a bit peevish about the want of wages whilst I was in Bedfordshire."

"You never! Oh fie, Tom." She looked at him sadly. "You might have told me."

He grinned at her again as he poured the tea, heedless of the drops liberally applied to the table and floor. "Never fret, only let us dash this off to Shaloe Brown, then we'll all be plump in the pocket and they will cease this muttering, you'll see. Now then, shall we set to work?"

Tom returned to his seat before the spinet, setting his teacup rather precariously on the top edge just by the exposed strings, and began to play with vigor, causing the cup to vibrate with each ringing chord. He called out the notes and listened with great satisfaction to the scraping of the quill on paper as Tess set them down at his direction. He was even more pleased to discover that she was amenable to his desire to set down the chords.

"And Jem said it couldn't be done!" he murmured to himself as Tess was writing. "I knew he was lying, the dog."

They moved on to setting down the words, and Tom sang out the final line, "If ever I return again, I will make you my bride." Suddenly he paused, cocking an ear in Tess's direction. "My dear, are you unwell?" He frowned as he heard Tess give a hiccupping sort of sob.

"No, I am quite well, thank you," she replied in a strangled, low voice.

With some concern, Tom felt his way toward her and pushed aside the small writing desk, then placed his hand on her cheek. "But you're crying!" he exclaimed, kneeling before her. "Whatever is the matter?"

At this, Tess's brittle composure cracked at last, and to her mortification she burst into a more violent flood of tears, clinging to Tom's hand, which still cradled her cheek.

"It's Jane," she choked out at last. "Jane, she's gone. Run off to marry the son of the squire of Rum-something or other. I couldn't read the note. She always had such dreadful handwriting. And it's not even that puppy who flirted with her at Culverleigh; it must be someone she only just met. Now she's gone, oh how could she?"

Tom embraced her tightly as she was wracked with yet another round of sobbing.

"A curse on her, the false lying jade!" he cried, then pulling away from her slightly, he added, "Tess, forgive me! You come here to tell me this sad news, and here am I prating away like a fool, making you do my copying-out without even asking how d'ye do. It was monstrously selfish in me, and I do humbly beg your pardon."

Tess shook her head, sniffling. "No, I'm ashamed to appear before you in such a sorry state. I am the fool. We quarreled so often, but still I believed we would make it up somehow. Now I must wear willows again, and be subject to prying looks and idle gossip." She sighed, wiping ineffectually at her face with a sodden handkerchief. "Tell me, Tom, was there ever a sorrier fool than I?"

Tom grasped her hands, still kneeling before her. "Don't say such things!" he chided her. "You are the loveliest, most talented woman in Covent Garden, in all of London, and you are still the toast of the beaux! Don't I hear your name all over the Piazza? Let Miss Carlyle become a fat old frump in a country house with a parcel of bawling brats. You still have a glorious career ahead of you."

"And be at the beck and call of every patron with a little cash," she added grimly.

"Not if you don't wish it," Tom suggested, although they both knew that there might come a time when she had no choice. "Come, the shock of it has lowered your spirits, but do not repine. You may, and I make this offer as a, ah, as a gentleman, I say as a *gentleman*, you may stay here if you are so inclined." Tess stared at him without answering. "If you wish it," Tom added, and Tess noted with surprise that he seemed apprehensive of her answer.

"But you have just rid yourself of all your house guests," she said after a pause. "You were forever complaining of the noise and want of privacy."

"Ah, well, you may call me inconstant, but now I find it strangely quiet and lonely with them all gone. And I would do all I can to rally your spirits. Tess, you are my very dear friend, and it pains me to see you so dreadfully cast down," he replied in all earnestness.

Tess was deeply moved by this display of concern, yet she was still puzzled as for an answer. Was he asking her to become his kept mistress or his legal wife? And which did she truly desire? She stared into his long, thin face, so familiar and dear to her, yet could not come to a conclusion that would satisfy both her desire and her better judgment.

"I take the invitation very kindly," she said at last, "but for the moment I find my present lodging will suffice."

Tom stood up quickly and stumbled back toward his seat before the spinet. "Of course, of course, never mind. But you must call here as often as you like, and if you should like to take your dinner here, I will have Susan prepare a fine beefsteak."

They finished the composition at last rather hurriedly, and Tom departed with Frankie to deliver it to Henrietta Street. Tess insisted she could see herself out, but in fact she had an ulterior motive for remaining behind. As soon as she heard the front door shut, she sought out Matthews and asked to see the book of household accounts. As she feared, it was in a terrible muddle. Ordinarily the task of keeping accounts would be the sole reserve of the head of the household, but in this case, a variety of hands had made haphazard notations, and it was impossible to tell how much was coming in and how much going out. But it seemed clear that the latter far exceeded the former.

After struggling over the book for some while, Tess closed it with a sigh. "Tell me the worst," she demanded. "How much is owed and to whom. All of it, if you please."

From anyone else this might have counted as impudence, but none of the servants had forgotten who it was had hired them. Matthews answered in detail, and a sad long list it was: baker, butcher, fishmonger, tailor, draper, and more, all, all had considerable debts, some many months in arrears.

"And that ain't even including the rent," Matthews concluded glumly. As he uttered the words, as if summoned by the admission, Mrs. Bracegirdle herself appeared at the door, hammering loudly and clearly expecting to be turned away.

"Don't take me wrong, I'm grateful for all you done for him, that I am," Mrs. Bracegirdle said to Tess, once she had recovered from the shock of being politely admitted, and was ensconced in the front parlor over a pot of tea. "Mr. Finch's affairs is much more orderly and gentleman-like since you've taken him in hand, Miss Turnbridge. But he's owing three months on the rent now, and with Mr. Handel indisposed and returned to the continent, well, if you don't mind my saying so, prospects ain't good at all for the coming season."

Tess sighed unhappily. It was true. After Lady Gray's kind intercession, both Tom and Tess had hoped to be employed again at the Theater Royal, Covent Garden for the summer season, but Mr. Handel had just recently suffered a fit of apoplexy and had departed to the spa at Aachen to take the cure, leaving his latest opera unfinished and the season in doubt. Tess marveled at the speed and accuracy with which this news had reached the landlady's ears, but she could not deny it.

"Here," she said, opening her purse. "I know it's not the full amount, but I can give you three guineas today as a guarantee on the rest. Will that suffice?"

Mrs. Bracegirdle's round face was suffused with smiles; it would suffice indeed. "You are very kind to him," she said, "better than he deserves. As far as I am concerned, you are welcome in this house at any time," she added, looking meaningfully at Tess.

Tess saw her out hurriedly, wondering at that last remark. How could she have known of Tom's offer of just a few moments ago? Was the whole world conspiring for her to go into his keeping? Yet it was a kindness; the landlady could just as easily have called her a whore and turned her out.

This business over, Tess saw herself out as well, leaving behind a shilling for Matthews, and one more for Susan and Dorcas to divide between them, which also increased her consequence among them inestimably.

Tess had saved up a good deal when she had been the kept

mistress of Charles FitzRoy, the second Duke of Grafton. A goldsmith's shop handled her accounts for her, and she could afford to be open-handed, at least for now. But for how much longer, if she could not find employment? It was kind of Tom to speak so highly of her talents, but she always harbored a lingering fear that the moment she was unable to secure a part in the coming season, her career would be declared over. She was all too aware of former prima donnas reduced to beggary in their later years.

As she walked briskly back to her rented lodgings across the Piazza, Tess wondered over the absurdity of Tom proposing to take her on as his mistress, when she was the one with the money, and he had a pile of debt. Was there ever anything so preposterous? She gave a short laugh.

CHAPTER THIRTEEN: ROSELINDA

For all her intentions of maintaining her independence, Tess found her resolve to keep to her own lodgings lasted less than a week after Jane's departure. She had errands enough to occupy her during the days, inquiring after her accounts and scrupulously paying her bills. But the nights were lonely and cold; for two nights running she kept herself awake with bitter sobbing, shedding tears not only for her lost companionship but nearly equally as much for her wounded pride, although she was loath to admit it to herself.

This will never do, she thought on the third night, willing herself to greater fortitude, but although she kept the tears at bay, still sleep would not come. She rose the next morning to discover that her only maid had run off, helping herself to a few pieces of plate and a small terra cotta statue of a shepherd on her stealthy departure. It was bad enough to awaken to a cold grate, no breakfast, and the remains of the previous night's supper still on the table, but when Tess discovered the theft, she felt the last of her forbearance snap, and with a cry of frustration, she hurled an earthenware pitcher against the wall, where it smashed into several pieces. Unable to bear the apartment for another moment, never mind cleaning up the mess, Tess stormed out, slamming the door behind her.

She walked around and around the Piazza for nearly an hour before she felt sufficiently in possession of her spirits to call again at number eight Maiden Lane. Upon being admitted by Matthews, Tess discovered Tom still at breakfast, but he invited her to join him with great solicitude.

"Would you care for a bloater?" he offered. "They're particularly fine today, I find."

Tess sat down stiffly. "I have come about your offer of the other day," she said without preamble, then before he could reply, she charged on, "It was very kind of you, and I tell you I hesitated not from any antipathy towards you, but from what I may blush to call niceness of manners, at your rather ambiguous invitation. However, it has come to my attention that you are in want of funds, and I own my lodgings are not quite as ideal as I might have described them previously. In short, I propose that I take a room here as a lodger. Is that acceptable to you?"

"But of course," he replied seriously. "Whatever arrangement suits you best is agreeable to me. Now let us make ourselves easy, and I will have Matthews set a place for you so you might partake of this excellent breakfast." This being done, he added, "I have some happy news for you as well. I have secured positions for us both in the coming season."

"Indeed?" Tess set her butter knife aside with some trepidation. With Mr. Handel on the continent for the coming months and no other reputable production in rehearsals, she had decided that she would rather perform at Vauxhall Gardens and at assemblies than risk her reputation with a lesser company, but the eager note in Tom's voice made her hold her tongue.

"Mr. Highmore at Drury Lane has engaged some Italian fellow to write a new opera, *Roselinda*, and you are to play the part of Roselinda herself. Ain't you amazed? Jem will step round in a quarter of an hour with the score. No, I tell a lie. I hear Matthews letting him in at this very moment," Tom said, cocking an ear toward the door.

"Really now, it's all so sudden," Tess replied faintly. "Who is this Italian composer?"

"A Signor Veracini, I believe," Tom said. "Are you acquainted with him?"

"Veracini, but he is a madman!" Tess exclaimed with a sinking heart.

"Aye, a madman indeed!" Jem cried as he swaggered into the room, tossing his tricorne hat to Matthews behind him and dropping the enormous conductor's score on the table with a resounding thud, causing the dishes to jump.

"So you know of him, then?" Tom asked, his long fingers feeling the edges of the score with satisfaction.

"He's a violinist of some minor talent. I know he was dismissed his appointment in Dresden," Tess answered.

"So he was," Jem corroborated, helping himself to the remaining bloaters and toast. "It were on account of a duel. He still walks with a limp after leaping from a second storey window, ha ha! But he is a cove of some talent, and this new *Roselinda* will be a roaring success, I warrant."

"Roselinda," Tess mused, flipping through the score. "The name sounds familiar to me."

"As well it might," Tom said. "It's borrowed from the play *As You Like It* by Mr. Shakespeare. You know, the pastoral one, where Roselinda dresses as a boy to escape her pursuers."

"And I am to play this part in pantaloons, forsooth?" Tess asked, feeling increasingly set against this production.

"I can think of no one better for the part," Tom said, grinning broadly. "Highmore was very happy to get you back, to wipe Mr. Rich's eye."

Tess was on the point of setting out her objections, when Jem added, "It will be a great step up for Finchy as well. Did he not tell you? He's to be the conductor, not only the music master. But rehearsals start the day after tomorrow, so we must get to work on learning the score."

Tess found that despite her misgivings, she could not deny Tom this important new appointment. She set herself along with Jem to the task of playing through the score so that Tom might learn it, running over and over it through the entire day and the next, while Tom's servants carried her belongings over from her rented rooms. Upon hearing of this interesting new development, Jem only raised a questioning eyebrow in her direction, but ignoring him, Tess turned her attention back to the spinet.

Despite her frequent removes, Tess had acquired a not insignificant collection of furnishings, the addition of which to number eight Maiden Lane pushed the house dangerously close to respectability. Unlike Tess, Tom did not give a straw for the appearance of his house and had no notion of entertaining visitors, or at least visitors of quality, nor did he have much use for the usual appurtenances of gentility. His home, although now more tidy than before, was still quite bare. Tess added to it among other things a fine chiming clock, which she placed on the mantle in the front parlor, a silver tea service, and a full-length looking glass, which she had set up alongside her featherbed and wardrobe in the bedroom Tom had given her, down the hall from his own. Her own *private* room, he said with gravity as he gave her the key on her first night there, a gesture she found unexpectedly gallant.

Playing through the score of *Roselinda* was heavy going. Veracini, for all his skill on the violin, was clearly unaccustomed to composing for voice. At first when Tess stumbled over a particularly awkward passage, they assumed there had been a copyist's error, but the same intervals occurred over and over, and eventually they conceded it was simply his style. It was plain the composer had no knowledge of the *passagio,* the perilous border between the chest voice and the head voice, nor of *tessitura,* that is, which notes sat most comfortably for singers. To her shame, Tess found her voice cracking more than once as she ran through the parts. Tom was kind enough not to remark upon it, although he had difficulties of his own. His seemingly extraordinary ability to hold an entire opera in his head at once, all the instrumental and vocal parts, was less a matter of memorizing each individual note, than simply knowing the rules of composition, which arranged the notes in familiar patterns endlessly repeated with only minor variations. But Veracini's unexpected turns and leaps were exceedingly difficult to fix with any certainty. And when at last they had fought their way through to the end, they found the score unfinished: Roselinda's final aria was missing, with only the hasty note *da decidere in futuro* scrawled in its place.

Jem banged out some concluding chords on the spinet in frustration. "Dammee, Finchy, I am almost sorry we've been dragged into this nonsense," he said.

Tom shrugged as he sprawled in an elbow chair, his head lolling against the back. "Work is work. In any case, it's one less wretched aria to learn tonight. Tell me, will you stay for supper? Unless I am very much mistaken, I believe that is the aroma of a boiled ham wafting in from the kitchen."

But Jem astonished both Tom and Tess by refusing for perhaps the first time in his life.

"Nay, there's a fine lady a-waiting me at the Nag's Head, a prime article, ha ha, and it wouldn't do to leave her all alone, would it?"

Tom tilted his head to the side inquisitively. "That fine lady wouldn't happen to be a princess, would she?"

"She would indeed."

Tess glanced between the two of them, Tom holding back laughter, and Jem blushing with embarrassment but attempting to put a bold face on it. "A princess, whatever do you mean?"

Tom grinned broadly. "Jem was quite taken with one of the mollies we met at Mother Birch's, name of Princess Seraphina. I wouldn't know, but he tells me she goes about rigged like a high-born lady."

"The finest lady you ever did see!" Jem blustered, uncharacteristically defensive. "You're coming it mighty high for one who fancies women in trousers. And you can't even see 'em! I'll have no more flings from either of you." He clapped his tri-

369

corne hat on his head.

"Never in life!" Tom raised his hands in surrender.

"Now if you'll excuse me, I have an appointment to keep." Jem swept out the door with his nose in the air.

"I wish you the joy of it!" Tom called after him.

Supper was an uncharacteristically quiet affair, with Tom and Tess each preoccupied by private thoughts. Tom was apprehensive for the rehearsals of the unfinished opera, and what sort of man this Veracini might prove to be. A fiery temper and tendency towards libertinism did not concern him, but if the composer could not bring off an ending, if he had no sensibility for his own art, they would all be in for a sad time of it.

Tess as well was refining on the coming rehearsal, but as the pudding was served, her thoughts ran on in a different direction. This would be only her second night at number eight Maiden Lane. The previous night she had been preoccupied with directing the servants in the arrangement of her room; unpacking her things had taken until quite late. She found it awkward to manage without a lady's maid, particularly in the article of her dress, but she was in no hurry to introduce a young girl to the household. Her own presence here was unconventional enough; she was determined to make do on her own at least for the moment. She was even more determined to set a precedent for friendly but virtuous conduct, but she was having difficulty striking the proper tone when retiring for the evening. Ought she to curtsy, even though Tom could not see it? Or shake his hand? Or offer a hug and a kiss, as if to a brother?

The meal came to an end and the cloth was drawn before she had come to any definitive course of action. They retired to the music room with glasses of port to practice a bit longer, but at last the candle guttered down. Tess was fighting back yawns when Tom suddenly stood without any ceremony and announced, "I believe I shall turn in," then strode through the darkened hall and up the stairs. Tess was about to offer to him a candle out of habit but caught herself just in time and instead merely followed him up the stairs. She paused for a moment before the door to his room, which was standing fully open, and in the flickering light cast by the candle in her hand she could see him untying his cravat and opening his shirt.

"Tess, is that you?" he asked.

She paused before answering, chastising herself for gaping at his bare chest revealed by his open shirt. "Yes, I-I wish you a good night."

"And to you," he replied, favoring her with an utterly disarming grin, and extending his hand. Without thinking, she placed her hand in his, and with a single deft move, he raised her fingers to his lips while pulling her in close to him.

"I want you to know how sensible I am...of your kindness to me," she said, somewhat unsteadily.

Instead of replying, he merely kissed her hand again, his eyes closed and mouth curved in a smile. Tess felt heat radiate through her from the touch of his lips on her fingers, burning away all her reservations and better judgment. She leaned forward impulsively and kissed him boldly on the mouth. As if he had been expecting her advance, Tom entwined his arms around her. Hardly aware of what she was doing, Tess kicked the door shut and led them towards the bed, where they fell onto the counterpane in a heap. She just managed to set the candle down safely beside the bed.

As they were struggling frantically to loosen their clothes, Tom paused for a moment. "Are you certain?" he asked her, his brows raised in concern.

"No, I am not," she said shortly. "Pray do not ask me again." She pushed him down, kissing his smooth broad chest.

He answered with a tight embrace, then rolled away from her to open the drawer of the bedside table. To her surprise, he produced a small sheath with a ribbon on the open end. Tess knew very well what it was, having learnt through bitter experience the value of such devices. Indeed, Tom had mentioned that he always used one, but she had not truly believed him.

"Do you mind?" he asked softly.

"Not at all," she replied without shame. "I am glad for it." She secured it for him with a practiced hand.

She gasped with delight as he pulled her breasts from her stays, kissing them and driving all thought from her mind. His sensitive fingers ran along the curves of her body, studying her form and teasing out her most intimate secrets. Tess shivered as his touch sent tremors through her. Never had she felt so minutely examined, the subject of such intense and focused desire, but far from ashamed, his attentions only stoked the heat within her. Just as she felt she could wait no longer, he lifted her skirts and without a word she granted him her last favor.

The pleasure was far, far in excess even than what she had imagined, and not only the rush of heat, but the look of intensity on his face, ordinarily so hard to read, with what she fancied to be a look of love, and it moved her beyond all expectation. When at last they had finished, he flung himself down beside her with a deeply satisfied groan and curled his rangy form around her much smaller one, embracing her tightly, and burying his face in her dark brown curly hair, which had come partially undone. It was sweet, unimaginably sweet. The candle, now fully burned down in the socket, gave a final dim flicker and went out, leaving them equally in darkness.

But as Tess gradually came back to herself, she gave a fretful sigh.

Tom hugged her even more tightly. "Do not begin to repine and say I cruelly seduced you against your will," he said softly. "I could not bear it."

Tess kissed his forehead, smoothing the hair that had come loose from its queue. "Nay, I shan't blame you," she said. "Only I do not desire the servants to know."

"Never trouble yourself on that account, madam," he replied. "They know very well who it was as hired them and who still ensures the timely distribution of wages. Besides, they are very much attached to Miss Turnbridge."

Tess smiled. "Even so, if I were to be discovered here come morning, it would excite more comment than I care to countenance. Do not take it amiss if I bid you goodnight."

Moving hesitantly through the darkness, with her dress and hair hanging in disorder about her, Tess crept back to her own room and to her cold, empty bed.

CHAPTER FOURTEEN: THE MAESTRO

Tess awoke to a languid, sunny morning, the previous night's pleasure still lingering. As Matthews entered her room with hot water for the wash stand, she was struck with a sudden idea.

"Bid Dorcas come help me dress," she instructed, pleased that she had found a solution for her lack of a lady's maid. She would pay the washer woman extra, and there was likely to be no grumbling.

As she was washing her hands and face, she found herself singing a broadside she had previously copied out for Tom. It had a lurching, strident, but still pleasant tune, although when she realized the words she was singing, she paused, staring at her reflection in the glass.

Oh Johnny, lovely Johnny, don't you mind the day,
You came to my window to steal me away?
You promised to marry me above all female kind,
Oh Johnny, lovely Johnny, what has altered your mind?

Oh Annie, lovely Annie, it was all but a jest,
For I never intended to make you my best,
I never intended to make you my wife,

Oh Annie, lovely Annie, all the days of my life.

With great effort, Tess put the unlucky words out of her mind and finished dressing, with the dour assistance of the aged laundress.

Upon descending to the dining room, Tess discovered Tom already at table enjoying his breakfast, but he rose and greeted her with a happy grin that elevated her spirits considerably. Throughout the meal, he did not make any reference to the previous night, out of courtesy, Tess realized, to her request not to alert the servants, who stood in attendance behind their chairs as they ate. Once again Tess found herself regretting that they could not share an intimate glance; as always he appeared somewhat removed.

As they finished the meal and Matthews cleared away the dishes, Tom listened for his retreating footsteps, and on ensuring that they were alone, he reached across the table for her hand, squeezing it warmly, which persuaded Tess to let go at least some of her trepidation regarding their new intimacy. She was on the verge of speaking of it, but a moment later, Jem came bursting in, with only a perfunctory announcement by a disapproving Stinson. Jem helped himself to the last of the griddlecakes remaining on the table and offered to run through the overture once more before the first rehearsal of *Roselinda*.

"Dammee, but it's a bollocksy mess of an opera," Jem declared. "But bad work is better than none at all, ain't it?"

Tom smiled thinly. "Well, we shall see what Signor Veracini has to say for himself."

The weather had turned foul, a thin drizzle that turned to a steady rain by the time they had crossed the Piazza to Russell Street. As they crossed Bow Street, the rain dripped off the rim of Tom's tricorne hat and soaked through Tess's calash. They arrived at the theater sodden and bedraggled, smelling of wet wool.

Inside, the singers and musicians milled about on stage,

but the noise of their chatter and the flickering candles did little to dispel the damp chill of the cavernous theater. Tess left Jem and Tom at the conductor's stand to join the company onstage. As she ascended the stairs, she caught the sound of a distinctive high-pitched laugh.

"Signor Farinelli!" she cried, curtseying politely. "You honor us with your presence," she added, wondering privately how Mr. Highmore had convinced the most celebrated castrato in London to join this makeshift production.

"Signorina Turnbridge," he replied in his uncanny woman's voice. "Likewise, I am delighted to see you here. Perhaps this opera may not be a complete fiasco after all."

There was uneasy laughter all around, the superstitious actors strongly disliking such an unlucky utterance. Tess glanced down at Tom, who was running his hands over the conductor's stand and talking with Mr. Brookings, the first violin from their days at the Rose. This was another hopeful sign, for Tom and Brookings worked very well together. Brookings said something she could not catch, that set Tom laughing, and her heart rose at the sight of his open, unaffected grin.

Suddenly the far door at the front of the house opened with a bang, and Mr. Highmore, manager of the Theater Royal, strode down the rows of empty seats toward the stage, surrounded by a bevy of servants, secretaries, and stage hands, and followed closely by a small, glowering man in a full-bottomed wig, who walked with a pronounced limp.

"What a bloody racket! A God-damn Whitechapel wedding!" Highmore shouted as the company scrambled to take their seats. "Pipe down, the lot of you! No better than a common mob," he muttered under his breath. But as he approached Tom, his mood lifted slightly. "Tom, my lad, what cheer?" he cried as he clapped him on the shoulder. "Come up in the world, ain't we? We have high hopes for you."

Tom stepped off the conductor's box carefully, using his walking stick as a guide, and bowed stiffly.

Highmore assumed a more formal air. "May I introduce Maestro Francesco Veracini." Tom bowed again more deeply, as the composer elbowed his way through the small crowd in the aisle. "Signor Veracini, I present our esteemed conductor, Mr. Thomas Finch, lately of the Theater Royal, Covent Garden."

"Your servant," Tom murmured, bowing for a third time. As he straightened, he heard a pinched, angry, heavily accented voice demand, "What is the meaning of this? *È cieco!* Is this a joke?"

A pox on Highmore for not telling him in advance, Tom thought angrily as he listened silently to Veracini's increasingly strident expostulations and Highmore's hesitant reassurances.

"No, it is impossible!" Veracini had worked himself into high dudgeon. "How can *il cieco* be conductor?"

"I have the entire score in here already," Tom asserted, tapping his temple with a finger. "At least as far as it is completed..." There was an uneasy silence, and he felt Jem elbow him hard in the ribs.

"You've copped it now, cully," Jem hissed in his ear.

There followed a confusion of voices again, Veracini shouting in a most vulgar manner, and Tom was aware of even more bodies squeezed into the narrow aisle, then Tess's clear, strong voice carried over the din.

"Maestro Veracini, how delighted I am to make your acquaintance at last, and may I say how sensible I am that you honor us with your latest composition," she chattered away in her Neapolitan Italian, curtseying and allowing him to kiss her hand.

Veracini favored Tess with a lascivious glance. "Signorina Turnbridge, I have heard tales of you. Does the company here in London know of your scandalous reputation, I wonder?" he asked, also in Italian.

Tess blushed to the roots of her hair and could not find an answer. What had he heard from her family? Was the maestro threatening her with blackmail?

Highmore had not quite followed their words but Tess's reaction boded no good. "And have I mentioned the extraordinary profits from *Il pastor fido*?" Highmore said loudly, in an attempt to steer the conversation in a better direction. Veracini's gaze snapped back to him. "All seats sold, every performance, thanks to Miss Turnbridge's virtuoso performance."

"You are too kind, sir," Tess said in English, recovering her composure. "But it was due entirely to the instruction of Mr. Finch. I would trust my artistry to none other."

"As the Signorina says, Mr. Finch is a man of talent. Pray let us put this disagreement behind us and commence the rehearsal," Farinelli added.

"No! You promised me Signor Holden of the Rose," Veracini insisted, his eyes growing wild again.

Highmore put an arm around Veracini and attempted to draw him somewhat away from the crowd, although privacy was impossible with the entire company leaning over the edge of the stage and crowded in the aisle. "Mr. Holden is taken ill of a putrid fever," he said in a low tone, still perfectly audible to the many eager listeners. "I assure you, we do not desire his presence here. Now Mr. Finch has been music master at Covent Garden and the Rose, and helped to earn them a pretty penny. What's more, we may pay him less than Mr. Holden, thus increasing our profits. Now what say you?" Veracini peered suspiciously around the larger man at Tom, who was still standing woodenly beside the conductor's stand.

"This opera *will* open according to schedule," Highmore added in a more threatening tone. "Every day that we must delay the opening occasions a significant loss of revenue. Now then, shall we begin the rehearsal, or must I continue to pay the players to stand about gawping?"

"Well, damn him for a miserable foreign scrub, anyway," Jem muttered to Tom as Veracini stalked off to a seat in the middle rows and the company rushed back to their places.

Tom ground his teeth and gave a tight smile. "I fear we shall all have a sad time of it," he replied in an undertone, feeling about for his baton. As he tuned up the orchestra, he was sharply aware of Veracini sighing and shifting about in the seat behind him, but the overture went smoothly enough. No complaints, only muffled harrumphing, which Tom realized would likely be the only expression of praise.

Highmore had done very well in assembling a company who knew their profession; there was none of the fumbling about and missed notes as in *Il pastor fido*, even among the chorus. Most of them had performed with Tom either at Covent Garden or at the Rose, and had grown quite attached to him. Still, Veracini cried out in irritation from time to time that a note had not been sung just so, or that he wished the violins to play more sweetly.

Even Tess did not manage to avoid incident. When it came time for Roselinda's first entrance, Tess stood confidently from her chair and sang out the first notes, only to realize a moment later that Farinelli had also sung the same notes with her. The two singers stared at each other, appalled. Sniggers erupted around them, and Tom brought his baton down.

"I-I beg your pardon," Tess whispered and sat down again, her cheeks flaming. How foolish she was to think the part of Roselinda was for her. The leading roles always went to the castrati, with their pure tones and powerful barrel chests. Not for the first time, she felt how unfair it was that the best roles always went to the men. But Roselinda was a female part! She had been certain that this time she could be the lead, not second best to a male soprano.

Tom rapped on the stand with his baton, then turned behind him to where he assumed the manager was seated. "Mr. Highmore, there appears to be a misunderstanding. Is not Miss Turnbridge to play Roselinda?" he inquired.

Highmore snorted. "Upon my word, what are you thinking, Mr. Finch? The role of Phoebe is for Miss Turnbridge. Roselinda spends the better part of the opera disguised as a man.

Or would you have Miss Turnbridge appear on stage in pantaloons?"

The entire company burst into undisguised laughter. To cover his confusion, Tom turned back to the stage and raised his baton again. "Very well then, Mr. Farinelli, if you please?"

"I can't believe Farinelli spoke on my behalf to Veracini, after that fling I wrote against him," Tom remarked over a very late supper of meat pie and a grateful bottle of sack at the Essex Serpent.

"He still ain't twigged that it was you who wrote the broadside, I warrant," Jem replied.

"Well then, pray he is never relieved of his ignorance," Tess put in wearily.

Even later that night, after Jem had departed for another assignation with Princess Seraphina, and Tess somehow found herself in Tom's bed once more, Tom added, "I am grateful to you, dearest Tess, for your kind intercession, and for inducing Farinelli to speak for me."

Tess tightened her embrace around him, resting her head on his shoulder. "It was monstrous of Veracini to use you so rudely. I tell you, I was so angry, I could have struck him." Tom only laughed.

"How can you laugh so?" she demanded, her anger returning at the thought of the ugly scene. "How can you bear such insults?"

Tom laughed, rolled her over and kissed her lightly. "Dearest Tess, I own I was angry at the moment, but the man is clearly mad, and not worthy of our regard. Did you not hear him cursing at the chorus for failing to sing his impossible notes in the way he has imagined them? No, I find the only means to live a peaceful life is to not to dwell on such slights. He insulted you as well, if I'm not mistaken? What did he say to you?"

To his surprise, Tess turned away from him and made as if to get up out of the bed. He grasped her arm and pulled her back. "What? No, please do not leave. What was it? Tell me!" Tom had expected to hear some trifling insult. He did not know what to make of the strength of her reaction. Was she weeping?

She said in a choked voice, "There was a scandal in Naples. That's why I left. He threatened to reveal it to the company."

Tom brushed the hair away from her face. "Was it really so terrible? You can tell me, I shan't think any less of you."

Tess drew in a deep shuddering breath. "I allowed myself to be seduced by the son of my mother's cousin. I was under the protection of my uncle, and when he found out, he said I must either quit the stage and be wed, or be turned out. So I left, and the family has disowned me."

Tom gave a short laugh, to Tess's consternation. "Is that all? I assure you, no one here cares a jot for such a trifle."

Tess did not reply. She had not thought on the matter in some time, but now it came rushing back. Somehow she could not put into words the heartbreak and shame of that time, nor could she say that after her second cousin refused the marriage, her uncle had made it clear she was never to return for any reason.

At last she said, "That is easy for you to say, as a man. I am a girl alone in the world, and if the theater owners decide not to cast me for whatever reason, I am ruined."

"Nonsense," Tom said, gripping her tightly again, embracing her with his whole body. "You are not alone in the world. I don't know about Naples, but here in London, audiences love a bit of scandal, and the theater owners know it. There is nothing Veracini can say against you that will damage your career, I promise you."

Tess sighed raggedly, the tears stopping at last. "I know. But you see, I have never been able to resist temptation, to my detriment. And here I am again in the same posture."

"Have I not been perfectly discreet, as you requested?"

When Tess did not answer, Tom changed the subject. "I am sorry for your embarrassment during the rehearsal. It's my fault for leading you to believe you were to be Roselinda."

Tess groaned, for the shame of that was still with her, although at least it took her mind off the more distant past. "No, I should have read the score more carefully," she said. "At least I am spared having to appear on stage in trews."

"More's the pity," Tom replied with genuine regret.

Tess pushed him over and propped herself up on one elbow, staring into his face, illuminated only by the moon shining in through the window. "Upon my honor, I do believe that was your intention from the beginning!" Tom grinned. "Mr. Finch, I declare you are the most depraved libertine in all of London," Tess exclaimed, swatting playfully at his shoulder.

He laughed, and embraced her again, sliding his hands from her waist down her thighs.

"Such shapely legs, it would be a shame not to show them off."

Tess surrendered herself to him again, willfully pushing all questions of her reputation and his constancy from her mind. True, he had promised her nothing, but then she was not certain what she wanted from him either. To marry and raise children? She could scarce imagine a path for which they were more ill-suited. For now, this new intimacy pleased her, wherever it might lead. She would speak to him of his intentions tomorrow.

CHAPTER FIFTEEN: THE ARIA

The next morning, Tess once again she found herself seated across from Tom at breakfast, watching distractedly as he searched about on his plate with his fork for a stray bloater. She was just contemplating how she might open the delicate subject of his intentions toward her, when Frankie banged the door to the dining room open and announced in a toneless voice, "Visitor to see you."

Tess winced. She was endeavoring to teach the boy gentle manners, with only limited success. Before she could admonish him to keep the visitor downstairs until they were ready to receive him, or at the very least, to announce his name, a lithe figure in a burgundy surcoat, pink and yellow brocade waistcoat and stylish peruke slipped in behind the boy, crying out in a heavy accent, "*Hélas*, my arrival is too soon! Forgive me, Thomas."

Tom slowly lowered his fork. The voice was familiar, but so unexpected, it took him a moment to be certain. "Henri?" he ventured, pushing the chair back with a scrape as he rose from the table.

"Thomas, 'ow 'appy I am to see you again!" Henri d'Angoulême strode forward and embraced Tom with brotherly affection, then turned to Tess and bowed politely. "And Mademoiselle Turnbridge! What an unexpected pleasure."

"No more unexpected than the pleasure of your visit," Tess

replied, also rising and extending her hand to be kissed.

"Indeed," Tom said. "Pray be seated, and Matthews will bring you tea. To what do we owe this happy visit?"

Henri's round face went pale, his blue eyes showing anxious concern as he sank slowly into a chair. "But you did not receive my letter?"

Tess looked at Tom, but he showed no sign that he knew what Henri spoke of. Since Tom had been a guest at the d'Angoulême family home in Rouen, the two men had enjoyed a friendly correspondence, although the subject of their letters was more often music than personal matters. "The last letter I had of you was some time ago, but you said nothing of a visit," he said.

Henri tugged at his cravat in agitation. "But I am *désolé*! Ashamed! Ruined! Please, forgive me, I beg you. I was certain you were informed of my arrival."

Tom waved his hand nonchalantly. "Think nothing of it, my dear Henri. You are welcome here at any time, announced or otherwise."

At that moment, Frankie reappeared in the doorway, relaying the coachman's demand to know what he was supposed to do with all the bloody baggage, expletive included. Tess stared at Henri. It appeared this was no social call; the man intended to stay for some time.

Tom, however, was delighted to see his friend again, no matter how unexpectedly, even more so when he learnt that part of the baggage included a case of the finest burgundy wine. He immediately rose from the table to show Henri upstairs, directing Matthews to bring up his trunks and deliver the wine to the cellar.

"You may have this room here," Tom said, groping about for the handle and opening the door. The small room was fitted out with bed, wardrobe, and washstand, with some unlikely feminine touches, such as prints pasted to the walls, and ribbons lying about, the relics of Charlotte's stay. "I'll have Dorcas make up the bed for you. The room just across the hall is my own," Tom explained, gesturing towards the door. Visible within was a half-open wardrobe with clothes spilling out onto the floor, and a nightshirt tossed on the unmade bed. "And that room at the end of the hall is Miss Turnbridge's." The door was chastely closed; Tess remained downstairs finishing her breakfast.

Henri turned to Tom, his eyes round with disbelief. "Are you not...? I mean to say...I assumed, as Mademoiselle Turnbridge is living here with you...that you had wed?"

Tom laughed lightly. "Wed? Heavens, no!" Still the question hung in the air, and Tom paused. It suddenly occurred to him that Tess might be less than pleased if he were to reveal that she had come to him in her shame after her female lover had jilted her, and that he had taken advantage of her grief to convince her to lodge chastely with him, then promptly seduced her. No, that might fall under the category of indelicate gossip that she would prefer to keep private.

Henri clapped him heartily on the shoulder. "Never mind, I apperceive the *circonstance complètement!*" he cried familiarly as Matthews and Frankie squeezed by them bearing a large trunk, the first of several. "But tell me," he continued in a low whisper, "is it the custom in England to keep one's mistress in one's own home?"

"Mistress!" Tom burst out, then lowered his voice as the servants passed by on their way downstairs for the next trunk. "I assure you she is no such thing."

"Well, what then?" Henri laughed. "If she hain't your wife, she must be your mistress!"

Nettled, Tom had no answer to this, but only led Henri back downstairs to the drawing room where Tess was waiting with the tea service. As this also served as the music room, there was much for Henri to exclaim over: broadsides, folios, and sheaves of loose notes to riffle through, flutes of various sizes, a battered old fiddle to pick up and try, as well as the humble spinet.

"What a delightful instrument," Henri remarked in French,

running his fingers over the worn keys and teasing out a tinkling series of runs.

Tom discovered to his dismay that his previous facility in French had waned significantly through disuse, and their conversation had a halting, macaronic quality. "You flatter me," he replied in English. "Surely you have finer instruments at home?" Tom knew this for a fact, having played the d'Angoulême harpsichord many times.

"Ah, but it is the novelty. I find travel quite invigorating, don't you?" Henri said in French, pounding out a gavotte. The slender table on which the spinet rested trembled slightly.

"Yes, indeed," Tess replied, more at ease with French than Tom was. "Is it that to which we owe the pleasure of your visit? A diversion? Or have you some business here in London, if I may make so bold as to ask?"

"*Hein?*" Henri stopped playing and turned his attention to his tea cup. On finding it empty, he stared at the ceiling abstractedly. Several times he seemed on the verge of speaking, only to clamp his mouth shut and start over again. Tess attempted to press him further, but Tom declared he had no wish to discommode their guest; Henri was welcome to stay as long as he pleased, whatever his business.

An awkward silence settled over the music room. Tess was about to suggest ringing for more tea when the door banged open unceremoniously to reveal the slight, disheveled form of Frankie again.

"Jem, uh, *Mister* Jem Castleton to see you," he said, then added after a lengthy pause, "sir." Tess glared at him and he added, "Madam," in a whisper as he backed out the door.

"Blimey, Henry!" Jem cried, making no attempt at the French pronunciation. Henri rose and they clapped each other on the back familiarly. "Damnably good to see you again!" Jem said, throwing himself into a chair. "What brings you to Covent Garden?"

"Henri is visiting as my guest," Tom interjected, feeling about carefully on the tea tray. "Now where is that bell? I'll just ring for more tea."

"Nay, Finchy, you know I ain't one to deny your hospitality, but it's time for rehearsal. I just came to fetch you over," Jem said.

Tom bolted upright from his chair. "The rehearsal! I had clean forgot. My dear Henri, you must excuse us."

"*La répétition*?" Henri inquired. "You is still engaged in the opera?"

"Why yes," Tom replied. "It's a new version of *As You Like It*, called *Roselinda*, put on at Drury Lane. The composer is Signor Veracini, don't you know."

"Tom is to be conductor," Tess said pointedly, vexed at Henri's sigh of disappointment. "It's a very big step."

"Yes, someone must pay the bills, or the landlady comes calling," Jem added with a laugh.

"My congratulations, then," Henri said, although he still appeared unconvinced. "Only I was certain that by now you would be a full composer in your own right. An oratorio, a symphony, even! You 'ave the materials already," he said, gesturing at the bookcase and escritoire overflowing with manuscript pages.

For a moment, Tom appeared bemused, thinking over Henri's suggestion, until Jem put a hand on his elbow and urged him toward the door.

"Yes, yes, it's very kind of you to say so," Tom said hastily. "Please forgive us, but you may make yourself at home. When we return I shall treat you to a fine British beefsteak, if you don't mind dining so late."

Leaving Henri to his own devices for the afternoon, Tom, Tess, and Jem hurried over to the theater, arriving just in time for Tom to take his place at the conductor's stand. Tom heard Veracini mutter "Eh, *il cieco*!" and shift restively as he walked by the composer's seat on his way to the stand in front of the stage, but they exchanged no further greeting, and Tom did his best to ignore him.

As the rehearsal went along, however, Tom realized that the reason they were not treated to a fit of temper as before was that Veracini was out of favor with Highmore. As the dancing master positioned the chorus about the stage, Tom overheard an angry, if whispered, conversation behind him between the manager and the composer, to the effect that the final aria still was not completed, indeed not even begun.

During the break, when the company and most of the orchestra disappeared backstage to wolf down a few bites of bread, or pass around a private flask, Tom bade Jem accompany him to the harpsichord in the pit.

"Take down the notes, would you?" Tom instructed. "We shall see if we can't help the maestro along to a happy conclusion for his little *spettacolo*."

He began playing a simple tune, feeling his way through the chords, adding embellishments and variations here and there. Every few minutes, he asked Jem to read him the lyric (for the libretto was long finished) and he would adjust the tune to fit the words more easily.

Tess wandered down from the stage to stand beside him, leaning on the edge of the harpsichord and watching him play. Tom did not seem to notice her, but played on with a look of intense concentration on his narrow features. He was frowning slightly, his face tipped up and away from the keyboard, his blue-white eyes turned toward the ceiling. She stared openly at him, feeling the warm glow of tender affection. He was dressed plainly in a green surcoat and buff waistcoat, his hair neatly tied back and curled at the sides, but she thought she had never seen him look so handsome.

Gradually, however, she realized that she was hearing different words in her head than the ones Jem was singing gracelessly—not Italian, but English words.

Oh Annie, lovely Annie, it was all but a jest,
For I never intended to make you my best,
I never intended to make you my wife,

Oh Annie, lovely Annie, all the days of my life.

Tess gasped, and Tom stopped playing.

"Tess, is that you?" he asked, turning toward her.

"That song!" she cried. "It's 'Lovely Johnny' isn't it?"

"Yes, of course," he replied, playing another variation. "You've been singing it about the house these past few days." Tess put a hand to her mouth. Had she been singing it under her breath? She hadn't noticed.

"What's this?" Highmore demanded, striding across the stalls to the pit, Veracini reluctantly limping along behind him. "Sounds like you have your final aria, hey?" Highmore rounded on the composer, drawing himself up to his full height and daring the smaller man to oppose him.

"But it is not a proper aria, a mere vulgar tune," Veracini protested.

"Precisely. The audience will love it all the more because they recognize it," Highmore insisted. "That's what Mr. Gay did in *The Beggar's Opera*, and it earned a mint of money for him and for Mr. Rich, I assure you."

"Ain't you heard, *The Beggar's Opera* made Gay rich and Rich gay, haha!" Jem added, grinning. Veracini scowled at him, but his eyes held only petulance, not the glint of madness as the day before.

"Yes, yes," Highmore waved his hand at Jem's repetition of the tired old saw. "Now I want this written up and delivered to Signor Farinelli by tomorrow," he ordered, then stalked off to find the stage manager and resume the rehearsal.

"Damn them all to hell anyway," Henri slurred, clasping Tom about the neck and spilling ale down the front of his waistcoat as he gestured enthusiastically with his tankard. In reply, Tom belched loudly and grasped the table before him with both hands, in a vain effort to counteract the unpleasant sensation that the bench beneath him was sliding sideways. He wondered for a brief moment where he was...ah yes, the

Labor in Vain. After the rehearsal, they had returned home to enjoy a late supper with Henri, then offered to show him the pleasures around the Piazza. After the first drink at the Essex Serpent, Tess had retired, and sometime in between the Nag's Head and the Labor in Vain, Jem had disappeared. Now only Tom and Henri were left, and judging by the diminishing sound of the crowd, the hour had grown quite late.

"They must recognize your talent!" Henri continued.

Tom only shrugged, slowly relinquishing his grip on the table. "Highmore does want to use my composition for the final aria."

Henri waved a hand dismissively. *"Eh bien*, but without your name, no? Where is the glory in that?"

"None whatsoever," Tom replied ruefully. "But I have never sought for glory for myself."

"No, it will not do!" Henri exclaimed, once again clapping an arm about Tom's shoulders and shaking him. "I tell you, my friend, you need a patron. And I, Henri d'Angoulême, shall be that patron!"

Tom laughed. "But my dear Henri, have you any money of your own?"

"I am the richest bourgeois in Rouen," he declared, then added, "or I shall be when I inherit from my father. But then, ah yes, then you shall write the finest symphony the world has ever heard!"

Tom merely smiled and reached for his tankard, only to find it dry. "Another round?" he suggested.

"I can scarce recall the last time I was out like this," Henri remarked, releasing Tom from his embrace and gesturing to a serving girl.

"Nor can I," Tom replied. "It's a pity Tess retired so early."

"Ah, Mademoiselle Turnbridge," Henri said contemplatively, then suddenly leaning towards Tom and poking him in the chest with a finger, he continued, "You know what you should do? Marry her!"

"What?" Tom exclaimed.

"*Oui!* Marry her now, or I shall marry her myself!"

"You? But you already have '*une belle amie.*' Ain't one enough, by God?" Over the course of the evening, Henri had gradually revealed that he had come to London in search of a wife, the girl selected by his father being distasteful to him. After several more bumpers, it became clear that he was in pursuit of one woman in particular, a comely young widow by the name of Mrs. Emilia Coates, a Catholic recusant who had settled in Rouen. Upon the death of her husband, she had returned to England, and Henri had followed, very much against his father's wishes, to press his suit with her. Henri gave a lovesick sigh and leaned back against the wall. He had removed his wig several rounds earlier, and now he ran his hand over his short ash-blond curls.

Tom took a slow pull from his replenished tankard, thinking on Tess. It was a pleasant thought—her silky hair, the touch of her soft hand, the sweet sound of her voice, calling him by name... Slowly, through the drunken fog, a recent memory drifted to the surface. What had she said before she left the Serpent and returned home? All he could recall was her voice with an edge of steel in it, bidding him to enjoy his boozing. And he had, but perhaps that was not her meaning. He thought suddenly of their previous two evenings together, the spark of intimacy now burning hot between them. And yet he had left her at home alone.

Feeling about him for his hat and staff, he said, "Come, let us return home. I believe Tess may be angry with me, and if she is, then all this talk of marriage will be for naught."

But even the thought of an angry Tess was not enough to dampen their ale-fueled spirits, and as they staggered across the Piazza, Tom with his arm draped over the much shorter Henri's shoulder, they sang loudly,

Oh the blue-eyed stranger shuffled into town
with his fiddle slung over his shoulder, oh.
He seemed so shy that he caught the maiden's eye

but he proved to be much bolder, oh.
He said, "I can play the bagpipes, I can dance a jig,
I can jump the highest caper, oh.
I can play a tune that will charm the singing birds,
I'm the finest cat-gut scraper, oh!"

CHAPTER SIXTEEN: THE PROPOSAL

"So tell me, Tom, how go the rehearsals for *Roselinda*? I am quite looking forward to the opening night." Lady Gray smiled indulgently at her nephew as he methodically worked his way through a saddle of lamb.

"Very well, I thank you," Tom replied, swallowing. "And it's very kind of you to invite me to dine with you again, Auntie. I haven't seen you in London this age. But I do wish you had invited Miss Turnbridge as well. It would grieve me if she were to imagine any slight."

"Would it now?" Lady Gray said, laying her fork down slowly, her tone suddenly frosty. "If you care so greatly for her good reputation, then why do you allow her to live with you like a common whore?" Tom's mouth gaped open and closed in astonishment, but before he could speak, Lady Gray continued, "Oh yes, I know very well what you have been up to, and frankly, Tom, I am saddened to hear you treat her so. I hold Miss Turnbridge in very high regard, but you must know I could never receive her here while you carry on in this manner."

Tom attacked the meat on his plate more vigorously. "Father received her very well at Culverleigh," he argued, not without a trace of petulance.

"That does not signify; the case was entirely different. She went to Culverleigh as a companion to Charlotte, not as your kept mistress, and she was not living in your house at the time. Tom, you must put this right and marry her at once."

Tom reached for his wine glass, which he drained with alarming speed.

"I will not." Even as he spoke, he regretted the childish tone he was so used to adopt with his aunt.

"How can you be so pig-headed!" Lady Gray exclaimed impatiently. "Don't you see, my only wish is for your happiness."

"But Auntie, I am already happy. The opera will be a success, a̶   wine merchant wishes to be my pat   nest now, ain't that grand?"

"Bu   you are not married?" Lady Gray ir   Tom did not point out that she had   his many and many a year, since h   ed to the dropsy, yet she seemed

"You must understand, your prospects are not of the best," she continued in a moralizing tone. "It was your misfortune to be born in scandal and sin; still you have done nothing to improve your reputation. Mistress Turnbridge is a fine woman, well matched to you in every way, and yet you deny her the decent position I am certain she desires."

Tom frowned. Tess had hardly spoken to him since he had returned in the small hours of the morning after drinking with Henri. Her anger was palpable in the house, but what could he do? She could hardly expect him not to entertain his friends. No, he was certain marriage was the last thought in her mind at the moment. Perhaps she would even find her own lodgings again. The thought of her leaving his house disturbed him deeply, he suddenly realized, more deeply than he had expected.

Mistaking the reason for his dark mood, Lady Gray declared, "I see the force of my reason penetrates your willfulness at last. Promise me you will speak to her."

"I shall," Tom mumbled, his thoughts already running in a different direction. Would Tess really leave?

It was difficult to find the opportune moment to ask her such a delicate question, with Henri in the house, Jem stepping round at mealtimes, and endless rehearsals. At last, on the morning before opening night, Tom had just finished dressing when he heard Tess's unmistakable light step in the hall. He flung the bedroom door open and called her name; the step paused but she did not answer.

"If you please, my dear, I know you're there. Might we have a word in private?" he said, gesturing within.

"But Henri..." she began.

"Henri did not return home last night. I believe we may hear shortly of the success of his suit with the comely widow. I assure you, there is none to overhear our conversation."

Tess did not reply, but he felt the brush of her wide skirts as she walked past him through the open door, and heard the rustle and creak as she seated herself in the chair by the window. There was a lengthy pause, but still she did not speak.

At last he said, somewhat uncertainly, "My dearest Tess, it has been brought to my attention that you may feel I have treated you poorly, that I have insulted your modesty. I tell you, that is the very farthest from my intentions. Therefore I propose to make all right with you. Let us be wed. There, ain't you happy now?" He smiled hopefully in her direction, his arms open to meet her embrace. After a moment, he lowered his still-empty arms, and his smile faltered. "You know, it's devilish hard to tell what you are thinking when I can't see your face," he said with frustration. "Say something, Tess."

"Wed!" she burst out at last. "You must be joking. That is the very last thing I expected you to say."

"What then?" he asked, frowning.

"You might begin by apologizing for staying out every night, boozing and whoring. Is that what I have to look forward to as your wife?"

Tom's face reddened, his customary good humor deserting him for once. "A man is entitled to drink with his friend. I have done nothing for which I might owe you an apology."

"Oh no?" she shot back. "I am well acquainted with your inconstant ways. The moment a pretty young jade crosses your path, your hands are all over her. Even in the church, for shame! And you ask me to wed? Is this your confession of love?"

"I tell you, I have not been whoring, as you so elegantly put it. I have thought on no other but you these past weeks," Tom insisted.

"How easily you lie," Tess said, disgust evident in her voice. He heard a rustle and creak as she rose from her seat. "Even now, you still wear *her* garter to tie back your hair—" she gave it a tweak "—after how abominably she used you in Paris! How long has she been dead? And yet still you think only on her. Do you deny it?" The words came out in a rush, as though she had been holding them closely within her for a long time.

Tom felt the blood drain from his face. "Madam, you tease me beyond all endurance," he ground out between clenched teeth. "I will go out for a walk now, before I say anything we shall both regret." He opened the door with a bang and strode downstairs.

Later that morning, Henri returned, wig in hand, looking disheveled but pleased with himself, to find Tess sitting alone at the breakfast table.

"Bonjour, Madame! Excuse me for returning at such an un-accustomed hour, but I 'ave the 'appiest news…" Henri trailed off, noticing Tess's lowering look and the untouched place settings. He pulled out a chair to join her and set the wig on the table beside him. "But what is this? Is something the matter? Where is Thomas?"

Tess turned down the corners of her mouth as she pushed her crumbled but uneaten toast around her plate. "He asked me to marry him," she said darkly.

Henri gave her a sharp glance before helping himself to a slice of ham. "Eh, I understand now why you are cast down in

396

despair. *Quelle tragédie!*"

She glared at him, her dark eyes glittering with anger. "Do not sport with me, Henri," she said, pushing back in her seat and making as if to rise from the table.

"No, no! I am sorry. Please do not leave," he said hastily, but with genuine concern. "I fear this is due to my interference. It was I who suggested the idea of marriage. But is this not what you wanted?"

"I hardly know myself," Tess replied with a sigh. "He is dear to me, but you know very well how he is! No money of his own, too fond of drink, too free in granting his affections..."

"I know he is very fond of you," Henri offered.

Tess gave a snort. "However he may feel about me, that woman is always first in his mind. You know, Sally Salisbury," she added, when Henri did not seem to follow. "The one who abandoned him in Paris. She haunts this house still! Little mementoes of her everywhere, and I know he still goes to visit her grave."

"You are jealous of a dead woman?" Henri asked.

Tess slumped down in her chair, her shoulders sagging. "When you put it like that, you make me sound very mean-spirited."

Henri spread his hands in a shrug. "Eh, so? Let him think on her from time to time, what can it harm?"

"But how can I know he will not forsake me, or give me over for some other?"

Henri shrugged again, more deeply. "How can any of us know that?"

Tess was silent for many moments, her thoughts turning over and over in her head. Henri was right, of course, but the uncertainty plagued her. How often had she been jilted by those who professed to love her? It would be the undoing not only of her heart but her career as well.

"There is another matter that weighs on my mind, but I feel very low even mentioning it," she said after a long pause. Henri nodded, and she continued, not meeting his eye, "Are you acquainted with legal term couverture?" She pronounced it in the English way. He shook his head. "It means the husband and wife are one, in the eyes of the law. But in reality, it means the wife is completely subsumed by the husband. That is to say, all her money and property becomes his, to dispose of as he sees fit..." she trailed off.

"And the most of the money is yours, which you do not care to put in his charge," Henri finished for her.

Tess threw her napkin on the table, looking pained. "You must think me the most grasping, cold-hearted of women."

"Not at all," Henri replied, giving her a look of deep sympathy. "Only those with ample funds can afford not to think on it at all. You are wise to be concerned. But have you not heard? I shall be Thomas' patron! He will compose and have more cash coming in. That should set your mind at ease, eh?"

"Oh, indeed? Then you are to inherit on your return to France? Your father approves the match?"

"Ah, as to that..." Tess had not intended her remarks as an interrogation. Seeing Henri's distress, she felt badly for bringing up such a delicate matter. "I am certain he will approve by and by," Henri said. "It shall not be so very long before he turns it all over to me, and then we shall have some truly great music, you shall see."

Tess nodded slowly. This all seemed very uncertain. Furthermore, she did not want Tom to step down as conductor, not when he had at last risen so far, not even to compose, and regardless of Tom's own income, she had no mind to put her assets under his rather dubious control. Henri seemed to expect a reply from her, but she could only sigh and say dispiritedly, "The truth is I have already been to Hampstead Village, to look at those charming new houses on the high street, and I have been considering taking one to let. Perhaps I have been my own mistress too long to be married now."

"Nonsense! Everyone desires to be wed," Henri said confidently.

"Oh, but how rude of me! Henri, I am sorry, I did not ask if you have any happy news to impart."

"Oh indeed I have!" Henri's round face flushed pink with pleasure. "I have won my suit, and we are married."

Tess leapt from her chair to embrace Henri and kiss him on both cheeks. "Oh, how happy I am for you!" she cried. "But how can you marry here in London, and so quickly? Do you not need the blessing of your church?"

Henri laughed, squeezing her hand. "We exchanged our vows ourselves. We will be wed in the church when we return to Rouen, but in England we may consider ourselves married already."

Tess embraced him again and wished him every happiness, feeling her mood lighten just a bit. Henri had given her an idea, a possible way out of her dilemma.

Tom did not return home until late in the afternoon, and he returned to find the house in an uproar over his absence. Henri had brought Mrs. Emilia Coates, now Madame d'Angoulême, to call before going together to the première of *Roselinda*, but she had been left to wait in the front parlor, dressed in her finest blue sacque, while dinner went cold on the table, and Tess and Henri paced anxiously, waiting for the master of the house to return. Tess found Emilia pleasant enough, if rather dull, with the sort of flaxen-haired, square-jawed, toothy look so common among English women, and she wondered privately what Henri saw in her.

Soon Jem arrived, also rigged out in rum flash in anticipation of the opening night, but he too was made to wait, and all three only increased their collective anxiety to a fevered pitch. When at last Tom tapped his way up the stairs, all three set upon him at once.

"Where have you been? You said you were only going out for a walk," Tess berated him.

"We thought you was run down by a carriage," Jem added at the same time, while Henri tried unsuccessfully to introduce his new spouse.

Tom ignored all of them and groped his way rather unsteadily toward a chair, then sat down slowly as if in a trance. Jem placed a glass of wine in his hand, which he downed gratefully.

"Come on cully, we must hop it to the theater. There's no time to eat," Jem said as Tom held out his glass for more.

"Mr. Highmore will be in a passion if we don't go directly," Tess agreed.

Tom at last seemed to take notice of them, although he did not stir from his chair, but instead grasped Jem's arm. "I found her!" he said, still sounding rather dazed. "I found Miss Betty!"

If Tom was expecting a more dramatic response to his declaration, he was disappointed.

"Who the devil is Miss Betty?" Jem asked irritably.

"I believe she was his nurse," Tess offered.

"No, she was a sort of lady tutor, a governess, at Culverleigh, and a distant relation of my sisters," Tom corrected. "The old earl sent her away when my blackguardly brother got her with child."

Jem, uninterested in this line of inquiry, tugged at Tom's arm, trying in vain to lift him from the chair. "Come on, there ain't time for this. You have to shift your clothes—you look like you've been dipped in the Thames."

"Well, yes, a bit, I fell out of the boat chasing after her," Tom said.

"For heaven's sake! What were you doing in a boat!" Tess exclaimed, throwing her hands in the air in exasperation. "You said you were just going to take a turn around the Piazza."

"And I did, too, but then halfway around I realized I had a new suit of clothes ready for me at the tailor, for opening night, you see. I thought since I was already out, I would step out to Southwark to get it before dinner."

"By yourself!" Emilia, heretofore silent, looked horrified as the words escaped her lips in an undertone.

Henri patted her hand, shushing her. "I think you'll find M. Thomas wonderfully capable, my dear. He gets all about London on his own."

Tom paused for only a moment, a slight frown the only sign that he had heard her. "To Southwark, as I said. I was just stepping down into the wherry when one of the passengers already in the boat took my hand to help me down. It was her! After all these years, Miss Betty herself!"

There was an expectant pause, until it became apparent there was no continuation of the tale.

"What? Is that all? Did you at least speak to her?" Jem asked.

"No, I cried out to her, but she pushed past me and ran back up to the quay. I attempted to follow her, and half fell out of the boat. Luckily the ferryman plucked me from the water, but by then she was gone. Jem, you must help me find her!"

"What, based solely on you twiddling your fingers with some aged mort? How can you be certain it was her?"

"It has been twenty years, and you didn't even hear her voice," Tess added softly.

"Twenty-two years," Tom replied testily. "Never doubt the perception of a blind man's fingers. I know for a certainty it was her. Why else would she flee the boat when I spoke her name? If it were a stranger, would she not laugh and say I was mistaken?"

Jem and Tess exchanged a glance.

"Oh bloody hell," Jem said with a scowl, looking trapped. "Right, I promise to look for the old trot if you only move your arse and get to the theater before we're both given the sack."

CHAPTER SEVENTEEN: THE ANSWER

Come write me down, ye powers above,
The man that first created love,
For I've a diamond in my eye,
Where all my joys and comforts lie.

"I do believe I know that song." Henri d'Angoulême turned from the fireplace, the fire tongs dangling from one hand, a glass of claret in the other.

"It is tolerably well known," Tom replied from behind the spinet, playing through the verse again. "Did you get that, Castleton?"

Jem, seated at the escritoire, merely grunted in reply as he scribbled down the notes. Wads of crumpled paper littered the floor by his feet, and there was a large ink stain on the frilled cuff of his white shirt.

"But after your great success, I thought you might compose something new, something wholly original," Henri protested, gesturing with his wine glass, so that the wine lapped over the edge and dripped on the carpet. He blinked at it in surprise, steadying himself on the fire tongs like a cane, which left sooty smudges on the floor. It was far from his first glass of the day.

"Hmm, perhaps one day, but the broadsides are more satisfying than all that Italianate frippery, and I'll be damned if I write for a castrato," Tom replied, banging out a bold close harmony. "There, how d'ye like that?"

"But your recent triumph..." Henri trailed off.

The opening of *Roselinda* had gone very well. A large crowd had turned out to see the famous madman, but Veracini had disappointed them by merely bowing politely and sitting quietly throughout the show. For an opera knocked together in a few weeks, the performance had relatively few missed cues and sour notes. Tom found it pleased him to be on the conductor's box for the actual performance, to hear the applause of the audience from the center of the house, and not just the far side of the stalls. He had been greeted and congratulated by a surprising number of people after the show. It seemed Emilia, Madame d'Angoulême was quite well-connected and had put it about that he was the true composer of the final aria. The resulting fame also agreed with him very well. Now Shaloe Brown, like a solitary, somewhat thin and shabby Fury, was pursuing him for a new broadside.

Ignoring Henri's remark, Tom played on.

"I'll give you gold; I'll give you pearl,
If you can fancy me, dear girl.
Rich costly robes that you shall wear,
If you can fancy me, my dear."

"It's not your gold shall me entice,
To leave my pleasures to be a wife.
I never do intend at all
To be at any young man's call."

"By the by, I am sorry to hear that Mademoiselle Turnbridge has engaged lodgings in Hampstead Village," Henri observed, his voice overloud in a sudden lull in the music.

Tom hit the keys with a dissonant clang. "She what?" At

last Henri had his full attention.

"Oh dear, had she not told you?" Henri said, stricken.

Jem glanced up from his work. "The infamous jade! Dammee! I never thought she would go that far."

Tom sat silently, his face pinched up into a frown and his pale eyes rolling in agitation, but he did not speak. Anxious to atone for his unfortunate revelation, Henri blundered on.

"My dear Thomas, there is still time to set this right! I know women, and they do not move house easily nor speedily, oh no, I assure you." This was spoken with the bitter ring of intimate experience, for Henri was impatient to quit England and take up his rightful place at home with his bride (optimistically assuming his father would withdraw his objections once he heard his troth was plighted), but Madame Emilia was still preparing her considerable possessions to be transported over the Channel, and purchasing even more as a trousseau.

"Yes, talk to her, make her see reason," Jem added. "God knows why, but she truly does seem attached to you. You bollixed it up by putting it to her so plainly. A fine lady like Tess wants courting," he advised.

"When has she ever been fooled by flattery," Tom muttered.

"Not pretty words and empty flattery," Jem corrected. "But do recall, she's been the mistress to a duke. She does as she pleases and could have any beau she chooses. No, no, if you would win her, you must make her think the marriage is her idea."

Tom bent his head over the spinet and hammered out the underlying chords of the song he had been working on several times.

"Perhaps," was all he would say.

Despite the adulation for Tom's aria, *Roselinda* was somewhat less than a resounding success. Once word traveled round the Piazza that Veracini was unlikely to storm the stage in the middle of the show and entertain the audience like an inmate of Bedlam, attendance dropped off rapidly, and after only two weeks, Mr. Highmore announced the production would be closing.

The night of the closing performance, Lady Gray attended, as she had every night of the short run. It gave her the liveliest pleasure to see Tom on the conductor's stand, commanding the ensemble with assured and professional precision. That night, however, during the entr'acte, she excused herself from her guests, leaving a widowed baroness, a spinster cousin, and a retired navy admiral to their game of faro in her private box. Ignoring the macaronis with their tall wigs and painted faces loitering in the hallways, she swept downstairs, through the crowd, and to the dressing rooms beside the stage. Here even more dandies decked out in powder and lace lingered by the dressing room doors: would-be or established patrons, hoping for the favors of the members of the company. Only one door was free from such attentions; Lady Gray followed a small boy who knocked and showed her in.

Tess Turnbridge sat before a narrow and smoky glass as a thin girl in a smock pinned the curls of her immense wig in place. The thick layer of her rather garish stage makeup was already creased and lined with sweat, but as she turned and greeted Lady Gray with a smile of the most genuine affection, her natural beauty shone through beneath the artifice.

"Sue, if you please, wait in the hall," Tess directed, and the girl fled with a hasty bob.

Lady Gray greeted Tess warmly, clasping both her hands. "My dear Miss Turnbridge," she said, "I give you the joy of your success in this role. I could only wish the run were longer." Tess politely demurred, but Lady Gray interrupted, "I know you have not much time between acts, so I shall not detain you but come directly to the point. I understand my nephew has proposed marriage to you." Tess blanched—did the whole of London know of her private dealings?

"Never look so alarmed, my dear," Lady Gray continued. "There is very little that goes on in my family that I do not know of, and I make a particular point of minding Tom's affairs, as he has no one else to do so. Yes, I know of his proposal to you, and I also know he made a dreadful bungle of it and evoked your wrath, very deservingly, I am certain."

Tess paused with her mouth open, unsure even how to begin a reply.

"No, no," Lady Gray charged on, waving her closed fan at Tess like an accusing finger. "I know what you are thinking, that his affront to you was too great, but I am here to ask you to reconsider, in short, to beg on his behalf that you will marry him."

Tess still found herself speechless with surprise. "But," she began after a long moment, "Am I not a little too low? Your family...the earl...that is..."

"Nonsense! My dear girl, it is Tom who has placed you in an indecent posture by bringing you into his house. I am sensible of his profligate ways, but you have been a great steadying influence on him, and I know he cares for you sincerely." She stepped forward and put a hand on Tess's arm. "Nothing would make me happier than to see him wed to you."

Tess found herself strangely moved. "I confess I have been thinking on his offer," she admitted. "But how can I be certain..."

Lady Gray cut her off. "My dear, I assure you, no one is more aware of Tom's failings than I. But I believe that he would rise to the occasion, were you to be properly wed. He can be rather thoughtless at times, but his heart is always in the right place. Now I will take my leave before I cause you to miss your entrance. Pray do think on what I have said."

With a sweep of her wide skirts Lady Gray was gone, leaving Tess staring at the closed door. That was not what she had expected the honored lady to say at all.

The company ground its way through the concluding act of *Roselinda*, acquitting itself competently if not spectacularly. Tess found herself struggling to keep her attention on the notes and figures on stage, her mind even more prone to wander at the sight of Tom at the conductor's stand, a look of the most intense concentration on his usually blank face.

At the close of the show, Tess was surprised to find Tom had navigated through the general melee to her dressing room, no longer her own private quarters, but now crowded with stage hands, dressers, and wig makers carting off the costumes and properties.

Tom stood uncertainly in the doorway, fidgeting with his heavy walking stick, buffeted by stagehands entering and exiting. "Tess?" he called out.

"Yes, I am here," she answered. "Forgive me for not rising, but they are shifting my costume." Two girls were tugging at her laces while an older woman was hastily pulling the pins from her wig and storing them between pursed lips. Tess sat calmly swaying under their ministrations; a lifetime in the theater had inured her against foolish modesty.

"I thought that since it is the final performance, we might celebrate over a pint at the Essex Serpent," Tom suggested. "Henri and Jem are already on their way there, and they most particularly asked if you might join us."

In the past, Tess had never hesitated to join the men at a public house, but tonight somehow the thought of the noise and smoke was too overwhelming. "That is kind of them, but I believe I shall retire early tonight," she replied.

Tom stepped forward, his hand swimming in a circular motion, searching for her. "My dear, are you unwell?" he asked with concern.

"Not at all, merely tired," she said, with a twinge of guilt for not taking his outstretched hand.

"Then I shall return home with you," Tom declared, dropping his hand but standing more confidently, grasping his walking stick.

"Oh no, you mustn't on my account," Tess protested, as the wig at last was lifted from her head, leaving a strange sense of lightness. They argued back and forth as the rest of her costume came away and she retired behind a screen to don her own clothes. She knew how he enjoyed a drink after the performance. She would not deprive him of the company of his friends, realizing as she spoke that she had intended to do just that the week before. No, he insisted, there would be no pleasure at all if she did not come with them.

At last, Tess found herself escorted home on Tom's arm, the first time they had done so after a performance. Matthews let them in and handed Tess a candle to light her way upstairs, but she paused for a moment in the darkened stairwell.

"Perhaps a quiet drink before we retire?" she suggested.

Tom smiled and bowed to her with a flourish. "As you please, madam."

The dining room being cold and uninviting, they retired to the music room, where Matthews hastily stoked up the fire. Tom found his fiddle, or more precisely, Tess prevented him from sitting upon it at the last moment. In the flickering glow of the fireplace and her single candle, Tess watched him play a long, slow air as she sipped sweet sherry from a scratched goblet. She settled back in her chair with a sigh. It was pleasant, even deeply satisfying to watch him play, working out new variations on the tune as he went along. She had not expected him to come home with her so readily. Could he truly be satisfied with evenings such as this for the rest of their lives? Could she?

"It was kind of you to accompany me, but I am sorry you had to forsake your friends," she said.

Tom laid the fiddle aside and felt carefully about for his glass. "My dearest Tess, you are the only friend whose company I crave," he said. He reached for her, and she placed her hand in his. He drew it to his lips, kissing each finger in turn, his eyes staring up above her head. "Please," he whispered. "Do not leave. Stay here with me."

Tess leaned forward and kissed him, but they both knew it was no sort of answer. They kissed again and again, but Tom did not attempt to push her further. Instead he laid his head in the crook of her shoulder, pressing his face up into her hair and against her neck. She put her arms around him with a sigh. She was attempting in vain to find the words she wanted to speak when they heard the front door open and close, followed by scuffling and loud voices coming up the stairs.

Tom sat up with a jerk. "That will be Henri returning," he said, cocking an ear towards the door. Tess smoothed the front of her dress, vexed at the sudden interruption.

They heard more confused shouting, then the door to the parlor opened with a bang, revealing a somewhat disheveled Jem Castleton, florid with drink, with a distraught Frankie tugging at the front of his jacket.

"I want to tell him! You promised!" Frankie implored, his voice rising several octaves and cracking in his distress.

"Tell me what?" Tom demanded.

"Where is Henri?" Tess asked at the same moment.

"Henri went home with Madame Emilia," Jem explained, swatting at Frankie. "Tom, I'm come to tell you, we have located Miss Betty." Tom started from his chair as Frankie howled in frustration.

"You dog!" Frankie cried, pummeling Jem's chest with his fists. "I'm the one who found her."

"Found her where?" Tom grasped the boy's shoulder.

"She been living in Southwark, name of Mrs. Poole," Frankie said, drawing himself up. "Only it ain't a very genteel place, begging your pardon, sir."

"We must go there at once!" Tom cried, making towards the door.

Tess tugged at his hand. "What, right now? And frighten the poor woman to death by pounding on her door in the middle of the night?" If it is Miss Betty, and not a poor unrelated stranger, Tess added silently to herself.

"Miss Turnbridge is right. It's past midnight," Jem agreed. "We can go in the morning."

Tom was forced to concur, but neither was he ready to retire for the night. He paced about the parlor, running his hands through his hair and demanding of Frankie more details, which were pitifully few. The boy had made inquiries, first locating the ferryman who recalled both the blind cove and the mort who fled from him the other day, then tracing anyone who recognized the woman. The trail apparently led to a Mrs. Poole, in a tiny rented room in Southwark, but beyond that no one seemed to know.

"And what of the child?" Tom wondered aloud.

"I don't rightly know of no child," Frankie replied hesitantly, his self-importance at reciting his tale deflating slightly.

"Child no longer," Tess said gently. "Think, Tom, how many years have passed since Miss Betty was turned away from Culverleigh?"

"Twenty-two years," Tom admitted.

"Any child, if there ever was one, has long ago moved on and made his or her own way in the world, I warrant," Tess said.

Jem guffawed. "If it weren't sent straight to the parish the moment it were born. Still, it means you have a long-lost nephew or niece somewhere. Why, it could be someone you know already! What if it's Frankie here!" He pounded the boy on the back.

"Twenty-two years," Tess reminded him. Frankie was still barely fifteen. "For shame, Mr. Castleton. You have been reading too many romances."

"We shall go to Southwark first thing tomorrow morning," Tom declared, still pacing, and ignoring their exchange.

"No," said Tess, taking his arm gently. "It would be best to send Frankie to fetch her here, where you can greet her kindly and entertain her at your leisure, rather than storming her house in a pack. She will think the bailiff is after her. Now let us all be calm and retire," she suggested, tugging him towards the door.

Late the following morning, after what seemed an endless purgatory of waiting, a triumphant Frankie led Mrs. Poole into the front parlor, which had been titivated by the servants under Stinson's nervous haranguing. Tess hung back by the fireplace with Jem, who had somehow invited himself to stay for the night and through the next day without anyone taking notice. Tess quickly took stock of the woman entering somewhat hesitantly behind Frankie. Her clothes were worn and much repaired, and her face bore the marks of a very hard life. When she smiled nervously, Tess could see the gaps of missing teeth toward the back. Any reservations she may have had about the woman's identity, however, were instantly banished.

As soon as Frankie announced her as Mrs. Poole, Tom strode forward confidently and clasped her hands, crying, "Miss Betty!"

This time, rather than fleeing, she greeted him with great emotion. "Oh Tom, how you have come up in the world," she said, kissing him on either cheek. "How proud I have been to hear of you."

Stinson as well, standing unobtrusively by the door, appeared quite overcome. Propriety prevented him from making a great show like his master, and Miss Betty seemed rather shy of him, as he nodded soberly to her.

Tom introduced her to Tess and Jem, and seated her in the finest chair, with Tess's silver tea service set out beside her. Still he could not be easy himself, but paced about in front of the fire as they talked. He could scarcely reconcile himself to the idea that the long-sought Miss Betty, whom he imagined had been banished to a tiny hamlet in the countryside, was not only in London, but had all this time known of his career, while he knew nothing of hers.

He tried to ask delicately about what had happened, although she was clearly reluctant to speak of it, and her story came out only in pieces, but they could imagine the rest. It was worse even than Tom had thought: the earl had not sent her into hiding, but turned her out without a penny. The child, whom she had named Richard, had indeed gone to the parish, although at some point she had reclaimed him, or established a connection with him in some fashion during his childhood. She mentioned several men in passing, who may have been husbands or patrons, but she had clearly never regained her previous respectable status, and although she avoided saying so, it was all too clear what her career had been: prostitution while she was still young and handsome, and petty thieving once she was not. As for young Richard, he had proved his father's son, a villain from a young age, at last taken up and transported to Van Diemen's Land at the age of twenty for theft.

Tom stood before the fireplace, with his elbow resting on the mantle, his face turned toward the floor but with an attentive ear pointed at Miss Betty. So it was as Tess had predicted; there would be no joyful reunion with a long-lost nephew as in a romance.

"Why did you flee from me in the boat?" he asked.

"You've become such a fine gentleman," she answered, and it pained him to hear the coarseness in her voice.

Jem suppressed a snort of laughter, which Tess took as her cue to lead him from the sitting room, with Frankie and Stinson trailing behind her, leaving Tom and Miss Betty alone. When the door clicked shut, Tom strode across the room and knelt before her, grasping her hands.

"Be damned to the earl for his cruelty to you," he burst out. "His soul to the devil, and his wife too."

Miss Betty sighed. "It is far too late for that," she said. "I have hated him too, and Richard even more so. But our anger does no good. In truth, I was a foolish girl, and Richard but a child. Your father took me in as charity when my parents died, and I no more than a distant relation of his first wife. He owed me nothing."

Tom only shook his head. "You are too kind to the old earl by half."

She regarded him sadly. "No, Tom. You mustn't bear ill-will against your own father. He always said you held the greatest promise of any of his children."

"He said that?" Tom was startled.

"Do not repine on my behalf," she said, not without some bitterness. "My fate was my own; I was my own undoing."

It was a strange thing, Tom thought, to have here before him at last a figure he had thought on for so long, like a ghost resurrected from his childhood. He thought suddenly of his mother—the sound of her voice, the touch of her hand on his face as clear to him as if it were she who sat before him. He laid his head on Miss Betty's knee, as she stroked his hair.

"You always was remarkable, even as a child. Everyone could see it," she said in a faraway voice.

He laughed a bit and shook his head without lifting it up. "You flatter me. I believe you was the only one there who showed me any kindness. I was not then accustomed as I am now to ignoring the jibes and taunts of others who would make me feel low simply because I can't see. You've no idea how much your lessons in that little schoolroom meant to me. You opened the world to me."

"I'm so glad you escaped from Culverleigh and made your own way in the world."

"It's very kind of you to say so," he replied, his voice rather muffled as he still kneeled with his head in her lap.

"It's not just empty words," she said sternly, lifting his head with her fingertips under his chin. "I have heard other tales of you as well, things I won't repeat. You have come so far, despite everything; pray don't squander it in drinking and whoring, as your father did. You have it in you to be a much better man than he ever was."

She put her hand against his cheek as his tears streamed down, and wiped them away.

There was no question of allowing Miss Betty to return to Southwark. Henri's few remaining possessions were ejected from the spare room to be send to Madame Emilia, and Miss Betty installed temporarily, above her protests.

Several days passed in this new arrangement. Then news came of the death of Queen Charlotte, and the entire city was clothed in mourning. Worse still, as a result, the opera season was canceled for the rest of the year, throwing them all into further uncertainty.

Tom did not know how things stood with Tess. She was pleasant in the mornings at breakfast, but spent every day out of the house, saying she had business to attend to. Tom did not say anything, as he did not want to seem to be prying into her affairs, but after their former intimacy, he could not help but think there was yet some coolness between them.

For the first time in his life, Tom found himself wondering how it would be if he could see her face. Perhaps if he could see, he would have a better idea of her mood. Usually he found the voice more than adequately expressive, but his apprehension was interfering with his judgment. Would she really leave?

Miss Betty, on the other hand, stayed within, having no business outside, but Tom sensed that she felt ill at ease in his house. He could hear her wander about restlessly, fretting and sighing. He tried to return to composing, now that he had more time at home, and while he invited her to join him in the music room, her shifting about made it difficult to concentrate.

After nearly a week of this, one afternoon he banged out a few chords then turned about to face her.

"You needn't stay in this house if you don't wish it," he said without preamble.

He heard more rustling about, then at last she said, "I am sensible of the very great kindness you did in taking me in. I'm sorry I can't feel easy here, but it is rather difficult, I find. I am neither a relation nor a servant. I can't help but feel like the receiver of charity."

"No!" Tom's brow pinched up in concern. "I think of it as righting the very old wrong done to you by my father. I only regret I did not find you sooner. Please stay as long as you wish."

"I told you, I have forgiven him in my heart already. It's not your duty to repent on your father's behalf. Besides, what am I to do with my time here? It suits me ill to be idle."

Tom did not answer at first, but half turned back to the spinet and ran through a simple tune with one hand. "I believe Charlotte might be glad of your companionship," he said after a long pause. "She's still at Culverleigh. Shall I write to her on your behalf? I realize it might bring back unpleasant memories for you, but I was just there recently myself, and I assure you the estate is utterly altered." He continued playing idly as he spoke, thinking aloud.

Miss Betty said cautiously, "I should like that, but I doubt if Lady Bolingbroke would ever receive me there again."

"Perhaps not. But we might prevail on Aunt Sarah to set you both up in a neat little house of your own. She will agree to any plan that might prevent Charlotte from flinging herself into the arms of Lieutenant Welgarth, I warrant."

Miss Betty was amenable to this idea, and Tom was pleased to hear a note of eager anticipation in her voice for the first time. "I was always fond of Charlotte," she said. "And I believe Miss Turnbridge shall be glad for my departure."

Tom felt his face flush hot at the mention of Tess's name, and turned abruptly back to the keyboard to hide his confusion. "Aye, well, as for that, she may depart well before you," he muttered.

"Tom!" He heard her rise from her chair, then drag it along the floor to seat herself directly beside him. She placed a hand on his arm. "If you truly wish to atone for the misdeeds of your father, then you must treat her with greater respect than he did the women in his life. Why will you not marry her and give her a proper position in your home?" Her words were pointed but her tone held only kindness and concern.

He lifted his head and turned in the direction of her voice. "I tried!" he said miserably. "I proposed marriage to her and she refused. What else would you have me do?"

415

"Do you love her?"

"Yes!"

"Did you tell her so?"

"Did I...?" Tom's mouth hung open in surprise. Surely he had said as much, many times over. He was forever paying her a thousand little compliments, addressing her affectionately, as was his habit... but perhaps that was not enough. There was no one else whose companionship he desired more, he realized, and the thought of her leaving was nearly unbearable. Why had he not told her so plainly? Would she even still listen?

Several more days passed, and yet Tom could not seem to find the right moment to speak to Tess. She kept herself distant, and Tom found it surprisingly difficult to open a conversation with her. A lifetime habit of avoiding serious topics was not so easily unlearned.

Meanwhile, Henri called for a final visit before departing for home at last.

"My dear fellow, you must come back to visit us again," Tom said, toasting his health with the last of the burgundy Henri had given him.

"And you are welcome to stay with us in Rouen whenever you please," Henri replied, although as he had not sent ahead to his father with the news of his marriage, the state of his future household remained somewhat uncertain. Nevertheless, he continued optimistically, "I am forever in your debt for helping to unite me with my dear Emilia. Please do think on my offer. It would give me the greatest pleasure to commission a composition from you, an *original* work."

Tom promised to think on it. He had already delivered his latest work to Shaloe Brown, but the idea of a longer work intrigued him. Rather than simply tossing off a tune quickly as possible, creating something wholly new suddenly seemed appealing. Already the notes were beginning to take shape in his mind.

The next morning, Tess rose late and remained in her room even after Dorcas helped her dress. She lingered over her toilette, even as the sounds downstairs suggested the rest of the household had already risen and taken their breakfast. She was just considering how best to make her entrance when she was surprised to hear Tom clatter up the stairs and bang on her door.

She opened the door with some bewilderment, as ordinarily Tom made a point of never intruding on her. He was still dressed only in his breeches and shirt, his cravat hanging open. He waved what appeared to be a letter in his hand, his face wreathed in smiles, his brow raised upward in excitement.

"I say, Tess! I'm sorry to disturb you, but I've just had the most wonderful news!" He brandished the unfolded papers in his hand.

"Yes, I'm here. What is it?"

"A letter just arrived from Mr. Rich. Frankie read it to me, the clever boy. It seems Mr. Handel has decided the public is tired of Italian opera and castrati and such nonsense. He is writing an oratorio in English based on Milton's *Samson*, and he wants you to sing Delilah."

"That is good news, thank you," Tess said carefully. "But what of you? He must ask you to conduct."

"No," Tom replied, suddenly seeming a bit abashed. "He asked me to sing the part of Samson." He thrust the letter in her direction.

Tess plucked the papers from his fingers and glanced them over. The production was still rather conjectural but it seemed they were both being considered for the leading parts when the composition was completed. As she read the letter, Tom leaned on the doorframe with an elbow, his arm extended above his head, his head tipped up expectantly. She gazed up at him, feeling as if her heart would burst. His casual, half-dressed posture, with his queue tied untidily, his boyish eagerness to share the good news with her, all these little things about him were endearing beyond measure.

"We shall stand on stage together. I should like that very much," she said, but her tone was measured.

Tom dropped his arm to his side and cocked an ear in her direction. "Tess, what's amiss?" His brow wrinkled in concern and his eyes searched the air above her head.

"Nothing," she replied, although her heart suddenly hammered as she prepared to tell him the words she had so carefully rehearsed. She took a deep breath then said, "I have taken rooms in Hampstead High Street."

"What? No!" Tom reached for her and put his arms about her waist, then fell to his knees, pressing his face up against her. "Please, you mustn't leave. I do apologize most sincerely for treating you lightly, for ever giving you cause to doubt me." He tightened his arms about her. "I realize I have not always spoken seriously, but I don't know how to put it to you more sincerely. I wish to be with you always, and to endeavor to make you happy."

"I appreciate the apology," Tess said evenly, but already her heart was rising up. "Are you saying that you wish to marry me?"

"Did I not ask it of you? But you turned me down, most cruelly. I won't trouble you by asking again, if your answer is no."

"I did not say no," she protested. "I only answered as I did because I thought you did not ask me in earnest."

Still kneeling before her, he grasped the front of her dress in his two hands and tipped his head up at her. "But I was in earnest, and I still am now. I love you, Tess. I think on you night and day. There is none other who makes my heart gladder, with whom I would care to live." As he spoke, his face opened, shining from within, for once fully expressive, but more than that, Tess could hear in his voice the intensity of emotion and she at last felt certain.

"Then by all means, let us marry," she said, "but it shall be as I desire."

Tom grinned up at her. "Of course, madam, would it be any other way?"

Tess ignored his teasing, continuing in a serious tone, "I would not have it be in a church, to be given to you to become your property. We shall marry ourselves, as Henri and Emilia did. Jem and Miss Betty may be our witnesses, which will make it legal, but you must agree that my person and my property remain my own."

It seemed to him an odd sort of request, but Tom nodded. He had come to appreciate what a precarious position women like Tess held in society, in some ways even more precarious than his own. She took his hand and tugged on it, until he stood before her.

"And I do not wish to give up the rooms in Hampstead," Tess continued, leading him to the bed and sitting beside him. "They are quite charming and fashionable, and a calming change from the city. We shall remove there when there is no production and return here for the opera season."

"Can we afford to keep two houses?" Tom asked, but in truth he was merely relieved that she would not ask him to give up the house on Maiden Lane. He rather liked the idea of two houses, which they could alternate between.

"We shall both have to keep working," she replied.

"Why yes, of course. You still have a brilliant career ahead of you, and I would not have you give it up merely for my sake. As you said, it would be a great joy to sing beside you on stage."

Tess clasped his hands in hers as she sat beside him, her dark eyes shining brightly. "I can think of no greater happiness."

He felt for her lips with his fingers, then leaned down to kiss her, a long hard kiss with the promise of many more in the future. She wrapped her arms around him and pressed herself against his slender chest. His sensitive fingers traced along the side of her cheek, his eyelids fluttering as he kissed her, and she felt a great surge of love for him in her breast.

On a sudden impulse, she closed her own eyes and placed

her hands on his face, feeling each of his features with her fingers, from his even brows to his long thin nose and cheeks still with traces of stubble. When she reached his mouth, she felt him smile under her fingers and her eyes popped open.

"What are you doing?"

Tess suddenly felt self-conscious. "I don't know. I was just wondering how you..."

He grasped her hands tenderly, kissing her fingertips. "You mean how I perceive you? That's not it at all."

"Then tell me."

"Hmm." He caressed her hand and kissed her palm, inhaling deeply as he did so. "First, I think of your hands, so small and soft, but also quick and clever in the way you touch me. Then I think of your scent, like the rarest of perfumes." He leaned forward and placed his head against her shoulder, kissing her neck. "Then your hair, so smooth and soft, and your tiny waist and round breasts..."

She pushed him away slightly in mock outrage. "Sir!"

He laughed and embraced her again. "But above all it is your voice I think of. That pure rich tone, so full of emotion."

"Well, my voice is my only fortune," she said laughing.

"Indeed. And if I am to hear it every day, I shall consider myself the luckiest of men." Again he found her lips with his fingers and kissed her deeply.

They might have remained in Tess's room much longer, but they both heard Matthews admit Jem below.

"Our second witness has arrived," Tess said, tugging Tom to his feet. "Now let us exchange vows, and it is done."

Jem and Miss Betty were only slightly surprised to see Tess and Tom descend the stairs together, flushed and rosy, and to hear the news. Jem congratulated them heartily, while Miss Betty kissed both of them on either cheek.

The exchange of vows took place in the music room, which seemed only fitting. Tom wrapped his arms about Tess's waist and solemnly intoned the ritual phrase: "I do take thee to my wife espoused."

"I do take thee to my husband," Tess replied, and he leaned down to kiss her deeply. Then he felt for the chair before the spinet and sat down. She sat in his lap, as he played the tune he had just published as a broadside, and they sang together, delighting in the rich harmonies he had composed.

O stay, young man; be not in haste.
You seem afraid your time will waste.
Let reason rule your roving mind,
And unto you I will prove kind.

Their sorrow and trouble now are past.
Their joy and comfort come at last;
For the girl that always said him nay,
Now proves his comfort night and day.

AUTHOR'S NOTE

Life in early eighteenth century London was sometimes brutal and dangerous, but always fascinating, and with more libertine attitudes than we might expect, especially among people living on the margins of society. Many of the historical details in this novel come from the book *Wits, Wenches and Wantons: London's Low Life: Covent Garden in the Eighteenth Century* by E.J. Burford, which includes descriptions not only of the theaters and brothels, but also of male and female homosexuality, and contraception use. For descriptions of more polite society, I drew on *Behind Closed Doors: At Home in Georgian England* by Amanda Vickery. Prior to the Marriage Act of 1753, self-marriage (exchange of vows without posting banns or obtaining a license) could be considered legally binding.

The description of the rituals at the molly-house and attitudes about homosexuality come from this website which includes detailed contemporary accounts: http://rictornorton.co.uk/eighteen/index.htm. Captain Lindsey's defense of homosexuality is borrowed from the trial of William Brown in 1726, where the defendant said, "I think there is no Crime in making what use I please of my own Body."

I drew inspiration for the character of Tom Finch from the real lives of many accomplished blind men in the 18th century. These include composers Turlough O'Carolan and John Stanley, magistrate John Fielding, mathematician Nicholas Saunderson, poet Thomas Blacklock, and explorer James

Holman. They all rose to great professional heights in the era before institutionalization became the norm for people with disabilities. I borrowed Tom's method of cane use and echolocation from the biography of James Holman, *A Sense of the World: How a Blind Man Became History's Greatest Traveler* by Jason Roberts. Tom's method of learning music is similar to that used by John Stanley, who worked with George Frideric Handel, and even conducted many of his oratorios. Stanley only needed to hear a piece of music played through once to memorize it.

The ballad "London" that appears in the opening chapters was in actuality composed by Henry Carey, whose career was also an inspiration for Tom's. The illegitimate son of the Marquess of Halifax, Carey was a prolific writer of both ballads and opera, crossing low and high society. A modern rendition of "London" can be heard on the album *Rocket Cottage* by Steeleye Span, sung by the great Maddy Prior.

Most of the operas mentioned here can be easily found in modern recordings and performances, including *Dido and Aeneas* by Henry Purcell and all of Handel's operas and oratorios. Francesco Maria Veracini was also a real composer, and *Roselinda* does include an aria based on a Scots ballad, but there is no modern recording of the entire opera.

All of the ballads mentioned also have modern recordings, often many versions. "Sovay" is on the album *Sweet Child* by Pentangle. "Farewell and Adieu to the Worries of Life" is recorded under the title "One Morning in June" on the album *Flame of Wine* by Lasairfhíona Ní Chonaola. The ballad Jem composes about Sal is based on the "The Newry Highwayman" recorded by Solas on their self-titled album; the song also contains references to Covent Garden and John Fielding. "The Brown Girl" is recorded under the title "The Banks of the Bann" by Shirley Collins and the Albion Country Band on the album *No Roses*. "Blue-Eyed Nancy" is recorded under the title "How Can I Live at the Top of a Mountain" by the Bothy Band on the album *After Hours*. The two French songs Tom learns from Henri are "Quand J'étais Fille À Marier" and "Au Chant De L'alouette" recorded by Gabriel and Marie Yacoub on the album *Pierre de Grenoble*. "The Roving Journeyman" is recorded by Paddy Doran on the album *Celtic Mouth Music*. "Bean Phaidin" (Paddy's Wife) has been recorded many times; a lively version can be found on the album *An Raicin Alainn* by Lasairfhíona Ní Chonaola. A somewhat cleaned up version of "Three Drunken Maidens" is on the album *Summer Solstice* by Tim Hart and Maddy Prior. "Spanish Ladies" and "Pleasant and Delightful" can be found on the album *Roast Beef of Old England*. "Johnny Lovely Johnny" is recorded by Dolores Keane and John Faulkner on the album *Broken Hearted I'll Wander*. "The Blue-Eyed Stranger" is recorded by Ashley Hutchings and the Albion Band on the album *No Surrender*. "Come Write Me Down" (The Wedding Song) has been recorded many times but the best known version is by the Copper Family.

I owe a great debt of gratitude to the many people who helped me complete this novel. Thanks in particular to Annabelle Costa, Ruth Madison, Avery Kingston, Rowan M, D. Grigsby, Dre Garcia, Drielle Gonçalves, Mark Ahern, and C. A. Tatum. Your assistance was invaluable.

Made in the USA
Columbia, SC
18 February 2022

56449902R00257